LOVE IN THE FOREST

Earth and Sky Series

JANINA GREY

SOUL MATE PUBLISHING

New York

LOVE IN THE FOREST

Copyright©2021

JANINA GREY

Cover Design by Ramona Lockwood

This book is a work of fiction. The names, characters, places, and incidents are the products of the author's imagination or are used fictitiously. Any resemblance to actual events, business establishments, locales, or persons, living or dead, is entirely coincidental.

All rights reserved. No part of this publication may be reproduced, stored in a retrieval system, or transmitted in any form or by any means (electronic, mechanical, photocopying, recording, or otherwise) without the prior written permission of both the copyright owner and the publisher. The only exception is brief quotations in printed reviews.

The scanning, uploading, and distribution of this book via the Internet or via any other means without the permission of the publisher is illegal and punishable by law. Please purchase only authorized electronic editions, and do not participate in or encourage electronic piracy of copyrighted materials.

Your support of the author's rights is appreciated.

Published in the United States of America by
Soul Mate Publishing
P.O. Box 24
Macedon, New York, 14502

ISBN: 978-1-64716-239-9

www.SoulMatePublishing.com

The publisher does not have any control over and does not assume any responsibility for author or third-party websites or their content.

I dedicate this book to my Pagan family near and far, most especially my first and very beloved High Priestess, Lady Hawk, who taught me about magic, Spirit, writing, and life.

To my beloved chosen family of Crows, Willow Hill Circle, Ravenmyst, Church of the Greenwood, StarFire Coven, and all those sharing in my life journey . . . thank you for your hugs, wisdom, lessons, love, laughter, life altering rituals, soul thumping drum circles, midnight magic, bonfires, and dancing 'til dawn. For all the lifetimes we've lived, and those yet to come . . . thank you.

Blessed be.

Acknowledgments

For eight years I have been a part of the Soul Mate family. *A Soulie*. I can't thank my publisher, Deborah Gilbert, enough for the knowledge, education, life experiences, and opportunities she has provided me with this connection. Many thanks to my cover artist, Ramona, and that amazing team of Soul Mate editors. All of your dedication transforms my manuscripts into real live books! *Now, that's magic*.

Special thanks to Andrea Kaczor and our Thistle Dew Retreats family, MJ Compton, Kat Morrisey, and Nina Pietrafesa for your inspiration and guidance. Thank you, Central New York Romance Writers, and Romance Writers of America for all you do.

To my sister, Jeana, thank you for brainstorming, laughing, and loving me unconditionally, and for being a great Book Tour Manager!

To my amazing offspring, Anthony and Allie Rose, thank you for keeping me sane and helping me chill out when things get crazy, and for loving me and believing in me without question.

Most of all, thank you, David, for keeping things in order when I get lost in my writing, for keeping the magic alive, and best of all . . . for making my happily-ever-after a reality.

Chapter 1

Adirondack Foothills, Late Summer 2018

Crouching down, she held her daughters as close as their seatbelts would allow, shielding them with her body from the assault of luggage and fellow passengers being tossed throughout the cabin. As their plane nosedived into a spin, a quick glance out the window revealed ocean and clouds spiraling, spiraling, spiraling. Shouts and shrieks of horror drowned out the cries of her precious daughters as they clung to her. The acrid, smothering fog of smoke choked her until a plastic mask covered her face bringing the sickening, sweet smell of straight oxygen into her burning lungs.

Precious air.
More screams.
Flash of light.
Black.

"Babe!" *a woman's voice shouted, clearing away the fog.*

Brooke Meadows sat up straight, her heart pummeling against her ribs as her fight/flight/or freeze response kicked in. *Breathe. It's okay. It was only a dream.*

With the vision fading, palms flat against the boulder beneath her, Brooke searched the area for the woman who belonged to the voice that woke her. Seeing no one, she closed her eyes, inhaled a deep, steadying breath, channeling energy up from the rock and through her trembling body, then down through her hands as she exhaled slowly. After a few repetitions, the anxiety faded and her heart felt lighter. She opened her eyes. Goal accomplished; composure regained.

The Monday afternoon sun was warm on her back as she rolled over and slipped her hands beneath her face, cushioning her cheek like a makeshift pillow. The last hour had been spent dozing and soaking up sunshine on a gray, smooth boulder overlooking the lush valley far below the cascading mountainside, bright with an abundance of late summer foliage. It was here, in this almost-forgotten nook north of the Big Apple, Brooke Meadows had taken refuge for the last three years.

Reclining onto her back once more, Brooke caught sight of a flash in the sky and picked out a plane flying so high the drone of its engine sounded more like the distant hum of a bee. She closed her eyes tight, as a hint of her most recent vision clutched her heart.

A faint and forlorn locomotive whistle brought her back to the here and now, just seconds before the train chugged around a bend heading west as it came barreling through the valley far below. Her cue to get moving. The next train would be carrying the incoming group of campers scheduled for their three-week retreat at Earth and Sky.

Her booted feet hit the ground with a thud as Brooke slid off her rock. The 3 p.m. team meeting would begin soon and if she didn't hurry, she was going to be late. For now, she tucked away the remnants of the nightmare as she mentally prepped for the incoming campers. There was no doubt one of them belonged to the vision.

~ ~ ~

The Amtrak train swayed rhythmically, stopping at various depots throughout the four-hour ride from Penn Station to Demilune, the small village he'd be calling home for the next three weeks. Josh Quinn hadn't ridden a train in almost two decades, not since his daily trek on the LIRR as a newly-graduated business major into Manhattan and his first corporate job. Commuting from Ronkonkoma, Long Island to Penn had introduced a whole new life to him; a life full of promise, meaning, stability, and most importantly, love. These were things he'd never known fully and completely as a child. They were goals and dreams he'd worked hard for as a man. All the irreplaceable things he had lost three years ago.

A glimpse of sweet rosy lips, chocolate brown eyes, and long blond hair filled his vision, only to disappear when he blinked. His heart tightened as the memory of his wife was replaced with the sweet and sunny faces of their two young daughters, mirror images of their mom, laughing and giggling until he blinked again. He swallowed with difficulty, forcing his mind to go blank. This had to stop. He came here to heal, to regroup, to get ahold of himself—the self he lost along with his wife and kids in the plane crash three years ago. The plane he was supposed to be on as well, but wasn't.

And he had three weeks to do it.

~ ~ ~

"This group is a bit different. Don't worry. It's nothing we can't handle," Kyle said, scrolling down the screen of his iPad with his forefinger.

Brooke eyed her supervisor, trying hard to mask her trepidation as Kyle momentarily panned the disgruntled expressions of his staff gathered in the main dining hall awaiting their assignments. Glancing back to the roster, he reviewed and confirmed the client information, counting out loud. "Six. We have six people joining us for the next three weeks, all in dire need of down time, all looking to find the meaning of life. All desperately needing to get their groove back. We're their last hope. Any questions?"

"Um, Kyle?" Paulie waved his hand for attention. "Adults? Seriously?"

"Yeah. Dee and Doug felt this demographic required some one-on-one attention, and each of their sponsors are willing to pay triple what we normally charge. Considering the money they're spending, and the level of healing they're looking for, we've got to get our game on for the next three weeks." Kyle shrugged, shaking his head side to side. "Sorry, dude. You know how Dee and Doug can be."

"Kyle?" Cara began, her brow furrowed. "How the hell are we going to adapt what we do with children for adults with no time to prep?"

"All of you are perfectly capable of working with either adults or youths. You all have your degrees in counseling. You've completed the webinars and certifications we require. You can do this." He offered an unapologetic shrug.

"Well, I for one would like to know why we weren't told this before now?" Brooke finally spoke. "I came here to photograph children, not coddle adults. Our work is to help youths who—"

"I know what our mission is, Brooke," Kyle interjected, his voice stern, yet filled with understanding. He shot a pointed look at his fellow therapist, Alyssa. "Help me out here."

"This is what HQ wants," Alyssa said in her no-nonsense tone, the one she used for the teenagers who would sneak down to the beach after lights out. "They want us to do *exactly* what we do with the kids. It works, and they want a successful, proven program."

"Using our program designed specifically for youths doesn't make any sense. It's definitely not a good enough reason as to why we weren't given a head's up." Brooke jumped down from her seat on the wooden picnic table, her voice raised to a level she rarely exhibited. "This is bull. I don't want to work with adults. I came here to get away from people."

"Kids *are* people, Brooke, and you're great with them."

"Kyle! You know what I mean. People, yes. Their issues are real. They aren't a bunch of whiny socialites who are looking for pedicures and pampering."

"They won't all be looking for pedicures. As I said, there are four men and two women joining us." He perused the information filling his tablet screen with a scowl. When he refused to meet her gaze, Brooke stormed across the hardwood floor with heavy steps.

Alyssa jumped up to follow her, only to have Kyle bark out, "Let her go," before continuing to field the remaining questions from his team.

~ ~ ~

Five syncopated raps sounded on the wooden office door already propped open by a large speckled rock glimmering with Herkimer diamond chips. Brooke waited outside Kyle's office until he hung up the desk phone and motioned for her to enter. "You busy?" she asked, her voice hesitant.

"Not really," he replied, peering at her over the rim of his wire-framed glasses with one eyebrow raised. "What's up?"

"Well, first, I'm sorry for being so rude. The changes in program threw me off-kilter and I needed to process. Then, to be honest, I'm a little disappointed we had no time to prepare for such a drastic change in our program. I feel it's pretty unprofessional of Dee and Doug." She perched at the edge of his desk, both hands clasped lightly at her waist. "Even so, my response wasn't any indication of professionalism either. I'm sorry." She offered a cheeky squint in his direction.

"Apology accepted," he said with a wave. "Brooke, these sponsors chose *our team, our program,* out of all the competition world-wide, and out of all the other programs Earth and Sky offers across the U.S. They reviewed our program model and curriculum and offered *a lot* of money for us to provide exactly what we've done from Day One—because they think it'll work. It was the clients who asked for it to be done this way. They didn't want anyone harboring any pre-conceived ideas about the people they were entrusting to our care. You know the gossip and whining would have been non-stop if we'd given you a week's notice." He leaned back in his swivel chair, slightly rocking side to side. "Right?"

"You knew?" She glared at him. "And you didn't warn us?"

"I was told to keep quiet. They want you guys to do what comes naturally." He crossed his legs out in front of him, stilling his movement. "I have to do what they say."

"I s'pose." Silence settled between them and when it finally transformed from awkward to accepting, Brooke spoke again. "Well. Can you fill me in on the rest of the briefing? What did I miss? What am I dealing with?" She searched his desktop for the camper roster and Kyle picked up a black two-pocket leather binder from the wooden file organizer sitting on a shelf to his right.

"Nothing you can't handle," he said, turning to his computer as she perused the camper profiles.

"Seriously? Ned Andrews? From the cult mass suicide? His sponsor is . . . Cole Comstock? Isn't he the TV evangelist who . . .?" Her voice drifted off as she continued to read a bit more. "Geez. Wow. Wait. The CEO of Quirkyflirt.com? Really? Oh, freaking fabulous." She threw the binder on Kyle's desk with a flick of her wrist. "How is this more important than working with children who've lost their parents? Or have been sexually abused? What in the—"

"We aren't here to judge."

Not happy with being called out, Brooke poked some more. "C'mon, Kyle. Quirkyflirt!"

"He lost his wife and twin daughters three years ago in a plane crash." Kyle ran a hand through his prematurely graying sandy blond head of hair.

"*Plane crash?*" Bits of the forgotten nightmare swirled like mist in her mind. She tried to grasp the remnants, as they evaporated into air. *His wife and kids are already reaching out to me. Great.*

She sat down on the arm of an easy chair situated beside his desk and wiped her forehead with the back of her hand.

"You seeing things?" Kyle asked, staring at her while he waited for her response.

"It's been happening for a few weeks now." Her voice was a whisper.

With a light pat on her shoulder, he selected a folder marked 'Quinn, J.' off the shelf and handed it to her. "See? This is *exactly* what you're supposed to be doing. I was wondering if you'd gotten anything yet. Looks like you'll be spending time with Mr. CEO, our little Deathwalker." He winked at Brooke as she rolled her eyes at the sound of her team's nickname for her.

Brooke was the first to acknowledge her abilities were nowhere near as consistent as The Long Island Medium or John Edward. Still, so far, she'd been pretty accurate; connecting with the deceased relatives of clients coming here to work through their grief. Or rather, they connected with her. Hence, Deathwalker. As scary as it sounded to some, she liked the name, as it described exactly what she did: she walked with Death. That seemed way less intimidating at times than walking with The Living.

She thumbed through the folder, settling on the profile for Josh Quinn, aged 42, white male from Manhattan, founder of Quirkyflirt.

"Once again, life proves money can't buy everything," she said softly, after perusing his application, resumé, and bio. She examined the extra piece of information not normally included in each camper packet—a full color professional headshot sent along as if he were applying for a role in a movie. Of course, he was gorgeous, she groaned inwardly, noting the most captivating baby blues she'd ever seen.

Unsettled by the intensity and the way his paper gaze made her catch her breath, she snapped the folder closed and dropped it on Kyle's desk.

Blowing out a heavy breath, Kyle agreed as he glanced at his cell phone. "Spot on. It can't. However . . . it can pay for a three-week, life-altering stay at Earth and Sky Retreats. Which is what they're all about to get."

Curiosity got the best of her, and she opened Josh's portfolio once again. With a quick read-through, Brooke learned Quinn's wife and two twin daughters had been killed in the Flight 143 plane crash over Indonesia. "Whoa. Flight 143. They never found the wreckage, did they?"

Faint recollections of her dreams haunted her for the briefest moment, then faded behind a thick black veil.

"Nope. And, according to his sponsor, he's been unable to move forward with life ever since." Checking his iPhone one last time, Kyle stood up and waved toward the door. "The bus is turning into the main gate. Time to shine."

Together they headed over to the rec room where the rest of the team had gathered to wait for the bus to arrive. Some were reading; some were playing pool. Regardless, they all dropped everything when Kyle called for their attention with a whistle. "Game on, folks. Let's go change some lives."

They huddled together, heads bowed, as Kyle began their mantra, with the others joining in. "Strength of the earth, empower us. Winds of the sky, move us. Light of the sun, nourish us. Waters of the river, heal us. We are one with the Earth and Sky, from dawn to dusk, to when the moon is high. So mote it be."

"So mote it be!" each member of the group echoed as they jogged out to the front entrance, where the Earth and Sky Retreats' bus was now idling. Brooke made a detour to the cabin she shared with her female coworkers and grabbed her Canon.

Moments later, Brooke stood by the perimeter of trees, studying the silhouetted figures through the bus windows. Something was different, and it wasn't only the change in demographic. Gooseflesh rose along her arms, which she rubbed away absentmindedly, attributing it to the breeze whispering around her. The leaves rustled, the camp flag flapped to life, and a crow cawed as it flew overhead and landed in the oak she stood beneath. Some would consider the black bird an omen. But as it peered down at her, she lifted her gaze and silently thanked him for standing sentinel.

The bus made a loud *pshht* sound, just before the driver cut the engine. With a soft huff, Brooke tapped her booted toe impatiently, waiting for the doors to open, allowing the inhabitants to spill out into the hazy, late afternoon sun. Up until now, it was teenagers ranging from 14 to 17 years old who would emerge hesitantly, almost fearfully. Kids who'd had the life sucked out of them one way or another. Kids left with no reason to live, no self-esteem, unable to love themselves or anyone in their lives.

By the end of the three weeks, Brooke now reflected as she waited for the bus to unload, it was a whole different set of kids who boarded the bus and headed home. Newfound confidence, self-love, and forgiveness replaced bullying, lying, and self-sabotaging behavior. They learned to trust both themselves and others. Most importantly they remembered how to feel and receive love, and give it back in return.

Upstate New York Earth and Sky had built a reputation over the last few years due to the success rates they offered. This specific location and the core team members had made quite a name for themselves.

Brooke especially was recognized for her talents—with a camera *and* with youths who were dealing with the death of loved ones. Messages from "beyond the veil," as she termed it, often provided the affirmation and reassurance people sought. Those left behind drowning in their grief needed to know their loved ones were still close by—happy, free of pain, and transitioning into the afterlife nicely. These messages did more healing than any therapy session could.

After Dee and Doug had received numerous letters commenting on the transformation youths in her care experienced, they nicknamed her endearingly as "Deathwalker" during one of their visits from Sedona. Despite her best efforts to minimize the impact of her gift, she was recognized as an integral part of this location.

Dee and Doug had made a successful business out of alternative healing, with retreats similar to this branch of Earth and Sky all over the country. Regardless, none received the praise this team had garnered.

It was no secret among her peers that Brooke was different, in a good although sometimes spooky way. She did have to admit when it came to death, getting through the grieving process was a no-brainer for her. Death is a part of life. Give yourself time to heal properly, then make a commitment to move on. *Life is for living, so live it.* And if someone initially couldn't deal with it, by the time Brooke finished working with them, they were—at the very least—beginning to grasp what she was trying to share with them.

Chapter 2

Later that evening, the campfire roared as its yellow and orange flames undulated in a seductive dance against the coal black night sky. Occasional embers popped like miniature shooting stars, landing in the dewy grass. The burning wood created a smoky haze as it drifted low, encircling everyone gathered around the campfire pit in the cool Adirondack night air.

Josh took in the shadowed faces glowing in the darkness, questioning why he was here. He was successful. Wealthy. Powerful. With the last word, his heart clenched and he exhaled deeply, as if breathing out would release the pain. It didn't. Time had proven he wasn't as powerful as he had always believed. All the power and money he possessed hadn't been enough to save his family. Or get him through these last few years.

Life had been great. He and Rosalie had everything other couples struggled to grasp, even fleetingly. Both sets of in-laws loved them. They had two beautiful twin daughters—Rhianna and Sophia. His heart constricted again and a soft groan rumbled in his throat. With a fleeting glance, he eyed each woman flanking him to his left and right, while they stared into the fire unmoving. Maybe he had imagined the sound. Maybe it was his heart groaning and only he could hear it.

Struggling to stay seated, to interact and do this healing thing he was mandated to do, he searched for something safe to settle his brain on. Work. Work should have been a constructive topic to think about. Yeah, but no. Not with it being the reason he was here. His board had actually offered him a retirement package to step down if things didn't change after this retreat. *Step down!* From serving as CEO of his own company *he himself* built! *No pressure there.* What could three weeks in the woods with a bunch of tree-hugging hippies possibly do for him? For the last three years he'd hopped from therapist to therapist, all specializing in different theories and practices with no one figuring out how to help him. How was this going to be any different?

He shook his head to clear the thoughts and studied the flames once more. Campfires were a distant but pleasant memory from his childhood, probably one of the few happier experiences he'd collected. His family relocated frequently, giving him little opportunity to create lasting friendships. His mother enrolled him in Scouts as a young boy, so he always had a troop he could join wherever they lived. As a result, he never had the focus or opportunity to participate in meetings or to complete the projects required to earn his badges. Occasional sleepovers were the only memories he'd held on to over the years. That and the nights spent sitting around the campfires, telling stories, bragging about badges, and listening to the sounds of the fire crackling.

All around him, the other five campers were chatting with their mentors, doing the usual 'getting to know you crap'. He stayed silent, preferring to observe, rather than participate in the nonsensical chitchat. Watching from behind his sunglasses was safe, if not difficult in the dark. He'd grown used to seeing things through the shaded lenses. It was no one's business how he was feeling, and unfortunately, he'd been told regularly his eyes were mirrors to his soul.

Throughout the late afternoon and earlier in the evening, if anyone suggested he remove the shades, he'd offer a curt one-word reply, followed by silence. It wasn't awkward silence, well not as awkward as the usual silences he tended to create with people—women especially. So, as a result, neither his mentor—*Alyssa? Melissa?*—or this other woman who'd been tagging around him like a puppy since dinner, attempted to strike up a conversation now. He was quite good at shutting people down.

This whole trip was nothing like Derek had sold him. He was more than surprised when he showed up at Penn Station to find three other men and two women, not the all men he'd originally been told would be joining him. He thought this was going to be a man thing. Men helping men. He did not expect women. To be assigned to a woman on top of it all was *totally not cool.* None of this was what he signed up for, had agreed to, when Derek threw this at him.

Derek. His best mate and closest thing to a brother he had. And Quirkyflirt's board president. *Ha.* Josh thought back to the last time he saw Derek at their favorite pub, sharing a couple of Happy Hour beers. Was it only three Fridays ago Derek extended this ultimatum to attend a wilderness retreat or consider an early retirement? Josh had thought at first his friend was joking. Derek's demeanor changed quickly as he insisted he was serious.

~ ~ ~

"The board decided the company's continual losses need to be addressed. We can't look the other way anymore waiting for the old Josh to return. We need our CEO back," Derek said flatly, staring into the mirror behind the bar as he caught Josh's gaze.

"Addressed how?" Josh asked slowly.

A deep groan was Derek's response as he studied the brown bottled longneck IPA in his hands. He scratched his forehead, blurting out, "They want you to retire. They're giving you three months to get your shit together or they want an early retirement."

Josh laughed, the sound echoing loud and harsh, and for a moment there was a lull in all the various conversations previously buzzing immediately around them. "I'm only forty-two. There's no way in hell I'm retiring. It's my friggen company. I built this baby."

This is true, Derek had reminded him. He built the company, and now the board controls it. There were shareholders to look out for, who wanted action. And employees. And a name to uphold. And he wasn't cutting it anymore. Not since the plane crash.

"Look, man. I get it. The board gets it," Derek said, turning his full attention on Josh, squared off, eyes locked. "I can't imagine what you went through, bud. It's been three years. Time to—"

"You seriously think three years is long enough to get over the death of your wife and two kids? There's a time limit now? I'm supposed to just—what?" Josh had asked, his voice cracking, as he snapped his fingers. "Get on with it?"

"They want you to try this wilderness healing thing. Candace said her husband's brother out in Arizona did it when his wife left him. He started abusing prescription meds to deal with the divorce and got hooked. He came back a new person. Been clean a whole year." Derek stretched out his hands in offering. "Give it a try, man. See what happens. You never know."

"Three years of therapy. I haven't missed a day of work in what, a month now? I have my shit together. You know it." Josh took a swig of his beer. "This is bull."

"You're back physically. Your heart isn't in it anymore. Your head definitely isn't in it. You're taking up space, man. We need our leader back. The old Josh."

"The Old Josh is dead!" Josh slammed his bottle down on the smooth glossy wood and it teetered, nearly falling

over as Josh pushed away from the bar and stormed through the crowd, leaving Derek sitting in the pub alone.

~ ~ ~

"You okay?"

Somewhere in the distance, a soothing voice coaxed him back to reality. Josh tilted his head and took in the woman sitting to his right. His vision was hazy, his head was foggy, and for the briefest moment he was confused.

Campfire. A circle of strangers. This woman sitting next to him. The retreat. She was the camp photographer. He'd seen her earlier, taking pictures from the cover of the trees as he and the other passengers disembarked from the bus into the partially shaded, late afternoon sun-lit circular driveway.

She was at it again, snapping away at the dining hall while they were eating dinner. He recalled she, like him, preferred to eat alone, set off from the rest of the crowd. So, they'd shared a table without talking. His mentor—*why the hell couldn't he remember her name?*—was also a camp therapist, doing double time heading things up with the other camp therapist, Kyle. Dinnertime found him sharing a table with the camp photographer. He should tell Derek to ask for a partial refund.

"Yeah. Thanks. I think I'm gonna turn in." He stood up without saying another word and headed toward his cabin.

~ ~ ~

Brooke glanced at Kyle across the crackling flames, gesturing to the empty path Josh had taken and disappeared down. Kyle gave a simple shrug as he shook his head.

From the moment Brooke had laid eyes on Josh Quinn, she observed the deep scowl etched across his otherwise handsome features. His perpetual frown, combined with his brooding silence, immediately defined his norm. Not to mention the black Ray-Bans he'd worn since she first saw him getting off the bus and stepping into the shady canopy of the trees. Brooke had held her breath as he turned his head in her direction, spying her as she half-hid behind the massive oak tree. She didn't need him to remove his shades to know those gorgeous heart-stopping baby blues were staring at her. She'd felt a full-on body flush from head to toe, so she raised her only line of defense, her camera, and began clicking away.

Six adults warily stepped down the bus steps and into Brooke's life. Two women and four men, all polished and perfectly coifed, hiding behind their name brand sunglasses, designer labels, dye jobs, and tanning salon perfection. After the campers had finished disembarking, Brooke's gut knotted as Kyle introduced himself, followed by Alyssa, and finally the rest of the camp staff. After dismissing the travel attendant who'd met them at the train station to accompany the campers here, Kyle paired off the two women with two female mentors. Josh was assigned to Alyssa, and the other men were teamed up with the three male Earth and Sky mentors.

When Kyle called out "Josh Quinn," Brooke had straightened up, mesmerized momentarily by the man who stood apart from the rest of the group, dark blond hair curling around his nape. The Ray-Bans hid his eyes and made him look way too cool for her. Behind the sunglasses his face read disappointment, maybe even disgust. With what? At being paired with a woman? Brooke raised her camera again and snapped, catching his disdain forever.

From the moment he arrived, the butterflies sleeping in her belly since forever had fluttered awake, and had not settled down. She was human, yes, but her lack of composure was unsettling and confusing. She was *the* team Deathwalker—an honor requiring a certain degree of detachment honed with an innate sense of empathy. This was her calling and why she was here in the great scheme of things. Divinity had guided her to Earth and Sky to help people cope with the loss of loved ones. To help them come to terms with a reality they did not choose, or want to live in. To help them find a reason to go on.

When it came down to it, she was getting paid to take pictures, even though she was way over-qualified. Running away and hiding from the world for the rest of her life took priority over her career and was her original intention when applying for this position. Once she came here to Earth and Sky, she realized everything happened for a reason. She'd been brought here for her own healing, yes. And to help others with traumas way more serious than her own.

Like Josh Quinn losing his wife and children. Yet, the loss he could experience if Earth and Sky failed him was huge as well. And for some odd reason, the responsibility of preventing this from happening had been handed to her. Yes, even though she was not officially his mentor. I'm here to chronicle and record, she reminded herself. *Nothing more.*

Liar. The dreams wove him, like countless other people in the past three years, into her life, thereby making him her responsibility, and making her more than just a record keeper.

And until she delivered the message meant specifically for Josh Quinn, there was nothing she could do about it. What his message would be, she had no idea.

Chapter 3

Breakfast had already been served by the time Brooke ventured over to the dining hall. She'd spent the early morning hours reviewing, deleting, saving, and cropping the pictures taken the day before. Categorizing them by day, subject, and camper in folders on her Macbook desktop kept things orderly and organized. This gave her down time away from everyone, allowing her introverted self to not worry about being outgoing and friendly. This alone time she needed to prepare also gave her time to transition from Brooke, the woman struggling with her own crap to Brooke, the cheery photographer. Brooke, the upbeat team player responsible for coaxing everyone out of their shells. The perky optimist whose job was to get the campers to think they were happy to be here as she clicked away, recording this segment of their life for eternity.

As the wooden screen door snapped behind her, Brooke scanned the tables as she familiarized herself with the faces, attempting to recall their names. The fire was roaring in the huge fireplace spanning nearly the whole wall at the far end of the building. It was necessary to ward off the chill Adirondack early morning temps. The clatter of forks against plates, the hum of conversations, and the smell of freshly brewed coffee greeted her as she searched the gathering of staff and campers. One by one, people caught her eye and waved, and she returned their gestures with subdued enthusiasm. As she was about to grab a table in the corner, she spotted him. And her heart skipped a few beats.

Sitting at the far end of the same table the two had silently shared at dinner the night before, well-distanced from the rest of the group, close to one of the exits, sat Josh. Once again outfitted in his sunglasses, he focused on his scrambled eggs, bacon, and biscuits.

A few minutes later she sauntered over with coffee and her own plate heaped with scrambled eggs and bacon. It was her job, along with being camp photographer, to pick up the slack when campers alienated themselves. She was also responsible to help Alyssa out when needed. Even aside from the dreams connecting her to Josh Quinn, it was part of her job to pair up with him when necessary and there was no way around it. She did her best to make the most of it, slipping onto the attached bench across the wooden picnic table facing him. He wore a pale lavender, button-down shirt with the sleeves rolled halfway up his forearms, leaving the top two buttons undone. She imagined he wore dockers similar to the tan pair he'd worn upon arrival—it seemed like a sort of casual uniform for him. She fought her urge to confirm her suspicion by catching a glimpse of what was hidden beneath the table. "Fancy meeting you here," she offered brightly.

Without lifting his head, Josh raised his eyes and glanced over his shades to stare at her for a moment before focusing on his breakfast once again.

Without giving his behavior a second thought, she scooped a forkful of eggs into her mouth, acting as though his snub hadn't bothered her. His attempt to alienate her was a pretty standard defense mechanism, and had come to be expected of the youths she worked with who had lost someone dear. They did not want to be here because they really didn't want to heal. The pain they wrapped themselves up in was a constant reminder of how much they loved the person they lost. Their greatest fear of forgetting the person who meant everything to them prevented them from engaging. If they let go of the pain, they'd be letting go of their loved one.

Healing is so hard. Probably the hardest part of losing someone you love. Brooke reminded herself different people handled their grief in different ways. Unfortunately, she had witnessed this first hand. Forcing her own memory away, she turned to the man sitting across from her hiding behind his Ray-Bans. It was unfair he was so good looking. Thank goddess she didn't have to deal with his baby blues just yet.

"How'd you sleep last night?" Brooke asked, sipping her coffee as she waited for his response.

After a long pause, he spoke. "I didn't. Anyway, what business is it of yours?" He kept his focus on his food. "Don't you have somewhere to be? Some pictures you have to take?"

She nearly picked up her plate and left. Until a vision of two blond girls floating face-down forced her to stay seated. "Did you not sleep well last night? Is there something wrong with your accommodations? I can let Kyle know and—"

"No."

"Oh. Not a morning person, eh?" She smiled brightly, swallowing what she really wanted to say as she chomped on a slice of bacon.

He ignored her, so she concentrated on her eggs, letting the silence settle between them. She got it. Hopefully in time he would open up to her. Hopefully.

Some people might look at three weeks at Earth and Sky as a vacation, a perk for being a CEO of a major company, or a wealthy families' way of dealing with life issues. This wasn't it at all. Earth and Sky's program was like an emotional bootcamp, providing people the opportunity to just 'be.' Most often, 'just be-ing' provided the downtime needed for some deep soul-searching, leaving nothing to hide behind when trying to avoid the transformative pain required for healing. Maybe the task was something he was coming to terms with. Maybe he had memories of camping with his family. Maybe he hates eggs. It didn't matter. When he was ready to talk, he would, Brooke reminded herself, looking around for Alyssa, who was nowhere to be seen.

"Can I have everyone's attention?" Kyle blew a whistle and glanced down at his iPad, and back up at the crowd as conversation quieted and everyone turned in his direction. He waved his arms, energy and excitement in his voice.

"Welcome to Earth and Sky Retreats!" Kyle called out as the last remnants of chatter stilled. The only sounds filling his pregnant pause was the crackling fire and the distant clatter of dishes, pots, and pans coming from the kitchen.

"I hope everyone slept well last night because we've got a busy day ahead of us." His broad grin beamed like a burst of sunlight glimmering over the expectant crowd, as he rested his gaze momentarily on each person. Finally, he came to Brooke, locking eyes with her as if fueling her motivation with his confidence in her.

Brooke dipped her head in acknowledgment before looking away. Kyle knew her well, and as far as bosses go, she could do worse. He was tough and kind at the same time. One thing for sure, he was extremely empathetic and the wellbeing of his team was top priority. Still, she was disappointed he and Alyssa hadn't considered the anxiety she struggled with regarding men, especially male authority figures. It was pretty apparent, even so early in the session, that Brooke was going to be spending a lot of time with Josh. As far as Alyssa's absence this morning, yes, she was probably setting up for morning yoga, which wasn't out of the ordinary. But until Josh began interacting with the other campers, it meant Brooke would be sharing at least breakfast with him.

As Kyle reviewed the day's events outlined on the tablet he held in his hands, Brooke tried to ignore the impatient drumming of her breakfast companion's fingertips on the table.

While Kyle laid out the workshops and activities offered throughout the next three weeks, a female camper sitting in front of Josh shifted continually on her bench, letting out a loud huff. When the woman muttered something about this sounding more like work than a retreat, Josh snorted and caught Brooke's attention, mouthing silently, "What the heck?" Caught totally off guard, she bit her lower lip, suppressing a grin, and shook her head.

He leaned in and whispered, "She probably hasn't worked a day in her life."

Brooke widened her eyes and shushed him with a finger over her mouth.

Moments later, as the group was dismissed, Josh turned to Brooke. "Does Alyssa require we wear special clothing for yoga?"

"Whatever's comfortable and allows you to move is fine, as long as it's not pajamas." Brooke added softly as an afterthought, "Or business suits."

"No business suits. Got it." Josh nodded. "I'll definitely take note to keep the suits packed."

As she gave him a thumbs-up, she turned her attention to the rest of the campers.

"Okay, everybody!" Brooke called out, waving her hands. "We're going to head over to the Sunshine Pavilion for yoga and meditation with Alyssa. Follow Paulie. See you all in about fifteen minutes."

As Paul rounded everyone up, Brooke turned to the man beside her and asked, "You want me to wait for you to change? I've got to run back to my cabin and grab the rest of my equipment."

She studied his face, well the bottom half of it anyway, as he set his lips in a thin line while contemplating her offer.

"Yeah, sure." His head was trained toward her and she could feel him studying her reaction.

Brooke's heart fluttered a bit with his words, unsure how to reply. "Very well. Go on. I'll go grab my bag and tripod. Hey, I might even put you to work and have you carry my stuff for me."

"No problem. Unlike the princess," he said, jerking his head in the direction everyone else had gone, "I like work."

"Yes," she said, leading the way out of the dining hall, wondering if he'd just removed the first brick from his wall. "I imagined you would."

Moments later, they met up at the path. "Wow. You actually came back. I'm impressed," she chided, handing over her camera bag with the tripod tucked neatly in the side strap. He could have stepped out of a men's magazine ad, dressed in black Adidas pants with the white stripes down the legs, and a crisp white V-neck tee shirt.

A sardonic raise of an eyebrow over the black plastic frame of his sunnies was his only response. Her heart thumped a bit as she forced herself to look away.

Silence enveloped the two until they came upon a large, octagonal wooden structure bearing a wooden sign marking their destination as the "Sunshine Pavilion." The oak floor was polished to a shine, and the roof appeared thatched with fronds and ferns, with a solid ceramic-tiled barrier peeking out here and there. There were no walls, allowing the space to feel airy and bright.

"Alyssa, want me to set up your music?" Brooke asked, wondering why this hadn't been done already. She motioned to the side table and asked Josh, "Can you drop my stuff over there?" As he laid the equipment down, she added, "Thanks for your help."

Alyssa gave a quick nod toward Brooke and began explaining to everyone else her routine and what was expected of them. Josh stood by the table where he'd placed her bag and tripod, sunglasses in place. He shook his head ever so slightly when Brooke waved at him, motioning him to go stand with the rest of the campers.

Offering an indifferent shrug, Brooke turned her attention to the collection of CDs, searching for Enya. Once selected, she popped it into the CD player and adjusted the volume with a remote.

"CDs. Wow. Blast from the past. You'd think with the money you guys charge us you could update your sound system." Josh spoke in a low tone, just over her shoulder. His voice was not quite a whisper, laced with unexpected amusement, his resonating timber stirring her to her core.

She jumped at his unexpected proximity, then gathered her composure and offered a cheeky glance his way. "Oh. You do stand-up, too?"

"No."

She studied his face for a moment, feeling his eyes lock onto hers through the black plastic impenetrable wall of designer sunglasses. He picked up one of the remaining mats and laid it in a spot at the back of the room by the exit.

As the campers began stretching, guided by Alyssa's direction, Brooke turned on her camera and scanned the crowd. Noticing an unused mat, she caught Alyssa's eye and joined her at the front of the class.

"Ned," Alyssa said in a low voice. "It goes against his religious practice. Kyle said he could stay in the meditation room for his morning prayers instead." In a louder voice, Alyssa called out the next set of directions for the class.

Biting her lower lip, Brooke focused on capturing the group's first morning session of yoga and began shooting. She made no bones about shooting Josh who sat cross-legged on his mat, his back resting against the half-wall, not participating at all.

After an hour of stretches and beginners' postures, rounded off with a five-minute guided meditation to relax and center, the campers and staff rolled up their mats, and Josh immediately stepped into action, offering Alyssa his help. At her request, he began to collect the yoga mats everyone had piled in a corner. "We'll meet you back at camp, okay?" Alyssa said to him, as she turned to Brooke. "You got this?"

The two women studied one another briefly, then Brooke gave an 'ever so slight' shake of her head. Apparently, Alyssa chose to ignore this as she gave a wink and waved, leading the crowd back to camp with the counselor everyone fondly called Barefoot Dan at her side.

"I guess you are stuck with me for a bit," Brooke said in a monotone as Alyssa and Dan brought up the rear of the group.

After a moment, Josh asked, "How is exercise against religious beliefs?" He finished rolling up the mats, one by one returning them neatly to their shelf as Brooke packed up her equipment. She didn't reply until they began the walk back to the dining hall, where immediately following yoga Mandy had directed everyone to go for her art session, Hearts and Crafts.

With her camera still slung about her neck, Brooke carefully chose her words while Josh kept in step beside her, camera bag and tripod slung casually over his shoulder. "Some people believe yoga is part of a religious path and considered a sin."

"Is yoga a religion? I don't think I've ever thought about yoga before, let alone as a religion. If anything"—he paused, humor lacing his words—"it's more like a hippy New Age thing."

"It's what you want it to be. Some use it to tap into spirit. Others use it for exercise. Some consider it bowing to their Gods. Here, at Earth and Sky, it's exercise. Nothing else. We don't proselytize."

"What would you be proselytizing anyway?"

"Nothing." With a shrug Brooke followed him up the porch steps as he held the wooden screen door to the dining hall open for her, motioning her through.

Each of the six tables had been set up with plastic cups of Sharpie permanent markers, colored pencils, and white card stock. A refreshment table along the back wall offered a glass decanter of cucumber water and one with lemon water alongside napkins and wineglasses.

As they passed the decanters, Josh whispered with a snort, "Zinfandel wineglasses for our water drinking pleasure. Fancy. So that's what my board is paying you for?"

After waiting a moment for her response and receiving only a pointed glare, he handed Brooke her camera case and tripod. Picking a spot at the table closest to the door, he left her without another word.

Once everyone was seated, Mandy spoke up, addressing Brooke as she flexed the tripod in the far corner and positioned herself to shoot the class. "Brooke, can you team up with Josh? Alyssa and Kyle are on a conference call with Dee and Doug." Without hesitation, she continued to the rest of the group, "Today we'll be introducing ourselves to ourselves."

A protest bubbled up automatically within Brooke as she glanced at Josh, noting his grimace. Apparently, he was as unhappy with Mandy's directive as she.

A collective murmur rose and fell among the group and Mandy paused patiently until the room was silent once again. Brooke took her seat with Josh.

"Everyone should have two pieces of cardstock," Mandy began. "Each of you will take turns drawing the outline of your partner's hand on the first piece. Teamwork. You are not allowed to trace your own hand. Mentors draw camper's hand, and then camper will draw their mentor's hand. You can begin." She turned her back to the class, flipped a switch on the audio system, and soft instrumental music filled the room.

Reaching for their pencils at the same time, Brooke squinted at Josh as she waited for him to place his hand on his cardstock. He didn't. Instead, he dipped his head back at her, gesturing for her to put her hand down first.

Age doesn't really matter when people are struggling with control issues resulting from death, Brooke noted, biting her tongue. Rather than cause a scene or argue, Brooke gave him this bit of control, as she would have with any of the younger clients she worked with previously.

Part of the healing process was coming to terms with the fact you have no control, then learning how to take control in a healthy manner when you can, she reminded herself.

The damn sunglasses were still in place, so all of this was supposition on her part anyway. How could she know what he was thinking if she couldn't read his expression? The thought of having to look into his eyes made her heart skip a beat and her breath catch.

Maybe he didn't hear mentors were supposed to draw first. Who knows? Watching him through veiled lids, she noticed his actions were mechanical and stilted as he traced the contours of her fingers and thumb. In a failed attempt to ignore the fluttering in her belly as the pencil tickled her skin, Brooke jerked her hand away as he finished the outline.

This was a simple exercise Mandy did every opening session, and on occasion Brooke had filled in with some of Alyssa's young campers. It was pretty much a no-brainer. Unfortunately, the exercise felt way different—much more intimate—with Josh than all the other times she'd completed this task with youths.

She bit her lower lip as she cast a quick glance at the man sitting across from her. His lips were upturned ever so slightly as he rolled the pencil between his thumb and forefinger methodically. He raised his eyebrows and tilted his head down to his hand as he offered it toward her, waiting patiently for her to accept.

Her cheeks warmed as she grabbed the pencil, an electric shock zapping them both as their fingers touched. "Oh! Sorry!" she chirped as she began what had suddenly become a monumental task of tracing someone's hand as the soothing strains of Van Morrison's "Into the Mystic" played softly in the background.

When everyone had finished and set their pencils down as instructed, Mandy continued her explanation for the next part of the activity. Brooke was finding it difficult to understand the directions as her head was foggy and there was a slight buzzing in her ears, similar to a white noise machine. She was only able to continue because she had done it so many times before.

They were to write a word in the palm of their drawing. For the campers, this word was reflective of how they felt just before stepping off the bus the day before. For staffers, it was how they felt the moment before the campers arrived. "Discuss these feelings with one another before you commit to the word you want to write," Mandy said.

Brooke knew the purpose of this exercise was to get the campers to begin dealing with their emotions, and in order for it to be effective, the mentors needed to complete the exercise with total honesty. She'd learned by watching. And doing. Kids were inordinately perceptive.

"When you write your word, use the markers to complete the hand, using colors, shapes, or symbols to reflect how you feel about where you are at this point in your life," continued Mandy.

"Once you're done, follow the same steps on your second pieces. Only instead describing how you felt, I want you to consider what you hope to get out of this retreat. Decorate your paper palm using the colors, symbols, shapes to reflect on where you hope to be at the end of three weeks."

"You go first." Josh directed Brooke with the authority and confidence of a CEO.

"I think we're supposed to talk *together*, and work on this *together*. So why don't we talk about what we may want to write *together*," Brooke directed. The buzzing had stilled and she was now ready to take control of the situation from the CEO.

"Very well." Josh paused for a moment, leaning back slightly, bracing his hands on the edge of the picnic table. "Pissed off. I was—*am*—really pissed off I have to be here."

Brooke inclined her head and peered into his Ray-Bans. "Why?"

"You said we are doing this together. So, I believe you have to tell me how you felt." He bent his arms, leaning his elbows on the table, resting his chin against his upturned palms, waiting.

She studied the fireplace across the room, where the morning's flames had died down and now only charred embers glowed. "I was angry, too."

An eyebrow quirked in disbelief above the dark lenses. "Oh, really?"

Nodding, she searched the black mirrors of his sunglasses.

"Why were *you* angry?" he said in a huff of disbelief.

"It's your turn. Why were you pissed off?" She jutted her chin out, holding her ground.

"I really don't need to be here." He scratched his head, then ran his middle finger along the darkened pattern of vein-like lines spreading throughout the wood grain of the tabletop. "It's ridiculous, and I have a company to run. I don't have time for all this tree-hugging, hippy crap. Seriously. What is drumming and yoga going to do for me three years of—" He stopped with another huff, reminding Brooke of a horse locked in a stall unable to reach his grain trough.

"Of—?" She tilted her head and waited for his response.

"Nothing. Your turn."

Honesty. How could she be honest without insulting him? "Can you take off your shades? It's really frustrating."

"No."

She pursed her lips and let loose. "Fine. There're young children out there who *want* to be here. Kids who *need* to work through their grief, who couldn't do anything as they watched their mother or father die a slow, agonizing death as they battled an illness. Or who lost their brother or sister to cancer or some other unplanned death. Or their grandparent or aunt or uncle who had a heart attack or stroke and lay in a coma for weeks before passing. I didn't sign up to work with adults. And I was angry I have to."

"Wait. You work with kids?" His brow furrowed thoughtfully.

"Yes, well sort of. I photograph them." She nodded. *And talk with their dead relatives.*

He leaned forward and bent his head toward her, his autumn sky blue eyes peering intently over the dark rims of his shades, and whispered, "You know what I do, Miss Photographer?"

Brooke attempted and failed to swallow a thick lump nestled in her throat, her green gaze locked onto his baby blues. *No one could be this sexy without knowing it.* Brooke held her breath waiting for him to continue.

"I promote the hook-up culture. And make money off a people getting laid. Lots of money." He sat back and released a short chortle.

"Yeah. I know." Her cheeks warmed yet again as she finally spoke.

"Sex makes me a lot of money." He leaned close once more and whispered again. "And being here hugging trees is keeping me from making money."

She could *not* tear her gaze away from his mouth. And it riled her even more. "Money isn't everything, Josh. It can't buy you happiness, can it? And as far as I know, we haven't instructed you to hug trees. Yet." She broke the tension—and the lock on his lips, picking at a cuticle on her thumb. She chose to ignore his comments about sex, although the butterflies in her stomach apparently heard his every word. He was deliberately toying with her.

"True." He nodded and brought his attention to the window.

They remained silent as Josh picked up two black Sharpies, handing one to her. He scrawled in the middle of his palm, *Pissed off.* Brooke followed suit and quickly jotted, *ANGRY.*

He colored his palm green, while Brooke left hers blank. When Josh pointed out she hadn't finished her drawing, she laid her marker down with purpose.

"Yeah, I am."

"We have to color paint them. I did mine green for the money I make. What're you going to color yours?"

"I'm not coloring mine. I'm leaving it blank."

"Why?" Confusion knitted his brows together above the bridge of his sunnies.

She offered simply, "Because all I felt was empty when they told us about the change in campers two hours before your bus arrived."

"No time to prep?"

"Nope." Brooke took the two remaining pieces of cardstock and placed one in front of Josh on the table and kept the other for herself. "So. What do you hope to get out of this retreat?" She chose to disobey the rules and traced her own hand. She couldn't risk contact again. She might sizzle up and disappear in a poof of smoke. Like a July 4th sparkler.

Silence was his only answer. He bent his head down as if studying the blank paper on the table in front of him.

His chest rose and fell with each breath as he toyed with the Sharpie, rolling it back and forth between his right-hand thumb and forefinger.

Mesmerized with his action, she waited for his response.

"I want to keep my job," he said, as he scribbled his goal not bothering to even trace his hand.

"And?"

"And what?"

"All you care about is your job?" She peered up at him, studying his mouth, waiting for a great revelation she knew would not come. At least not today.

"What do you expect?" His hands came down flat on the table as he leaned in and slammed the Sharpie down with a crack, barking his question at her.

Struggling not to rise to his bait, she breathed in for a count of three, and exhaled for a count of three. "Something with a little more substance. A little more depth of character. A little more human."

He threw his head back and laughed out loud. It was not a happy sound. It was harsh. Cold. And it left Brooke with a thickness in her heart, struggling for a reply. Before she could find the words to respond, he untangled himself from the table and stormed out the door, leaving Brooke staring wide-eyed as he left the building taking two porch steps at a time.

Chapter 4

Standing at the shoreline, sun hidden behind the scalloped mountain terrain, Brooke sunk her bare feet into the wet earth. Moments earlier, she had quickly excused herself without explanation from the Friday drumming workshop, escaping to the shore in search of solitude.

Picking up a stone, Brooke threw it into the water with a loud splash. "Get. A. Grip. Brooke Meadows. What the hell is wrong with you?" She shouted to no one.

Josh. Josh was what was wrong with her. How could this be? He wasn't the first man she'd come in close contact with since . . . since . . . Richard. But he was the first man who made her stammer and blush. The first man to make her forget what she was saying mid-sentence. The first man she thought about at night, as she lay in bed while sleep eluded her.

She was not prepared for the unexpected connection striking her like lightning almost immediately. Never had this happened to her, not even before she'd sworn off all men three years ago. None of the men who'd come on to her since relocating here had interested her one bit. The guys she ran into in town, single dads of the kids she worked with. Occasional reporters looking to cover E&S. The answer was always the same. No. She was not ready to trust any man just yet.

She paced, feeling caged even though the whole lake lay in front of her, her thoughts racing in time with her steps. *And then he had to show up.* It felt as though he watched her every move, but it had to be her imagination. He was here because he couldn't get over the death of his wife and daughters, not to hook up. He was vulnerable, and having these thoughts made her feel almost predatory. *Just like . . . Nope. Not going there.* She pushed the memory out of her mind.

And those freaking dreams. Brooke stopped pacing and covered her face with her hands. The last few nights found her waking up at three, four, and 5 a.m. Most of the dreams had her reliving wispy bits of terror—both from her own past and from a past she knew didn't belong to her, only to have them blend together and dissipate into her subconscious.

Some of these dreams were not terror-filled at all. Some of them, well . . . It was as if she were a cat in heat, she thought in disgust as she brought a closed fist to cover her mouth in reflex. It was like she was watching subconscious porn with the actors switching between her and Josh and then Rosalie and Josh. And sometimes all three. Tossing her head, she forced the thoughts away as she paced some more.

If she didn't get it together, Brooke was sure she would not survive the next two weeks. She would be surprised if she lasted until Sunday.

Walking over to the line of trees bordering the lake beach, she picked up a fallen branch. Determining it fell from the willow she stood beneath, she rested a hand on the rough bark of the trunk and whispered a word of thanks. After stripping away the leaves and bits of growth, she used her camp knife she kept sheathed at her side to whittle away the nubs, then sharpened the end until it was straight and smooth.

Returning to her previous spot, she faced the west where the orange glow of the setting sun had faded to a faint shimmer on the mountain ridge. Taking a deep cleansing breath, she exhaled slowly, repeating the action three times. When her thoughts were at last void of anger and confusion and fear, she turned to the north and placed the tip of the makeshift staff on the sand.

Spinning clockwise, she drew a circle around her body. When the circle was complete, she crouched and placed her hands palms-down along the cool, damp ground while whispering words of healing for herself and for Josh. And for Rosalie and the girls. She stayed there unmoving, her spirit in the Astral, until the dinner bell sounded. Like an audible cord, the faint tinkling brought her back to the here and now.

Slowly she rose, unbending her legs to stand as she turned counterclockwise, stick in hand, retracing the circle in the sand in a backwards motion. When she was done, she stepped out of the circle still drawn in the sand, feeling much less heavy-hearted and much more at peace.

~ ~ ~

"Sorry I'm late." Brooke ran into the dining hall, nearly colliding with Kyle as she barreled through the doorway.

"Whoa! Where's the fire?" Kyle caught her by her shoulders with a chuckle, peering beyond her into the yard. "You okay?"

Brooke felt her face flush, as she avoided his eyes.

"No fire, just got distracted and didn't want to be late for dinner. I'm okay." She took a step back and twirled. "See?"

"You need to talk?" he asked, catching her gaze.

"Nope." She shook her head. "I'm good."

Kyle eyed her while she perused the dinner buffet. Once she had selected her choices she glanced back. Alyssa had joined him, and Brooke continued to feel the heavy weight of now both their attention while they spoke. Alyssa waved as Brooke set her tray down on the table and took a seat with Mandy, Cara, Louisa, and Renee.

~ ~ ~

The drummers were out and in full force as the campfire crackled and popped at the center of the circle. Alyssa and Maddy were up and dancing to the beat, and some of the campers had picked up their drums and joined in as they attempted to follow the different rhythms. Brooke and Josh sat near one another, and as usual, spoke little. His Ray-Bans were annoyingly in place. The drums were lulling at times, energizing at times, and a source of laughter when people screwed up and had to start over.

"How come you're not dancing?" Josh asked, motioning his head with a nod to the women now numbering four as they swayed around the fire.

Brooke shrugged. "I prefer drumming."

"Why aren't you drumming?"

"Why? Do you want to drum? I can get—" When she started to rise, Josh briefly placed a hand on her arm. Her knees nearly buckled and she collapsed back into her chair.

"No. I'm fine. Curious, but okay." A brief glimmer of a smirk faded into the shadows.

"Another night, then. There'll be plenty of time to drum. It feels good sitting back and taking it all in for a change." As she spoke, she absentmindedly rubbed away the tingling imprint his hand had left on her arm. She knew he'd been watching her, and her face grew warm with the realization of her actions. He peered at her in the darkness over his shades. Unable to look away, she licked her lips and tried not to remember her dreams.

"You're not required to take pictures at these events?" He cocked his head and waved his hand at the circle, breaking the trance.

"Even I get a night off sometimes," she said, offering another shrug.

He dipped his head in understanding, then asked, "Why're you stuck here babysitting me?"

Ignoring him and the ire he ignited within, she stared into the fire as she swallowed a retort. Finally, she spoke. "So, what did you do on your break?" Brooke offered an open-ended question as an ice breaker and conversation starter.

"Nothing." Josh leaned to his right and picked up his water canteen sitting on the ground beside his chair.

"You had to do something. Even if you napped, it's still something. Isn't it?"

"I don't nap."

"Okay," Brooke said softly, peeking through the shroud of silence hanging between them.

After a few moments, Josh spoke. "I also don't do well with open-ended questions. I don't do well with cognitive therapy. Or behavioral therapy. If you want to talk to me, talk to me like a person. Not like I'm your class project for your Psych 101 crash summer course. I get it now. Are you a returning student, interning here, and shooting photos for cash or a class assignment?"

"What the hell? I don't talk to you—"

"Yeah, you do, Brooke. I'm not one those kids you guys can pick apart and rebuild. I'm an adult. I'm a man. I've got shit I'm dealing with. But I'm dealing with it. If you want to talk to me, talk to me. Don't dissect me. Okay?"

It was all she could do to stay seated and act like nothing was wrong. Had she been treating him like a case study? No. A fragile human being? Maybe. He was no different than all the other adult campers here on their journey of healing. "Okay. Let me clarify a few things. We don't pick apart and rebuild anyone. Kids or adults." She waved at him when he started to interject as he raised a hand and opened his mouth to speak. "Let me finish, please."

Josh raised his canteen in salute and took a gulp.

"I understand you're dealing with *stuff* or you wouldn't be here. This is what we do. We help people deal with what they're going through. We help them figure out how to embrace it, acknowledge it, then redefine themselves without it. This is the only way you're going to live a healthy, productive life again, Josh." She kept her eyes on the fire roaring and dancing before them. "You choose. You can get something out of this and go back to your comfy CEO couch, or you can sit here and sulk for the next three weeks and look forward to your early retirement." She sucked in her breath, surprised and dismayed with what she'd verbalized, and checked the circle to see if Kyle or anyone else had heard. Everyone seemed absorbed in the music and laughter. She exhaled and slunk back into her chair. Outbursts like this could not happen again.

"I see." Josh set down his canteen and cleared his throat. The moments dragged by, but then he asked, "So, what did you do on your break?" With one fleeting swipe, he slipped his shades off his face. His blue eyes stared intently into her own. She blinked, swallowed, and reminded herself to breathe. They were as mesmerizing in life as they had been in his photograph. Ironically, she wished he'd put the sunglasses back on.

After a moment she broke his gaze and trained her sight on the flames. She wasn't sure if it was the heat of the fire, or her answer warming her cheeks. "I worried about you." Her words were barely audible, even to her own ears.

He nodded. "Me, too."

They locked eyes until Brooke spoke. "I'm a little out of my element here. Except for my co-workers, I've gotten used to talking with usually only kids."

"I know."

She shot him a sidelong glance, wondering what he knew? Was it so obvious she was out of her element? Or was he referring to the fact she'd already told him she worked with kids. Did he find her incapable?

"So, if I sound condescending," she continued, "or if you feel like I'm treating you like a child, I'm sorry. It's not intentional. And I'm not babysitting you for Alyssa. She's your mentor. I'm only here to fill in the gaps."

"She has a lot of gaps." He grimaced.

True, she seemed to have more than usual, Brooke noted silently.

"This isn't about me and Alyssa, though. It's about you. So?" She offered him an invitation to speak.

"No." His answer came quick and sharp. "Sorry. No." He paused before continuing. "I don't want to have to go through the whole 'get to know you' phase all over again. It's been a bit difficult working through all of this with Alyssa, then having to do it all over again with you this whole week."

She studied his eyes, dark orbs smoldering and burning, reflecting the flames. She could easily lose herself in them. But the anger. The grief. It was almost as tangible as a piece of cooled and hardened lava. Surely, if she held his gaze too long, she'd melt from all the emotion. The minutes ticked by as she collected herself.

"How was your dinner?" Brooke asked, opting for something safer.

"The food here is exceptional. Not at all what I expected." He brushed a smudge of ash off his leg.

"What did you expect?" She grabbed a bag of M&M's someone passed her as they shimmied around the fire clockwise, offering her and Josh the bag of treats with an outstretched hand.

"Hot dogs?" He laughed.

"Well, I'll warn you now. Hot dogs are on the menu with the Survival Wilderness themed lunch we do later in the program."

"I'll call out sick for hotdog day."

She shook her head, and in an amused voice said softly, "No calling out sick."

He hesitated and studied her for a moment. A slip of a smile turned up his lips. "So, I guess I should ask right about now how your dinner was."

She poured a handful of M&Ms into her palm, before handing the bag to him. He mimicked her action and passed the bag to the person to his left.

"It was delish, as always. Although our chefs were trained around the world, they specialize in local, down-home, feel good comfort food cooking. No escargot, or sushi, thank goddess." She ended with a quick chuckle and shake of her head.

"I hear ya on the sushi. I'd take a hot dog over raw fish any day." His laughter warmed his gaze.

Killer eyes and a killer smile. No man had the right to be this good looking. Refocusing, she continued the conversation before her awkward silence consumed her, and asked, "So, what did you think of your first few days?"

Studying the flames, he took a long pause before answering. "It's been both what I expected and dreaded. At the same time, it's been all right."

"Well, I'll take 'all right' any day." She picked up her canteen and took a swig of the still-cool water.

"What did you think of my first few days?" He continued looking ahead.

She smiled at his profile in the darkness, shadows and light playing off his features, and gave a non-committal lift of her shoulders.

He turned toward her with dark eyes as he waited for her response. "C'mon. You see everything from behind your camera lens. I bet you don't miss a trick."

She couldn't hold back the shimmer of a smile as it broadened into a full grin. "Well. Everyone gets off to a rough start, some more than others." She couldn't face him, so she searched the sky for stars, trying to still her heart, before setting her canteen on the ground beside her chair.

How could any man have this quick of an impact on her? He was so out of her league. How was this even possible? For the first time in years, Brooke was trusting a member of the male species again. The butterflies in her stomach flitted a bit with the thought, and she adjusted in her chair, hoping to crowd them out and settle them down.

"And?" He cocked his head to one side, waiting, his eyes burning with curiosity.

If they'd been at a bar, Brooke would have taken this exchange as flirting. Everything about this man was sensual, sexual. Or was she simply reading too much into him? How could she be attracted to a man who was still suffering from the loss of his wife and children and had been left in her care? How could she even think he was flirting?

Clearing her throat, she realized she'd been blatantly studying his features in the darkness. "I think if you keep an open mind and heart, and trust us, you'll be able to work through all those things weighing you down, keeping you from a healthy life."

"It's difficult to think of life without them, without grieving them. It seems so selfish." Even though his voice cracked, Josh refused to break her gaze.

"Just remember, Josh. Life is for living."

And just as she thought he'd taken another brick out of his wall, he gave his full attention to the fire, slipping his Ray-Bans back into place.

Chapter 5

A steady, gentle rain saturated the early Saturday dawn, enveloping the woods and lake in a soft gray veil. Rather than opt for her morning meditation routine, Brooke decided a jog around the property in the misty morning rain would bring her the much-needed cleansing relief she sought.

She'd had another nightmare last night, as she had every night for the last five days since Josh arrived. And, as usual, by the time she'd gotten up, gotten dressed, and nearly completed her jog, any recollection had faded into the back recesses of her mind. All she could recall was the terror she felt, and the sound of screams.

She forced the thought out of her mind, concentrating on the steady rhythm her feet made as they pounded the jogging path lacing the perimeter of the property. The rain fell softly around her, on her, washing away her fears, cooling her body, and bringing her back to a state of peace.

By the time she returned to the main yard, she was drenched to the bone, water cascading in rivulets down her forehead and cheeks; her nightmare forgotten. As she jogged past the entrance to the dining hall, she noticed Josh sitting on the porch swing, cradling a mug in both hands. She felt his eyes—once again masked by his sunglasses—following her as she sprinted past. She waved in acknowledgement, not stopping until she was up the steps and in the haven of her own cabin.

~ ~ ~

"I didn't know you jogged," Josh offered as he slipped onto the bench across from Brooke, his ceramic E&S mug freshly filled with steaming hot brew cradled gingerly in his hands.

"There's a lot you don't know about me, Mr. Quinn." She took a swig of coffee, trying not to sputter as he slipped off his Ray-Bans, folded them and placed them on the table between them.

Bright blue, crystalline eyes. Cool and piercing to her soul. Her stomach fluttered.

. . . I got this thing about blues . . .

Her brain whispered the potential line of a poem and she tried to memorize it until she could jot it down. *It could be about all things beautiful and blue. Autumn skies, the ocean; a lovers' eyes.* Only he wasn't her lover. *Geez, Brooke!* She blinked hard to clear her brain.

His voice brought her back to the moment and the line was forgotten. "Apparently. For instance, you know my last name," he said, pointing to her nametag and reading aloud, "Ms. Brooke with an 'e'. But I don't know yours."

"There's no need to know my last name," she said, her eyes flitting between his nametag and his face. He'd not shaved in a few days, and a stubbly growth had filled in his jawline and chin. She struggled to ignore the fluttery feeling deep inside. *Why did not shaving make him hotter than he already is?* Her body temperature rose a degree or two as she squirmed in her seat.

"Not fair. Especially since you're getting paid to pretend we're forming a friendship." He tilted his head to one side, catching her gaze.

She swallowed a large gulp of her coffee and glared at him. "Ouch? Where do you come up with these insults? I'm getting paid to photograph and chronicle this retreat. The friendship's pro bono—*by choice*."

"Just pointing out the obvious. Ms.? Mrs.? Brooke with an 'e' and no last name."

After a moment's hesitation, she offered, "Meadows."

He cocked his head, eyes laughing. "Brooke Meadows. So, let me guess. You were conceived at Woodstock or something?"

"Continue." She chuckled and held his gaze.

"It's the perfect hippy name. All New Agey. Were your mom and dad hippies?"

"Actually," she snorted softly. "Yeah. They were. Sort of. And, by the way, I was *not* conceived at Woodstock."

"Sure, sure," he said, in full-on jest-mode. "Do you have a sister named Moonunit and a brother named Forrest or something?"

"Did you do a background check on me?" She shot him a mock look of horror.

"No way! You have a brother named Forrest?" He squinted in disbelief as he slapped his palm on the table. "I knew it!"

"I don't have any brothers or sisters." The look she gave him would wither a cactus on a rainy day, and her voice was as dry. "I was joking."

"Touché." He stared at her, his eyes lit with mischief, his mouth lopsided with an ever so slight grin.

She studied his face and sighed softly, enjoying the banter. Probably too much.

"I imagine you've been to Woodstock though." He turned and caught her gaze again.

"Are you telling me or asking me?" she queried, her eyes warm.

"Stating a fact. You've been to Woodstock. You probably smoke pot. You hug trees. You garden. And when you aren't here, you're probably living in a commune with a bunch of other hippies saving the bees or something." While his face was deadpan serious, his eyes matched hers in mirth and warmth.

"Yes. Sometimes. Yes. Yes. No. And yes, I'm seriously concerned about the bees." She laughed while he matched her answers with his statements, as he raised his brow in surprise.

"So, who'd you see at Woodstock?"

"It's actually called the Bethel Performing Arts Center now, and it's located in Bethel, New York. Not Woodstock. It's got an amphitheater and vendors and a museum. It's really cool. You should go."

"It's not in Woodstock? What the—? Hm. You know, maybe I will. We could go." He avoided her eyes and studied his coffee. "I mean, like a field trip. With the other campers."

Brooke's breath hitched in her chest with his initial comment. As he finished his suggestion, she willed herself to breathe again. *Stop reading into things.*

"It would be fun. However, we've got our itinerary all set for the rest of the retreat. You should definitely check it out at some point. They've got their line up on their website. Remind me to give you their URL."

"Great. I'll give you my number and you can text it to me."

"No worries. I'll email it to you with the email address you have on file. Or you can Google it. Bethel. Performing. Arts Center."

Although his autumn sky blues were bright and unwavering, he conceded and said, "You're good."

"And you are terribly naughty." How she was able to still speak—let alone think after their most recent exchange—was beyond all logic at this point.

"Seems it's what I do best." He stood up and stretched his arms high and wide. "So, where do you think Alyssa will have us doing yoga this morning? I can't see the princess walking all the way to the pavilion in the rain." He stared out the window as the rain fell nearly horizontally, battering the windows like pellets from an air gun.

"A little rain is cleansing. It will do you all good." She turned her attention to the window as well.

"Rain sucks."

"I like to think of it as liquid sunshine."

"You must be an eternal optimist."

Eternal optimist. She used to be. Once upon a time. A while ago. Nowadays all Brooke saw was loss, sadness, sorrow. It was so difficult to be positive all the time, to play the role she had to play for the kids. And adults as well. And her team members. She couldn't ever let them know the demons she battled and the grief she kept in check. Only Kyle and Alyssa had been privy to her private information. And Dan. And this was why she ran; why she was faithful about her yoga and meditation. Why she focused all energy on healing others. It was the only peace she ever got from her memories.

"Hey. Earth to Brooke." Josh waved a hand in front of her face.

"Sorry. Yes. Eternal optimist. You pegged me." She stood up and motioned for him to follow. "Rec room. Let's go see if she needs any help setting up. And to answer your question, no. We won't make you walk too far in the rain. Goddess forbid you delicate flowers get wet."

~ ~ ~

The rec room had been reorganized, with the couches, chairs, and occasional tables pushed back along the perimeter of the room. One of the maintenance crew had retrieved the yoga mats, which were piled on one of the leather couches. Alyssa greeted Brooke and Josh at the door, holding it open as they climbed the porch steps.

Brooke hung back, fiddling with her camera, reviewing the last shoot she'd taken, deleting the blurry or unflattering shots while Alyssa and Josh rearranged the remaining furniture. When their task was completed, Alyssa had Josh place the yoga mats on the table by the entrance. When he was finished, he came to stand by Brooke as she stretched to the soft strains of Enya. Picking up the CD case, he studied it and waited until she was done with her routine before he spoke.

"I used to jog." His gaze never left the CD case in his hands.

"Oh? Can't picture you as a runner. Treadmill, maybe?" Brooke teased.

"Before Rosalie."

"Your . . . wife?" she asked, knowing the answer already from her review of his file. Her name echoed as Brooke heard her brain whisper it back.

He nodded. "Life got too busy. The business took off surprisingly fast. And then she was pregnant." His voice cracked.

"I understand. Sometimes life gets in the way of our own self-care and before we know it—"

"It's gone." He turned toward her, his gaze clouded with pain.

"Well. I was going to say 'it's tomorrow and another list of excuses has popped up.' I get it. I'm really sorry for your loss. Truly. I understand what you're going through." She placed a hand on his shoulder, and he immediately jerked away.

"Do you, now? How do you know? Have you lost your wife and kids?" His quiet demeanor flared into rage as he turned on her. "Well? No. You haven't. So, you *cannot* possibly understand what I'm going through." His words were sharp and came in a staccato downpour, sounding as brittle as the rain falling on the rec room roof.

"No, Josh. I can't." She paused and inhaled deeply before continuing. "I can't begin to understand the grief you're experiencing with the loss of your wife and daughters. I do understand grief and pain, and suffering and guilt. And I'm here if you need to talk. It takes time, and the pain never goes away. Eventually you have to start living again."

"What if I don't want to live again?"

A pregnant pause hung between the two as they stood there, eyes locked. Brooke whispered softly, her voiced strained. "You don't stop looking for a reason to try."

Similar conversations had filled the last three years working at Earth and Sky, hundreds of times, only with children who had their whole life ahead of them. Trying to make a grown man who had already experienced a good part of his life figure out how much adventure was still left to experience . . . This was out of her ball park. Sure, the same mechanics of counseling applied. The same understanding of grief therapy applied. But she was not his therapist. She was not hired for a counseling position. Sure, she was qualified, and had all the correct degrees. She didn't want this responsibility anymore. She was the photographer, and taking pictures suited her fine.

How could she show him there was so much to live for, when she herself was struggling with the exact same concept?

"What if I don't want to?" The waver in his words tugged at her heart. She wanted to throw her arms around him and hug him until his pain went away. She didn't, of course.

"You try anyway. And you keep trying. Until you find a reason to succeed." A lump formed in her throat as she reached out her hand. "Trust me. It sucks. I know it sucks. It will get better one day. It will never be the same, though. You'll see. It'll get better."

He squeezed her hand and when he spoke, his voice cracked. "How can you be so sure?"

Brooke locked onto his gaze and mustered all the strength she could find in her body to sound completely convincing. "I just know. You have to believe. And be patient."

With a slight nod of his head, Josh closed his eyes briefly and when he opened them, they reflected his pain and confusion. He reached into his breast pocket for his shades, masking himself once again.

Chapter 6

"How'd your visit with Kyle go?" Brooke had been rocking the last half hour away on her front porch swing, immersed in a romance by her favorite author when Josh came meandering around the corner. He took the steps two at a time, and joined her on the swing. Although the rain had stopped after three days of periodical showers and overcast skies, the morning was still cloaked in a muggy, misty shroud.

"Rough."

Brooke closed her paperback and waited for him to continue. He said nothing. A chipmunk scurried across the battleship gray porch floorboards, climbed up a column, and jumped onto a disk-shaped bird feeder overflowing with sunflower seeds. A few of the black-shelled seeds slid off the platter and onto the porch. The chipmunk paused under the scrutiny of his audience. Ever so cautiously, he picked up a seed, nibbled, threw a sly peek at Brooke and Josh, nibbled again, then peered up at the humans once more. When he'd finished stuffing as many seeds in his cheeks he could possibly hold, he took off down the column and under the porch.

"You see this little guy? Hey, Chippie," she called out to the furry brown critter. Brooke couldn't be sure where Josh's attention was, as he was still wearing his sunnies, so she reached out an arm and pointed.

"Yes." His voice was monotone, his posture rigid even as the swing gently moved back and forth all by Brooke's effort.

"I think my life is like Chippie's life. And all those seeds are like all my life experiences. I see a goal. I go for it, thinking I've got it all together. And *just* when my goal is in reach—basically living a happy life—I realize it can all be snatched away. Or it starts to crumble and those seeds start falling. Some seeds are empty husks. Others are full. And as they fall, I can't do anything to stop it. So, I take what I can and get the hell out as fast as possible, making sure I don't lose anything else. I'd rather stay hidden, satisfied with the seeds I stored away, rather than risk losing everything by taking another chance."

"What happens when you realize all you're holding on to are empty shells?" Josh croaked.

"You tell me."

Josh reflected in silence, his face an emotionless mask. "You go out and keep looking for more seeds?" He bit his lower lip between his teeth so hard it lost color. He clenched his two hands into together, his knuckles whitening.

"Yup."

They sat there on the swing in silence for a long while as the mist broke, and the afternoon sun caressed the dampened lawn and trees. When Josh finally spoke, his voice was gruff. "I'm going to skip the afternoon drumming circle today. I don't like to drum. I don't want to drum. I can't drum."

With a knowing smile, Brooke asked softly, "Do you have a heartbeat?"

A curious frown was all he offered.

"Well? Do you?"

"Of course I do. What does this conversation have to do with anything?"

"If you have a heartbeat, you can drum. It's the most primal, most ancient, most soothing beat in the Universe. A beat we first heard in our mothers' wombs. If you have two hands and a heartbeat, you can drum." Her lips lifted on one side, offering him a crooked smile, as her eyes twinkled in merriment.

"You don't understand. I suck at music. I sucked at band. I was a computer geek. And a bookworm. A nerd. I love music. I just can't play an instrument."

"Well, now is a good time to learn, isn't it?" She stilled the rhythmic rocking of the swing with her sandaled foot and stood up. "C'mon."

"What?" He remained on the swing as she descended down the steps.

"I'm going to show you how to drum."

With a wave of her hand, Brooke coaxed Josh from the swing. And even though he shook his head, protesting, he followed.

~ ~ ~

"See? I told you." Brooke laughed as they ended a very fast-tempoed rhythm beat out on two djembes they had selected from the music closet in the rec room.

"You're good. I never would have thought I could do this." Josh stared at his hands resting on the drum head.

"You have to trust me. Trust yourself. Trust the drum. And trust your heart." She stared at him, suddenly uncomfortable as his gaze turned to her lips while she spoke. Even after she stopped talking, his eyes never moved. "It's what I tell all the kids I teach when they're here. Trust your heart. It's good advice." Trying to explain herself only made it worse.

As she babbled on, Josh offered a lopsided grin. "Uh-huh. I see."

"Yeah, well. I don't think you do." The flush of her cheeks was spreading to the rest of her body.

"Thank you." Josh put down his drum and pocketed the sunglasses he had placed on the seat beside him. He leaned forward, his elbows resting on his knees, sharing her personal space as he stared into her eyes.

"For?" Her breath caught as she noted, being this close, that his baby blues might actually be baby teals, something she'd never noticed before now.

She scooted her metal folding chair backwards, then beelined to the storage shelves. Pausing for a second, she shook her head to clear the crazy thought he'd been about to kiss her. Her drum made a solid thud as she set it on the shelf. After finding the nearest window and opening it, she scanned the wall for the overhead light switch by the door and headed in that direction. The room had darkened considerably as another storm blew in from the southeast.

"Teaching me how to drum. Reminding me what it's like to feel again. I haven't felt anything in a long time." He rose from the folding chair and carried his drum to the shelf Brooke had placed her drum on. After setting the djembe next to Brooke's, he joined her by the door.

She watched his every move; the graceful way he unfolded himself from the chair; the casual yet commanding way he sauntered across the rec room; to the way he studied her face, his eyes settling on her lips as he halted by her side.

Her heart pounded wildly and her breathing lost its normal flow as he reached for the wall switch and shut the lights so they stood in the shadows once more. "Thank you. For teaching me how to drum," he said, his voice barely audible.

"You're welcome," she said in a breathless whisper. She cleared her throat and continued. "It's getting dark. Storm's blowin' in." Brooke's voice cracked and she swallowed thickly. "We should go."

"We should, shouldn't we?" His words came softly, cloaked in a husky timber.

"Yes." She answered too quickly as he took another step closer.

He had a regal profile and in the shadows his silhouette appeared as though an artist had traced him, a soliloquy of perfection. Her legs grew wobbly as he filled her personal space with a velvety soft reality she'd not known in an awfully long time. He was so close she picked up his scent, like a heady incense. He smelled of fresh air, and rain . . . and man.

A rumble of thunder rolled around the mountains, and the lunch bell rang out in the distance, far off and faint. His eyes were warm and inviting. He smelled so good.

"Brooke?"

Reality returned with the sound of her name. She blinked and noticed he was studying her with an intensity that turned her insides to melted butter. His dimples cut deep and his teal blues were bright with amusement.

"Uh. Yeah?" She practically grunted, unable to speak.

"Lunch?" A corner of his mouth turned up on one side ever so slightly. "Unless you prefer to stay here in the darkness."

At first, she thought he was mocking her, but his energy didn't seem chiding at all.

"We better get going," Brooke said, leading the way by putting as much distance between them as possible, without waiting for him to follow.

~ ~ ~

Dan, Alyssa, and Kyle were involved in a quiet conversation while cradling gray and green E&S mugs of steaming coffee by the coffee station when Brooke approached them in the dining hall after depositing her used plate and utensils in the collection bins by the kitchen. Although she wasn't exactly sure what to say, it needed to be said.

"Hey. Got a sec?" Inhaling a deep breath, she focused on the trio, then over her shoulder at Josh, who was walking back to their table with a second helping of barbecued ribs.

"Sure. What's up?" Kyle turned full body away from Alyssa and Dan, directing all his attention on her.

"Um." Brooke shifted from foot to foot, at a loss for words, suddenly not sure what it was she needed to say and why it was now so urgent.

Alyssa and Dan focused on the coffee bar, poured their warmers and engaged in conversation as they provided Brooke the privacy she needed. Kyle waited quietly as she collected her thoughts.

"Um." She began again, not sure how to define her concerns. "I'm—I'm not comfortable working with Josh. Or maybe it's too comfortable? I don't know. It's confusing me." There it was. Her face warmed as she ducked her gaze to avoid her boss' scrutiny. She glanced over her shoulder at Josh, and he waved at her from across the hall, never hesitating as he gnawed through his second pile of ribs.

Alyssa had stepped up beside Kyle as Brooke spoke, and now reached out a hand, lightly patting Brooke's shoulder as Dan sauntered off to a nearby table. "Has something happened? Did he do something—?"

"No! Not at all. I'm not good with adults. Especially. . . *especially* . . . You know—"

Raising a finger, Kyle spoke. "Wait. You are good—no, *great*—with adults. I've seen you interacting with the parents of the children who we serve. You are awesome with adults. Don't underestimate yourself."

"No one is forcing you to spend time with him, Brooke." Alyssa spoke softly. "Isn't this what you do when loved ones reach out to the kids you work with? You're not doing anything wrong or different."

"I know. . . he searches me out, and I feel bad for him. And . . ." Her voice trailed off knowing she searched him out as much as he kept an eye out for her.

"And how is this different from the twelve-or fifteen-year-olds you work with?" Alyssa studied Brooke's face.

"Seriously, Alyssa?" Brooke pinched the bridge of her nose with her thumb and forefinger and shook her head. "Just look at the guy. Geez."

"Well. Yeah." Alyssa sighed in a failed attempt to suppress a giggle.

Brooke studied a ragged bit of cuticle on her thumb, tugging until it tore and a little droplet of blood formed.

"This is your forte. This is what you do best. You're our Deathwalker. We need you. *He* needs you," Kyle reminded her gently, raising his brows and shoulders as he spoke.

"The dreams. They're starting to feel real. Like. Uncomfortably real." Brooke couldn't bring herself to tell them the complete content of the dreams and why they disturbed her more than usual.

"Have you told him about them yet?" Alyssa prodded softly, her voice a soothing coo.

Tossing her head side to side, Brooke widened her eyes and glanced back at the man who she knew without a doubt was going to upset her reality if she allowed it.

Just under two weeks had passed since meeting Josh Quinn. Being this close, and—in a sense—so intimate with a man, was an experience she had avoided for more than three years. If he had been old, or smelly, or arrogant, or . . . or . . . or anything except the CEO and founder of a company created to *promote the hook-up culture,* as he had so eloquently put it, maybe it wouldn't be so bad. He was too cool. Too . . . everything she needed to stay away from. He radiated sexuality and confidence despite the gruff exterior he wore like armor; despite the Ray-Bans he hid behind. Although lately he was hiding behind them less, at least when he was alone with her. And this was not cool. *So not cool.* She did not—no, she *could not*—allow herself to trust a man she hardly knew. Not again. Never. Well maybe not 'never.' Just not now. It was still too soon. And besides *all of this,* she knew his wife. Sort of. Well, his dead wife. And Brooke was not sure how Rosalie would feel about *all of this*.

The awkward silence permeating the trio while Brooke mentally sorted things out was broken as Alyssa leaned over and offered a light hug. "I don't know what you want us to do?"

Do? He's your charge, not mine! Do your damn job and stop pawning him off on me. Brooke grimaced, unable to utter those words.

"We can talk about this later. And if you still can't sort things out, well, we will figure something out. Okay?" The coaxing soft smile and raised brow from Alyssa came across as pity, irking Brooke even more.

"Thanks," she mumbled. Brooke didn't feel thankful. She felt frustrated. Apprehensive. Like a failure. How could any of those emotions translate into thankful?

Chapter 7

"Does anyone have any questions about the different uses for the plants we're growing in the gardens and around the camp? We've got our edibles, our medicinals, and the poisonous ones." Paulie took in everyone gathered on the back deck for his Fun Times with Foraging group and waited for questions.

Louisa raised her hand. "It's been a long, rough week. Do any of them get you high?"

A chittering of laughter sounded and Paulie and Mandy, Louisa's mentor, exchanged a shared suppressed look of amusement.

"Ah. If they did, you really think I'm going to tell you all?" He winked at her, and more laughter erupted.

Checking his watch, Paulie began closing the textbooks laid out on the table he was seated at and pointed to a stack of envelopes, field guides, stenographer notebooks, and Fujifilm Instax instant cameras and packages of film. "Your assignment, so to speak, is to identify as many of the plants we discussed today and photograph them. I can tell you one thing for certain. Every plant we reviewed is located within a half mile of base camp." He peered around once more. "Last chance. Any questions?"

When no one spoke, Paulie offered, "No? All right. Should you have any issues with your cameras, Brooke here is the expert. You get to keep those cameras by the way. You can get more film on Amazon. They'll be packed up with the rest of your things when you head home."

Brooke waved her hand from the back of the room and smiled.

"Let's do it." Paulie clapped his hands and gave a thumbs-up. "Class dismissed. Enjoy the rest of your Thursday, everyone." He pointed to Craig, his charge, and added, "Craig, can you make sure everyone gets a tote to put their supplies in?"

Craig nodded and joined him at the desk, reaching into a box to retrieve canvas bags with the Earth & Sky logo imprinted on each side.

While packing up her camera equipment, Brooke eyed Alyssa and Josh walking together, engaged in conversation. With a wave, Alyssa left his side, heading toward the main office building, leaving Josh standing alone. As Brooke broke down her tripod and tucked away the Polaroid camera she had planned to use when foraging instead of her Canon, he came up to stand beside her.

"Want to use our half-hour break to start looking for plants? Alyssa has a meeting." His blue eyes were narrowed and warm, squinting against the sunlight.

"Thanks. I'll probably get to it later, though. I'm her meeting." Brooke avoided his gaze, peering into her tote as she assessed its contents. Another line of her poem came to her just then. Where was her damn pad? . . . *lose myself in memories of autumn sky blue eyes . . .*

"Mm-hm. You? All these meetings. Sounds important." Side by side, they made their way to the dining hall. Alyssa's and Kyle's offices were on the far side of the building, near the infirmary.

"It's nothing, really." Her answer came too quick even for her.

"A meeting about nothing. Sounds like the Quirkyflirt board." He chuckled and allowed his eyes to drift toward the tree line at the perimeter of the base camp field. "Important nothing, or check-in nothing?"

She shrugged. "Just . . . check-in nothing."

"You seemed upset when you were speaking with Kyle and Alyssa the other night. Does your meeting have something to do with your conversation by the coffee bar?" Concern etched across his face, replacing the scowl he wore less and less these days.

He was a CEO. A keen business man who didn't miss a beat. Of course, he *would* notice. Besides, she wasn't the type to mask her feelings well at all. "They call it 'deprocessing.' Making sure we don't hold onto anything we are helping the campers sort through. All staff are required to participate. It's like, you know, checking the nails in the floor boards to make sure they don't come loose."

Those teal-blues studied her soul without wavering. "I see. So . . . word is your nickname is Deathwalker. It was interesting to hear the campers share stories they heard about you."

Brooke snorted softly, pointing to the counseling office, where Alyssa had been standing watching the pair walk across the camp. "Oh. You'll have to fill me in one of these days. But right now, Alyssa's waiting. See you at lunch? Maybe you can regale me with the gossip?" She gazed up into his eyes, and when they crinkled warmly, she tilted her head in confirmation. "Enjoy your free time. I might be a little late for lunch. See ya later." She gave a quick salute then made her way toward Alyssa.

"Sounds good. Have fun at your nothing meeting." He waved back and headed off toward the verandah lined with green wooden Adirondack chairs.

~ ~ ~

The office décor was sunny and bright; pale yellow walls were peppered with decals of butterflies and a rainbow. In the corner was a table, joined by a shelf filled with art supplies including clay, paints, canvases, coloring books, glass and wooden beads and jewelry supplies, and other little boxes Brooke had never found the opportunity to explore.

She sat on a peach, linen-covered easy chair, clutching a bright orange pillow in her lap as she faced the camp therapist she also considered her friend. "I can't do this." Brooke shrugged and shook her head as she squared off with Alyssa, who had eased into a similar chair across from her. A walnut coffee table rested between them, offering a vase of orange day lilies and a bowl of red and white peppermints.

Responding in a soothing tone, Alyssa asked, "Do you want to talk about what part of 'this' it is you think you can't do?"

"The dreams. Josh. The rape. It's all blending into one. I can't tell what's my reality or his or Rosalie's anymore. I'm tired. Let me take pictures and not worry about anything else."

A heavy sigh sifted from Alyssa as she leaned over and grabbed Brooke's hand, patting it reassuringly. "Let's unpack everything, okay? What chunk do you want to deal with first?"

"I don't know. I want to be able to sleep."

"What about the dreams?" Alyssa leaned back and waited.

"I can't remember a lot of it. As usual. Night terrors. Screams. I want to say I'm in a plane crash, then me and Rosalie are having tea like we're old buddies. She keeps telling me something I'm not able to hear. Then I look at her and it's because she's underwater—drowning. Or sometimes I can't hear her because I'm being dragged away and held down with a pillow over my head. I won't even get into the plane crash. I know a lot of this is probably because I'm feeding off Josh's guilt."

"You know these dreams are a gift, right? A gift given to you to help others." Alyssa offered this consolation, which Brooke refused with a flip of her hand.

"It's not a gift. It's a curse. I don't want to feel or know what others were thinking when they were dying." Her eyes welled up with tears as she searched Alyssa's face for some semblance of understanding.

"It's who you are. You can't deny it any more than you can deny having brown hair and green eyes."

Brooke chewed at the cuticle on her pinky nail, and a droplet of blood surfaced. She sucked it away and applied pressure with her thumb.

"I'm super attracted to him," Brooke replied in a wavering voice, changing the subject. "I think it must be his wife channeling through me."

"Channeling? Does this normally happen?" Alyssa smiled kindly, with a slight tilt of her head. "Maybe you're attracted to him."

Brooke drew a shaky breath. "I've never channeled before like this. I'm absolutely not attracted to him! He's . . . He's . . . He's kind of domineering, he wants to control everything. And . . ."

"And so are you." Alyssa laughed. "And all the kids you work with want to take control. It's part of the survival tools and healing process. This isn't any different."

"Yeah, but. No. It *is* different, Alyssa. He's not a kid. He's . . ." Brooke felt her face warming.

Leaning forward, both hands clasped, Alyssa prodded. "He's gorgeous."

Butterflies battered the lining of Brooke's midriff, and she hesitated before answering, offering a slight affirmation with a nod. "He's. . . he's the *founder* of Quirkyflirt, for goddess's sake."

Alyssa laughed and nodded. "Yeah. I can see why his company is so successful, hm?"

Brooked buried her face in her hands and groaned in frustration. "See? I can't do this!"

"And 'this' is?"

"He flirts! I don't think he realizes it even! I think it comes naturally!" Brooke flailed her hands as she spoke.

"Well, he came here to get past his grieving, no?" Alyssa's eyes glimmered in sympathetic amusement.

"I-I-I don't know!"

"Can we talk as friends? Not as your boss?" Alyssa leaned forward and caught Brooke's eyes.

Brooke shrunk back, on alert, then leaned into her friend. "Maybe? It depends. I don't know what to do. I don't understand."

"Just answer this. What are you afraid of?"

The question although softly spoken, jarred Brooke to the core. "Are you asking as a therapist or friend?"

Alyssa remained silent, waiting.

And, as if on cue, Brooke filled the empty space. "I'm not afraid of anything!"

"With Josh. What are you afraid of?"

A long sigh echoed, sounding loudly, accompanied only by the ticking of a clock.

"I have to stay professional."

Alyssa nodded.

"He came here to heal. I can't screw up his life. I need to stay focused." Brooke rubbed her eyes with one hand.

"Yup."

"I don't like being alone with him."

"Has he been in appropriate?" Alyssa straightened up, eyes narrowing.

"No! Not at all. Well." Her face flamed as she recalled their private drumming session. "No. Not really."

"Is this a trigger for you? Because of what happened at your last job?"

A thought-filled moment passed and Brooke shook her head. "Not exactly a trigger. Well. In a way, yes. I can't trust him. I don't want to trust him. How can I be there for him if I can't trust him?"

"You two seem to get along really well?" Lifting a palm upward, Alyssa sliced through the air with her question.

Brooke's shoulders slumped with her words. "Is it obvious, hm?"

Alyssa bit her lip and her eyes glittered with laughter.

"This is totally not cool," Brooke whined.

"This shouldn't have any impact on your job, Brooke. You're not a therapist, or a life coach. You're our photographer." Alyssa offered a sympathetic smile. "Having a relationship wouldn't exactly be—"

"I don't want a relationship! Don't you get it?" Brooke gulped. "I'm afraid of him. Of me. Not of him. Of me, and what I might subconsciously be telling him. What if he reads my empathy as permission to take advantage of me? What if he doesn't respect my boundaries because I'm subliminally telling him I'm attracted to him? What if he thinks I'm saying okay and he—he . . ."

"He . . .?"

"Um." Brooke struggled with her words. *"Takes advantage of me."*

"He's grieving his wife. And kids. I don't think you have to worry about history repeating itself here."

"I don't want to take any chances, Alyssa. Richard played on my consolation, my empathy, my concern for him. And he . . . he . . . took advantage of me."

"He *raped* you. No questions asked. When you were vulnerable. His mother just died. He *raped* you in an act to gain control of the situation. It won't happen again—especially here."

"Death makes people do crazy things." Brooke inhaled deeply, and released a slow, steadying breath, her hands clutching the arms of the chair she sat in.

"I don't think Josh is like this. And even though he's still caught up in grief, I think he's beyond a senseless reaction type of thing. I don't think he'll take advantage of you. This is the first time since Richard you've worked with a man who is dealing with the death of a loved one. Of course, this is going to be triggering."

"I'm not imagining it. He flirts. I know what flirting is. And he *sells sex*. He *told* me himself! Sure, he may be grieving his wife. It doesn't mean he's celibate and doesn't go out and have sex with any woman he wants!"

Knitting her brows together, Alyssa spoke slowly. "Maybe he's not the only one who needs healing here?"

"What? What do you mean?" Brooke scoffed and rolled her eyes, unable to meet her friend's gaze.

"Are you afraid Josh is going to sexually assault you? Or are you afraid he may want a relationship with you?"

"Ha! First off. I *know* he doesn't want a relationship with me—I'm so not in his league. I'm a photographer. I take pictures. And he's a CEO of one of the most successful businesses *in the world!*" She waved off any thought of a relationship with Josh Quinn. Or with anyone right now. Anyone. "How ridiculous can you get? Besides, I would never!"

"So, you're concerned it's more likely he will take advantage of your kindness and sexually assault you, rather than develop a fondness for you and want to build a relationship?"

A pregnant pause settled between them, until Brooke dismissed those two concerns with a shake of her head. "Both of those scenarios seem kind of lame, don't they?"

"The first, maybe. The second, yes. I seriously doubt he's going to physically hurt you." Alyssa wrinkled her nose and shrugged. "I didn't mean I don't think he could be interested in you. I meant . . ."

"He *is* freaking hot, isn't he?" Those butterflies continued to beat their wings against her belly.

"Unfortunately, yes. He is." Alyssa laughed and shook her head. "So, what are you afraid of, Brooke? Him or you?"

"I guess, me." She wrapped her arms across her chest and hugged herself hard.

"While I don't envy you, I do believe in you. You can handle this. Try and do your best to keep it professional. Try not to beat yourself up, though. You're human, after all."

The lunch bell sounded and Brooke searched Alyssa's face. "I still don't know what to do."

"Well. I think this is easier to deal with than you realize. As far as the dreams go, start journaling again, if you aren't already doing so. And maybe share what's happening with him?"

"No. It's not time yet. She hasn't given me any message. Or if she has, I don't remember it."

"Okay, try the journaling and see if it helps." Alyssa stood up and Brooke followed. "And as far as Josh. Well. We all grow from every life experience we live. Maybe this one is difficult because it's your turn to heal as well. See where it goes. You can be professional and friendly. Who knows what the Universe has in store for us? Do what you do best—let life flow. You got this. Remember. Everything happens for a reason." Alyssa offered a knowing smile, and stretched. "I don't know about you. I'm starved. I think I smelled greens cooking."

Chapter 8

"I think I'm skipping kayaking today." Josh announced his decision near the end of lunch on Friday, to no one in particular, after spending most of the meal pushing his uneaten potato salad around on his plate. Half a turkey club lay untouched, as did the shiny, red Gala apple.

"Why do you want to skip?" Brooke asked carefully, keeping her voice low. Alyssa apparently hadn't heard, as engrossed as she was in her deliberations with Dan over which brand of camping hammocks was superior.

He tossed his fork onto his plate and rested his forearms on the table, clasping his hands tightly in front of him. "Just don't feel like it. Do I have to have a reason?"

Silence slipped between them for a moment. A quick glance at the discoloration of his knuckles as he clenched his hands told Brooke otherwise. "Yeah. You do. Do you want to talk about it?"

Pressing the tips of his three fingers against his forehead, Josh closed his eyes and exhaled a loud sigh of frustration. "God. I don't want to talk about everything all the freaking time." He dropped his hand to the table and glared at her. "I don't *feel* like it. Why does there have to be a goddamn discussion for everything?"

At this point Alyssa and Dan ceased the hammock debate, as everyone at the table grew quiet. Dan started to speak, but Alyssa laid a hand on his forearm, silencing him.

"Because that's what we do. We're here to help you. Remember?" Brooke offered gently. She clasped her own hands lightly in front of her to keep from reaching out to touch him.

"Whatever." He pushed back from the table and started to stand up, then reclaimed his seat as Kyle called on everyone's attention for afternoon announcements.

"Okay, let's get moving. Go change into your swimsuits and head down to the lake. We'll be combining Recreation and Journaling today. There's a small island we'll be kayaking to, where we'll be doing some self-exploration, have a snack, then head back to camp by four. Any questions?" When Kyle was finished, and the group began buzzing again with small talk, Josh stormed out the front door.

"What happened?" Alyssa asked as she helped Brooke collect their lunch plates and utensils, including those Josh left behind.

With a slight lift of her shoulders, Brooke raised her open palms, offering only, "I have no idea."

As she spoke, a flash of water engulfed her, and a memory belonging to someone else her caught in her chest, robbing her of her breath.

"Brooke?" Alyssa grabbed her shoulder and shook her.

The sound of her name, the feel of Alyssa's grasp lifted Brooke from the watery wave washing over her reality. "I'm okay!" she gasped, patting her chest in a few solid raps with her open palm.

"They drowned, Alyssa," she said in a voice barely above a whisper. "Remember?"

The camp therapist exhaled slowly. "We should have considered this. Will you stay back with him if he doesn't change his mind?"

"Hello? I can't. I have to take pictures," was her only response before heading to her cabin to get changed and to grab the gear she'd need to shoot the event. She was really getting tired of Alyssa constantly pushing Josh onto her.

~ ~ ~

Brooke headed down to the lake, swimsuit under her khaki shorts and green camp shirt, a nylon backpack slung over her shoulder. In it she carried two journals, two water bottles, two individual serving packages of mixed nuts, tissue packets, and two pens. Two of everything in case Alyssa directed her to stay back with Josh. She would make him work through whatever was blocking him.

"You okay?" Kyle approached her, his life preserver open and flapping around him, a concerned frown etching his brow.

"I'm good. Where's Alyssa?" She avoided his gaze, scanning the crowd.

"She said she'd be down after checking on Josh." As he spoke, he lifted his chin in the direction of the path behind her. As Brooke turned toward the sandy walkway flanked by thick vegetation separating the beach from base camp, Kyle waved and called out to Josh and then Alyssa who was following a few steps beyond.

Josh stepped into the clearing and onto the lake shore beach area donned in mid-thigh length swimming trunks patterned with brown, yellow, and green leaves on a sky-blue background, along with a sleeveless yellow tank, and light brown leather docksiders, with sunglasses in place. He sauntered across the sandy strip of beach toward them, his face a mask of resignation.

"Okay, let's get moving. Everyone else has already pushed off. You two"—Kyle pointed to Alyssa and Josh—"can grab this tandem here, the two-seater. All the singles are used. Sorry, you know the early bird gets the worm." Kyle jogged over to his personal red kayak, decals covering the front deck. "Let's go." He waved them on, tucked his backpack in the compartment, picked up his paddle, then dragged his kayak to the water's edge and slipped inside.

"Kyle?" Brooke called out. "What am I supposed to do?"

Looking to Alyssa, then back to Brooke, he responded, "Alyssa, figure it out. I've got to catch up with the rest of the crew."

Josh headed over to the two-seater while Alyssa trudged over to Brooke. "I'm going to hang back, since it looks like there isn't room for the three of us." She searched Brooke's face and offered a feeble smile. "Besides, he can paddle and you can take pics. It works out perfectly."

With a roll of her eyes, Brooke turned her back on Alyssa and, saying nothing, stormed off to where Josh waited beside the kayak. She bent over the hatch and stored her backpack, then grabbed the paddle he offered. Together they maneuvered the kayak to the ankle-deep water and as she moved to step into the rear, he directed her to the front seat. "I'll steer."

"I usually take the back when I'm in a tandem." She made no move to follow his direction, and—despite Alyssa's comments—she was quite capable of taking pictures and steering.

"Because you work with kids. I'm not a kid."

Brooke hesitated, closed her eyes, and counted to five.

"Please? Let me do this." His request was barely audible, his lips pulled taut.

"Fine." And although her voice was filled with compassion, if he hadn't said please, she argued with herself, she would not have relented.

They donned their preservers, and after a few minutes of power paddling, caught up with the rest of the gang. The next half hour was spent enjoying a leisurely trek to Center Island, located halfway between the two sides of the lake. "It's not exactly center, but, hey, I didn't name it," Brooke explained to Josh as if he was one of the youths she'd brought along this journey so many times before. He remained silent the entire trip.

Once they docked the kayaks onto the island's sandy beach, Rob, the mentor in charge of journaling, gave instructions. While he spoke, Brooke climbed out of the kayak, and camera poised, began filming video of the others as they climbed out of their kayaks. After Josh had secured his vessel, she directed him to grab his journal and pen from her backpack and start without her, then pointed to Rob, who was already explaining the goal of this excursion.

"Find a remote spot to talk using the list of questions provided. Mentors, I want you to lead. After each discussion, journal your thoughts and write about this experience," Rob said. "Remember, conversation, not interrogation. Have at it, guys."

With a snap of a salute, he wrapped up the instructions. "We'll head back to camp in about two hours. Once you finish here, feel free to explore or take some alone time. Try not to interfere with the others until you know they're done."

A short while after, Brooke found Josh on a secluded patch of beach, and sat down cross-legged beside him. She accepted her copy of the questions Rob had distributed while she'd shot photos, which Josh offered her without a word, then retrieved her own journal from her pack. A quick review of the assignment while Josh slipped off his shoes and dug his feet into the sand showed it would be a pretty simple effort.

"It's a 'get to know yourself' type of thing. Nothing too complex," Brooke offered to a reticent Josh who remained focused on the lake's horizon, arms resting on bended knees. "What element do you relate to the most? Do you prefer sunrises or sunsets? Favorite thing to do on a rainy day? Favorite vacation spot. Stuff to help us share our lives."

"I know. I reviewed them while you were off shooting pictures. Why don't we skip the small talk and get down to it?" He picked up the black leather-bound journal and fanned through the empty pages before tossing it on the sand between them.

"And what would 'it' be?" She stared at the journal—a 5x8 leather-bound three-ring binder, now covered with bits of sand.

"I guess I'm supposed to want to open up to you and find some remarkable healing aspect of this little jaunt?" His voice was as dry as the sand they sat on. "But isn't this Alyssa's job? You're the photographer, no? The PR person?"

"Wow. Gee. Thanks." Brooke took a deep breath and tried not to take it personally. "I'm not your counselor, and I don't want to be either. I can just be your friend, here to listen. But, if you insist on being an ass, well, I have no problem ending this conversation here."

She could feel him looking at her, even though his eyes were masked by black shields of plastic. As hard as it was, she picked up her journal and pen, and began writing.

"I was being an ass," he said after a few moments of silence.

"Yeah. I know." Pen poised, still focused on her page, Brooke waited for his response.

"We had kayaks."

Brooke snapped her head up quickly, waiting for him to continue. This wasn't where she expected the conversation to go.

"Tandems. Mine was red. Rosalie's was green. We'd each take one of the girls. From the time they could walk they knew how to swim. We never went anywhere dangerous. We wore our life preservers. Always. To make sure they'd be safe." His voice cracked and he hesitated. "I always kept them safe."

Brooke swallowed. The lump in her throat stayed put, preventing her from speaking.

"So, yeah. Now you know why I didn't want to kayak. My last good memories of them. And then the way they—"

He grabbed a handful of sand and let it pour back onto the beach from his closed fist.

She nodded. "I'm sorry."

"We kayaked our last vacation. They loved the water as much as I do—did. I haven't kayaked since."

"I—" She started to apologize again, as he shook his head, effectively silencing her.

"I forgot how much I liked it. Being so close to the water, smooth gliding, basically effortless. The cool spray. The fresh smell of water and air. It was like mini-vacations sometimes. I'd get off work early and Rosalie would have the girls ready, cooler packed. All I'd have to do is hook the SUV up to the trailer with the kayaks and we'd be gone. I'd forget everything, all the bullshit of the week, when I was out there with the girls. Talk about therapy."

"And now? This isn't therapy, is it?" Her voice trembled a bit as she whispered the words.

"No," he said, his voice hitching again. "I miss them so damn much. I don't want to enjoy this, or anything. It's not fair to them."

"To not enjoy it is even more unfair to you. You're alive. Life is for living. They would have wanted you to—" Brooke stopped short as a flash of brackish green water, frothy with whitecaps, engulfing her caught her breath. The beach tipped and momentarily was replaced by an unending ocean stretching out to the horizon, before righting itself. "*Time to heal, babe,*" echoed like frothy wisps in her mind. She blinked and the vision was replaced with the serene deep blue lake reflecting a nearly cloudless sky before her.

"What's wrong?"

She swallowed thickly and shook her head. "Nothing. I'm fine. They would have wanted you to heal and go on with your life. Wouldn't you have wanted the same for them if it was the other way around?"

Josh nodded slowly, still trained on the horizon. "I s'pose so." He picked up his journal and began scribbling fiercely.

~ ~ ~

Later in the evening, as everyone sat around the Friday night campfire laughing, chatting, drumming, and dancing Josh decided to check out. Instead of joining in the revelry, he kept his sunglasses in place and fixated on the flames dancing, leaping, and swaying, climbing higher and higher up the four-foot stack of wood as it roared with life. *Life is for living,* Brooke had said. *And she was correct.* Life was indeed for living, so why even bother if all he did was exist?

He'd lost count of the number of times he contemplated ending it. Pills. Applying for a pistol permit. Hanging. Slicing his wrists. So many ways and so many times he thought about taking his life. He couldn't though, because he was a fighter. He was not a quitter, and he knew suicide, although it took someone with conviction and strength to follow through, would be his way to avoid coping and dealing with the shit he was living. Avoidance was never his thing. He met life head on. Always.

Alyssa's voice echoed in the distance, interrupting his reflections. "Do you want a cuppa tea or coffee? Mandy's taking orders."

"Nah, thanks." He reached down to the ground by his folding chair and lifted his Hydro Flask half-filled with water. "I'm good."

"Remember our coffee station stays stocked around the clock on the weekends, *FYI*." Alyssa stood up and stretched. "Just in case you change your mind."

"Yeah, no thanks. I'm probably going to head to bed." He cradled his water in his lap.

"Okay, then. Have a good sleep if I don't see you." She waved at him and then disappeared into the border of darkness beyond the firelight.

A few chairs to his left, Brooke sat with a drum nestled between her legs, lost in the beat, the fire, the dancers. This was her element. Her face appeared impish in the firelight, with her hair pulled into a pony tail at the top of her head.

As if he summoned her, she paused in her drumming and glanced up. He watched as she searched his face, and his heart did double time as their eyes locked. Brooke had somehow managed to find a way into his heart; something no one had been able to do in a long while. Since Rosalie. He set down his flask, forcing himself to look away, and focused on the fire once more. The few drummers ended their beat and the dancers slowly came to a halt, shouting, "Thank you, drummers!" The drummers responded in kind, calling out, "Thank you, dancers!" Everyone laughed like it was some secret joke. He didn't understand what was so funny.

Another beat began, lulling him into a hypnotic state as he gazed at the fire, not speaking or moving. Brooke had passed her drum on to someone else and now sat hugging her knees to her chest, staring into the flames. *What the hell am I doing here?* Sitting around a campfire drumming and dancing was for hippies, not a city guy. He missed the lights, the noise, the incessant screech of tires and honking horns; the wail of sirens. He wanted a beer. He wanted to be sitting down at the local pub, eating nachos and downing a beer with Derek. *Derek!* Right now, all he wanted to do was kick Derek's ass. It was more than a month ago Derek had broken the news to him at their favorite bar during happy hour. And he had no choice. The only choice he had was to take Derek's offer or be forced out of his position.

He unfolded himself and stood up, heading toward the path back to camp. As he passed Brooke, where she now sat curled up in her chair, legs tucked beneath her, he muttered, "I think I'm going to turn in."

"Too much fresh air?" she asked, her eyes wide and glittering with amusement as they reflected the firelight.

"No. Not at all. A little exercise isn't the reason." He tapped his foot and scanned the circle. "Just. Too many people. I'm gonna call it a night." He continued walking without waiting for her response. It had been a long day, filled with too many difficult memories. He was torn between wanting to escape the real world by sleeping, and staying by the side of this woman who was helping him feel something other than anger. What it was, he wasn't sure yet.

He hadn't even made it back to base camp when he heard the patter of sneakered feet padding the path behind him.

"Wait up!"

Recognizing Brooke's voice, he paused for a moment as his heart did a double beat, then he continued walking. He'd committed to escaping with sleep. Sleep had always been the much safer option. He wondered what she got paid an hour to babysit him when Alyssa wasn't around. He felt a stirring, knowing he didn't look at her as a babysitter. He wanted more from her, and this bothered him on so many levels. The conflict was not something he needed right now.

"Yo!" She reached him and when he continued to walk, she kept pace. "You forgot your flask." She held up the container, her voice tinged with disappointment. "I probably should have left it there."

"It's not like anyone's going to steal it. Not out here in the sticks. Unless there are bear and raccoons wanted for petit theft?" He didn't even glance at her. He was not going to give her the chance to sweet talk him into joining her again by the fire.

"I thought you might be looking for it during the night. You know, if you wanted a drink. If not, I'll go put it back by your chair." As she turned to leave, he reached out quickly and grabbed the flask from her hands.

"Thanks. Good night." He barely said the words before he started off again in the direction of his cabin. To his dismay, so did she. "Listen. I'm not in the mood for chitchat. Do you mind?"

"Wow. For your information, I'm going to help Mandy with the coffees and hot cocoa. Do *you* mind?" Her voice sounded strained in the shadowed darkness.

Josh watched her lithe body storm passed him, moving to the end of the shadowy path, into the clearing, across the base camp, and into the dining hall. For a moment—the briefest of moments—he regretted his rudeness. As he neared his cabin, he dismissed any guilt, thinking of nothing else except sleep.

Unfortunately, the distant heartbeat of drums filtered through the woods, across the camp, and into his cabin via the screened windows, settling around him in the darkness. It kept time with his breathing. It synced with his own heartbeat. It lulled him, and at the same time mesmerized him enough to keep him awake.

He thought about the private drum lesson Brooke had given him, and how she came alive when she played. And how he had wanted to kiss her. Gone was her professional façade. Gone was the carefully selected phrases and barricade keeping him from connecting with Brooke, the person. Brooke, the woman.

He wasn't here to connect with a woman, he reminded himself. He was here to get his shit together so he didn't get his ass fired from his own company. *His own company!*

The Quirkyflirt concept was something he'd envisioned before dating apps even existed. He built it himself, as rudimentary as the first version was. He tried it out on his friends. And then their friends tried it and before he knew it, he met Rosalie—the biggest success of the whole project. Shortly after they started dating, they were married. Within a year, they had two beautiful twin daughters. All because of Quirkyflirt.

He'd been pretty crass with Brooke when describing his company. And deliberately so. From the moment he stepped off the bus he was drawn to her, try as he might to fight it. Her hair had been pulled into what now seemed to be her customary ponytail, flecks of red highlights glinting in the afternoon sunlight. She'd stood apart from the other staff members, hands cradling a camera, scanning the crowd as they disembarked from the bus, shooting pictures of the crowd, the staff, and their initial first impressions and meetings. She didn't look too happy. It was more like she was observing a play as the events unfolded. He couldn't take his eyes off her, and when her name was called as camp photographer, he felt a twinge of disappointment she wasn't going to be his assigned mentor. His blood warmed at the thought of spending the next three weeks with her.

For three years he'd managed to anaesthetize himself from the dating scene. He tried once, and it ended in a disastrous one-night stand. It felt as if he was cheating on Rosalie, even though two years had passed since her death. In the end, even making all the right moves, he couldn't finish the act, and left the hotel room literally deflated—mind, spirit, and unfortunately even body. He hadn't wanted or attempted any personal intimacy with a woman since.

Until now.

However, he was not about to experience another failed lovemaking session. Even though he might make a living out of selling sex, he was petrified he would never be able to perform again; unable to escape the feeling he'd be cheating on Rosalie. The thought of making love—or attempting to make love—was terrifying. Not exactly what the world expects from the CEO of Quirkyflirt. If word got out, it would destroy his reputation and business forever.

A quick glance at the digital alarm clock by his bed showed him it wasn't even 11 p.m. He'd been tossing and turning for an hour. The drums beckoned him until he sat up, deliberating going back to the fire. Ripping the sheet and blanket aside, he swung his legs over the edge of the mattress, feet planted firmly on a plush throw rug.

He was here to get his shit together. He was here to finally let go of his grief for his wife and daughters. He would always love them, yes. What good would it do them if he lost everything? What good would it do them if he became a miserable, old hermit, detached from everything? Even if he took his own life, which at one point seemed to be the only way out of this misery, what then? Would he even ever see them again? What sense did it make taking such a chance?

He sighed and rubbed his head vigorously trying to make sense of what he was feeling.

Life is for the living, Brooke had said, and her words rang in his mind ever since. He slipped back into his khaki shorts, slid his feet into his docksiders, and headed for the door.

Life was for the living. It was time he started living again.

The walk to the firepit took less than six minutes, with every step feeling like an eternity. What would he say to her? *I'm sorry I was so rude?* He wasn't a person who normally made apologies—not because he couldn't. He rarely did anything he had to apologize for—most of the time. He was straightforward and honest, and never needed to apologize since he always tried to be tactful yet considerate. Until he came here.

He stood in the shadows watching the crowd. The dancers were still going at it, the drummers providing the music inspiring them to express themselves as they swayed and twirled around the fire, which was still roaring high into the night. His chair was now occupied by Paulie, who sat talking to Kyle, who now filled Alyssa's chair. Alyssa, he noted, sat on the far side of the fire, next to Dan. She had returned as well.

The seat beside Brooke was the only available spot void of bodies, sweaters, canteens, and other personal items. He made his way toward it, his eyes never straying from her image. She had taken up her djembe again and was keeping rhythm with the other drummers. Her eyes were closed, and she swayed with the beat, smiling and looking quite peaceful despite the noise. He moseyed toward the camp chair until he stood beside her, then slipped into the adjacent seat practically without sound. As his weight settled, the canvas chair groaned briefly, causing Brooke to open her eyes and glance toward him. Without missing a beat, she offered a quick wink, her hands never faltering. She closed her eyes once more, focusing on the rhythm.

After the music had stopped and the dancers and drummers had expressed their customary gratitude, Brooke turned to him. "What brings you here?"

Suddenly as tongue-tied as a teenager asking his crush to prom, Josh drank in the woman beside him and shrugged. "Couldn't sleep with all this racket."

"Ahh," Brooke said, training her sight once again on the flames. Barefoot Dan, the mentor who oversaw the drumming circle, picked out a simple beat as he invited everyone, the campers especially, to echo his rhythms. Brooke followed along a few times before offering her drum to Josh.

"Nah. Thanks. I'm fine observing," he said, as held both hands up, declining her offer.

"Cool," she replied and repeated the most recent beat offered by Barefoot Dan.

A twinge of *something* erupted in Josh's gut when Dan winked at Brooke as they bantered rhythms between them, almost like a musical game of tag. Josh witnessed her face brightening as she smiled broadly back at her fellow drummer, echoing his beat, and the *something* rose in his throat, leaving a lump that was difficult to swallow.

Barefoot Dan had long sandy blond hair, bound in a braid reaching down his back. He wore a sleeveless white tank top and red wrap yoga pants, and true to his name, nothing on his feet. His broad shoulders and muscular arms gave evidence to the power rumbling through the night with every bass blast released from the drum carved to look like a dragon coiled in a resting position. Blue gems for dragon eyes reflected the firelight. Dan's drumming was sure and strong, commanding the crowd. He wondered if Brooke and Dan had something going on. *Not my circus*. The last thing he needed was to get involved in a triangle, at worse, or a relationship with someone he'd never see again, at best.

He was here to get his life together. She was here to take pictures. End of story.

Mid-tempo, Brooke stopped drumming and handed her djembe to Josh, urging him to try. He shook his head, as she gently prodded him. "You know you got this. You did so well when we were alone. Can't you try, for me? Please?" She crooked her head, her expression sincere and coaxing.

His reserve melted like a stick of butter sitting on one of the stones in the circle marking out the pit. After nestling the djembe between his legs—and forcing himself to not think about where the drum had rested moments earlier—he listened to the beat a few times then joined in. Beaming with confidence, Brooke kept rhythm with her foot tapping the ground, as he stumbled through the first few beats then caught on and followed along.

It was then she rose slowly from her chair, swaying with each step as if the fire were beckoning her. For a long moment she remained solo, barely moving to the hypnotic rhythm. Alyssa soon joined her and the two swayed in unison. Soon Brooke was swirling and flowing, undulating like the flames dancing at the center of the circle.

As Josh followed her with his eyes, he continued drumming a very simple beat. Brooke caught his gaze from across the fire, and held it as she undulated in time with his tempo. Lost in the moment, he sat trance-like as she shimmied and swirled before him, swept up in her primal fire dance. It was as if the flames breathed life into her as she spiraled gracefully, dancing for him and only him.

The other drummers sped up the beat as the song played on. And as it continued to increase in speed, Brooke's arms rose and fell as she clapped and twirled, accompanied by Alyssa, Cara, and Mandy. When the song finally ended abruptly, everyone broke out in laughter, shouting out their thanks, as Brooke collapsed in the chair beside Josh.

The soft curve of her breasts rose and fell from her exertion, as she giggled and gulped air, her face filled with delight. "Awesome! And you kept up! Great job!"

His body warmed with her compliment and he nodded in appreciation, determined to keep his focus on her face. "I thought you didn't dance."

"I usually don't. Sometimes the fire beckons me." Her eyes were two dark orbs, mysterious and knowing, and he willed himself to not get lost in their depths. She was an enchantress, with her hair spilling out of her ponytail and cascading down her shoulders and back. It would be so easy, so right, if he leaned over and claimed her with a kiss. He licked his lips, then forced the crazy notion away.

"Well, you seemed like you were having fun." His words felt stiff and forced. This woman was smart, funny, talented, artistic, and made him feel completely out of his element. How was this even possible?

"I was. Were you?"

He handed her drum back and dipped his head in confirmation. "Yes. I was. Thank you."

"You are most welcome. Anytime, Mr. Quinn. Any time."

Chapter 9

The toaster hummed as Brooke watched the red coils slowly brown her plain bagel placed in the center of the steel rack. When the oven *dinged*, Brooke flipped open the door and precariously poked and slid her toasty warm breakfast onto her plate, spreading butter and honey across both halves. After grabbing a napkin, she joined her team and waited for the Saturday Morning In-house Briefing—*SMIB*—to begin.

This was where and when the team reassessed the week's progress, gave input and insight about each of the campers, and offered feedback to anyone on the team who was struggling with an issue. And even though Brooke was not an official mentor, she was included and her input valued due to the relationships she often developed with all of the campers. Alternately blowing on and sipping her steaming black coffee, Brooke peered over the rim of her green and white ceramic Earth & Sky Retreat mug as she waited for Alyssa to begin. Barefoot Dan joined her to her left and as soon as he was seated, Alyssa spoke.

"Good morning, everyone! What a beautiful day we've got today! How're we all doing?" Alyssa peered around the table from where she stood and picked up her own mug, taking a gulp as she acknowledged the automatic echo of replies.

"Great. Who wants to start?" she asked as she sat down. Dan raised his hand in answer, swallowing a mouthful of bagel before speaking. "Lance. Wow. His life could be made into a movie. He's struggling with a lot—I mean *a lot*—barely getting through it. The journaling and drumming's okay for him. He told me the yoga and meditation are *really* helping him. He's even doing the guided meditation CD you gave out the first day. He does it every night before bed. Thursday was the first time in a year he didn't have nightmares," Dan said, nodding as he spoke.`

"Everyone should meditate and do yoga regularly. It's amazing the benefits these simple practices offer," Alyssa responded. "He mentioned the chamomile tea and lavender infuser was helping also."

"Yeah. He's working through it all. I definitely see an improvement." Dan fist pumped the air and winked at Alyssa.

"Great news. Next?" She tossed him a grin, holding his gaze for a moment before sweeping her sight around the table, and one by one the mentors gave their reports.

Rob, the camp poet, provided feedback about the second week, which wasn't much better than the first. His charge, Ned, had spent their entire time quoting Bible scriptures about Armageddon, continuously repeating the same passages used as the catalyst for his fellow brothers and sisters 'Of the Mount' who had taken part in the mass suicide. "His guilt over not drinking the 'Holy Water' is really strong, and his fear of burning in Hell keeps him awake most nights," Rob explained.

"At last week's workshops all of his writings included sketches of fire and demons. He's cried through most of the campfires and drumming, and yet, he refuses to leave. He said it was his punishment," Rob explained, in exasperation. "This week he skipped the campfire and the only thing his journaling reflected were dates and empty pages. This is a tough one."

"Yeah, he was uncomfortable working with a woman therapist. He made it quite clear at the start of our first session last week. He explained to me his religious path teaches women are either vessels for breeding and serving men, or are doing the Devil's work. Oh, and only men should have positions of power and healing. I offered to switch him over to Kyle. He declined, insisting he was with me for a reason and, maybe he was supposed to help me see the light." Alyssa shook her head and agreed with Rob. "Ned's a tough one. Good luck."

"And his mat remains empty at your yoga class, Alyssa. Yoga's a sin," Brooke offered quietly as Alyssa nodded in confirmation.

Mandy took her turn next, and described the second week with Louisa as going fairly smoothly, noting that she only caught the model forcing herself to vomit after a meal once a day by Thursday. The first week had started out with catching Louisa in the bathroom breakfast, lunch, and dinner. "She explained butter made her nauseous. The smell of turkey or roast beef killed her appetite because it smelled like animals. She couldn't eat tuna because it reminded her of all the dolphins being killed. She has a story for every food she was offered. We do a lot of hugging, which seems to be helping her. And the kayaking totally built up her confidence. She's petrified of drowning."

Raising his hand, Paulie practically shouted, "Craig's afraid of the dark. Like 'consumed with immobilizing fear' afraid of the dark. He keeps every light on in his cabin, and *will not* go outside after sundown unless I'm with him. It was like pulling teeth getting him to join us at campfire."

"Yeah. I had him Wednesday when the big storm blew in, and as my office started getting dark, he demanded I turn lights on. He's got a lot he's dealing with and rightfully so. Sexual assault in a dark alley at night would traumatize anyone," Alyssa offered with a sigh.

Everyone fell silent for a moment, then Brooke spoke. "Ya know. I don't see what we're expecting to accomplish in three weeks. These people are struggling with major trauma, and three weeks in the woods cannot possibly be enough time to effectively help them. We aren't expected to cure the kids we work with. What are we seriously hoping to accomplish here? This feels insane."

Tilting his head in silent understanding, Kyle spoke for the first time since the start of the meeting. "Brooke, I think Dee and Doug believe we're laying the foundation for healing—proper healing—*to begin*. No one is expecting miracles. Just a little more progress than traditional therapy has been making. I don't think these individuals are damaged beyond repair. I think they have roadblocks preventing them from healing. We're here to help them identify the roadblocks so they can create a new course to maneuver around them."

"It still feels impossible." Her scowl underscored her doubt.

"Well, how about you fill us in with things by you? What are you getting from everyone?"

One by one, Brooke recounted her interactions with each of the clients, and summarized where she thought they stood at the end of two weeks.

"Okay. You guys are making good progress with all of them, well, except for Ned. No?" Kyle marked a check by each of the campers' names and then asked, "What about Josh? He seems to like spending time with you. What do you think?"

"Hmmm. Ya think?" She wrinkled her nose and laughed. "He calls me his babysitter, and is a bit annoyed he doesn't spend more time with Alyssa. Sorry, Alyssa."

"This group is way too involved for me to have been assigned a charge. I'm sorry, Brooke. He seemed like the best one to step back on since he's coping with the death of his wife and kids. You're the one naturally to pick him up for me. And thanks, Kyle, you've been great also."

"True. And I get it totally. He doesn't understand, though." She picked at her thumbnail in agitation. "And I've made it quite clear I'm not replacing his therapist."

"No. He's got me for that. But it's good you've been making time to work through some of the exercises with him. Thanks," Kyle said, before continuing. "Have you talked with him about your dreams yet? Have you gotten any messages to convey?"

She shook her head. "No." It was uncomfortable for her to talk about her ability with the others, so she chose not to elaborate.

Barefoot Dan spoke up. "It looks like you two get along really well. He follows you around like a puppy dog. Even during down time."

"Well. Yeah. He's definitely not as bad as say, I dunno, Ned?" Brooke gave a nervous twitter. "And at least now he sometimes shows a sense of humor. Maybe twice, I think." She rubbed the frown on her forehead away with one hand, offering a feeble smile to her group.

"What happened last night at drumming? I saw he left and came back, right?" Dan prodded.

"I don't know what happened? We haven't spoken much since then. He's probably still sleeping," Brooke said, glancing at the clock. "It's only 7:30."

Kyle grimaced. "He was pretty angry in our first session. Totally pissed off that his best friend—who's also his board president—forced him into this 'summer camp for adults' as he put it. He's worried he's the target for a takeover. He doesn't understand why he's not allowed to grieve the death of his wife and two daughters."

"Why isn't he? The poor guy. I wouldn't want to live if my partner and kids died. I can't imagine ever getting over it." Cara asked, a look of confusion marring her face.

"He doesn't show up for work, most of the time. He's ceased all social engagements except for occasional happy hours on Friday with his friend—the board president. Hasn't dated. Lost all contact with his family and friends. Has anger issues. And he's run through traditional therapists like water.

Derek said he also believes he's contemplated suicide more than once. He doesn't have any concrete proof, though." Kyle spread his hands wide. "We're like his last chance."

"Wouldn't taking his job away give him more reason to contemplate suicide?" Cara noted with a cluck of her tongue.

"Derek said he used the job as an excuse to get him here. His biggest concern is Josh following through with a suicide attempt. Derek said he didn't know how to talk about it with Josh, so he threatened the early retirement because he knew it would get him to take action. And it did."

"He's grieving though, for God's sake. Can't they cut him some slack?" she reiterated, still looking confused.

"If not for anything but his looks alone. God, he's gorgeous. I wouldn't mind consoling him," Mandy murmured with a smirk. "Alyssa, you've hit the jackpot with this one."

"Not me. Brooke's the one he migrates too constantly." Alyssa gave a knowing nod toward Brooke with her chin.

"Guys! Seriously?" Brooke slapped a hand down on the table. "Enough!" She offered this as a reprimand even though she totally got what Mandy was saying. "His looks have made it a bit difficult though." She chuckled softly. "No lie."

"And now he's hardly ever hiding behind his shades. Geez. How do you handle those baby blues?" Mandy feigned a swoon and giggled.

"Hello, ladies? You still haven't answered my question about why grieving is so wrong," Cara interjected.

"It's been three years since the plane crash. He was supposed to be with them. At the last minute, he cancelled his ticket for a board meeting and planned to join them the next day," Brooke informed everyone. "He's totally incapacitated with survivors' guilt."

"Ah, wow." Dan exhaled as the rest of the team voiced similar sentiments. "Well, good thing we got you,

Deathwalker." He patted Brooke on the back, and she shot him a glare.

"Well, even though it's been three years, he's gotta lot of guilt to let go of," Cara offered softly.

The group fell silent for a moment.

"Oh, yeah. Speaking of which. Josh mentioned he's heard stories about me and how I got my name, Deathwalker. Care to elaborate?" Brooke glared around the table, mildly amused, but still needing to call her peers out.

"Not many people we know talk to dead people, Brooke," Mandy offered in a meek voice.

"We were hanging out waiting for class to start one day and Craig was freaking out about how dark it gets at night. Not realizing his phobia, the rest of the gang started regaling him with spooky moments they'd experienced. Everyone loves a good ghost story, right?" Cara continued.

"It's freakin' cool," Dan said. "Brooke, even you have to admit it. We have someone who talks to dead people on our team."

"Not to mention a witch!" Paulie laughed.

"Guys! I don't want the campers knowing about my private life. We've been through this before. I hope to goddess you didn't say anything. My spiritual beliefs are *my business!*" She narrowed her eyes at Dan. "I've got dirt on every one of you. You don't see me sharing it with the campers."

"No one mentioned you being a witch, honest, Brooke. Sorry." Paulie shrugged.

"Even though I'm out of the broom closet, I decide who I want to tell, get it?" Her voice was stern and she hoped she'd made her point clear. Her mouth curved ever so slightly as she relaxed in her chair and murmured, "Don't make me get out my poppets."

Her teammates chittered nervously as an awkward silence filled the room.

"Or reveal who has been practicing secretly with me." She pursed her lips, observing each one through narrowed eyes, most if not all of whom had participated in a ritual with her here and there.

"Okay. So, where were we?" Alyssa abruptly changed the subject as she called for attention by clapping her flattened palm twice on the tabletop.

"Renee, my charge, blames herself for a huge wildfire she set accidentally. It took out her family's 150-acre vineyard in Napa Valley," Cara stated in a matter of fact voice. "No official charges were brought against her. However, her family lost their home, distillery, barns, livestock, and fifty acres of the best grapes ever grown to produce the number one selling California wine. As a result, they disowned her. She was having an affair with one of the staff, and they met for a tryst in the barn. As she described it, in uncomfortable detail I might add, they got a little, uh, vigorous, should I say? She had set up candles and lanterns on hay bales for ambiance and knocked one over."

"Wow." Brooke stared wide-eyed at Cara, lost for words.

"She cried the whole session on Tuesday," Alyssa offered. "I couldn't understand a word she said. But I think we made real progress. I think this last week will put her in a good place."

"Who the fu—sorry—*hell* would put a lantern on a bale of hay? Nothing wrong with a good old flashlight." Dan searched out a pencil-thin black cylinder from one of the side pockets on his khaki cargo shorts and held it up for inspection, standing it upright on the table in demonstration. "Great invention."

The team sat silent for a moment, taking it all in. Alyssa stood up and lit a wand of white sage, walking counter-clockwise around her staffers, circling the room until she hit the perimeters, fanning the walls in a ceiling-to-floor effort, signaling the end of the client update portion of the meeting.

Dan grabbed his and Brooke's mugs and headed for the coffee pot. "So, what's planned for this coming week? I wouldn't mind doing a fire every night and drumming. Might be what this group needs."

"Yeah, Kyle and I were thinking the same thing." Alyssa followed behind Dan with her own mug.

"I can offer guided meditations during the hour break before dinner, to help everyone process any crap they've encountered during the day," Brooke offered in a tentative voice.

"No. You guys need your down time. We're not going to start imposing on your self-care this late in the game. We can't afford to lose any of you to burn out." Kyle shook his head emphatically before adding, "We appreciate the offer, Brooke. But, no."

Dan handed Brooke her mug and she lost herself for a moment in the steam rising in wispy trails as it mingled with the smoky haze left by the burning sage.

"Okay. I have an idea," Brooke began slowly. "What if we work on a more themed type of curriculum for the rest of the retreat? Like tie in the meditation to the art work, the nature walk, the dancing, and release everything at the last campfire."

Kyle and Alyssa nodded at one another, then back to Brooke. "Go on," Alyssa prompted.

Brooke thought for a moment. "We can use Monday's guided meditation to discover and explore the paralyzing thought process keeping them from moving on with life. In art therapy, Mandy can talk about the importance of creating a visual of this thought process and do whatever it is she does with art therapy so well." Brooke laughed.

"I get it," Mandy exclaimed. "We can collect things like leaves or twigs, stones, and moss during our nature walks so they can use them in their art project."

"Or we can use those twigs as symbols of what they want to release and burn them in the fire?" Barefoot Dan bopped in his seat barely containing his excitement, drumming a five-beat riff on the table in emphasis. "We can burn the art project in the fire!"

"How about we teach them how to make their own fires? With bow drills. If starting their own fire doesn't promote manifestation, nothing will," Paulie said, enthusiasm pinging in his voice.

"And I can choreograph the dance to do around the fire after we burn everything," Cara offered enthusiastically. "I love this idea!"

"We can work on the words during journaling they need to say to release whatever it is they're releasing," Rob said slowly.

"And we drum the crap out of it Saturday night! Yeah!" Dan nearly burst out of his seat, amped up and ready to roll. "We got this!"

"Looks like we have our work cut out for us. Nice job, Brooke. Let's do this." Kyle grinned broadly at his team.

"So, let's talk about you all now. What are you planning today for self-care?" Alyssa studied each of the team members individually.

"Me and Cara are heading into town to shop. Anyone want to join us?" Mandy shot a questioning glance at Alyssa and Brooke. "We can do a girl's thing. Maybe get our nails done?"

Brooke shook her head and held up her hands, revealing well-kept and unpainted nails. "I'll pass. Thanks."

Alyssa agreed with Brooke, suggesting they hit the village shops and meet up with the Mandy and Cara for dinner.

When Alyssa caught Brooke's eye, Brooke gave her a thumbs-up, asking, "Can we do Mexican? I could really use a margarita."

"You? Margaritas? Since when?" Dan asked with a puzzled expression.

Licking her lips, she tasted the sweet and sour blend of tequila and lime. "I don't know? Weird. I'm totally craving a margarita!"

"Awesome. Margaritas it is!" Kyle laughed and jumped on her suggestion. "We're going to catch a movie, so why don't we all meet up for dinner at Casa Bella say around five-ish? I'll put this one on Dee and Doug's tab. I think we earned it these last two weeks."

"I'll be DD and drive the bus, so have at it, gang. Margarita's for all, thanks to Dee and Doug," Barefoot Dan offered. "And I'll man the fire tonight, Kyle, so if you want to get loopy, feel free."

"Thanks, Dan. I'll be keeping you company as co-DD." Kyle winked at his number one drummer and fire walker. "I want to say you all totally blew me away with the challenge you were given. I'm proud to call you my team. Dee and Doug have been talking about a really great thank you for all of you. But I can't say anything just yet. Meeting's over. Team dismissed. Enjoy your day, and I'll see you tonight at Casa Bella. I'll make the reservation."

Moments later, Brooke was in the yard, embracing the sunlight with eyes closed as she soaked in the warmth. The last thing she wanted to do was go to town. But the margarita—as unusual as it was for her—would make it worthwhile. Definitely. She licked her lips and swallowed.

"Sleepwalking?" Josh's voice jarred Brooke from her thoughts. He came up behind her in stealth-mode, catching her off-guard.

"Ha! No!" She jumped, startled. "Just soaking up this gorgeous sunshine! Good morning! Did you eat breakfast? How'd you sleep?" Brooke turned her attention on a smiling Josh, noting the humor in his voice was evident in his blue eyes, void of their protective barrier.

"I actually slept really well, thank you. No breakfast yet. They're taking us into town for breakfast. Shopping. A movie. You know, fun stuff." He scowled. "I would rather sit by the lake and read my book, but this is a mandatory 'fun' outing. It will be good for us, *they* said."

They were the interim counselors brought in today to provide the opportunity for staff to enjoy some downtime to practice self-care. "You don't sound too thrilled," Brooke offered with a sympathetic smile. "I do get it, though. I'm being dragged into town too. Meanwhile, I've got this rock up on the summit calling my name."

"A rock? Interesting." His quizzical frown eased and he kept pace alongside her as she continued making her way to her cabin.

"It's a flat boulder, great for taking naps. And it overlooks the valley. You'll get to meet it on the final group hike this week. It's an extraordinarily personable old boulder. Quiet, respectful. Inviting." She grinned widely. "Maybe I'll introduce you two before the planned jaunt."

"Sounds like a great ole fellow. The pleasure would be mine." He returned her grin, just as a high-pitched trill sounded across the camp.

The day counselor, Greta, let go of the whistle on the lanyard hanging from her neck and hollered to the rest of the campers mulling about the yard. "Bus is at the gate. Let's go, people!"

Josh turned his attention briefly to the woman with gray hair and clipboard in hand, before facing Brooke again.

"Well. We're being corralled. Enjoy your day. I'll see you tonight at the fire?"

"You're planning on going to the fire?" She tilted her head up at him.

"I thought it was mandatory." He removed his shades out of his shirt pocket and slipped them on.

"No, not on the weekends. Encouraged, not mandatory." She peered into the black mirrors, seeing only her reflection.

The whistle blew again. "Let's go! We have a schedule to keep!"

Brooke bit her lower lip, her voice tinged with amusement. "You'd better get going before you have to sit in the front seat for time out."

"Right? Have a good day. See ya tonight."

"You, too." She watched him walk methodically toward Greta and the bus as it idled curbside. He peered over his shoulder once, waved at her, and she waved back.

As he reached the bus steps, he threw a quick glance at her one last time. She waved again and as she did so, he reached up and took off his shades, locked eyes with her momentarily, and nodded before turning and boarding the bus.

The butterflies in her belly waved frantically as well. Brooke took a deep breath in an attempt to calm them down, but they continued to wave ferociously.

Chapter 10

Two margaritas, a belly full of burritos, and a healthy serving of guacamole later, Brooke sat on the bus, lulled by its rhythmic sway as it lumbered down the backwoods roads leading to the Earth and Sky campground.

Licking her lips, Brooke could still taste the salt and lime, feel the residual warmth of the tequila lingering throughout her body as she stared out the window at the black outline of forest against the summer evening sky. She felt a bit fuzzy from the alcohol. It had been a while since she'd drank, and almost never since she'd had a margarita—probably senior year at college. Honey mead or merlot was her usual choice of beverage when alcohol was served.

Dinner had been fun, if not a bit crazy. Mandy and Cara had taken the opportunity to let their hair down, and eventually resorted to doing shots of tequila while the rest of the team sang "La Bamba." Brooke had declined, content with sipping on her margarita as she watched her co-workers get raunchy and rowdy. Josh was always a sip away in her mind, and even though she was physically sitting at a table with her co-workers, mentally she was lost in thought, caught up in teal blues and sunnies, wondering what he was doing and if he was having a good time.

"Penny for your thoughts," Kyle offered as he sat down next to her at the table, bringing her back to the moment.

"Just enjoying life," she said, as her face grew warm. She tipped her glass and took a swallow of the cool, pale green liquid as remnants of crushed ice bumped against her teeth. She ran the tip of her tongue over her lips, flicking at the little granules of salt that had coated the rim of her glass.

"How's things going?" Kyle grinned, nodding at her nearly finished drink. "Need a refill?"

"Nah. I satisfied my craving. If I order a third, I'll be passed out for the night. You'll have to carry me off the bus," she said, a sheepish grin brightening her face.

"Good to see everyone relaxing. You all are doing a great job, even with the surprises. This is our way of saying thanks." He raised his glass of water and tilted it in a toast in her direction.

"It's getting easier with each day. It's sorta helping me deal with my own stuff too. So, thanks back, I guess?" She avoided looking at Kyle and instead poked with a toothpick at the half-slice of lime floating in the remnants of her margarita.

"Great. You know I'm here if you need to talk, if Alyssa's not available." He motioned toward the other camp therapist with a nod of his head.

"Yup. I appreciate it." She continued poking at the lime until it was submerged under the melting bits of ice.

~ ~ ~

The smell of campfire permeated the air as the bus arrived back at camp shortly after 9 p.m.

"Smells like the day staff got the fire going for us. Hopefully they grabbed the drums as well," Kyle said after getting a whiff of the smoky air. "I'll see you all down at the pit, say by nine-thirty. Sound good?"

It was 9:15 now, Brooke noticed after taking a quick glance at her iPhone. She surveyed the base camp and saw no life, heard no drumming, and wondered how Josh had fared. Would he be joining them around the fire, as he said he would? Or would he bow out, since learning it wasn't mandatory?

"I'm going to change my clothes. I'll meet you guys in a few," Brooke called out as she headed to her cabin. All she wanted to do was sleep. It had been a long day, and going to bed early would have been her first choice, especially since this was technically their off day. She shed her 'town clothes' as she referred to her floral sundress and hemp sandals, and slipped on a pair of Levi's, an Earth and Sky tee, and her socks and hikers.

. . . losin' myself in the cool feel of Levi's . . .

Another line of her poem about blue popped into her head. She jotted it down in the journal by her bed, then reached for her Earth and Sky sweatshirt on a peg by the door, made her way out of her bedroom and down to the fire pit.

All the camp chairs had been set up, with drums placed sporadically, but there was no sign of Josh and Alyssa anywhere. Brooke noted the rest of her co-workers, most of whom had already hooked up with their counterparts as they filled one another in on their days' events. She paused in front of Alyssa and Josh's empty chairs, with her own chair next to his, and silently called his name.

"Hey."

As if she'd summoned him on cue, Josh stepped beside her, two steaming mugs in his hands. No sunglasses.

"Thought you might like some fresh java," he said, offering her one of the mugs before claiming his red camp chair.

Cocking her head to one side, she grabbed the cup of steaming coffee, nodding in appreciation. "Wow. How thoughtful. Thanks."

"You sound surprised." He peered at her over the rim of his mug as he gingerly sipped the brew, his gaze amused and unwavering as she claimed her green folding chair beside him.

"I am," she chirped after settling in her seat and cautiously tasting the steaming liquid. "You remembered how I like it."

"Black, no sugar makes it pretty easy."

"Yeah. I'm pretty easy."

"Are you, now?" His eyes were smiling at her, his mouth hidden as he took another drink of his coffee.

"*Going*. Easy *going*." She pointed to a drum she did not recognize, placed between their chairs, and offered a quick change of subject. "So, did you do this, too?"

"Yeah. I figured I'd give it another try. A real try, not being forced into it by the resident slave driver drummer." His words were laced with a hint of dry humor as he studied the fire.

Dan and Kyle prodded the tinder with pokers, sending sparks flying as they added logs and readjusted the mound to keep the flames dancing.

"What changed your mind?" she asked as her gaze followed the sparks wafting up and disappearing into the night sky.

"We stopped at a shop and they had a drum circle going outside. Everyone was having fun, laughing, dancing. Drumming."

"Beats 'N Things."

"Yeah. Cool shop. Lots of unique gifts and what a collection of drums. I saw this and that was it." He lifted up the blue, teal, gold, and black *darbuka,* and handed it to her.

"I love Beats 'N Things!" She accepted the drum and settled it between her legs, rubbing her palms around the goatskin head in a circular motion. "This has great energy." She patted out a simple rhythm, then laughed as she handed it back to him. "It's a happy little drum you got there."

"You can have it," he said, "since it makes you happy."

"Me? No, I can't. Thanks, though." She did not reach for the drum as he held it out to her, so he set it beside them on the grass with a shrug.

"So, yeah. It's my fave stop when we go to town. That

and Nurtured by Nature," Brooke began, attempting to ease the awkward silence that fell between them. "I love that place. I could spend a whole paycheck there if I'm not careful."

"Yeah. That was another great shop. She's got some beautiful pieces. I met the owner. Everything's original designs. She makes them herself," Josh said, as he slipped his hand into one of his pockets. "There were a few pieces that really caught my eye."

"Ah, yeah," Brooke followed his hand then looked up into his face, his expression unreadable, but penetrating to her soul as she attempted another subject change. "I ended up getting a full body massage and taking a nap in the hot tub at the day retreat health spa the girls dragged me to. And, against my will, I got a mani/pedi." She held out her unpainted, neatly-trimmed fingernails as a change of topic. "The guys went and saw some action flick. We ended up doing Mexican for dinner. If you like margaritas, this is *the* go-to place in all of Upstate New York. They're known for their margaritas. I can still taste it if I think hard enough," Brooke said, licking her lips and laughing. "Margaritas are the nectar of the gods."

When silence was Josh's only response, she grew quiet and turned to him. "Josh?"

"What did you say?" His words were sharp and his voice low. His hand left his pocket as he gripped the arm of his chair.

"Say? Why? I don't understand?" Thoroughly confused, Brooked fumbled for an answer.

"Rosalie." His voice cracked. "She loves margaritas. I mean. She used to . . . she loved them. They were her *go-to* drink." He shot an accusing glare at Brooke. "She used to say they were the nectar of the gods."

"Oh. Dear. I'm . . . I'm sorry." Brooke closed her eyes as she felt electricity shoot through her from head to toe.

The campfire disappeared, the chatter from the campers and mentors faded, replaced by the roar of the ocean, tinkling of music, sand, and surf filling her senses. Through the haze she saw Josh staring at her. In her mind, she heard Rosalie say softly, *"I'm so sorry, babe. It's not your fault. You have to let it go. Let us go. Don't ever let go of your dreams."*

Josh froze for a second, then yelled, "What the fu-!" He sprung to his feet, knocking his chair over as he threw the ceramic coffee mug at the campfire, shattering it. Without another word he took off running into the woods.

Brooke was frozen in time, as if suspended by strings like a puppet, unable to move. Suddenly the haze lifted, the taste of margaritas gone. And so was Josh. "Where is he?" she asked, her voice hoarse and reverberating around the otherwise silent circle. "What happened?" She noted his overturned chair and watched Paulie and Kyle running toward the thicket of trees. Everyone was staring at her.

"You said *something* to piss him off." Cara narrowed her gaze. "You okay?"

Brooke felt her stomach knot as a wave of uneasiness swept over her. "I'm not sure—I think—Rosalie. I think Rosalie came through. I'll—I'm okay," Brooke said as her voice wavered. "I'm not sure about him." She stood up, slightly off balance for the briefest moment, remembering Rosalie's words. She'd never experienced communication like this before. The messages usually came in the form of a dream, which she would deliver to her charge. But this . . . Had she actually channeled Rosalie this time?

"Did you . . . *you know*?" Cara whispered, looking around at the other people within earshot.

"Maybe? I have to find Josh. If he comes back here, text me, okay?" She held up her phone and went running in the direction Kyle and Paulie had disappeared.

~ ~ ~

When Josh finally stopped running, he found himself at the edge of the lake. Dark velvet midnight blue sky above, splattered with stars, the mirror-like lake at his feet. The waters faded into blackness where he knew trees like sentinels lined the far shore. At this moment all he saw was water gently lapping at his feet, reaching into eternity as it blended into the canopy of sky overhead. A loon cackled in the far-off night, interrupting the cacophony of tree frogs whirring and burping their nightly song. He buried his face in his hands, failing miserably at coming to terms with what had occurred minutes earlier.

What kind of parlor trick was this? How could they even pull this off? How could Brooke mimic her voice? *Her voice! Rosalie, Rosalie, Rosalie!*

And her catch phrase, what she constantly told him, told the girls. *Don't ever let go of your dreams.*

He smoothed his face with his hands, bringing them together as if in prayer, tapping his forehead against the tips of his fingers.

This whole thing was a farce. *They're in on it with Derek and they're probably charging a hefty fee for making it appear like I'm going crazy. Once they confirm I'm nuts, the board will fire me for good.*

I'm not nuts! I heard you, Rosalie! I heard you!

"How did Brooke do it? How did she know? How did she get your voice so perfect?" Josh paced back and forth along the shore muttering aloud.

"Josh!"

He froze in his tracks and searched the dark sands of the lake shore, lit only by the stars and the silver moon. On the edge of the trees lining the lake beach stood Paulie and Kyle. Josh looked on as Brooke wave them off, then strode toward him while her co-workers faded into the woods. "Go away, Brooke. Leave me alone!"

Chapter 11

Brooke continued toward him with a purposeful stride, obviously not at all deterred by his words. "Let me explain."

"No!" Josh held his hands up and she stopped dead in her tracks. "I trusted you."

"You can still trust me. I'm sorry about what happened back there. I have no control over it. It just happens. I don't know why, but—"

"Brooke! Stop talking. Stop lying to me. I'm not stupid! I know what's going on and I'm not going to let you do this to me." He confronted her, face to face, her features clear despite the darkness of the night. There was pain, confusion . . . and something else . . . in her eyes.

"I was beginning to trust you. And then, you do this?" He spread his hands wide.

"I didn't *do* anything to you. What purpose would it serve me to hurt you?" Her voice trembled as she squinted up at him.

"I wouldn't put it past my board to pay you off to prove I'm crazy. If they're orchestrating a takeover—" The sound of her gasp cut him off.

"Josh! We're a reputable organization. We're in the business of healing people, not taking them down. Earth and Sky is not conspiring with your board. I know this sounds nuts, but if you don't want to believe me, I don't know what to tell you."

She started to leave, but for some crazy reason he couldn't let her walk away. He grabbed her by the shoulders to stop her, and a quick burst of static electricity shot through his hands, causing them both to jump.

"How did you do it? How did you copy her voice?" His voice came out a low growl. The questions were hard to articulate, but he had to know.

"I didn't *do* anything. It just happens. It has for a while now. The stories you mentioned? This is what they're gossiping about. Why they call me Deathwalker."

He held her fast until she shrugged off his grasp and half-ran to the picnic table where she sat watching him.

He didn't move. He wanted to believe her. He wanted to believe she was not double-crossing him. Today was the first time in a long time he missed someone other than his wife and children. He thought about her all day, hoping to catch a glimpse of her. And when he did, he found her standing at the drum circle in her sundress, looking like a woman and not his babysitter. He wanted to run over and scoop her up and kiss her and not stop until they both needed to breathe.

His memory was interrupted as Brooke patted the space to her right. "Josh. Please. Come sit with me and I'll do my best to explain."

He took two reluctant steps toward her. "I . . . don't understand what happened. You sounded *exactly* like Rosalie. How did you know about the margaritas? And she always said not to let go of my dreams. How did you know?" His voice cracked under the weight of his broken heart, memories threatening to shatter what remained and burst it to pieces. "I miss her so fucking much. Derek, my board tell me to let it go. Now you—or you're trying to say that *Rosalie*—is telling me to let it go. How? How?" He climbed up on the table and sat beside her, dropping his head into his hands, finally releasing gut-wrenching sobs that had been building since boarding Amtrak nearly two weeks ago. "I don't know. I don't know what to believe anymore," he said, his voice crackling with his confusion.

When her arms came around him, he melted into her embrace, resting his head on her shoulder as he continued to purge all the sorrow and anguish he hadn't shared with anyone for the last three years. Tears he was not supposed to cry because he was a man. Tears filled with guilt and anger at fate, at Rosalie, at himself. Tears he didn't deserve to cry because he had chosen to not be with his family. And they died. Leaving him alone.

The moon climbed along the horizon as his sobs quieted down, and he sat there beside her, spent. Brooke slipped out of her sweatshirt and handed it to him. "You're all snotty and I don't have tissues."

"I can't—" Mortified at his breakdown, he was even more repulsed with the offer of her shirt.

"Yeah, you can. Think of it as a full-sized handkerchief fashioned into a sweatshirt. All my kids use it when this happens. Trust me. It's seen worse." She gave him a lopsided half smile, took the sleeve then leaned into him and gently wiped the tears away from his eyes. "Don't worry. It's clean."

He groped his pockets, searching the table and surrounding area around for anything else to do the job, and failed. In the end, her sweatshirt was it. Tentatively, he accepted the garment and wiped his nose. "This is disgusting. I'm so sorry."

Her voice soothed him as it settled like feathers through the night air. "Don't be. We can walk back to camp and get tissues if it's too gross for you?"

"No. Please. I don't want to go back. Not yet." He wiped his nose, wadded up the shirt, and set it on the table beside him. "I'll buy you a new one."

"Don't worry. It's camp tradition. It washes well." She put an arm around his shoulders and squeezed hard. "You okay?"

He blew out a hard breath. "Better than I have been in a long time. I guess I needed the release. Thank you."

"Tears are cleansing. And healing."

"I cried at their funeral. Well, memorial. We had one for all three of them. My girls." His voice cracked. "I don't remember anything from it. Except their three photos. I couldn't even say goodbye to them." His voice broke again as he closed his eyes.

"Saying goodbye is tough. Not saying goodbye is tougher." She gave another quick squeeze of his shoulders and when he opened his eyes, he sought out her gaze, needing a lifeline.

"Now it's too late. They're gone." His whisper echoed across the lake before dissipating into the night sounds.

"No, they aren't. I mean, physically they may be gone. But they're still here, all around us. In here," she offered as she placed a hand over his heart.

"You think so?" He squinted doubtfully in the darkness.

"Yeah," she offered simply with a nod.

As he cocked his head to the side, he caught her eyes. By day they were a brilliant green. Now? They were dark caverns he could absolutely lose himself in, if he allowed it. He held her gaze, mesmerized, and as he willed himself to breathe, he took in her essence. Jasmine, night air, and . . . woman. A deep groan sounded from within his chest as he bent his head and, without conscious thought, he brushed her lips with his. He needed to taste her. Electricity sparked between them at first touch, causing them both to jump and gasp.

This was not what he planned, and surely not what he wanted. He wanted to be angry with her. He wanted to believe the worst. She could be a fraud and manipulative, preying on his vulnerability. He'd come here to heal. Not to . . . to . . . "Sorry. I shouldn't have—" he began in a ragged voice, more upset with himself than her at the moment.

Quick as a cat, Brooke jumped off the table and walked

to the far side. "No, you shouldn't have." She looked around the empty beach. "We should go back."

"Brooke. I'm sorry," he called after her as she headed to the path. She waved him off and kept walking.

~ ~ ~

"Is he okay?" Alyssa asked. She, Dan, and Kyle were still tending the fire when Brooke returned in a huff, stomping her way to her chair.

"Is *he* okay? *He's* fine. More of an asshole than usual, but fine." She scooted her chair close to the flames, slunk down, and placed her feet on the large boulders marking the pit.

"What happened?" Kyle's chest puffed out as he straightened up, doing a quick head-to-toe scan on her.

"Oh, nothing I couldn't handle. Relax. He's just a—" Brooke was cut off by Alyssa's very loud and pointed greeting.

"Hey, Josh! Welcome back! Doing okay there?"

"I think you were going to say *jerk*. I'll finish it for you." He grabbed his chair and dragged it up beside Brooke, ignoring Alyssa completely. "Is that what you were going say? If not, I can think of a dozen other nouns we could fill in the blank with."

"That works." She folded her arms across her chest and refused to look at him.

She should have seen it coming. Just like Richard. What is it with men? She scrunched her eyes shut and blocked out the memory she could not deal with right now.

"Can we talk?" He leaned over, speaking in a low voice. "Please."

"No. If you don't leave me alone, I'm going to bed."

Kyle, Dan, and Alyssa all remained quiet, staring at the fire. Brooke knew they had all ears on her and Josh. And for that she was thankful. Would he hurt her? She didn't think so, now that she had made her boundaries clear. Did he trigger a bunch of crap that left her spinning? Hell, yeah. She just needed to think. But she didn't want to be alone.

"I can't believe you came back to the fire." She hissed at him.

"What did you come back for? I came back for my drum." He folded his arms and settled deeper into his chair. "And to give you this." He tossed her wadded up sweatshirt on the ground by her feet.

"Yeah, thanks. Well, there's your drum." She gave a toss of her head back to where his drum lay in the grass behind them.

"I don't know what came over me. I'm sorry." His voice was hushed, and he sounded way more sincere than Brooke wanted to hear at the moment.

Her recent conversation with Alyssa was pinging around in her brain as she reflected on what just happened. It was totally different than the whole Richard thing three years ago. Richard was way older, married. Brutal. She drew a fist to her mouth as she squeaked, forcing back the urge to cry or scream. She wasn't sure which.

Dan looked over his shoulder with the sound, and repositioned himself across the fire, so that she and Josh were in his full view. Brooke locked eyes with him and answered his unasked question with a slight nod of her head and a thumbs-up.

What happened with Josh was different than Richard. She wasn't interested in Richard. She wasn't imagining kissing Richard. She didn't find him attractive. She had never hoped he'd do those horrible things to her. Josh, on the other hand. She exhaled deeply and shot a furtive glance his way, only to find he was staring at her, as if willing her to look at him.

"I didn't mean to—" he started, pausing as she held up her hand.

Truth be told, she'd been thinking of kissing him just seconds before he took the initiative. That brief caress was her undoing. It took every ounce of willpower she possessed to not lay him on the table and kiss him back—and maybe even more. But out of the deepest, darkest, recesses of her soul the image of Richard, disgusting, leering Richard, pawing at her flashed in her mind.

And so, she ran. But who was she running from, really? Richard? Josh? Or herself?

Chapter 12

"Hey!"

Brooke swallowed a groan at the sound of Josh's greeting as she cut across the yard heading toward the clearing in the woods leading to the path she hiked every Sunday afternoon. This was her real self-care time. Her time to think, reflect, release, and heal. Her trip to the day spa yesterday was her way of caring for her team mates—of spending time with them and bonding as friends and co-workers. This was her time. Today she was planning on sorting through the gnarled strands of emotions and fears tangling up her mind and heart. Fate had been weaving this web—a strand here, a strand there—all week, and last night it had managed to trap everything into one tightly-wound ball of unorganized panic and disarray.

She had spent the morning finalizing the Hail and Farewell PowerPoint they traditionally showed to the campers at their last breakfast before boarding the bus home. It was hard to believe "So Long, Sunday" was only a week away. She left an additional 15 blank slides to be filled with shots from the coming week, the final ceremony, and the bonfire. Other than those minor adjustments, her work was done. As she browsed through the folder of photos she had collected, she reflected on the personal growth she had experienced this time around.

Her initial prejudice was evident in the first few photos she captured of sullen expressions and body postures that clearly proclaimed they did not want to be here. As the days progressed so did the mood of her photographs. She did not miss a smile, a tear, the comradery. Some learned how to laugh; some learned how to cry. And, hopefully in the next week they would put it all together and learn how to live again.

When the presentation was as finished as it could be, she focused her full attention on cleaning her room. Laundry, changing the bed linens, rearranging her personal items in her dresser drawers, and even taking down the window curtains and washing and rehanging them kept her occupied and away from the rest of the team and campers. It wasn't only due to her desire to avoid Josh. This is how she dealt with her Deathwalker duties. Retreat, release, recoup, re-engage.

And now it was her time. Breaking stride, Brooke paused a moment as she swallowed thickly and tried to still her now fluttering heart. Without turning around, she waited for Josh to catch up to her. Thankfully, her sunglasses were in place, two mirror/blue orbs of protection shielding her emotions and thoughts she knew could be easily read in her eyes.

Ironically, his shades were off, as he came around to face her, and tucked neatly into his shirt pocket.

"What's up?" She kept her question simple and monotone. The last thing she wanted was company. Especially his company. She attempted 'resting bitch face' in the hopes of keeping him at bay.

"Where've you been all day?" He reminded her of the lost puppy Dan had referenced at the meeting, and her heart sank with a twinge of regret, as if she'd abandoned him by a curb to fend for himself.

"Sunday's are downtime. You know, like last week. You're free to do what you want, and so is the team. I thought you knew." She moved a half-step toward the path waiting for her a few yards away. If only she'd left three minutes earlier. Two even.

"I did." His eyes trailed toward the path, then back to her. "The rest of the staff were at breakfast and have been hanging around all day. Me and Dan had a really good talk at lunch. I wanted to make sure you were okay."

"I'm fine," she lied. She needed to get away and, obviously, he wanted to talk.

"You going for a hike?"

With a glance at her day pack and walking stick, she bit back a sarcastic reply. "Yes."

This happened a lot with her younger charges. Especially after she had channeled their mom or favorite grandparent, or a sibling. It was natural for them to want to use her as a direct line of communication, which is why she had learned to set boundaries. Too often a similar scenario would happen with a little one catching up and wanting to tag along. And she'd usually let them.

This was much, much different.

She'd never been kissed by any of her charges. To make matters worse, she couldn't stop thinking about it. And, when she woke this morning, she realized she wanted more.

Nope. Not happening. It couldn't. He was leaving in a week and she'd never see him again. She wasn't sure if never seeing him again was a good or a bad thing.

"Want company?" He waved at the path, then back at her again. "Are you going to the rock you said you'd show me?"

She had offered, hadn't she?

"Yes," Brooke said again, glancing at his hiking shoes. "You'd need water and I really want to get going. I'm already running late."

Pointing to a canteen hooked to his belt, he smiled brightly. "Let's go."

Cancelling was not an option. This was *her* weekly ritual. But, could she chance being alone with him again? After last night? And what if Rosalie came through? Channeling is emotionally and physically draining for her. Brooke watched Josh take a few steps toward the clearing, pause, and wave back to her.

"Are you coming, or what?" he asked. "You're running late, remember?"

It was her hike, not his. He was not going to go all CEO over her and take control of *her free time.* With a scowl, she double-stepped to overtake the lead, motioning for him to follow. "We are *not* going to repeat what happened last night. So, if you're thinking—"

He raised a hand simulating the Boy Scout salute and offered earnestly, "Scout's honor. I want to see the rock you keep talking about. Nothing more."

Deepening her scowl, she led the way. Part of her was petrified to be alone with him. The other part of her needed to prove she could maintain control. And yet, another very small part of her called her a liar. She wanted to be alone with him. And she wanted to throw all control over the side of the mountain.

The climb was easy, as far as hikes go. This was Number Three of the 'Lower 'Leven' trails in the foothills leading up to the Adirondacks' 49 peaks people came from all over the world to hike. Brooke had completed all eleven options, but this was her favorite. It took about a half hour to reach the summit if she hoofed it hard, and was an easy breeze downhill to get back to base camp.

Along the way she silently pointed out with her walking stick different sites of interest, like a cave opening under a ledge, or the waterfall still flowing due to the unusually long, rainy season. They passed a clearing two thirds of the way up, with a little field boasting a patch of forget-me-nots which always brought to mind *Lady Chatterley's Lover* by D.H. Lawrence—the part where Mellors decorated Connie's private parts with forget-me-nots and woodruff. She pointed to the field of blue blossoms and smiled when he nodded back in silence offering a thumbs-up as his response. He got it. No talking. Which was more than she could say about the younger charges she shared this hike with on occasion.

Her heart soared as it did each time she reached the peak. She twirled slowly as she took in the 360 degrees of the breathtaking view of valley and town to the south, and the Adirondacks looming on the northern horizon. The sun gleamed brightly overhead as she greeted her rock with her longstanding ritual. Forgetting momentarily the shadow close by, Brooke placed two hands palms-down to tap into the earthy boulder energy and closed her eyes.

Rustling movements to her side brought her back to the moment, and she remembered she was not alone. Josh had mirrored her actions, placing both his well-groomed, tanned hands on the boulder, palms-down, with his eyes closed. Brooke hoisted herself up onto the rock, slipped out of her backpack and laid it on the smooth surface beside her. Rather than remain at the big boulder, Josh sauntered off and made his way to the edge of the cliff, and proceeded to pull out his iPhone, snapping photos at every angle. At one point, he took a panorama image, slowly turning to catch the 360-degree view. He found a smaller boulder, big enough for one person, and situated himself there, his back to Brooke.

She watched and thought for a moment about his suicidal tendencies, wondering if she should call him back from the ledge. "You okay?" she asked, and when he gave her a thumbs-up, she laid down, using the back pack for a pillow, and closed her eyes. It was like plugging a battery pack into a wall outlet for her.

She wasn't sure how long she dozed—probably just a few minutes—but when she awoke, she found Josh positioned beside her. Sitting up, she grabbed her water bottle and chugged. He remained laying down on his back, arms folded upward, with his hands forming a pillow for his head, sunglasses in place.

"You awake?" she asked when he didn't move, and immediately received a nod of confirmation. "Sorry if I was rude to you by falling asleep. It's my only time to—"

"I get it. No worries. No need to apologize. We apologize too much already." He sat up and swigged from his own canteen. "You know, you snore." He tossed a half-smile in her direction.

Shaking her head, she harrumphed. "I do not!"

He held up his iPhone and laughed. "Want to see?"

"You recorded me sleeping? Hello, Creeper."

He laughed again, denying the accusation. "Nah. I was only joking. I didn't record you."

"I want to see your phone." She grabbed at the sleek cellphone grasped in the hand he held high over her head.

"And if I refuse, you'll what? Give me detention?" His pearly whites gleamed in the sun.

"Maybe."

Waking the phone, he rested his thumb against the home button to unlock it, and poked at the Photos icon, revealing only images of scenery.

She harrumphed again and produced two granola bars from her pack, offering him one.

After chewing in silence for a moment, Josh spoke. "About last night . . ."

Here it comes. Brooke took a swig of water and braced herself. "Yeah?"

"I've been thinking. A lot. I want to believe what happened last night was real. That Rosalie and my girls aren't suffering, and that they forgive me." He raised his knees and rested his folded forearms, staring out at the blue sky and deep green mountain range.

She waited. And waited. And when he said nothing else, she peered at him over the rim of her sunglasses.

"But?"

"But I have so many questions. This isn't my reality. It may be yours, but this kind of thing doesn't happen in my world." He bent his head and caught her gaze over the black plastic shield of his own shades. "How do I know this isn't just a gimmick?"

"Do you believe I'm the type of person to make something like this up?" She forced herself to not look away, as intense his energy was at that moment. "Talk to me. Tell me what you need from me to help you understand this is real."

"I'd like to believe I'm not a rude person. I mean, if I started pumping you with questions, wouldn't that be like you offering me a cup of coffee, then me demanding you take me out for dinner?"

She didn't argue his analogy. "Most people want to know if I have any more messages."

"I trust if you do, you'll relay them. I think she got her point across. Rosalie was pretty vocal with her needs, and didn't dwell on things." He exhaled heavily, poking at an ant marching across the flat, sunbaked boulder.

"Oh?" Brooke swallowed hard, pushing down the sudden need to cry. She noticed a pulse beating in the side of his neck. She trailed her gaze along his tanned skin, to his perfectly sculpted ear, his strong jawline, his profile. She ducked her head and envisioned a plexiglass wall shutting down between them like a guillotine. With a deep breath, she exhaled all desire to weep, regaining her poise and strength. *Being an empath sucks sometimes.*

Grabbing a tissue from the front pocket of her backpack, she handed it to him, studying the horizon as he blew his nose and cleared his throat. "She was the love of my life. My rock. My wings. My motivation and inspiration. And then she was gone. And the girls. They were mini-Rosalies. So perfect. So precocious." He chuckled softly, sadly, shaking his head.

Except for nodding in encouragement to continue, Brooke waited, not moving at all.

"She begged me to not change my flight. And when I told her I had to, she begged me to allow her and the girls to postpone their flights, stay back a day so we could all fly out together. I felt horrible, having to put work before them again. We'd waited three months for this trip. We were packed, ready to roll. The girls were so excited. But when Derek and the board called an emergency meeting to approve a partnership expected to bring huge profits, I had no choice. I had to stay. I told her to go, and I'd catch the earliest flight out and be there by dinner the next night."

His breath hitched and he shook his head again, as if arguing with some inner demon.

Brooke bit her lip and placed a hand on his shoulder. Her heart lurched as if something had a viselike grip on it, and she brought her hand back to her lap fast.

The connection with Josh was strong, stronger than with anyone placed under her care, and she struggled to come to terms with this. Hands folded safely in her lap, Brooke spoke in a soothing tone. "No one knows why these things happen. They just do, and we can't blame ourselves for the choices we make in good conscience. You had no idea. They had no idea. It's life. And death."

"I get it now. Finally. You know, last night. I woke up this morning and I feel like someone turned a light on. Like I've been wearing a shroud this whole time and now the shroud's lifted. I can breathe again and it doesn't hurt. Here." He pounded the middle of his chest with a closed fist, then ran his hand through his hair.

"I needed you to connect me to Rosalie, so she could tell me she's okay, the girls are okay. I needed to know they don't hate me for abandoning them," he whispered, his voice cracking.

"They don't hate you, Josh. That's not how it works when we cross through The Veil. All human resentments and sufferings heal and pass as our souls evolve. That's what I've been led to believe anyway." She reached out again, offering a quick compassionate pat on his back before retreating, hands clutched in her lap once again.

"I've hated myself ever since it happened. Every damn day I get up and I'm alive and they aren't, and I hate myself for choosing business over them. I thought it was my fault. I guess this is the reason why I gave up on Quirkyflirt. Every time I'd go to work, I'd think *I chose work over them*. Now I see I can't control Fate."

Exhaling a long sigh, Brooke nodded slowly. "You got it."

"Now what?" He took off his shades with a quick swipe. "Do I get to leave?"

A short chortle was her initial response. "No," she said. "There's no early dismissal for finishing early. Besides, you just completed Stage One. Get ready for Stage Two."

"What was Stage One?"

"The Awakening," she answered promptly, continuing with a disclaimer. "Mind you, this is completely my own observation. It's not something Earth and Sky follows. It seems to hold true with many of the campers who come through here, regardless of age. If they make it through these three stages, they usually leave here healthier than they were when they arrived. And able to make it on their own."

"So, what are the other stages?" He lifted his palms in question.

"Well," Brooke continued, flipping her thumb up. "Stage one is The Awakening." Her forefinger shot out as she explained, "Stage Two is Understanding and Accepting. And"—middle finger displayed, she ended with—"Stage

Three is Manifesting Change." She held up her hand and waggled her digits at him. "No going home until Stage Three is passed."

"So, you guys really think you can heal people in three weeks? Make them functioning members of society?" He raised one eyebrow in disbelief.

"Well, yes and no. Yes, the healing process definitely *begins* here *if* the person is ready. If so, we help them build the foundation where they can continue healing. We can't force you guys to heal. We *can* show you how to begin to heal and how to keep healing—*if* you want to." She studied his face as he nodded thoughtfully.

"I think I'm ready."

"I know." She jumped off the boulder.

"Thank you," he said, remaining on the rock as his demeanor changed from sunny to cloudy. "For not staying angry with me about last night, about the kiss."

"No worries, thank you for believing me about Rosalie," she replied, capturing his gaze as she took off her sunnies. "Besides, I may have overreacted a little bit."

"No. You didn't. I don't force myself on anyone. I don't know what got into me. And I just needed to tell you I was sorry in the light of day, so you could see I meant it."

His sincerity seemed genuine enough for Brooke. And although his eyes were warm, she detected a hint of sadness. Or was it regret? Her butterflies flitted and she steeled herself against the impulse to pull him close and kiss him. *Talk about mixed messages.*

"Shh," Brooke said. "I accept your apology. But in the future, remember I'm super big on consent, FYI." She leaned against the rock and studied the toes of her hiking boots as he jumped down and stood beside her.

"So am I. And I respect you and admire you, and I trust you. And last night I totally blew it."

"Almost. Almost blew it. You weren't entirely wrong to go there. It was just bad timing." She wrapped an arm around his waist and gave a quick squeeze of a hug. "We'd just experienced something really emotional, and traumatizing, and in a way, it forged us together and—"

"Bad timing?" He cupped her chin, his eyes questioning.

She held her breath, her lips parted as she dropped her gaze to his mouth, wanting so desperately to ease away and replace the bad memory of their first kiss.

"Well. Yeah." She tried to speak but lost her ability to form a coherent sentence. All she could think about at the moment was how the world was right when he stood by her, how he wore fresh air like an expensive cologne, and how her body felt as brilliant as the first rays of the morning sun when he touched her.

"Is this what consent looks like, Brooke?" he whispered and dipped his head.

"I don't know anymore. I can't think when I'm around you," she said, lifting her arms to rest on his shoulders as he turned into her, drawing her close.

"This sure feels like consent," he murmured, closing his eyes, nudging her nose with his.

She molded into him, her hands cradling his head. His hair was soft against her fingers, his body hard against hers, his breath minty as he paused, waiting for her, she knew. Tipping her head up ever so slightly, she brushed her lips against his.

He leaned back, searching her face. "You sure?" His voice was wavering, hesitant.

You want this, she reminded herself, as her heart beat a steady rhythm against her ribcage. "Yes." Her answer caressed his lips just a hairsbreadth away.

He growled low and deep as he buried his face in her hair, nuzzling the vulnerable, tender spot just below her ear. He left a trail of kisses along the soft curve of her neck, her jawline, before he claimed her mouth with a gentle fierceness not unlike that of a late afternoon thunderstorm.

Desire like heat lightning rolled through her body as she responded, tracing her hands down his spine, over the hardened muscles sculpting his back, pulling him into her.

His kiss deepened, and she welcomed him, forgetting about everything she had run from, everything she hid behind, knowing this was where she was supposed to be. At least for right now.

Chapter 13

Brooke struggled to breathe and sat straight up in bed choking and coughing, trying to clear her lungs of the seawater. Her hair was soaked, her body was soaked, and for a moment she had no clue where she was. Panting, she clutched her throat and realized her night shirt was dry. There was no water. No ocean. The clock ticked. The katydids whirred. The bullfrogs croaked.

All was well in the Adirondacks.

Except it wasn't.

Trembling, she swung her legs over the edge of her bed, flinging the sheet and the maroon cotton weave blanket away from her body. Her legs were wobbly, and she was still trying to clear her throat of the salty remnants of seawater as she crossed the room. Her movements were slow, as if she was walking in water. But there wasn't any water, she reminded herself. She opened her bedroom door and tiptoed down the darkened hallway to the communal bathroom. Cara, Alyssa, and Mandy were asleep in their bedrooms behind closed doors.

Goosebumps prickled the skin along her arms as she reached for the wall switch. A row of globe bulbs lit up above the mirror hanging over the white porcelain sink, casting a soft glow throughout the small bathroom as a gurgling cough sounded from behind her. Frozen with fear, Brooke struggled to breathe, unable to even lift her eyes to look in the mirror to see who or what had joined her. As the gurgling cough drew closer, Brooke whimpered, and with a scream muffled by the seawater puddling in her own throat she forced herself to look up through veiled lids.

Standing behind her reflection in the mirror was the image of a beautiful, though water-drenched, woman. Immobilized by fear, Brooke stared at the corpse of what surely must have been Rosalie. Water poured from the woman's mouth like a faucet left on at full force. Her eyes were wide and filled with sorrow, her hair entangled with seaweed. She lifted an arm and pointed away from the bathroom, whispering fiercely, "Go, now!"

Brooke ran. Back to the safety of her bedroom, closing her door with a thud. *Go where?*

It had to be Rosalie. The woman had long, curly blond hair. She wore dangly emerald teardrop earrings, and an emerald pendant around her neck. Her dress was green also, and didn't look wet even though she apparently had drowned in it. Why else would she be wearing it? So, okay. If this was Rosalie, what was she trying to tell her? 'Stay away from my husband?' She said, "Go, now." Go to where? Go away? Go to bed? Go to Josh? What would she even say at this hour? *Yo. Your dead wife told me to come wake you up.*

Shaking her head clear of the horrific vision, Brooke sat on the edge of her twin bed, and checked the time on her iPhone. 3:13. She was breathing fine now. No gurgling in her chest, no struggle to cough up the sensation of fluid making her feel like she was drowning. Crawling back beneath the covers and keeping her back to the wall and her eye on the door, she dozed and woke on and off for the next hour, her room lit by the overhead light.

With the first morning song of robins, sparrows, and warblers, the first cawing of crows, Brooke dragged herself out of bed, resigned to the fact she was up for the day. She straightened out her bedcovers, slipped on her yoga pants and tee shirt, and ventured warily to the bathroom again, silently pleading with Rosalie to leave her alone. As she quickly splashed water on her face and brushed her teeth, Brooke kept her eye on the mirror, making sure she did not receive any visitors—especially dead ones.

Heading toward the dining hall, Brooke could smell the bacon cooking and the coffee brewing already, even though it wasn't even five o'clock. The vision of Rosalie—she was now sure it was Rosalie—was still fresh in her mind. From the long blond curls to the dangling emerald earrings, even in death she was stunning.

The dining hall was empty except for one lone coffee drinker. He waved at Brooke, his face etched in worry and weariness. From the looks of things, it seemed Josh hadn't sleep well either. Brooke wondered if he'd been visited by his dead wife as well. Armed with a freshly poured cup of coffee, she joined Josh at what had become their usual table, sliding onto the wooden bench after setting her ceramic mug down gently.

"You're up early," she offered, her voice weary as she squinted at him.

"As are you." He motioned to the clock hanging over the door.

"I couldn't sleep. Been up a few hours."

"Me, too." Josh frowned into his coffee, offering nothing more.

"Want to talk about it?" She studied the puffiness around his bloodshot eyes, the bright blue glittering more so than usual. He'd been crying.

"Not really," he answered too quickly, avoiding her gaze.

"It's okay." She wanted to ask him about Rosalie, what kind of jewelry she wore, what her favorite color was. To do so would be unkind, especially since it was pretty obvious he was struggling at the moment.

So, they sat together, not speaking. Just being there for one another. The sun rose, early morning light filtering in from the large, paned windows. Kyle and Alyssa arrived first, raised eyebrows and a nod their only greeting. Brooke watched them get coffee and sit at a table at the far end of the hall, peering over Kyle's iPad, murmuring softly between themselves.

When she glanced back at Josh, she caught him staring at her. Her face grew warm as she realized she wore no makeup and hadn't washed her hair since Saturday. At least she'd brushed her teeth.

"You're completely different from her, you know. Even so, I think she would have liked you." He twirled the gold filigree wedding band, slipping it on and off his ring finger, head bent.

"How so?" She watched him toy with his ring, mesmerized.

"You're both honest to a fault. She couldn't lie if her life depended on it." The worry etched in his face softened in recollection.

"You hardly know me. I could be the most consummate liar, and how could you tell?" She crooked her head to the side and waited.

"Your eyes." He leaned closer over the table, and rubbed his thumb over the wrinkled worry lines between her eyebrows. "And this. It scrunches up when you are struggling with something. When you finally speak what you're trying so desperately to hold back, it smooths out. I imagine if you lied, it would become a permanent fixture."

She shifted on the bench, moving out of his reach, and cleared her throat. His touch warmed her in places nowhere near her eyebrows. "Very perceptive of you. I didn't realize I had become a case study."

"Sorry. Not a case study. Just something I noticed." He eased back onto his side of the table. "Hey. I wanted to talk to you about something yesterday. I couldn't find the words. Or the right time."

"Yeah?" *Please don't ask me about Rosalie.*

"I haven't kissed many people since Rosalie . . . passed." He locked onto her lips, his eyes simmering and unwavering.

"Oh." He was staring at her mouth and suddenly she wanted to kiss him again. "I don't feel comfortable talking about this right now," she whispered, leaning close. "I shouldn't have. It was totally inappropriate and I'm sorry." She didn't sound at all convincing, even to herself.

"I'm not. And I think we should do it again. And again. With your permission, of course." He narrowed his eyes, burning a hole in her heart.

"I'm pretty sure kissing on a regular basis could be considered a breach of ethics." She fidgeted in her seat and watched as the team and campers slowly started filing in for a jolt of morning coffee to jumpstart the day.

"What if this is the next step in my healing process? You don't want to prevent me from healing, do you?" A hint of laugh lines crinkled in amusement around his eyes, but those baby blues were still brimming with sadness.

"This isn't the kind of healing we encourage. It's crazy and you have to stop talking about what we did. Someone will hear you," she whispered ferociously, looking over her shoulder. "It was an accident and it won't happen again."

He rubbed his face with both hands, then leaned in again resting his chin and jaws in his palms. He continued in a low voice. "I dreamed of her again. Last night. This morning."

"You did? What was she wearing?" Brooke gulped, afraid to hear the answers.

"She was wearing her favorite dress. She was beautiful. Her hair was perfect, her skin. Her eyes were bright green— Oh, wow." He scratched his head in confusion. "She had brown eyes, not green. You have green."

Brooke nodded.

"Well, in my dream hers were green. They matched her dress and her–"

"Teardrop emerald earrings? And matching pendant?" Brooke asked quietly as she leaned forward, locking onto his gaze, resting her elbows on the table, mirroring his posture.

He studied her a moment, before asking, "You saw her too?"

"Yeah."

"Did she say anything?"

"Not really. She told me to go."

"So, you came here?"

"Nah. I've been up since three."

"Me too. I just wanted to hold her. She sat on the edge of my bed and we cried together. When I woke up it was three. Actually, it was three thirteen. She hadn't been sitting on my bed, it was all a dream."

"I wouldn't be so sure, Josh. She followed me into the bathroom. She wore a green satin, sleeveless gown, dangly emerald earrings, and a green pendant."

Closing his eyes, he spoke. "It sounds like her favorite outfit she'd wear when we'd go to the opera or theater. Those jewels, I got them for her for our first wedding anniversary. They were her favorite. They were lost in the crash." As his voice caught, he cleared his throat and kept speaking, staring at her. "Did she say anything else? Were the girls with her?"

"Your daughters haven't come through with any messages."

He nodded in acceptance.

"Your wife scared the shit out of me though. She woke me up by pouring water on me. Not cool. Spirits never comes through like this. But Rosalie is really strong. And determined. I've only gotten messages in dreams before now. Definitely never had anyone come through in my bathroom before." She scowled and gulped the last of her coffee.

"Seriously? You saw her in your bathroom? Physically?" He pushed away from the table. "Why is she doing this? Is this normal? For you, I mean?" His curiosity seemed to be overshadowing his grief, which was a good thing.

"Yes and no. This time it's different. I've never had an encounter like this before. This is a whole new level. I feel like she's so determined to reach you that she's using all her energy and manifesting in ways I've never thought possible. Josh. These are things I've had a hard time believing could be real when I've heard other people share similar experiences." Just saying those words was overwhelming. Brooke rose and pointed to the coffee station. "I need a refill. You?"

He stood up to join her, gulping the last remnants in his mug. "How's it different? Isn't it the same for all mediums?"

"I'm *not* a medium!" Her words echoed in the dining hall, causing Kyle and Alyssa and a few others to glance her way. "I'm *not a medium!*" she hissed again for emphasis. As she poured her coffee, she asked, "Can we go outside?"

A few moments later they were sitting on top of the picnic bench down by the lake, watching the mist rise in spirals, greeting the morning sun in some ancient tribal dance. Wispy pastel clouds of lavender and peach wove in and around the distant mountain tops.

"How is it different?" he asked again.

"It's different because I feel like I know her. Because she's presenting herself as a full apparition. Not only that, but I feel like she's been preparing me for this for a while."

"Really? How so?" He leaned forward, resting his elbows on his knees, cradling his cup in his hand as he shot her a sidelong glance.

"I've been dreaming of drowning for a couple months. At least. It's been quite horrific. I wake up sputtering, really feeling like there's water in my lungs and I'm drowning." Her eyes were wide and her voice trembled. "But it's not me. It's her."

"So, you can tell me what she felt when she was dying."

With a quick shake of her head, Brooke dismissed him. "Please don't ask me to."

"I'm sorry." He held out a hand and wrapped his fingers around lower arm, squeezing lightly as his thumb caressed the soft pale skin and erratic pulse on the underside of her wrist. "Can you tell her to stop?"

"I normally don't. They usually have a reason. And it's usually to help their loved one." She raised her hands in prayer position to her mouth, exhaling the weight of it all, trying to still her racing heart.

"How does torturing you by drowning you help me?" He released his hold, resting his elbows on his knees, hands clasped around his coffee mug once again.

"Hmm. She's not drowning me. But she *is* making me relive her experience."

"Why do you allow this?"

"I don't. I don't know how to shut it off." She traced the edge of the table with her forefinger. "It usually stops when they've gotten their message through."

"How long does it take? And why would she come to both of us at the same time? At first, I thought it was all a dream. After talking with you, though . . . She was contacting me as well, wasn't she?"

"Sounds like it," Brooke said. "She told me to go. I think she was telling me to go to you. I should have. I didn't know what to say." She lifted her shoulders in reflection.

"Next time, 'want to get a cuppa coffee?' would work." He offered her a wistful smile. "I think Rosalie likes you."

"Don't be crazy." Brooke scoffed and dismissed him with a wave of her hand.

"No, seriously. I do. Rosalie was so territorial about the women I had to deal with on a daily basis. She wasn't the jealous type. But she made no bones about making sure everyone knew I was her man. For her to tell you to go to me at three a.m. The same time she woke me up. She has to like you. Maybe she thinks you'd be good for me."

"You're projecting, Josh. Our loved ones don't stand behind The Veil playing matchmaker." She hopped off the picnic table and he reached out and took her hand.

"What if she is? What if I'm here because Rosalie picked you to be in my life? To heal me?" His eyes were honest and earnest as he faced her.

"If this is the case, she doesn't understand ethics." She tried unsuccessfully to retract her hand, but he held on fast.

"Tell me you don't feel it?" He studied her mouth as she tried and failed to respond. "You can't," he whispered, as he leaned in and brushed her lips with a soft kiss.

"Josh. It's not right." Her voice cracked, but she didn't budge. Instead, she kissed him back ever so gently. "I'm here to help you heal. Not take advantage of you in your vulnerable state."

"I'm not vulnerable. I'm stronger than I've been in three years." He flexed his arm, showing off his muscles as he let go of her hand and laughed.

"You're making great progress. And getting involved with me would ruin everything." She straightened up a bit and stood akimbo as she tried to talk sense into him while putting safe space between them. *He's too kissable. Way too kissable.*

"Getting involved with you would make everything right. Or else Rosalie would not have brought us together." He stood, placing a hand on her shoulders.

"This will not work out. I'm telling you, it can't happen. These kisses are great, yes . . . but . . . this can't happen again. It goes against everything I believe. I don't get involved with clients."

"Hello? Your clients are usually twelve! We're adults, and I can make my own decisions." He dipped his head closer to her, his eyes sultry and full of desire.

"Decisions you think your dead wife is forcing you to make, you mean? I don't want to be with someone because his dead wife says I have to. Don't you get it?" She raised her voice as she stormed back to the base camp, leaving him standing in her dust. She needed distance. He lit her sacral chakra like a bonfire at Brushwood.

"Brooke! Wait!" he called after her and caught up in a moment. "You've got it wrong."

"I don't think so." She kept walking.

"Brooke! Stop and talk to me!" He barked out the order in a clipped, authoritative voice.

"Don't tell me what to do!" She whirled around and yelled at him. "No one tells me what I can and can't do! Ever." She stomped her foot for emphasis and immediately regretted it, feeling like a 14-year-old throwing a tantrum.

"I'm sorry. Really." He brought it down a notch and the two of them stood face-to-face under the canopy of trees dividing the beach from the camp. "I'm explaining it all wrong. I don't do this dating thing very well."

"Dating? Dating! We aren't dating, Josh Quinn. Since when did we start dating?" She flailed her hands at him and he backed up.

"Sorry! See? I'm a bumbling idiot these days when it comes to women."

"Ha! You founded the number one dating service around the world. You *sell sex, and people getting laid makes you money.* Remember?"

He visibly cringed at her reminder.

"Can we start all over?"

"Only if you can grasp the fact I'm not going to hook up with you because you think your dead wife is orchestrating this. Tell your Rosalie to stay out of my love life!"

Without a look back, she stormed off to camp, gaining as much distance as she could, as quickly as she could, to avoid melting into his arms and kissing him again.

Chapter 14

The rising sun was warm and the morning was alive and chattering with wildlife as Brooke greeted the new day dawning from her front porch. This had been her routine the last few days: skipping early morning coffee time at the dining hall, grabbing a quick bite to eat, scooting over to the pavilion to set up her camera equipment. Any offers from Josh to help were immediately declined as she struggled to avoid his questioning and confused gaze. *Like an abandoned puppy.*

Establishing these boundaries had been an exhausting although necessary effort for Brooke as she attempted to maintain control over her emotions, her life, and her professional relationship with Josh.

True, she was expected to spend time with the campers on a one-to-one basis, getting to know them, befriending them, being a confidant for the things they were finally ready to share. But this was way different when the person was a 13-year-old girl in braces struggling with the death of a grandparent who'd battled cancer for the last three months.

Josh was a totally different package. Whether he realized it or not. And she was pretty sure he realized it. Josh oozed sexuality, sensuality, and plain ole sex, even in his fragile, disconnected state. There'd been only one other time where Brooke had worked with a man of this status and power, believing he was good and moral. Trusting someone more than herself had ruined her life.

Successful, handsome men were out of her league, especially married ones. They were as dangerous as jumping into waves crashing on a pristine and picture-perfect beach without realizing there's a riptide.

Josh Quinn was like a gorgeous resort beach, offering a tantalizingly cool ocean to dive into at best, to dip her toes into, or maybe even wade a bit, at least. Nothing more. Life at Earth and Sky was safe, predictable, nonthreatening. It was *her* retreat from the world, and this was where she wanted to live out her life until her dying day. She had no need for fancy beach resorts.

After leaving Cali three years ago without regret, Brooke found her way to the East Coast mountains and never looked back. California and powerful men were two things she never wanted to encounter ever again.

She thrived in this world, surrounded by a thick physical and emotional buffer of 100 acres of forever wild lands. The only way to interact with anyone who hadn't been pre-approved by her bosses was to go into town. For three years, this had been her home, and she had healed herself as much as helping others heal in the time she spent here.

Earth and Sky was open year-round, with the program and staff adapting to the seasons. She had lucked upon the position by chance, and jumped at it immediately, securing the last interview Dee and Doug scheduled prior to closing the request for applications. Her years of experience as an event planner with a major bookstore chain, and her certification as a licensed social worker and life coach made her a prime candidate for the open position. Her time with Angels-R-Us made her a shoo-in. Doug called her and offered her the job before she had even finished the ride back to her hotel. Once she accepted, she called the packing and moving company back home and had everything delivered here and put straight into storage.

This job had been her salvation, and nothing was going to ruin it for her. Especially a whirlwind affair with a CEO of the most popular dating app in the world, *who admittedly makes his money off people getting laid.* There could be no affair, despite what her traitorous body was demanding.

The breakfast bell sounded, and with a sigh, Brooke rose and left the comfort of her front porch to start her day.

~ ~ ~

"Open your eyes when you are ready and come back to this reality. Gone are your stresses and worries as you continue to move forward in your journey of healing. Take your time, make sure you take a drink of lemon water before you go. Have a great day, everyone!" Alyssa ended the meditation wind-down part of her session, shut the CD player off, and placed the disc in its holder.

"Hey. Can we talk a minute?" Hugging his mat close, Josh came up behind Brooke, who had been standing in the back flipping through the digital photographs she'd taken during this session.

Biting her lower lip, she eyed him cautiously. He was not wearing his sunglasses, and this was a good sign—but sure to be her downfall. "Um. Okay. What's up?" Brooke glanced around the pavilion. She noticed Alyssa had finished packing up and was sitting on the stairs retying her sneakers.

Josh eyed Alyssa also. "Can we go somewhere and talk before the next session?"

"You see Kyle today, no? Are you all right?" She paused in her task of packing up her camera gear.

"Yeah. I'm great. I was hoping we could fix whatever happened with us—me and you." He motioned between them with his index finger.

"There's nothing to fix. We're fine." She shrugged. "You should probably get going to the next session. I'll be there in a few minutes, after I finish straightening up here."

"I'll help you—" he started as Alyssa called out from the entrance.

"Actually, Josh, I could use your help. I need to speak with Brooke, so if you could transport her gear for her, I'd really appreciate it." Alyssa waved at Brooke and shot her an 'I'm not taking no for an answer' look.

Brooke's stomach lurched, and anxiety churned in her gut. Was her relationship–or attempt at no relationship—going to jeopardize her position?

"Uh. You got this?" Brooke motioned to her camera bag and tripod.

He grabbed the equipment and waved her off as Brooke joined Alyssa and headed down to base camp.

"Everything okay?" Brooke asked as they made their way to a staff sitting room filled with floor to ceiling windows overlooking the back half of the property, including the distant view of the Adirondacks.

"I was going to ask you the same thing," Alyssa said, sympathy written across her features.

It was a comfy space with campy looking furniture, framed photos of all sorts of Adirondack weather and climate; sunrises, sunsets, snowy peaks, mist spiraling over the lake, autumn leaves painting hiking paths in brilliant hues of gold, orange, red, and brown. The furniture was rustic yet comfortable, with tree trunks for legs and framing. Soft, huggable, overstuffed pillows with autumn leaf patterns were tucked cozily into the corners of the sofa and chairs. Brooke took a seat on the couch, wrapping her arms around a burnt sienna throw pillow, legs tucked under her. She loved this room, but like her co-workers, she hardly ever came here with it being so removed from the everyday space normally occupied. She made a mental note to come here more in the future.

"Am I in trouble?" Brooke asked, frowning.

"Professionally, no. But we *are* worried about you."

"Why?"

"We thought your initial protests were because you were upset when Dee and Doug changed the rules. We didn't take into consideration, um, well, things you've had to overcome in your past. Since Saturday night when you and Josh disappeared, well, Kyle's noticed there's a bit of a disconnect with you and the team, and you and Josh."

"Am I in trouble?" Brooke asked again. She should have sucked it up with Josh and been firm, rather than avoid the situation for the last three days. Avoidance was so unprofessional.

"No, you are *not* in trouble. You are our priority. We didn't provide you the support you needed as a key team player, so I'm offering our support now. Do you need us to intervene with Josh? Did he do something you didn't consent to? I'm sorry we didn't come to you sooner." Alyssa's genuine concern seeped out in her words and from her eyes.

"No! It's okay. I mean, it's too late. We have less than a week left. I've had to establish boundaries. And it's more his wife who's causing the issue, not him," Brooke said in an attempt to reassure her boss.

Alyssa tilted her head in question. "His dead wife? Ah. So, you're still getting visits?"

"Yeah. She's persistent. He thinks she's trying to set us up." Brooke rolled her eyes and shook her head.

"Set you up?" Her question was filled with confusion, despite Brooke's explanation.

"I had to set boundaries. And I'd be lying if I didn't admit those boundaries were for me as well."

"He is a looker, for sure. Well . . . are your boundaries working? For you, I mean?" Alyssa asked slowly.

"I've had to avoid him. I'm sorry, I know you depend on me to step up, but . . . I can't. Not with Rosalie being so pushy."

"Sorry, I still don't get what you mean?" Alyssa's expression told Brooke she thought she was nuts, so Brooke could only try to explain, as embarrassing as it was going to be.

"Rosalie . . . Rosalie is, uh . . ." Brooke shook her head as she sought unsuccessfully for a way tactfully state what Rosalie had been doing the last few weeks.

"Yeah?" Alyssa furrowed her brow, waiting.

After a moment of silence, Brooke blurted out, "I think Rosalie wants me to have sex with her husband!"

Chapter 15

"What?" Alyssa shot Brooke a look filled with disbelief.

"I know, right?" Brooke jumped up and began pacing, flailing her hands as she continued. "She keeps making me have these dreams of her and Josh—you know—having sex for goddess' sake! Like, *I'm right there*. Sometimes I'm Rosalie, sometimes I'm me, watching on. And I'm seeing everything, Alyssa! Everything, down to the friggen mole on his butt!"

"Whoa! This was not where I expected this conversation to go." Alyssa shook her head and burst out laughing.

"It's not funny!"

"I know, I can't help it." She visibly shook with her effort to not laugh, tears rolling down her cheeks.

"Seriously?" Brooke's voice was monotone as she stared at Alyssa struggling to compose herself.

"I'm sorry. Really. But god, you're getting permission from a dead woman to bang her husband. You'd be laughing too if you were me." Alyssa pointed at her in accusation. "So, stop with the high and mighty indignation."

"Do you believe me?" Brooke tilted her head and waited.

"Yes," Alyssa whispered as she stood up and went to Brooke, wrapping her arms around her in a supportive hug. Brooke brought her arms up and buried her face in the crook of Alyssa's neck and began to weep.

"I don't know what to do." Brooke sobbed.

"How do you normally handle messages from loved ones?"

"I follow their lead and do what they tell me to do." Brooke sniffled.

"Oh, dear."

"Yeah."

"Well. Hmm." Alyssa untangled herself from Brooke's embrace and sat back down. "This is a dilemma, isn't it? Want to unpack this and see where it leads?"

"I suppose so." Brooke sat down as well, squaring off with her friend and mentor. After a few minutes of reflection, Brooke spoke. "He's hot. It's taken every bit of everything I have to not fall for him. Which makes Rosalie's messages even more irritating."

Nodding, Alyssa offered, "Technically, I'm fairly certain there isn't anything in the P&P prohibiting camp photographers from developing, um, *intimate friendships* with clients."

"Alyssa! We normally work with minors." Brooke cringed inwardly as she echoed Josh's words from the other day.

"Yes, and how many of your clients have you maintained a relationship with? At least one per group? You've even spent holidays with some of their families."

"Alyssa! You know it's a totally different situation. Wow. It sounds like you're trying to get me to engage in unethical behavior!"

"No, I'm not, because I don't think it's unethical. Besides, we can't control what your heart feels and if something's happened. Brooke, if he is harassing you . . . we want to be there to help you sort things out."

"Nothing happened." Brooke shut her down. "Nothing's going to happen. Trust me. It's the last thing I want."

"When are you going to start, you know, living again?" Alyssa waved her hands wide and groaned, continuing her lecture. "You have your whole life ahead of you. And you're wasting it away here."

"Wasting it away here when I could be getting laid by someone like Josh?" Brooke shouted at her.

"You're misinterpreting what I'm saying," Alyssa countered, not responding to Brooke's emotional outburst. "You're pushing him away because you're afraid of getting involved with him and it's affecting your professionalism. You're good at boundaries. But your fears are preventing you from doing your job. Maybe you should cut yourself some slack." Alyssa leaned forward and plucked a dead leaf off the ivy sitting on the coffee table.

"I haven't been totally effective at pushing him away." Brooke began slowly, avoiding Alyssa's scrutiny.

"Oh? How so?" Her friend leaned in, amusement and understanding lighting her eyes. When she received no answer, she continued. "It wouldn't be a bad thing, if you know, you two . . . did something."

"I can't even believe we are having this conversation!" Brooke jumped up and again started pacing the office. "You want me to date a client."

"Everything happens for a reason, Brooke! I want you to deal with what happened to you three years ago so you can heal and move on. What happened was wrong and horrible, I get it. By not allowing yourself to heal, by shutting yourself off, you're allowing him to have control over you. He was a monster and what happened was horrible. Not living again, not trusting again, is way worse, Brooke. You have so much to offer someone," Alyssa reasoned in a soft tone. "You're in the same place as Josh. Living in the past, afraid to move into the future. Maybe the two of you were brought together for a reason—to help each other heal."

Blood pounded in Brooke's head, blurring her vision and causing her heart rate to race out of control. "I can't even go there. I can't think about it."

"You have to start sometime. Three years is a long time to hide. Maybe it's time to start re-evaluating where you're at in your own healing process. I'm worried your inability to deal with what happened with you—after all this time—is keeping you from doing your job."

"And my job is to date Josh?" She snorted.

"You know your job is not to date Josh. All I'm saying is you're not his mentor, or his therapist. Your official responsibility is being the camp photographer. We get the extra perk of you being able to relay messages to people who've lost a loved one. But you're free to make friends with any of the campers, just as you have in the past. We need you to work more closely with Josh, especially since you're getting messages from his dead wife. Running away from him because you're attracted to him is not doing your job."

"I can't have sex with him."

"I'm not saying you have to. But if his dead wife is telling you this, maybe she knows something you don't?"

"I can't have sex with him," Brooke reiterated.

"Are you telling me or are you trying to convince yourself? Look, Brooke. You're human. You're alive. What do you say all the time? Life is for the living? Maybe you should practice what you preach. Stop hiding away from life."

Brooke made her way to the door. "We're done here, right?"

"Yup. Think about it, though." Alyssa stood up and followed Brooke. "Can I get a hug? I don't want you to be angry with me." She held out her arms and Brooke reciprocated. They stood there for a moment as Brooke's anger subsided and her heartbeat resumed its normal rhythm. "You deserve to be happy. And healed. And we need you. And love you. And want you to be healed."

"I get it. I'm sorry I'm not living up to your expectations," Brooke bristled again. "I don't know if I can ever get over what happened. I don't know if I *want* to." She took a step back and studied Alyssa's face.

"Just don't be mad at me for not understanding your request to reassign you when you first came to us," Alyssa explained, as she sat back down in her chair. "You're allowed to be human once in a while. You're strong and you're resilient. And we need you. Josh needs you. And you can't let one asshole define who you are and control the rest of your life."

"I don't think you understand. Richard raped me. My body. My reputation. My career," Brooke said, unmoving from her place by the door. "I tried to fight back legally, and he destroyed my name, called me a liar and a slut when I tried to go after him. *He said I came on to him!* The whole world read about it!"

"No, it didn't."

"It made headline news, Alyssa. The trial, the rape, everything. No one believed me because he was a prominent politician and married—with children." Brooke came back in to her office and sat down on the couch, burying her face in her hands as she wept, her whole body trembling.

Alyssa came and sat beside her, saying nothing.

"He killed me, all of me. And I don't know if any parts of me will ever be able to feel alive again. Maybe this is why spirits started talking to me, I don't know? Maybe I'm crazy? I don't know. What I do know is I can*not* trust any man right now. Especially one who is so casually offensive about sex and exudes such male privilege! I know a sure sign it will end in disaster when I see one. And you want me to drop everything and walk straight toward another tsunami as if I'm wearing a life preserver and it's a wading pool!" She leaned back and studied Alyssa's reaction.

"At some point you're going to have to be honest with yourself and stop running and hiding because you're scared shitless of trusting a man again. Your fear is preventing you from living." Alyssa threw back at her friend and co-worker, slapping her palm on the arm of her chair.

"I'm not afraid to trust men. I don't need men in my life right now. I don't need anyone!" Brooke shouted back at her.

"Keep saying it loud and clear and see what the Universe sends you, Brooke. You're going to die a shriveled up lonely old woman, with no one to keep you company except for dead wives!"

Brooke froze. She could only stare into Alyssa's blank face.

After mentally counting to five to regain composure, Brooke launched from her chair and marched to the door. "I need the afternoon off. Personal time." Brooke said as she closed the door behind her with a soft thud, ignoring Alyssa's pleas to not leave.

As Brooke headed toward her room to grab her purse and car keys, Josh caught up with her in the front yard. "Hey. Can we talk?" Sunglasses prevented her from seeing his eyes.

"No. I have to take the afternoon off. Sorry." She didn't hesitate in her gait.

"Were you fired? Is it because of us?" He placed a hand lightly on her arm and continued to walk beside her.

"There is no *us*. I'm not fired. Let it go." She shook free of his gentle hold, took her porch stairs two at a time, and disappeared into her cabin.

She wanted to leave Earth and Sky and never return. Picking up her keys and purse, Brooke thought about it. She could go into town, book a hotel room, write her resignation letter and be gone by morning. She didn't need this job. Her three years of savings would hold her over nicely anywhere she wanted to go until she landed a new position.

She paused and took a deep breath, recalling Alyssa's words. Was she running and hiding? It's what she did three years ago. But now? This was her home. She wasn't hiding anymore. She'd built a life for herself. She definitely was not hiding. Or was she? The rest of the staff worked only summers. Come autumn and winter, Brooke found herself with a whole new team as she picked up year-round tours of duty. Spring was the time of year Earth and Sky was refurbished for the new seasons, but even then, she stayed on and helped with the gardening and painting. Almost all her vacation and sick time had been accrued. She never went back to the west coast to visit with her family. Not even for the holidays. They had never approved of her life style choices. When the rape trial hit the news, family members didn't believe her. They accused her of doing it for attention and money, or to ruin his political career since she was more liberal and he was a top GOP official.

Looking down at her keys in hand, Brooke wondered if Alyssa could possibly be right. Was she still hiding? Running? Going into town would be running. Running would be quitting. And quitting would be letting down a lot of people.

Instead, rather than run, she set her purse and keys down, and checked the time on her iPhone. Seeing it was already past 11, Brooke took a deep breath, contemplating heading over to the Nature Center where Paulie would be doing his wilderness class. Maybe she was running and maybe it was time to stop. *Reconsider now so you don't regret later.*

Yeah, it was unethical for a counselor or therapist to fall for a client, but she wasn't either. She technically was *only* the camp photographer. The fun job. The easy job. The job where you get to be friends and chat. And, maybe in Josh's case, explore being more than friends. Her belly flipflopped. There was nothing wrong with being friendly with a client. Especially if his dead wife approved. *Right?*

She changed her clothes and slipped on her hiking boots. Her first thought to head into town, secure a hotel room, and comprise a resignation letter, she decided, was the coward's way out.

Maybe Alyssa was right. She needed to stop running.

Josh might be good looking and rich. And he may be so casual with sex he thinks he can proposition anyone he feels like. He's here because he is vulnerable, struggling, grieving, and he needs help. Not to mention, his dead wife has been summoning her for months now. She is exactly where she is supposed to be.

Moments later, camera in hand, Brooke opened the door to the Nature Center and Paulie paused in his description of how to whittle a bow drill.

He waved a piece of wood at her. "Was wondering where you were. Come on in. You're missing all the fun."

Nodding, she felt her face grow warm as she lifted a folded aluminum chair from the rack and placed it behind Josh and Alyssa sitting in the last row. Josh's gaze never wavered from Paulie, but Brooke noticed he sat straighter as she whispered, "Hey." He was wearing his sunglasses once again.

"I'm sorry," Brooke continued in a hushed voice to the back of his shoulder.

"You were pretty rude," he said quietly, staring straight ahead as Paulie directed everyone to line up and select the wood pieces they'd be whittling into their bow drill base.

Struggling to maintain a professional mindset, she acquiesced. "I'll give you that."

Chapter 16

Flanked by the other campers on either side of him, Josh felt totally out of place as he wondered why the hell he had to attend support group. These people were batshit crazy. They had no clue how to relate to what he was going through—had gone through. None of them had lost a loved one. They were a bunch of spoiled rich kids who had grown up into a bunch of spoiled rich adults and maybe—*maybe*—money and privilege were the only things they had in common. But even as he argued in his head, he knew he was not being completely honest with himself. He just didn't want to be in group.

"I never had time to be a kid," Louisa said, between sniffles. "I was always trying to be perfect, trying to be beautiful. It was like my mom wouldn't love me if I was ugly. I can't remember life before beauty pageants. All I ever heard was how beautiful I was."

"Well, you are," Renee replied, leaning over and placing a hand on Louisa's shoulder. "Being beautiful isn't a crime."

"No. But when your whole worth is defined by your lip color, hair color, weight . . . it's a life sentence. I've been wearing makeup since I was four years old."

With a sob, she continued. "Mother would yell at me if she caught me sneaking food out with my friends. She'd smell my breath when I came home. Not for alcohol or cigarettes like other moms, but for fast food or pizza." She bit her lip and hiccupped. "One time she came home early from church prayer group and caught me eating chips. She dragged me to the bathroom and shoved a finger down my throat 'til I threw it all up. Now she won't speak to me ever since my break down and my decision to leave modeling."

A few gasps were audible from the crowd, then everyone grew silent. Renee spoke next. "I'm struggling with something similar. My family has disowned me since the fire. And I don't think it's because of the fire specifically. I shamed them by falling for a paid hand. The fire was accidental. Falling in love with someone 'beneath our status' was a choice I made and they're embarrassed by me."

"Are you still with him at least?" Lance asked, his face etched in concern.

Renee bit her fist and sobbed, shaking her head. "They had him arrested for vandalism and forbid me to ever see him again. While he was in jail awaiting the trial, he couldn't make bail. He got into a fight and . . ." She closed her eyes tightly, and took a deep breath before continuing. "He got into a fight and when I went to visit him in the hospital, he told me someone had been paid to beat him up, and they told him it was a warning from my family. He broke up with me and said we were over."

Lance shook his head and gulped a breath. "I can't imagine not having family support through the tough times. I don't know where I'd be without my parents, my sister. Ever since I came home from Afghanistan, they've been my sole connection to the outside world. I hardly ever leave the house. I haven't picked up my Canon since my last photo shoot gone bad. And the nightmares . . ."

He buried his face in his hands, his body shaking.

"My family disowned me too," Craig confessed. "They said I asked for it because I'm gay." His voice cracked and he began to cry inconsolably. "They told me I was going to hell," he burst out, sobbing. "Who says this kinda crap to their son?"

"Parents who love you and don't want to see you go to hell," Ned said.

Craig cried harder as Lance defended him. "That was pure evil!"

"What's evil is having sex with men. The body is God's temple and he is soiling it. He's a sinner and—"

"Stop it," Lance shouted as he jumped up in Craig's defense.

"It's okay, Lance. I'm used to small-minded religious zealots," Craig said, wiping his eyes with his shirt tail.

Alyssa and Kyle exchanged a sidelong glance. "Ned, this is totally out of line," Kyle said, "and one of our guidelines is to speak with compassion and kindness and to not judge. Your religious beliefs cannot be used to harm someone."

"Just sayin' it like it is. Ya'll are too afraid to tell the truth. He's a sinner and he's goin' to pay for it. Just sayin'."

"What right do you have to cast judgement on him—or anyone?" Josh spoke for the first time since group began. He'd spent the whole session listening to everyone whine throughout this pity party, promising himself to walk out at any moment. This hit him hard.

"Why don't you take your shades off and tell me to my face, Mr. Hotshot? We heard about what you do for a livin'. You may as well be a pimp or own a brothel." Ned glared at Josh and stood, towering over him.

Remaining seated, Josh turned to Kyle and peered at the therapist over the rim of his Ray-Bans. "Are you going to tolerate this attitude in your so-called 'safe space?' He's not affecting me at all. However, I can't speak for the others."

Kyle slapped both palms on his thighs and stood up and announced the hour was up, and directed everyone to stand and center for the closing affirmation.

Ned laughed and stormed out of the room, muttering something about being done with sinners and hippies.

Not acknowledging the rant at first, Kyle led the group in their closing, before dismissing everyone for the evening.

"Hey, guys? Before you go, I want to say one more thing. I'm sorry you all were subjected to his toxic behavior. It will be dealt with accordingly. While Ned is struggling with his fair share, we all are, and his behavior is not what we hope to experience here. I'll reach out to your mentors and they will be available to talk, if you need them." Kyle bowed with a Namaste gesture, leading the campers out of the room.

~ ~ ~

Josh rapped lightly on the front door to the cabin Brooke shared with her co-workers. He'd been under the impression she'd be waiting in the dining hall for him. Apparently, he was wrong. After dinner, the two parted ways with Josh calling out 'see ya later,' and he thought when she waved, she was agreeing to see him tonight. So, where was she? He counted to 30 and was turning to leave when the door opened and Mandy greeted him. "Well, hello, Josh."

"Hey. Sorry to bother you all so late. Is Brooke around? Don't wake her if she's sleeping. It can wait 'til morning."

"Is everything okay?" She peered around him and past him, into the night.

"Yeah. I . . . Rough group tonight. I was hoping to bounce stuff off her. I can work it out with Alyssa tomorrow." He backed away and mumbled, "Goodnight." It had been foolish to look for Brooke. If she wasn't meeting him in the dining hall there was a reason and it wasn't any of his business.

"Um. Actually, she's not here," Mandy said in an apologetic tone. "I can tell her you're looking for her when she gets back. She shouldn't be too late."

"Oh. Nah. It's okay. We'll catch up tomorrow. Thanks, though." He ignored the way his heart felt heavy, the way loneliness enveloped him like a thick, smothering blanket.

He didn't want to go to his room. He didn't want to go to the rec room. So, he wandered around the camp, no destination in mind, until he heard the faint sound of drumming. It made him curious, because there had been no drumming or fires this week at night. Following it led him toward the lake, with the moon above guiding him like a beacon. As he drew closer to the lake the drumming grew louder, beckoning him. And with the drumming he heard Brooke's voice. He didn't know she could sing, yet he could tell it was her. He cocked his head and listened. It was definitely Brooke.

As he broke the clearing he stopped, not expecting the sight before him. Brooke and Barefoot Dan were seated cross-legged on the ground, drumming and singing within a circle of candles. Protected by the shadows of the trees he had not yet emerged from, Josh watched the two, even though he felt kind of creepy doing so.

They eventually stopped drumming and rose, setting their djembes on the ground beside them. Brooke picked something up and held it above her head, cradling it. Even with the bright light of the full moon he couldn't discern what the object was. She murmured something, Barefoot Dan repeated it, and she set the object down before them. His heart beat wildly, feeling totally uncomfortable spying, but curious as hell wondering what they were doing.

The silvery light of the full moon shone down on her as if it were a spotlight, as if painting her hair in shimmery white water, flowing down her body and spilling onto the ground around her. She was . . . magical. He stood mesmerized, unable to take his gaze from her sight. He remembered how he'd scoffed when Louisa mentioned she'd heard Brooke was a witch. He didn't think witches existed except in Hollywood. After tonight, he wasn't so sure.

She walked in a circle in a counterclockwise motion, arms outstretched. Barefoot Dan stayed close behind her as he extinguished the candles one at a time. In the moonlight, Brooke and Dan appeared to float to the water's edge, their black capes flowing behind them. After tossing something into the water they let out a whoop and a holler. Josh watched as they gathered up their supplies, the sound of laughter and chatter filtering through the night air as they placed everything in a basket. He took this as his cue to leave. Quickly.

What the heck were they doing? And why was she doing it with Dan? Were they a couple? As he traipsed through the woods, his steps measured and sure, these thoughts filled his mind. He'd thought Alyssa and Dan had had something going on. Now, seeing Brooke with him, he must have been wrong. Brooke was so good at keeping things professional. She was so good at keeping her private life private, it was difficult to get to know her. His lips tingled as he remembered their kisses. She had seemed as into it as he had been. Since then, though, she was cool and distant. Now he knew why. Brooke and Barefoot Dan were a thing. And even though he was CEO of the world's most popular dating app, Josh had morals—despite Ned's holy roller judgments. He knew the rules. Brooke was off limits.

Right now, he felt more alone than ever. He wanted to be the one on the beach with Brooke. He wanted to be drumming with her. He wanted to be by her side. He knew this now more than ever.

Chapter 17

"So, you were looking for me last night?" Brooke came up behind Josh and sat across from him, setting her steaming coffee cup on the table as she slid onto the bench. "Everything go okay at group?"

He had the morning paper spread open, reviewing the updated stock exchange news, and did not look up when he spoke. "Not really. No worries."

"We can talk about it, if you want." She sipped her coffee.

"I'm good," Josh said, closing the paper, wondering how he was going to approach the subject. He wasn't a 'beat around the bush' type of guy. "How was your night?"

Studying her coffee, Brooke answered slowly. "It was good."

"Yeah? Do anything . . . fun?" He searched her face and she peered up at him, her green eyes guarded.

"Fun is a matter of perspective." She chuckled softly and shook her head.

"Enlighten me," he directed with his usual authoritative tone.

"I wouldn't want to bore you with my dull existence. Besides, you were asking for me last night, and I wasn't there for you. I'm sorry. Mandy said you were a little out of sorts. What did you need?"

You. "Just to talk." This fencing was driving him crazy, and turning him on, even though it was obvious she wasn't interested in him and a had a perfectly good reason—Barefoot Dan.

"Why don't we get to the Yoga Pavilion early and if you feel like talking about what happened, we can do it there, before Alyssa and the crew arrives." Brooke glanced around the dining hall as campers and mentors filed in, grabbing coffee and finding their regular spots. "First let's eat. I'm starving."

~ ~ ~

"I wouldn't say it was traumatizing, but the crap he was saying, and how offensive he was to Craig, just cause he's gay? I wanted to pop him one. But I didn't." Brooke watched as Josh organized the mats in a pile by the entrance.

"Well, I don't think you were out of line saying something to Kyle. I imagine he will deal with it today." Leaning back against the table, she rested her palms on the edge as she spoke.

"Thanks. And I hope he does. At first, I thought everyone there had nothing to deal with compared to everything I've been struggling with for the last three years. But, man, they're all dealing with *a lot*. Even Ned," he murmured with a shrug, closing the cabinet door.

"Very perceptive. And empathetic of you, for the most part," Brooke said, with a chuckle. While Josh completed his task, she contemplated the change in him since Rosalie had delivered her message Saturday night. It was all she could do to keep from throwing her arms around him and hugging him. They locked eyes, and for the briefest instant Brooke saw a warmth and something else she couldn't name. Or refused to name. A 'something else' she felt deep inside as well.

The moment was broken when Alyssa called out as she joined them on the pavilion. "Thanks for setting up, guys. I feel like lately I'm one step behind myself all the time."

"You've got a lot to do, it's understandable." Brooke waved and offered a feeble smile.

"Yeah. I don't mind. I'm in good company." Josh's words were directed to Alyssa, yet his warm gaze never left Brooke's face.

"Thank you for understanding." Alyssa headed to the sound system as the campers filed in behind her, grabbing mats and taking their usual places on the floor.

Brooke and Josh each took a mat as well, taking their spots in the back. As class was ready to begin, Kyle came to stand beside Alyssa, asking for everyone's attention.

The normal chitchat ceased as Kyle continued to speak. "I'd like to apologize for any trauma Ned may have caused during his stay here." His eyes spanned the room, not settling on anyone. "He was driven to the station at dawn, so you won't be seeing him for the duration of the retreat."

The pavilion fell silent until Louisa exhaled a long breath, exclaiming, "Well, thank Christ for small miracles."

"Seriously." Lance put an arm around Craig, and pulled him close.

"Thanks, Kyle," Craig said softly, head down.

"It wasn't because of how he treated you specifically, Craig. Although, group *was* the turning point." Kyle headed toward the back of the group, grabbing a mat by the entrance, leaving one solo, untouched mat. Ned's.

~ ~ ~

Immediately following meditation, Alyssa pulled Brooke aside. "Renee asked to speak with me," she began.

Before Alyssa could request the favor, Brooke nodded and waved her on. "We'll clean up here," she offered, without hesitation.

"You sure?" Alyssa asked, glancing quickly at Josh, then back to Brooke, calling out for Renee to wait up.

"I'm good." Brooke offered a thumbs-up as proof. "Honest."

Brooke and Josh spoke little while they sanitized the mats with wipes, then stacked them in the cabinet. When the sound system had been covered, cabinets locked up, and she and Josh were heading out of the pavilion, Brooke spoke. "I'm sorry I haven't been around much this last week."

He paused, clearing his throat. "Of course. I understand relationships, and respect those commitments. I never cheated on Rosalie, and I would never expect anyone else to—"

"What are you talking about?" Brooke halted and did an about face.

"I was out of line for kissing you. I misread your response and I apologize. I didn't realize you and Dan-"

Brooke burst out laughing. "Seriously? Me *and Dan?* Where is this coming from?"

"You and Dan aren't together?" he asked, studying her through squinted eyes. She could almost hear the gears clicking in his brain. It was ironically funny they were even having this conversation. Dan spent the evening trying to convince her Josh was interested in *her*. And Brooke had vehemently and outwardly argued against it, even though in her heart she knew he was right.

"Why would you even think this?" She shook her head vigorously from side to side.

"Last night, on the beach. I was looking for you and I saw you two together." He shrugged. "I figured, full moon, alone on the beach. Hey, whatever works."

"You were spying on me?"

"No."

A deadpan glare was her response.

"Not intentionally."

"Uh-huh."

"I was walking to clear my head. And I heard the drumming, so I thought it was another circle. When I got there . . . I was caught off guard." As an afterthought, he added, "What in the world were you two doing, anyway?"

Choosing not to answer, Brooke continued toward the camp.

He followed in silence, until they were a hundred yards or so from base. "Everyone's saying you're a witch."

Brooke stopped so suddenly Josh nearly collided with her. "So?"

"Are you?"

"What does it matter if I am or not? I don't ask you about your spiritual practices."

"Being a witch is a spiritual practice? I thought it was, I don't know. Like a club."

Insulted and dumbfounded, Brooke's face contorted into a mask of pure confusion and disbelief. "A *club?* I've heard it called many things. Never a club. Your deduction's priceless!"

She hooted, her entire body shaking with laughter until Josh joined in, chuckling at first, then guffawing as heartily as Brooke. Finally, wiping tears from her eyes with an attempt at composure, Brooke offered, "It's not a club."

In mock surprise, he noted dryly, "Thanks. Not a club. So, what is it you two were doing? Were you sacrificing something? Tell me it was a doll, not a baby."

Brooke allowed him to finish asking his questions, noting how amusement crinkled around his eyes and how the hint of dimples appeared as he tried not to laugh. With a stern frown, she pointed to the rec room where Mandy was facilitating the art therapy session. "You are particularly good at diverting conversations, Mr. CEO. You're not off the hook for spying on me. And what I do in my personal life isn't the focus here. But if you must know, we were celebrating the Blue Moon. We did not sacrifice anything. It was an offering to Goddess. Satisfied?"

He cocked his head to one side as his face lit up. "You are one very interesting person, Brooke 'with an e' Meadows. Remarkably interesting." He followed her up the stairs and entered the rec room as she held open the door and waved him through.

~ ~ ~

"I don't see how I'm ever going to make fire with this." Josh shook his head and held up the various parts of the bow drill he had finally completed after working on it over the last few days. He sat cross-legged on the ground beside Alyssa, surrounded by wood shavings of various sizes. He had to admit, he thought as he admired his bow drill, his was definitely well-constructed, almost identical to the sample Paulie had provided as a model. This was normal, he thought as he ran a hand over the smooth contours of the wood pieces, no splinters sticking out anywhere. He never cut corners, always followed directions, and did not put up with shoddy workmanship with himself or anyone else. He kept high standards, beginning with his own efforts, and expected everyone around him to do the same.

"Paulie will show us. I've done it a few times. It's totally cool." Alyssa's smile was bright and reassuring as she put her completed bow drill parts into a box with her name written in Sharpie marker across the sides.

"Seriously, what's the purpose of all this anyway? I'm probably never going to camp, let alone make a fire with this." He lifted the bow drill parts in one hand and waved them at Alyssa.

"Well, Mr. CEO. I know it's hard to imagine a world where you would be unable to accomplish anything you set your mind to," Brooke butted in, stepping behind the two as she lowered her Canon. "This was more than busy work. More than a simple assignment. It's even more than learning a survival skill you might need one day to save your life. If you should ever find yourself lost in the wilderness with no matches to build a fire, that is." She winked at him. "You never know when this could happen."

"She's right," Alyssa interrupted. "I'm going to let you think about the purpose of *all this*." Her arms opened wide as she gestured to their surroundings. "Why don't *you* tell *me* what you learned, if anything, while you were here."

Reflecting on her words, Josh thought about the last two and a half weeks; the daunting tasks the mentors had put upon him and the other campers; and where he was at the first day compared to how he felt today. Some of the experiences could be categorized as first-time endeavors—like whittling a bow drill—he would have never participated in down in Manhattan. In fact, he would have laughed and called it doomsday prepping.

But in this environment, surrounded by . . . yes, the earth and sky . . . things were different. His perspective was different and, as a result, everything about him—Josh Quinn—was changing.

As he looked from Brooke as she towered over them, to Alyssa who sat quietly watching him reflect, he got it. He understood why he was here, why whittling a bow drill, drumming around a fire, identifying weeds—no, *wild flowers*—was so important.

The gray mist he had been hiding under the last few years was no longer a comfortable haven. As it lifted with the understanding of this part of his journey, he took a breath of the sweet-smelling Adirondack mountain air. The gray haze he once thought of as soothing and comforting had only been smothering him. For Josh, life had always been black or white. The day he lost his family, the black and white blended into gray. Right now, he was seeing life in living color for the first time in a very, very long time.

He no longer resented having to come to this retreat. Still, he was antsy to get back to work and life. He was ready to live again, to move passed the guilt he needed to let go of. Letting go of the guilt didn't mean letting go of the love he felt for his wife and kids. He understood now.

"Life." His voice cracked with the one-word answer as his eyes welled up with tears. He lifted his hand to his chest pocket in an automatic reflex, and when he felt the familiar frame and lenses of his Ray-Bans, he stopped and lowered his arm, and left the shades tucked away. He didn't need them anymore. It was okay to feel.

"Life is for living," he finished his thought when neither woman responded. Brooke had been a guiding light for him, making him realize things were exactly as she told him. *Life is for living.*

His heart clenched a bit as he watched the two women exchange glances. Tears welled up in Brooke's eyes as she dipped her head in confirmation.

Leaning over slightly, she grasped one of his hands with both of hers and held it tight. "Congratulations. You completed Stage Two," she said to him in a choked whisper.

Chapter 18

The final Saturday arrived in a flurry of excitement as campers, mentors, and hired staff prepped both emotionally and physically for the final bonfire and farewell/graduation party. At breakfast, Kyle gave the final directives for the day's schedule.

"We've got a lot to do, so after breakfast, let's move it. Campers, your manifestation project has got to be completed by tonight. So, anyone who hasn't finished, see Mandy and Cara." He pointed to the far end of the hall and the two raised their hands.

"Your rooms have to be packed up as well. Totes have been provided for you to take home any additional purchases, memorabilia, or any projects you completed. Those supplies are provided at the back of the dining hall." He motioned to the back of the room without hesitation. "Once your rooms are packed and projects completed, we will break for lunch at one today. Everything must be done by then. After lunch, everyone is required to shower and dress for this afternoon's and evening's activities." He stepped back and gave the floor to Alyssa with a sweep of his hand.

"After lunch, see me," Alyssa said to the group. "We've talked here and there about the manifestation ceremony we've been preparing for you all tonight. It actually starts with your shower, believe it or not." Her smile was full of mystery as she paused while the campers turned to one another murmuring.

"Is it going to be a communal shower?" Louisa raised her hand and twittered nervously with her question.

"No, of course not. The ceremony will begin with each of you individually, in your own shower. Solo." Alyssa emphasized the last word with a laugh. As an afterthought she added, "Great question, though. Thank you, Louisa."

After everyone quieted down, Alyssa continued. "You'll be given sage soap and shampoo to wash with. As you scrub your body, we want you to envision cleansing away all those old ideas you thought were healthy when you first arrived three weeks ago. Imagine they are a crusty covering and really scrub them hard, because this retreat has uncovered all of the unhealthy emotions and thought patterns hidden within. Now it's time to wash them away. It's time to let go of your sadness, self-doubt, anger, regret—everything. Everything you realized you were harboring serves no purpose in a healthy, happy life. Watch all negativity flow out of your life, flow down the drain. Say goodbye to the person you were when you stepped off the bus your first day here, and welcome the new you who'll be leaving us tomorrow. This is the person we will be honoring tonight."

Alyssa assessed the campers. "Everyone good?" Seeing the campers nod in confirmation, she continued. "Allow your bodies to air dry after your shower. Once you are dry, put on the garments I'll be giving out after lunch. They're really beautiful, and specially made for this event, and yours to keep after you leave tomorrow. We'll meet down in the field, where we'll begin the celebration."

After a brief pause, she added, "I'm really proud of all of you. This was a life-altering experience for everyone." She focused briefly on Brooke before continuing. "And each one of you sitting here today aced it. Can I see a show of hands from everyone who learned something about themselves this retreat?"

Raising her own hand, Alyssa waited and watched as everyone in the room followed her action, including mentors, and Kyle and Brooke as well.

"This has been a remarkable journey for all of us, and I hope it was as transformational for all of you as it was for me. Thank you everyone for putting your heart into this, and working to experience this metamorphosis of growth and healing."

Kyle took the floor. "Thanks, Alyssa. Okay, now everyone, let's eat. We have a lot to do!"

~ ~ ~

Getting up from her seat with a wide stretch, Brooke asked, "Do you have a lot to pack?"

Josh stood also and together they followed the crowd to stand in line for their breakfast. "Nope. Toiletries. These clothes. I've left out what I'm wearing tomorrow, and another shirt and pants for tonight. I didn't know you guys were providing us with . . . an outfit? Did I hear correctly?"

"Sounds like it. And you're happy with your manifestation project?"

"Yep." He grabbed a plate and piled on scrambled eggs, sausage, and bacon, handing Brooke the tongs as he finished each, and she followed his actions. "Are you happy with yours?"

"Yeah, I think so. It's not as in depth or thought out as yours. I'm really impressed with you. Didn't think you had it in you." She laughed and shrugged.

"Me either, to be honest." They made their way back to their table and sat opposite one another in their customary routine, minus Alyssa and Kyle, who were busy barking orders at various staff and campers. "It all came together so easily. And for the first time in a long time I *want* to move on. I *want* to heal. I *want* to live again."

"We're going to be throwing them in the fire. You heard her, right?" She scooped up a forkful of eggs as she spoke.

"Yep. It's not really anything I'd display back home anyway." He chewed on a piece of bacon. "I'll have to admit, it was therapeutic to make, though. It made me think about my life, what I want to let go of, and what I want to hold on to."

"We never really explained much while we were making them. I heard you saying something while you braided the twine." She paused midair, inviting him to share.

"Hope, healing, and love. Like Cara taught us. Put your intentions into every action?" He caught her gaze, his blue eyes searching and so intense Brooke had to look down as her heart clenched and the butterflies woke up in her belly.

. . . haunting blue eyes, so blue, so blue. I got this thing about blue . . .

She cleared her throat and continued. "And the rock?"

"The rock is my world, and all the weight of it. I wrapped the braided twine around it to embrace it and heal it. The pieces of twigs and wildflowers and things I hung from it represent all the hopes and dreams of my past, and the things *and people and feelings.*" He paused and caught her gaze again. "Everything I now know I need to let go. All the guilt, regret, and anger I've been holding on to."

"And the pebbles and the other little trinkety things you found?" Brooke prodded.

"It was crazy finding the things I did, but it worked perfectly. The coin is, of course, financial success—either with my company or in another venture. Who knows what the future holds, right? The black and white marble represents my sanity and is a reminder to keep balance in my life. The toy car wheel is a reminder to keep moving forward, no more wallowing. The rock is a reminder to stay grounded. The metal red heart—it looked like it was part of a child's ring or necklace—is of course, love." He wore a frown and his voice caught slightly as he explained. "I hope one day I find someone, not to replace Rosalie, but to live and love with. Life is for living, like you've been telling me. It's also for loving."

"Wow. This is pretty intense. I would have never thought you'd come this far when I first met you. You've done well, Mr. CEO." Her smile was warm and sincere, and as she studied his face, she thought she saw his cheeks color slightly.

With a scowl, he brushed her compliment off with a roll of his eyes and a wave of his hands. "I figured all the things I want to release are burnable. But those little objects will withstand the fire to some degree. Well maybe not the tire." He set his fork and knife down and wiped his mouth with his napkin, resting his forearms on the table's edge as he grew reflective. After a moment, he asked, "What about you?"

"I made a basket." Concentrating on scooping up the last forkful of eggs, Brooke added thoughtfully, "Wasn't nearly as creative as you."

"I thought it was beautiful. It's a shame to burn it."

"Yeah. Well. I can make another. But this one is special. Every reed and branch represents—" She couldn't bring herself to finish as her eyes welled up and her throat constricted with the words. Avoiding Josh's eyes, she folded and refolded the napkin in her lap.

"Represents?" He prodded her softly.

She blinked away the tears, and cleared her throat, swallowing the pain and inability to speak. "Just stuff. Life lessons. Things I want to manifest in order to let go of . . . things. You know, that brought me to where I am today. That make up my life. That I probably don't need anymore."

When he didn't respond, she filled the vacant silence with further explanation. "The basket is full of empty, invisible things I've been choosing to hold on to for years. I think I'm ready to dump it all now."

"Such as?"

His eyes were blue and clear, like a lake where she could jump in and completely wash away her past. And inviting.

She caught her breath and locked onto his gaze, struggling to repress the urge to kiss him.

"Brooke with an 'e.' I wish you would open up to me." Josh leaned forward and whispered the words.

Brooke followed his hands as he reached toward her and she was thankful she had kept hers in her lap. She was sure he would have grabbed them in his. One more glance into his baby blues and Brooke felt as though she was drawn into his soul. It was difficult to look away. Difficult to not tell him things. These last few weeks had redefined their relationship from adversarial, reluctant players in a production neither had auditioned for, to two people developing a bond and connection. Brooke worked hard to keep the bond professional. Yet, as every moment passed it had grown increasingly difficult. Now he was leaving tomorrow, and she wished she had made the most of every moment. Their opportunity was nearly gone. Nearly.

"I'm fine." She smiled brightly and pushed back from the table. "I'd say you've got the morning to yourself since your packing is finished and your project is done. What are you going to do?" She stood up and grabbed her plate and waited for him to follow.

He didn't answer until they were standing outside in the sunlight. "I was hoping, if you were free, we could take one more hike up to the rock. I'd like to say goodbye to the ole fella."

The first and only time they had hiked to the rock together was the day after he had kissed her. She thought he was planning to kiss her again, and she'd set him straight if he tried. It would be nice sharing time with him without an argument. It would be a good memory to hold on to. And she had a feeling once he left tomorrow, she was going to be searching for memories to hold on to for a lifetime.

"I think it's doable. I'm sorry I cancelled the group hike.

The weather made the decision for us. We can go today if you want. We've got until 1 so we won't have to rush."

"Awesome. Let me change into my hikers." He headed toward his cabin. "I'll meet you back here in ten."

Chapter 19

"Okay, Mr. Smarty Pants. What's this patch of flowers here?" Brooke pointed at a low ground covering with violet flowers growing along the path, tucked in the shaded areas.

He squatted and studied the plant, scratching his head in thought. "Hmmm. Violets? No! Wait. Hmmm. Periwinkle? Or forget-me-nots?"

"Ahhh. Yes! It's lobelia,forget-me-nots. Well done, Four out of five." She held her open palm up, waiting for him to stand and high five her back.

"Thanks for taking me to your rock one last time." He joined her back on the path. The rest of their climb was in silence, with no sounds except for an occasional bird call, the chitter of squirrels, and their feet thumping along on the well-worn path.

When they reached the summit, Brooke veered off to her rock and placed her hands palms flat, soaking in its energy and balancing her own. Josh retraced the path he'd followed the first time he climbed, finding the smaller slab to sit on as he scanned the horizon. She climbed up on the warm, smooth boulder and sat crossed-legged as she soaked up the sun.

"I thought about jumping the first time you took me here," he started slowly.

"Well. Thank you for not ruining my day, which would have been pretty sucky of you." She kept her eyes nearly closed, head tilted toward the sky, as she eyed him through her lashes.

"I'm so glad I didn't. I would have missed so much.

Especially my shot at healing and beginning life all over again." He glanced over his shoulder at her.

"Are you ready to start over? Really?"

"Maybe? There are a few things I have to sort out."

Her heart skipped a beat. "Like what?"

"I think it's time to sell my place. It's too big and has too many memories. And I'm not really sure I want to remain CEO at Quirkyflirt anymore. For now, yes. In the meantime, I think I'm going to explore my options." He stood up and joined Brooke on the rock, his legs dangling over the side of the boulder.

"Those are awfully big steps to take, maybe think about smaller steps. Baby steps. No need to make such drastic changes all at once." She studied two ants as they scurried along the length of a crack separating her and Josh.

"The last three years I've put my life on hold. I'm tired of being on hold. Of being in Limbo. I really think I'm ready to start living again." With his left hand palm-down on the rock between them, his thumb traced along the crack where the ants had just traveled, the length of his hand resting an inch or so from her thigh.

It was only his pinky, for goddess' sake, but Brooke could swear she felt his body heat radiating from it. It ran up her leg and through her body, warming her faster than the sun had once they had stepped away from the shadowy shade canopy of the pathway.

Mesmerized by his hand, she forced herself to speak. "What?" she asked as her face warmed beneath his scrutiny.

"Do you ever think about making changes? About going for it, when you barely know what 'it' is?" His gaze never wavered.

Swallowing with difficulty, Brooke tried to find her voice. "Not in a while," she squeaked.

As he leaned forward, so close his breath fanned her face, he whispered, "You've never thought about doing something so crazy it doesn't seem like you?" His lids lowered and he offered her a sleepy, sultry, knowing look, immediately melting her sacral chakra.

Drifting her gaze from the smoldering heat of his teal blues to his tantalizingly close, oh so close, mouth, she licked her lips and pursed for a kiss. She was under a trance, it seemed, and nothing she could do would be able to break it, she was sure. Silently, she shook her head slightly back and forth, closing her eyes, her breath shallow in anticipation. She lifted her chin ever so slightly, and waited.

"Me either. Not in a long time," he whispered again. "Until you."

A flutter of a kiss, soft and testing tickled her lips ever so lightly. She hiccupped a breath, then leaned back and opened her eyes to see if he had truly kissed her once more, or if it was her imagination.

The warmth of his breath caressed her cheek as his face stayed close and slightly tilted to the side, while his hands came up behind her head, guiding her parted lips to his again. She closed her eyes and leaned in, welcoming him without reservation or hesitation.

How could anyone taste like fresh air? She wondered savoring the moment. *Spearmint and fresh air* was her last conscious thought. Brooke lost herself in his essence, their auras blending as their soul energy mingled like morning mist rising up through the valley.

His fingers wove in her hair so neatly caught up in a ponytail, tugging it free, combing through her tresses as they cascaded around her shoulders in ringlets. He rested his hands on the back of her neck and her shoulders, holding her near to him. He deepened his kiss, answering her response.

Adjusting from sitting cross-legged, Brooke turned into him, wrapping her arms around his torso, her hands resting on his waist. It had been a long, long time since she'd allowed herself to feel. And he made her feel so good. She could not stop thinking about kissing him again, wondering what it would be like to feel his body against hers. To let down the façade she kept up and allow herself to be free in the moment. She hadn't been kissed like this—*toe-curling, butterfly catching, breathlessly divine*—in a very long time. He was the first man she trusted enough to share such an intimate moment with in, well, forever.

They both drew back at the same time, searching each other's faces, their eyes melding—her green eyes, his blue, like earth and sky.

"Thank you," he whispered, reaching down and covering her hands resting in her lap. "You know, I wanted to kiss you since—at least since our first campfire. And every time we do, I just want more."

"I know." Her cheeks warmed and her lips pursed in a knowing smile. "It's been so difficult fighting this. I didn't want to take—"

Leaning in, Josh lifted both hands to cradle Brooke's face. Before he could kiss her again, she placed her palms on his tee-shirt clad chest.

"I'm not sure we should be doing this, Josh." She tossed her head side to side, her voice breathless and unsteady.

His confusion was evident. "I leave tomorrow."

"Exactly. I'm not sure I can finish anything we start." Her words trembled in a soft whisper.

"We don't have to finish anything, Brooke. I'll wait 'til you're ready." His voice was low as he straightened up, his eyes crinkling with warmth, passion, and understanding. "I'm not looking for a hook-up."

She fell silent and bent her head, unable to look at him. "Good. I'm not really a hook-up kinda gal. Besides."

"Yeah?"

With a groan she dismissed him with a wave. "Forget it. We should get going." Her heart tugged as she caught sight of his wedding band. Rosalie. A vision of the woman, her beauty radiating beyond the grave, filled her head. She straightened up and lifted her gaze to study the horizon, blinking away the image.

"You just admitted you've been feeling this for a while now." Josh followed her line of sight toward the valley out in the distance.

"I have. But thinking and doing are two different things."

"I understand. Which is why we're here today. I've been thinking about this all week."

"You invited me up here to kiss me? What happened to saying goodbye to the ole fella?" she said in a mock-stern voice, her eyes twinkling.

"Hey. Your tone might work on your younger charges. Not on me." He called her out, but his expression was filled with amusement.

"And while this flirting might work with all your other women, it won't work with me. I'm kinda old fashioned." She laughed, her cheeks warming.

"Other women?" He laughed outright. "What do you think I am?"

She paused, trying desperately to not throw the phrase back at him she'd been unable to let go of since he uttered it three weeks ago. Losing the inner battle, she said quietly, "CEO of a dating app used world-wide to get people laid."

It seemed her words even silenced the wildlife around them.

"I'm sorry," he offered simply.

"For?"

"Sometimes I can be an ass." His eyes turned to a daddy longlegs spider climbing over the edge of the rock, walking toward Brooke. "Can you please forget I ever said those words? I only did it to push you away when I first realized I wanted you."

She slowly slipped her hand down to her calf, where the spider had climbed up. He crawled onto her outstretched palm, and up her forearm before she picked him up with her other hand and set him on the rock in the direction he'd been traveling.

"Wanted me?"

"Yeah."

Except for a long exhale, Brooke remained silent.

"So, you feel it, too? It's not just me?" He caught her eyes again and held her gaze.

After what seemed like forever, she summoned her courage to speak, never breaking his hold on her eyes. "I feel it." Her heart fluttered as she understated his effect on her.

"Now what do we do?"

Shrugging, she stared, at a loss for words, now turning her head and squinting in the sunlight.

"Do you ever come down to the city?" His question came hesitantly. With a shake of her head she answered, "Not often, usually end of year—around the holidays. Dee and Doug throw an annual gathering for all the Earth and Sky locations, usually in a hotel on Times Square. Which is really weird because we're so nature based. Hey, it's their dollar."

"Around Christmas?" She could see the wheels in his brain turning through his eyes.

"Anytime between Samhain—Halloween—and the New Year. Once they threw a masquerade ball and invited clients and staff. Total blast. Another time they hosted a Thanksgiving feast. I gained about ten pounds in four days." She rubbed her belly and grinned.

"I'll bet. How long does it last?"

"Usually a week, all expenses paid. They try to make it a full New York City experience. They take us to the opera, to see a musical, and a play. We visit the museums. We've gone ice skating in Rockefeller Center. It's a good time."

"So, you like the city?" His words were laced with hope.

"No. I hate it. But I can take it in small increments."

"Kinda like me and the country." He waved a hand around them with a forlorn sigh.

"You don't like being in nature."

"I don't mind it, as long as it's in small increments," he echoed. "When the girls were younger, we tried to take them to the state parks, and hiking, and boating. I've always loved being outdoors. So did Rosalie. But business got busier and getting away together seemed more difficult each year. This retreat was a huge reminder of how I failed as a husband and father."

He grew quiet, and Brooke stayed silent for a brief moment. "You seem like you were a great dad and husband. They were lucky to have you in their lives, Josh."

A feeble smile briefly touched his lips, then faded. "Well, it's over. Any shot I had is gone now. All I can do is move forward."

"It's really all any of us can do. Learn from yesterday, plan for tomorrow. Live for today." She played with a rough cuticle on her thumb, hyper-focusing on the jagged edge to avoid looking up at him.

"So, you're a country girl."

"And you're a city boy."

She wrinkled her nose at the huge chasm between them, reflecting. "If I was a city girl, I'd never have met you and helped you with this part of your journey." Her heart ached. Any kind of future together was not a reality, and this conversation was proof. Even dating seemed too absurd to even consider.

"How do you do it? How do you stay so optimistic?" He scowled in the sunlight, shading his eyes with his hand.

Not feeling overly optimistic, she forced a bright smile and asked, "What other way is there to be?" With a hop off the rock, she stretched and pointed toward the trail. "We should probably head down to camp."

"Not yet. Please."

"We aren't kissing again, so don't try anything funny, mister." It wasn't easy to push away the sadness tugging at her heart, even though she'd had a lot of practice hiding disappointment throughout her life. Her laugh lilted like a butterfly and he smiled in reply.

"Why not? You're a great kisser."

Her cheeks warmed as if the heat of his gaze had kindled a fire on her skin.

"Seriously. I want to thank you for everything you've done for me. I couldn't have gotten to this point without you. I know I have my work cut out. It's going to be hard when I leave here. You've given me a foundation of healing and I know I'm only going to keep moving forward." He hopped down off the rock and stood beside her.

"It was a team effort."

"Nope. Don't discount your gift, Brooke. Getting Rosalie's message to me. Your friendship. Your wisdom. You're what made this retreat so transformational. I would not be where I am right now at this moment if you hadn't come into my life. I know it. Thank you."

Brooke felt her face flush even more deeply with his praise, and as she started to protest, he placed a slender finger on her lips and shushed her. They locked eyes once more and she swallowed thickly, knowing if he kissed her, she would not stop him.

He didn't. Instead he hugged her in a polite yet thorough embrace and stepped back. "Can we get a picture?" he asked as he retrieved his iPhone from his pocket and hit the settings for a selfie.

"Maybe," she said, grinning. "If I give you my email address will you send it to me?"

"Ya know, Brooke. Texting would be easier." Stepping into place by her side, he wrapped an arm around her shoulders and leaned toward her, with the valley stretching wide behind them. Lifting his other arm, he cocked his head in her direction, directed her to "say, 'cheese,'" then snapped the photo. Not releasing his embrace just yet, they viewed the image together.

As Brooke unwound his arm from her body and regained her personal space, she shot him a thumbs-up.

Raising his eyes from his phone, he asked, "What's your number?"

Biting the inside of her lip in deliberation, she finally relented, spewing out the digits. Rather than simply type her number into a blank text and send the image, he opened his contacts, saved her name, sent the photo, and stated with a wink, "Now we can go." He turned toward the path.

"If I hadn't been told you were a CEO," Brooke said, following behind him, "I'd have guessed it."

"How so?" he asked over his shoulder.

"Because you're so friggen bossy."

Their words and laughter stilled the chirping crickets and twittering of birds and wildlife. After a long moment, life in the Adirondacks continued as Brooke and Josh meandered back down the path to camp, and to the last 24 hours of their time together.

Chapter 20

It had been a long day, an emotional day. A healing day. By late afternoon, a sense of peace, fulfilment, and confidence seemed to have settled over the entire camp. The ramped-up energy of finalizing projects, packing, and getting last minute photos of one another had been grounded and dissipated as everyone gathered around the fire pit, projects in one hand, their written words of manifestation in the other.

Each person spoke about their project, what it represented, and what they hoped to achieve as they moved on in life. One by one they cast their projects and notes into the fire. As they did this in a clockwise effort, they linked hands until the circle was formed.

When Brooke felt Josh's grasp, she reflexively jerked away in reaction to the jolt of electricity coursing from palm to palm. He held fast as she tugged, looking down into her eyes as a faint smile curved his lips. The butterflies must have felt the jolt also, as they began pounding away in her belly. It was difficult to relax, to not think about the heat generating from his touch as she studied the fire, her hand snuggly and securely tucked into his. There it remained as everyone reflected on their projects, their hopes, and dreams, and what they were determined to release, finishing with the goals they planned to manifest when they returned home.

As the ritual drew to a close, the circle was opened as each person, moving counterclockwise, released their clasp of each other's hands. Josh held tightly to Brooke, his grasp becoming firmer for a moment before letting go. She held her hand up for inspection as he watched on, his eyes smoldering and intense.

"I didn't want to let go," he whispered.

"It's normal," she whispered back. "Trust me. What you're feeling is normal. It will pass."

He gave a slight shake of his head, giving Kyle his full attention as the main therapist spoke. "You guys are amazing. Seriously. The effort and thought you put into your projects . . . it blows me away to think how much progress you've made in three weeks." As he spoke his gaze took in each person in the circle, making eye contact with every man and woman there. "Our work here is done. Great job! Let's go grab some grub!"

Josh hung back, watching the last of the flames die down. Brooke stood a few steps behind him, not knowing if she should leave him alone and take off with the rest of the crowd or go to his side.

"Thank you for waiting," he said moments later, turning to find her still there.

"I wasn't sure if you'd want company."

He filled the space between them in two strides, suddenly a hairsbreadth from her, close enough to feel his words on her lips as he spoke. "I don't mind your company. Ever."

Before she could respond, he kissed her. There with the fire dying behind them and the sun setting behind the trees, the aroma of the evening meal wafting throughout the camp, and the laughter and chatter of their fellow campers off in the distance, he kissed her.

At first it was just a caress of his lips, a reminder of their afternoon on the rock. It soon became a query, asking permission for more. Closing her eyes, she gave it. It wasn't a conscious action, it was more an automatic response, like magnets drawn together by forces unseen. Cupping her hands behind his head, nudging him closer as he moved against her, she melted into his embrace. She trembled as his hands moved along her shoulders before trailing down to rest on her lower back, molding her to his hardness. This was so much more . . . thorough . . . than before.

He tasted so sweet, still like spearmint and air, but even better as his lips beckoned and coaxed her response. She knew she should stop this right now. The more her mind yelled, the more difficult it became to listen. Ever since their private drumming lesson she had wanted to taste his kiss. Instead, she had pushed her feelings aside and focused on helping him, despite his constant flirting, attention, the constant companionship, the teasing and joking, the looks. The accidental and probably now looking back, not so accidental touches. Since their first kiss, the need she felt for him was constant and grew more difficult to ignore with every passing moment.

She eased back enough to look at him and drew a deep breath. Her eyes widened as she searched his face for any sign of strength he was going to stop. He had to be the one, because she knew she couldn't.

"I leave tomorrow," he reminded her again. His voice was soft.

"And I don't." She bit her lower lip to keep it from trembling. It was difficult to remember what life was like prior to three weeks ago. Prior to the first time she saw his face through her camera lens.

And then *click*. It had passed. Three weeks gone before she barely had time to refocus and shoot again. They stood suspended in time, lost in the sight of one another, eyes locked, as each memorized this last moment before it faded into dinner and campfire and drumming, then sleep and the morning rush to gulp down breakfast and hop on the bus. The bus taking him away from her forever.

~ ~ ~

The tables in the dining hall had been rearranged from their traditional rows, to complete a rectangle three tables long and two tables wide. A few people were seated, and some were standing on the food line waiting for dinner to be served as Josh and Brooke entered. The energy was different, more boisterous than usual. Campers and mentors were not paired off as they had been the last three weeks. People were mingling and sitting with other campers or other mentors, as if this were more of a social gathering than a healing retreat.

This was new, Brooke thought, tossing Josh a confused look and a shrug. "Thank goddess the presentation is finished and the CDs and thumb drives are done. Thanks for your help," she said, as they surveyed the hall.

"It was fun," he said, removing his arm from the small of her back as they wandered through the dining hall. Alyssa was off to the side engaged in conversation with Dan and Lance. Cara and Mandy were sitting with Kyle and Paulie. Louisa and Renee were chumming it up with Craig. Brooke wasn't sure where to go, not really wanting to leave Josh's side just yet.

They headed to a space at one of the tables which she and Josh claimed in an unspoken agreement. It was wide enough for the both of them and placed them conveniently between two of the smaller groups.

Brooke focused on Louisa and Renee, attempting to join in on their chat, only to end up listening with a feigned interest, not saying much at all. It was difficult to think and follow along, let alone add something intelligent to the conversation when without warning all of her senses were suddenly tuned into Josh and only Josh.

With the weight of arm now absent, Brooke's back felt exposed, naked and chilled. The heat from his thigh so tantalizing close to hers and the smell of his cologne, woodsy and musky and clean, distracted her beyond recovery. It was his kiss, the gentleness, the passion, the fierceness, the claiming, the way it completed her and answered all of her questions that was at the center of her undoing.

How was she ever going to get over him?

You won't, a voice whispered in her head, but she dismissed it when his thigh pressed against hers in a caressing fashion, jolting her out of her musings. She stared at him, but his head was averted as he listened to something Louisa was saying, seemingly totally oblivious to the sparks he'd lit between them. It was only when she hiccupped a deep breath, attempting to compose herself did she notice the slightest twitch of a smile touch his lips. Ever so subtly, his hand dropped from the table to his lap, and from his lap to her thigh, giving her a gentle squeeze.

He felt it too, she thought, pressing her leg against his in answer. Too quickly he removed his hand, placing it back on the table, leaving a coolness where the heat of his touch had just seared. She sighed again, looking down at her thigh then up at his profile, wishing everyone would disappear. She stretched her leg out, wrapping it around his beneath the table, suddenly uncaring if anyone saw.

Tilting his head slightly toward her, his eyes alit with laughter, he asked softly, "Why the sigh? Bored?" His baby blues penetrated her core and she shook her head ever so slightly, still unable to put a coherent thought into a sentence. She was consumed with desire and could only think about him. *Inside her. Now.*

Looking away, Brooke felt her face grow warm. Her head was buzzing, her body was tingly, the butterflies were thumping, and suddenly it was all too much for her to handle. *Flashbacks of making love. Flashbacks of kayaking. Flashbacks of lying in bed, silk linens draped over her long tan legs.*

She glanced down at her hand resting on his thigh and caught sight of her engagement ring and matching wedding band, golden and brilliant in the sunlight, the two-carat diamond blinding as it reflected the summer sun's rays.

Feeling faint, realization washing over her like cold lake water, Brooke erased the vision belonging to someone else with a shake of her head. Regaining her equilibrium, she placed her hands on the table and straightened her spine. Still overwhelmed with the amped up energy flowing through the dining hall, the feel of his muscular thigh pressed against her, arousal burning throughout her body like molten lava, and the memories in her head she knew were not hers, she excused herself. She had to cool off. She had to cool the fire. She had to wash away these feelings of someone else's past.

"I'll be right back," she called out to no one in particular as she slid off the bench and headed to the exit.

Even Alyssa questioning where she was going didn't give her pause. She tossed a quick wave and kept walking, ignoring the wispy voice pleading in her head.

Please, don't.

Once out in the cool dusky air, Brooke picked up her pace, heading for the lake. "Leave me alone!" she shouted.

Her body was on fire, her head felt like it was going to explode, and the only thing she could think of was to get to the lake. By the time she broke into the clearing she had lifted her sweatshirt over her head, tossing it to the sandy ground. She paused long enough to kick off her sneakers, making a beeline for the water, leaving a trail of clothing behind her. Freed from her clothing, she sloshed into the ankle-deep waters ebbing along the shore with a splash. Even the cool temperature did not slow her down. Diving head first she went under, swimming toward the center of the lake, consumed with a need to cleanse and purge, to wash away the intensity and desire, the fogginess, the lust and ache she felt for the man who belonged to someone else. Even if this someone else was no longer flesh and blood.

Just once. For me. Please.

"No! Leave me alone!" Brooke surfaced and screamed at no one, taking in a gulp of air before diving below again.

You want him as much as I do. Please. You can have him forever. All I want is one more night.

Brooke swam deeper, trying to get away from the voice of the dead woman whose husband she had fallen in love with in just three short weeks.

Her lungs were tight and she opened her eyes to see only blackness, thick forests of kelp, and occasional fish and bubbles. How deep had she swam? Suddenly she realized she needed air and she shot up, heading to the surface before the reflex to gasp would overtake her, filling her lungs with water instead of precious air. She was a good swimmer. She could do this. She'd been a lifeguard in high school, for goddess' sake.

She raised her eyes to the surface and saw the bright halo of sunlight shimmering through the murky water, and she aimed toward it, kicking and paddling ferociously. Get to the light, she told herself. *You're almost there.*

As she propelled upward, she realized it couldn't be the sun. It was dusk, the sun was setting as she'd ran to the beach. What then? She peered into the light and saw a woman.

Rosalie! Rosalie?

Just inches before clearing the surface, Brooke screamed. Water filled her body and a second later she broke through, thrashing as she went under once again. As she sank into the watery depths, Rosalie coaxed her to the surface. *Follow me. I'll save you.*

It was a trick. Rosalie didn't want to save her, Brooke thought, confused. She couldn't focus, couldn't breathe, couldn't think. Couldn't swim. She closed her eyes and let the darkness embrace her.

Chapter 21

Josh wanted to follow her, but his actions would have been way too obvious. Unless she was hoping he'd join her as she jogged across the campsite toward the lake. From his seat at the table, he kept her in his sight as he gazed through the screen windows. She broke into a sprint near the lake path, and he fought the urge to join her, forcing himself to remain seated.

Damn. He hadn't felt like this since Rosalie. He was so hot for Brooke it was all he could do to control his urges. And even then, he was failing miserably as he recalled the heat of her leg against his, the tingling in his fingertips as he caressed her thigh. For the first time in forever, since his unsuccessful attempt at sex with the one-night stand he'd entangled himself in, his desire was strong enough to overcome his fear of failure. He was ready to make love, and Brooke was the woman he wanted to share this with. Tonight. He drew a deep breath, remembering her scent—jasmine and honey. And sunshine. And air.

Air. Rosalie's voice sounded in his head. *Go, now! Josh, she needs you!*

For the briefest moment, Josh sat stunned at the sound of Rosalie's voice reverberating in his mind. A second later, he pushed away from the table with such a force it rattled the dishes and cups and startled those seated nearby. He sprinted across the dining room in a few short strides, calling out Brooke's name. Something was wrong. He could feel it as he ran to the exit. Alyssa shouted after him, but he didn't respond. He had to get to the lake.

Hurry, babe!

Each step felt as though he were stepping in shore sludge, the in-between border of beach dividing water and sand.

"I know! I'm going!" Behind him, he heard Alyssa and Dan shouting for him. He heard the thud of their feet as they followed.

Spotting her sweatshirt and the trail of clothes, his knees buckled, threatening to give out as fear overtook his body. Without a second's thought he ran into the lake fully clothed, kicking off his docksiders before hitting the water with a yell. "Brooke!" he called out repeatedly, swimming toward the center of the lake, not knowing why. He dove under the water, trying to catch a glimpse, dreading to find her, yet hoping he did before it was too late. Maybe she was not in the water at all.

He broke surface and heard splashing behind him. Throwing a quick glance over his shoulder as he continued toward the center, he saw Alyssa and Dan had followed him into the water as well. He dove under once more only to see Brooke's body shoot up to the surface propelled and surrounded by a blinding flash. He came up with a yell as he reached her lifeless form. As she began to sink again, he hollered.

"No! Don't you die on me! Don't you die on me!" he continued shouting as he started swimming back to shore, dragging her while keeping her head above water. It was slow moving, and finally Alyssa and Dan reached him and took over. "Help me! Help her! Please, oh my god! Help me!" He was shouting and crying and lost. She couldn't die. Not this way. Not her too.

"We got this. Get back to the shore. Make sure someone got a blanket. Kyle's calling 911." Alyssa huffed as she and Dan swam through the murky lake waters with Brooke safely tucked between them.

Josh reached land first, joining the other campers and mentors as they watched Alyssa and Dan struggle to the shore weighted down by their soaked clothing and Brooke's slumped body. As soon as they were out of the water, they laid her down in the sand on her back. Josh went to her side, grabbing Brooke's hand as Dan bent over her face, bringing his ear close to her nose and mouth. "She's not breathing!"

"Do something!" Josh yelled.

Dan picked up her wrist, and when he couldn't find her pulse, he cried out, "No! Brooke don't fucking do this!" After five seconds of searching but finding nothing, he shouted for Alyssa. She knelt beside him and began chest compressions, counting and watching the lack of response of Brooke's upper torso, then checking her breath. When she still did not react, Alyssa tilted Brooke's head back, pinched her nose and covered her mouth with her own.

After puffing life sustaining breath into her friend's body, Alyssa began chest compressions once more, yelling at her to wake up. "God damn it, Brooke. Come on, girl. Don't you give up. Come on! Breathe!"

"C'mon, Brooke. Please don't leave me. Not now," Josh whispered, mostly to himself, willing her to breathe as he watched Alyssa working methodically, focused intently on the woman who lay lifeless between them.

After struggling unsuccessfully, Alyssa reached a hand out to Dan, and they switched roles. Dan began alternating chest compressions and mouth to mouth in an effort to give Alyssa a rest. He had no luck either and was in tears as Alyssa touched his shoulder, ready to resume her effort. Everyone else hung back in horrified silence as they watched the two attempt to literally pump life into Brooke's limp body.

"I called 911. They dispatched someone but it may be a while. I told them we had CPR-trained staff," Kyle shouted as he ran out of the wooded path toward the group gathered around Brooke. "Is she okay?" His voice trembled as he handed Dan a deep blue cotton weave blanket to cover Brooke's naked body. Visibly shaken, Josh stood up as Kyle came to his side.

"Alyssa's got this," Kyle said. "Brooke *will* be okay." His voice was firm and full of conviction.

Josh knelt beside Alyssa wrapping his fingers around Brooke's lifeless hand, watching every move Alyssa made.

"She can't . . . do this . . ." Josh clutched Brooke's hand tighter, willing life into her body and soul. "You have to breathe, Brooke!"

As if on cue, water began gurgling out of her mouth, and Brooke's lungs began working, pumping air on their own. Alyssa leaned back on her heels, calling for everyone to give Brooke room.

Gasping, coughing, and crying all at once, Brooke sat up with Dan's help, clutching her chest, choking, trying to clear the remnants of water out of her lungs.

"Stand back, everyone, give her some room!" Kyle echoed Alyssa's command when no one moved, motioning the campers and mentors to step back.

"Breathe, Brooke. Breathe. It's okay. You're okay. You got this." Alyssa held her close, murmuring in her ear, tucking the blanket around her shivering body, trying to calm her down as she continued coughing, her eyes wide with terror.

As Josh sat back on his haunches, struggling to calm his own breathing, he watched the tenderness the two friends exchanged and felt totally helpless and out of place. And terrified at the thought of how close Brooke had been to death. Drowning. Just like his wife and two daughters.

With air filling her lungs once more, Brooke regained control of her breathing and, still wide-eyed, turned to Josh. "Rosalie," she whispered. "She saved me."

Nodding, his eyes watery with tears, Josh answered simply, "I know."

The air around them grew thick and quiet with the realization that Brooke nearly drowned.

"Okay, everyone. Let's go finish dinner," Kyle directed, waving the crowd toward base camp. Before leaving, he turned to Brooke and Josh, Alyssa and Dan. "You guys all right?"

They each nodded, as Kyle studied Brooke intently. "You gave us a scare, you know."

"I'm sorry." Brooke dipped her head and continued, "I'm not sure what happened." She shot a sidelong glance at Josh, who held her gaze without blinking.

"I think I hear sirens. Must be the paramedics. They're going to want to take a look at you." Kyle turned toward the main camp. "Get some clothes on. Someone give her a shirt or something."

"I'm fine. I don't need to be seen." She started to wrap the blanket around her body like a cloak, making sure to cover all her private bits and pieces. As she struggled to stand, Dan and Josh rose to their feet, each slipping an arm around her waist for support. She attempted to push them away, refusing to be coddled. "Guys. I'm okay."

"I've got her. You guys should get out of those wet clothes. We'll meet you back at dinner in a few." Alyssa barked the order at both men, shooing them away as she offered her support to Brooke.

"Seriously, I'm okay," Brooke offered in a small voice, watching Dan and Josh walk ahead.

"I know. Humor me, will ya?" Alyssa took in her coworker and friend with a long look. "What the hell happened?"

Brooke studied the ground as arm in arm they clung together taking one slow step at a time to their shared cabin. Finally, she offered, exhaling one word, a name. "Rosalie."

"Josh's dead wife?"

With a nod, Brooke silently tried to piece it all together. "You're saying Rosalie tried to drown you?"

"No. But she was trying to take me over—"

Alyssa stared, dumbfounded. "What are you saying? Like she possessed you? Like on TV?"

"No. Well, yeah. Sort of. I don't know!" Her face warmed with the suggestion Rosalie had presented. Was she crazy? This didn't happen in real life.

They continued on in silence until they reached their cabin's porch steps. "Are you going to be okay? The paramedics are going to have to check you over." Alyssa motioned toward the circular driveway where Kyle stood speaking with two EMT's by an ambulance. The distant echo of chatter filtered out from the dining hall.

"I'm fine. I don't need to be checked out. I just want to take a hot shower, bundle up under the quilts, and go to sleep. I'm freezing. And I'm so tired. And embarrassed."

"I don't think you have a choice. Sorry." Alyssa delayed Brooke for a moment, nodding toward Kyle and the two EMTs walking in their direction.

"I don't really want to see anyone."

"Not even Josh?" Alyssa crooked an eyebrow at Brooke as they waited.

"Him, I'll see." She shot back as one of the EMTs waved at her.

"Hello, miss. I heard you had a bit of a scare at the lake?" The paramedic wore a name tag revealing her name as "Donna."

Brooke eyed the name tag, then addressed Donna, stating without hesitation, "Yes. But I'm fine now and I don't need to be seen."

"Kyle here told me I'd have a hard time with you. Protocol requires we at least need to check your vitals. If you could come back to the ambulance, miss, we'll check you out and be on our way." Donna motioned to the ambulance as she retraced her steps, expecting Brooke to follow.

"Uh. I'm okay, Thank you. Really. I just want to go back to my cabin, shower, and go to sleep." Brooke waved and turned to enter her cabin.

"Miss? We're required to check you out to make sure you're okay. It won't take more than a few minutes." The second EMT was emphatic, his tone polite.

As Brooke opened her mouth to argue, Alyssa nodded to the paramedic. "They're right, you need to be checked out, Brooke. Let's change your clothes, and then they can check you out. Let's go."

Moments later they met back in the living room, Alyssa in fresh jeans and tee shirt, carrying her hoody. Brooke was swathed in her robe, towel and toiletries in hand as she headed out of the bathroom.

"I didn't think you were going to shower." Alyssa shot her an awkward grimace. "If I'd have known . . ." She glanced down at her own body.

"All I had was a blanket and I wasn't getting in clean clothes after being covered in lake water. Besides I was freezing."

Brooke called over her shoulder as she headed to her bedroom to get changed. "After I see the EMTs, I'm coming back and going to bed. I am not up to dinner and a fire tonight. I'm serious. I don't need people gawking at me all night."

"Fine. Do what you need to do," Alyssa called, stepping on the porch to wait for her.

Chapter 22

The sun had completely set and Brooke was regrouping on the loveseat in front of the fireplace, swathed in a quilt when the screen door squeaked as it opened, jarring her from an almost hypnotic dream state. A fire burned quietly, gas-fed with no muss or fuss. Josh entered her cabin with two plates of food covered in aluminum foil. "I knocked. You didn't answer."

"Just dozing. Sorry." She waved him over and he came to stand beside her.

"I hope you're hungry." He offered a sheepish grin and Brooke suddenly knew how his company got its name. Josh was the quirky flirt. Peculiar and endearing at the same time. Unique. Drop-dead gorgeous, and a geek. Great combo.

Brooke reached out and grabbed the plate he offered, peeled off the tinfoil, balled it up, and tossed it onto the coffee table.

He squeezed onto the little space left on the love seat, forcing Brooke to uncurl her legs and sit up. They both stretched out, using the coffee table as a footrest. After wadding up the tinfoil covering his own plate and mimicking her previous motions, Josh pulled out of his shirt pocket two sets of utensils wrapped in napkins.

"She wouldn't leave me alone."

He stared at the flames licking the sidewalls of the fireplace. "I'm sorry. I thought I put her memory to rest."

"The workings were to heal things on your part. To help you heal and let go." Brooked sighed softly, staring at her untouched plate. "We haven't done anything for her."

Reaching for her hand, he wrapped his warm fingers around it and gave a light squeeze as he spoke. "Is she why you went to the lake?"

"Sorta. She wasn't trying to kill me. I don't know what happened. I was trying to . . ." Brooke couldn't find a way to say the words.

"Yeah?" He dipped his head and caught her gaze, waiting.

"You're going to think I'm crazy."

"After what I've experienced these last three weeks, let me be the judge." His eyes were warm but filled with curiosity.

Gulping, Brooke blew out a long, cleansing breath, and tried to explain. "She wanted to be inside of me and have sex with you one last time."

Brooke watched him process the concept. He blinked and cocked his head with a quizzical look on his face. "Huh?"

"See? You think I'm crazy."

"No! It's just . . . Rosalie was extremely territorial. We were offered plenty of threesome opportunities and she was adamantly opposed. To want a threesome now seems . . . contradictory to the living Rosalie."

"You think I'm lying? Why would I make it up!?" She pushed away from him and started to stand up. "I knew you wouldn't believe me."

Reaching for her hand, Josh tugged her back down to the sofa, slipped his arm around her shoulders, bringing her close to his side. "I believe you," he whispered as he pressed a kiss on her temple.

Her head rested against the firm expanse of his chest, and with her ear positioned this way she could hear the soft thud of his heartbeat, slow and steady. It mesmerized her and lulled her, easing her anxiety.

"I was trying to wash her out of my body," she whispered back, and a firm hug was his response.

A light rap sounded on the door, and Alyssa and the girls peeked in. "Hey, we're heading down to the fire pit, if you two are interested," Alyssa offered as they each made their way to their rooms. "Just grabbing jackets. It's a bit chilly out tonight."

"If you want to go to the fire, you can go. You don't have to babysit me. I'll be fine." Brooke spoke softly, waiting for his decision.

"I'm not leaving your side. If you want to go, we'll go. If you want to stay here, this fire is fine for me." He jutted his chin toward the gas flames burning in the fireplace.

It was his last night. His last campfire. His last drumming circle. To miss it would be selfish on her part. "No, we can go." She started to move as he tightened his hold.

"Not yet," Josh said. "I'd like to enjoy the peace and quiet for a few more minutes."

"Understandable." She relented and settled back into the crook of his arm. "We'll be down in a few," Brooke called to her roommates as they headed toward the door.

"We'll grab your drum. See you there," Cara called, waving her hoodie at them.

~ ~ ~

Jasmine and honey. She smelled so good. Her hair was so soft against his cheek. Her body so warm and inviting, curled up against him. He wanted to kiss her. Again. But he couldn't. He couldn't, knowing Rosalie might at any moment pop into Brooke's head. Or his.

For the first time since Rosalie's death, Josh desired someone other than his wife. And it didn't feel like cheating. It felt like living. *Life is for the living* had been Brooke's mantra, and she was so right.

"I can't believe I'm going to ask you this. But I don't know how else to put it." He breathed her essence and closed his eyes, reveling in the woman he held in his arms.

"Just say it." She leaned forward and grabbed their plates. "We haven't eaten a bite. I don't know about you, but I'm hungry." Handing Josh his plate, she waiting for him to continue.

"I don't want tonight to end." He searched her eyes, feeling like a bumbling teenager.

"So . . . what's your question?" She dipped her head and gave him a cheeky glance out of the corner of her eye.

He dug down deep inside for the nerve to share his thoughts and took a deep breath before he spoke again. "I was wondering if we could keep in touch after tomorrow."

"Keep in touch?" Her expression was blank, and Josh was at a loss as to how to clarify his request.

"Yeah."

"Like . . .?"

"Like." He huffed, never expecting this conversation to be this difficult. "Like, I almost lost you. And I don't want to lose you. Ever."

Her eyes lit up, crinkling around the corners in question, and he fumbled for words, wishing he could retract his last statement. "What I meant was—"

No help was coming from the woman by his side as she stared at him, waiting. Saying nothing, he lost himself in the flames reflecting in the dark orbs of her eyes.

"Yes?" She bit her lower lip, as she looked down to her lap where the dinner plate rested, and pushed around the now cold steak tidbits, baby potatoes, and carrot slices.

"I'd like to call you sometime. Visit. Have you come down to the city. Text. I want to get to know you." He watched her as she evaded his gaze, wanting to throw the damn plates aside so he could draw her onto his lap and kiss her. Instead, he speared at a piece of meat, and after chewing thoughtfully while waiting for her response, he added nonchalantly, "You know. To see where this goes."

"Okay." She pierced a piece of potato and popped it in her mouth.

He waited, not sure what to say when nothing else was offered. He'd thought about asking her earlier in the day. Numerous times. But with the whole lake thing? Now he knew losing her, not being in her life, not having her in his were no longer viable options. It took everything he could to say this. And all he got was an 'okay.' She was driving him crazy. Without a doubt.

"I hear drumming." She speared another piece of potato and waved at his dish. "Come on. Eat."

Chapter 23

A veil of sparks scattered like fireflies against the black night sky as Dan crouched on his haunches, prodding the remnants of the once roaring fire. He rolled the last log over with a stick he'd been using as a poker, its pointed end now blunt and charred. Retrieving his pocket bellows from a side pouch in his pants, he tugged on the metal tube, expanding it. Then after inhaling deeply, he put the tube to his lips, leaned near one of the smoldering logs resting on a pile of embers. He blew hard and the flames rekindled, fed by his breath.

"Who's staying up 'til the fire's out? I will if no one else wants to, but to be honest, I'm beat." He slipped a narrowed gaze at Alyssa, collapsed his pocket bellows, then glanced back at Brooke and Josh. Everyone else had retired, leaving these four the last of the group enjoying the cool evening air and fire.

"I'll hang if you want me to. Otherwise, I was about to get ready to head to bed." Alyssa stretched and yawned. "What about you, Brooke?"

"I'm not ready to go to bed yet. In fact, throw another log on, will ya, Dan?" She stretched her leg out and tapped his calf with the toe of her sneaker.

He swatted at her, but followed her directions. When the log caught, he saluted and bowed, laying the poker on the ground in front of the remaining pair. "Don't stay up too late kids. We have an early morning." He directed his attention to Josh specifically. "Bus leaves at nine o'clock sharp."

Josh nodded as he, like Brooke, watched the pair head off to basecamp with Alyssa in the lead.

"How long have they been together?" Josh asked as he turned his attention toward the fire.

"Who?" Brooke snorted softly. "Dan and Alyssa?"

"Who else is there?" He leaned over and picked up the poker on the ground at their feet.

"Huh! You're crazy. They're friends, for goodness' sake."

"If you say so." He jabbed at the log, repositioning it at an angle so the air seeped beneath it, feeding the coals.

"I do say so. Trust me. I would know." Brooke scoffed the notion away with a frown and a wave of her hand.

"Uh-huh," was Josh's only reply as he settled back into his chair. He reached out and grabbed Brooke's hand without taking his gaze from the fire. He felt her tug gently at first, then relax and curl her fingers around the warmth and strength he offered. "So. How are you so positive? Are you sure you and Dan—?"

"Nah. I told you before. He's like a brother. Never thought about them as a couple, though. But . . . now you mention it . . ."

He watched her sift through the memories searching for confirmation. With a shriek, she gave a nod of agreement. "Dan is why she saddled me with you so much. I think you're right!"

She glanced down at their entwined hands and he lifted them up for closer inspection. "You okay with this?"

"Mmmm. I guess."

The fire crackled then, as if prodded with Dan's poker that once again rested on the ground before them. Straightening his back, Josh felt chills run from head to toe, as though someone had poured ice water down his spine. "Brooke?"

"Yeah?" Her whisper was hesitant.

"Something's happening?"

"Yes, it is, *babe*." Her voice was at first a monotone, but ended sounding like Rosalie. Brooke's gaze was unwavering as the fire roared and spit, flames popping and licking in a whirlwind of energy. And then it died, leaving the two logs simmering as spirals of smoke curled up from the embers and charred wood.

"What the—?" Josh started to get up, then settled back in his chair as Brooke woke from her trance and wove her fingers tighter around his, clenching his hand so tight it throbbed.

"Josh." Brooke's voice was hoarse as the gray outline of a woman began to form on the other side of the fire. The smoke from the simmering logs grew denser, and twirled and wove a spiral, until it became a full specter of a woman—Rosalie.

"What the actual *fu-?*" Josh yanked his hand from her grip, shouting his dead wife's name.

Brooke jumped up as well, looking ready to run and as confused as he felt. "Is that you, Rosalie?"

With her question, the flames roared to life once more.

Brooke and Josh glanced at one another, then back to the apparition, motionless.

"*Baaaabe.*" The night grew completely silent, with not a peep sounding from the peepers, or frogs, or crickets.

Josh blinked back the tears threatening to flow and his voice was nothing more than a trembling whisper. "I'm so sorry. I'm so sorry," he repeated, his voice echoing in the night as the specter floated beyond the fire, watching them.

"*Thank you, Brooke. For hearing me. For bringing me peace. Take care of him for me.*" With Rosalie's words, Brooke began to weep.

"*Babe. It's time. I have to go. I will always love you. Remember her words. Life is for living.*" Rosalie raised a diaphanous hand to her lips, reached out to Josh, and blew gently on her fingertips. Sparks like stardust swirled and danced between them, settling around them in a scattering of silver embers before fading away.

In a fiery flash of flames, Rosalie's image exploded against the night sky, lighting the entire circle as if it were daylight. As the flames in the firepit died down, the night grew pitch dark and a thick silence blanketed the area. Enveloped in a hazy veil, Josh and Brooke watched the smoke twist into a spiral, floating upward until it dissipated in the darkness. Once more the crickets chirped. The peepers peeped. The bullfrogs croaked.

"What just happened?" Josh's voice waivered as the logs flared up again and slowly rekindled themselves to a low burn. A look of disbelief shadowed his face.

"I've–I've—never seen anything like this b-b-before," Brooke stammered, staring at the spot where Rosalie had materialized moments earlier. The concept of reality was suspended as they both tried to explain away what had just happened. There was no logical way to debunk the fact that Rosalie had paid them a visit. And left them with a very definitive message.

"She's gone," he offered finally, gently tugging Brooke into his embrace. He brushed a light kiss over her forehead. "She's gone."

"You okay?" Brooke asked as his hold tightened around her body.

"I don't know. I feel like I just lost her all over again. I haven't really had her here for the last three years, though. Have I?" His voice caught with his revelation. "I feel empty. At the same time . . . this sounds horrible . . . I feel free. Like I've been released from prison or something. It sounds so bad." He screwed his eyes shut, trying to make sense of everything he'd experienced, everything he was feeling. "I'm exhausted."

She looked pointedly at the fire, once again burning brightly. With a sigh of regret, she reminded him softly, "You can go to bed if you need to. I understand. I promised I'd stay until the fire went out."

She stepped away from him and bent over to pick up the poker.

"I don't want to leave you. We can stay here all night. I wouldn't mind. I don't want to be alone." He returned to his chair, watching her silhouette against the fire's orange glow as she rearranged the logs and the flames crept higher.

Moments later, they sat side by side, arms resting on their chairs, hands dangling together, fingers entwined. The crackle and pop of the fire filled the air around them as they reflected on what had just happened. All the while they held hands as the moon traced her path, arcing across the night sky, dipping low along the horizon.

. . . always hopin' for a blue moon that for once really looks blue . . .

"I don't want anyone to know what happened today—especially tonight. With Rosalie. Okay? Please don't make her a part of Earth and Sky's sales pitch." Josh squeezed her hand tight. "I still don't know what to think. I need to process this. I'm not sure where to go from here."

"I understand," Brooke began slowly. "You know. I came up here to get away from the world. From men. I'm not really a one-night stand kinda gal, Josh." She flipped her right hand and rested her pointer against her temple, shaking her head.

"This wasn't what I was looking for either, Brooke. For the first time in three years I feel alive again. I *was not* expecting this." He ran his free hand through his hair, focused on the flames.

How could we make this work? How can I be thinking like this? The idea of even sharing his life with another woman was difficult to wrap his head around.

"I had a couple one-night stands *before* I was married. They never felt like this." His words came slow and low, unsure how to express what he was feeling. "I don't want this to be a one-night stand."

She caught her breath and hesitated. After a moment, she chuckled, her words dry as the Adirondacks in early August. "Is this what you say to all your women?"

"I don't have other women."

"I'm sorry. I know."

A lone howl sounded off in the distance, maybe a wolf, maybe a coyote. Josh couldn't be sure. "So, who did you come up here to get away from?"

A pregnant pause was his answer as she squirmed in her seat. She eased her hand out of his grip and stood by the pit, focusing on poking at the fire.

He waited until she was back in her chair before he continued. "You know so much about me. You probably have a file this thick." Josh lifted both hands and held them about six inches apart, shoulder height. "And I know nothing about you. Except you were conceived at Woodstock. Not the concert of course."

He winked at her, but it was lost as her sight never left the fire. He hoped she could hear the humor in his words. "No worries. You don't have to talk about it. We have a lifetime." He settled back in his chair and stretched his legs out, crossing them at the ankles as he folded his arms behind his head.

"A lifetime? You sure?" Her lips curved slightly upward.

"What's so funny?" he asked quietly. "Lots of animals mate for life. Eagles, wolves, swans."

"You're serious."

They locked eyes in the darkness of the night, with the fire settling down, and the moon setting low over the jagged horizon of mountain peaks and plateaus. "I might be."

"You don't even know me. You said so yourself."

"So it's your fault if we don't work out, isn't it?" He leaned over the arms of their chairs, nuzzling her nose with his, aching to taste the sweetness of her kiss once more. She inclined her head ever so slightly, just out of reach. He growled low and stood up, scooping her in his arms as he claimed her lips fiercely at first. Her taste, her touch soothed him, as they molded together as one, joined gingerly by the varying peck and plummet of their kisses. Moments later, she cuddled her head close against his chest, as he rested his cheek on her crown. She wrapped her arms tightly around his torso, her breathing in sync with his.

When she did eventually step away (Josh would have stood there all night so as not to let the evening end), he watched as she crouched by the pit one last time, rolling the remnants of the logs apart. The charred bits split and scattered as she pushed them to the outer rim of the stone circle, where the coals had died into nothingness and sand. She scattered the remaining red embers, and leaned back to grab her canteen by her chair. Still on her haunches, she twisted the top off and poured the remaining water over the red and black simmering and glowing bits. It made a hissing, fizzling sound as steam coiled like smoke, dissipating into the cool evening air. When the smoldering heap no longer appeared to be a threat, Brooke stood up and faced him, reaching out.

Accepting her invitation, he wrapped her hand in his and nudged her to his side, where they stood for a moment surveying the circle of empty chairs. The weekend volunteers had collected the drums, cups, and any debris left behind, so there was little else to pick up. "I will never forget this place. You. Drumming. This firepit. What happened tonight."

Leaning her head against his arm, she sighed softly. "Me either."

"You? Are you going somewhere?" He slipped a finger under her chin and lifted her face to his.

"No. I meant I will never forget what it was like with you here. Very different, to say the least." She raised up on her toes and left a lingering kiss on his mouth, then settled back onto the balls of her feet.

"I'm not gone yet." Gathering her closer to him, Josh nuzzled her nose with his. "We have until sunrise."

A soft giggle was Brooke's response, as she nose-kissed him back.

Studying her in the darkness, he wondered how the hell he was going to board the bus out of her life tomorrow. He tilted his head to the side and brushed his lips against her mouth, her cheek, the soft and tender skin at the hollow of her neck. As she angled her head to the side, welcoming his kiss, he drank her essence, and his body came alive with desire. He cupped her bottom close, drawing her to him as her hands splayed across his chest. She offered her parted lips up to him, and he captured her in a deep and searching kiss as she slipped her arms behind him, resting her hands on his lower back.

They parted, breathless, his body aching with need, and he turned to leave, guiding her behind him. Silence ensued as they headed toward basecamp, entering the wooded path separating the firepit and lake from the camp. Brooke paused, tugging him to a halt.

It was so dark in this patch of forest Josh could barely see Brooke as he turned to face her.

"I . . . I don't know if I can do this," she stammered, her voice soft and doubtful.

"It's okay, Brooke. I can promise you, this won't be a one-night stand."

"It's not the only reason why."

Josh waited for her to continue. When she didn't, he lifted their still-clasped hands and pointed toward the cabins. "Let's talk about this inside, where it's warm." He started to move, but she remained in place.

"Brooke? What's going on? Are you married or something?"

"Oh, my goddess, no!" Still unmoving, Brooke clenched his hand tightly, as her breathing quickened.

Enveloping her in his arms, Josh held her close and whispered against her head. "It's okay. Whatever it is, it's okay."

She took a deep breath, and spoke into his chest. "I. I." She inhaled again, then expelled her secret in one breath. "I was sexually assaulted a few years ago, before I came here."

With her words, Josh froze momentarily, until an overwhelming need to protect her thawed his blood. He held her at arms-length, searching her face, trying to figure out what to say or do. Finally, he could only offer, "I'm so sorry."

She buried her face in his chest and started to cry. "I'm sorry. I thought I could do this. I can't. If you were hoping we—"

"Hey, hey, hey. I wasn't planning on doing anything. Lifetime, remember? This isn't the end of us." He bent his head and came right up close to her face. Her eyes were glistening with tears.

"Do you need to talk about it?"

"No. I think we should go to bed. We have an early morning." She hung her head low and spoke in a whisper.

"I understand." He hugged her hard one last time. They plodded silently through the woods and into the clearing. As they came to the crossroad of the path ushering the way to their respective cabins, he held her one last time, brushing his lips against her forehead. "Get some rest. I'll see you soon."

She nodded, and murmured, "Good night."

The next 150 feet to his cabin felt like a mile. Each heavy step led him away from the woman he wanted desperately to hold, to make love with even though he knew so little about her.

She'd been sexually assaulted! It explained so much. She was tough. But she was fragile. She was independent, but was her independence born out of fear of getting close to someone? She was intelligent and funny, talented. And sexy as hell. With those thoughts he climbed the steps to his front porch, the screen door, and his empty bed.

As he placed his foot on the last step, he heard the distinct sound of running footsteps behind him on the gravel and as he turned around, she shot up onto his porch, taking the four steps two at a time, nearly colliding with him.

Totally confused, he could only stare at her as she caught her breath.

"I don't want to be alone tonight," she confessed with a gulp. "Can we grab a cuppa coffee? I think I want you to get to know me better."

He grinned, affirming the option with a quick dip of his head. "Sure. But we only have a few hours."

"We'll make every minute count," she offered hoarsely, as she slipped her hand in his and led him back down the stairs to the dining hall and the 24-hour coffee station.

Chapter 24

"My whole family is in California. I don't talk with them anymore." Brooke offered this slowly as she poured a mug full of coffee.

"I don't have much family either," Josh countered as he handed her his mug and waited. Together they steered as if on autopilot to their table, with no one in the dining hall at all. Even the morning cooks hadn't arrived. It was eerily silent.

"How do you want to do this?" She studied his face as they slipped onto the benches at their favorite spot.

"Whatever way makes you feel most comfortable. I don't want to pry," he said simply.

"I agreed to answer your questions, and I mean it. For the first time in a long time, I feel like I've found someone I can trust completely."

Josh nodded and agreed. "I feel this way, too."

They remained silent for a moment, as Brooke bowed her head and studied her reflection in her coffee. "He was a prominent public official. Handsome. Charismatic. And married. I was not interested in him *at all*."

"Wow. Sorry. I didn't see this coming." Josh gave a quick shake of his head before urging her to continue.

"Neither did I. Am I making you uncomfortable?"

"Nope." He motioned for her to continue.

"All right, then. I was working at Angels-R-Us, volunteering while getting my Death Doula certification." She paused, and took a steadying breath. "I was called in by my volunteer coordinator and told there was a woman who was nearing her time. She asked if I could make arrangements to stay with the family—probably for not more than a few nights. The son, she explained, had made a sizable donation to the Angels-R-Us Foundation and requested someone be at his mother's side day and night. So, I went."

She cradled her mug and took a stabilizing gulp before continuing. "You sure I'm not boring you yet?"

"Never. Go on." Josh sat immobile, his entire being trained on only her. His energy gave her the courage to continue.

"When I first got there, Audrey was nowhere near death's door. I stayed with the family on and off, mostly on, for about a couple weeks. I got to know the children, a young boy and a young girl, his wife—who wasn't living there as far as I could tell, and of course . . . *him.* In fact, when I first got there the kids were staying with their mom at their beach house. He worked and she didn't, he said." She blinked hard and grimaced, pausing a moment before continuing.

"They seemed like the perfect family at first, and I didn't even realize they were separated until he told me. Not a care in the world. No money problems, loving and happy, no dysfunction. But the longer I stayed, something felt . . . icky."

Brooke bit her lower lip and studied Josh's face for a sign to keep going, or to stop.

"If you don't want to tell me anymore, I understand," he said softly, grabbing her hand.

"I'm good." She paused, collected her thoughts, and continued. "Once I was there full-time, I started noticing how the kids spent more time there, too, but they avoided being alone with him. When I was with their grandmother, they'd stay in her suite with me, reading or playing on their phones or tablets. When I was alone, even in my quarters, they'd be my shadows. I thought it was because their mom was taking advantage of having a live-in babysitter."

She set her coffee mug down and clasped her hands on the table. Josh closed his eyes, then slowly opened them to study her, guarded curiosity filling his baby blues.

"Audrey was frail, yes, and although she didn't seem to be terminally ill when I first arrived, her condition deteriorated over time. She had a team of private doctors and nurses who would tend to her. We spent her every waking moment together, but days passed, those waking moments grew less and less." Brooke picked up the paper napkin lying beside her mug and started fidgeting with it, rolling it and unrolling it as she spoke.

"She started sleeping more than she was awake, and my role as a volunteer took on more of a household assistant. I contacted Angels-R-Us and told them what was happening, but because his donation had been so substantial, they asked me to stay on. When I told them I couldn't continue to volunteer, as I needed to get back to my real job—I was a guidance counselor—they told me the Senator had spoken with them about hiring me as a full-time aide, and if I wanted, I should speak with him. Since it was summertime, I was technically on vacation. They pointed out all their other volunteers had full-time jobs, and they would really appreciate it if I stayed on and considered the offer."

She took a swig of coffee, cradling her mug. "I didn't want to, but I was growing very fond of Audrey and the two kids. I felt like they needed me, needed my protection. From what? I don't know. So, he came to me and said Angels-R-Us had called and told him I might be leaving, and he offered me a huge amount of money to stay. It paid for the rest of my death doula training with a quite a bit to spare, so I agreed. When I wasn't sitting bedside with Audrey, I was staying with the kids, going in their built-in pool or playing video or board games with them, while Richard was flying back and forth to D.C. and his wife was playing around at the beach house. It was a pretty easy deal. And I'd truly started to care for Audrey and the kids."

"Nothing in life is free," Josh offered slowly.

"Yup. Then one Saturday morning . . . the kids were shopping with their mom. He was in his study going over some proposal or something. I was sitting in Audrey's room reading *Gone with the Wind* to her, she loved when I read to her. And as I got to the part where Rhett was asking Scarlett to be his mistress—have you read *Gone with the Wind*?"

Josh shook his head.

"Oh. You should. Anyway, as I read the scene Audrey told me, 'Thank you, dear Brooke. What a fine way to go.' And when I looked up to ask her what she meant, she was gone. It was so unexpected I wasn't sure what to do. No one had ever passed away on my shift. So, I got up and searched for the Senator. When I told him his mother had passed, he began crying uncontrollably. It was so sad, so I hugged him, trying to console him. He became really angry and started yelling at me and shaking me because I didn't get him before she died. Next thing I know, he's . . . he's hitting me. Pushing me. He—"

Brooke stopped short, staring off into the darkness outside a nearby window. Josh said nothing.

"I tried to get him to stop, but he was blinded by his grief and anger. I got away. He caught me and dragged me back to Audrey's bed. And then right there—right there he, he—beside his dead mother!"

Brooke buried her face in her hands and began sobbing uncontrollably, muttering, "Right there! Right there!" Josh came to her side, gently rubbing her shoulder, until she stood up and turned to him. He wrapped his arms around her, and there she stayed until her sobs ceased.

"Hey," he murmured, nudging her face up to look at him with his finger crooked beneath her chin. "It's going to be all right. He can't hurt you now."

She reached into a pocket and fished out a tissue, blew her nose, and shoved the soggy Kleenex back into her pocket. "I'm so tired. What time is it?" She searched for her phone as he reached for his and checked his first.

"It's not even four."

"Do you want to go to the rec room, maybe watch a movie or relax? I'm so tired." She stretched and yawned.

"We can go back to my cabin and turn on the fireplace. My couch is pretty comfy." He raised his hands in offer.

"No funny stuff?"

"Cross my heart," he offered, crossing his heart.

Chapter 25

The minutes ticked on bringing dawn ever closer as Brooke lay curled up in Josh's embrace talking about everything they possibly could, until they had fallen asleep midsentence. Now, feeling confusingly safe, she rested her head against his chest, as she listened to the steady rhythmic beat of his heart and breathing.

It felt good to trust a man enough to fall asleep in his arms. Especially one who smelled so good. She tilted her head a bit and inhaled his musky scent, closing her eyes and snuggling closer.

Tentatively, she splayed her hand over his solar plexus chakra, between his chest and stomach, reveling in his warmth and the energy surge she experienced. He was more muscular than she'd expected, she realized as her fingertips traced over the ripples of muscle and skin hidden beneath the taut olive-green cotton Earth and Sky tee-shirt he wore. It felt good and right to be sitting next to him here, held by him, touching him. At least for this very surreal moment.

Too much time had passed since she'd allowed herself to trust a man, to trust herself enough to be this vulnerable. This felt good. Real good. Rubbing her cheek against the broad expanse of his chest, she placed an impulsive, feather-soft kiss as an afterthought.

He murmured something in his drowsy sleep-state as he drew one arm tight around her shoulders, holding her close. She felt his chest rise and fall, felt him stretch slightly then relax as he drifted awake and planted a return kiss on the top of her head. Rubbing his jaw against her forehead, he asked softly, "You up?"

"Mm-hm," she replied, feeling her heart quicken.

Grabbing his iPhone, he checked the time. "We didn't sleep hardly at all. It's not even five."

"Wow. I thought it was later," she said, her head resting against his chest.

"You can go back to your cabin if you need sleep," he offered slowly, rubbing his hand along the curve of her hip, down her thigh, and back up to her waist.

"I don't need sleep. This feels too good to pass up for sleep." She tightened her hold around him.

"Yeah, it does," he whispered. His hand trailed along her body, ever so softly caressing the underside of her breast. He nudged her forehead with his nose, beckoning her to lift her gaze to him. When she did, he captured her lips in a slow, deep kiss.

She stretched and leaned into him, the butterflies somersaulting in her belly in response.

Tentatively, she returned his kiss, parting her lips as she met his increasing ardor. Her fingertips trailed from where her hand rested on his belly, up to his chest, then smoothed across the broad width to his shoulder and arm, where his muscles contoured naturally in perfectly sculpted form.

Their breathing picked up in sync, as they adjusted and molded to one another, his knee parting her thighs as she turned to him and pressed her softness against his hardness. The early morning crept closer as the fireplace flames danced and threw their shadows against the walls.

She arched against him, wanting more, wanting much more.

Unfolding from her spot within his cuddle, Brooke climbed onto Josh's lap and tucked her legs around him, sinking into the overly stuffed couch. True, he'd promised no funny stuff. But she'd done nothing of the sort.

He clasped both hands around her jawline, cupping her face close, and whispered, "Are you sure about this?"

She groaned and answered with a heated kiss, bringing her hands up around his head and pulling him nearer to her as she raked her fingers through his hair, whispering, "Oh, yes, I'm positively sure about this," against his lips.

His touch smoothed the contour of her back, cupping her bottom close with a squeeze as she tightened her thighs into his. As she pressed her body against his hardness, he leaned back and paused, studying her face.

"Say my name," he directed softly, his heavy-lidded eyes never leaving her lips.

"What?" she asked, startled by his request.

"My name." A slight smile curved his lips as she responded to his demand.

"Now tell me you want me," Josh directed in a husky command as he bent his head to nibble her neck, just below her ear.

"You're driving me crazy," she murmured with a quiet groan, tilting her head for better access. "Can't you tell?"

"I want you to tell me," he whispered, nibbling her lobe.

Understanding finally where this was coming from, and where they were leading, she followed his request. "Yes, love. I need you," she offered, raining kisses along his jawline. "I want you. I want this. Us. I'm okay. I promise."

With her words, he smoothed his hands along the underside of her thighs, his fingertips teasing her most feminine bits. She groaned again, moving against him, finding his lips with her own, claiming him in a deep, demanding kiss.

It was his turn to mutter something unintelligible as he stood up, holding her to his chest, as she wrapped her legs around his waist and her arms around his shoulders. He carried her into his bedroom, and laid her gently on his bed, studying her face in the pre-dawn morning shadows as he slipped out of his Levi's, kicking them to the floor. Pushing off the bed with her feet, she lifted her bum and slipped her jeans down over bended knees, off her legs, and followed suit by kicking them to the floor also.

. . . losin' Levi's, findin' skin against skin . . .

"I want you too, Brooke." Crawling onto the bed beside her, he half-covered her body with his own, one leg parting her thighs, kissing her soundly and fully.

Fevered kisses rained over their curves and contours, while roving hands gently caressed and explored this new, recently unchartered territory. Gone was any sense of propriety, any concern for unethical behavior. They had these few precious hours left of the morning, and then he'd be gone forever. After today she might never see him again, and this thought spurred Brooke on. Rolling over onto her side, she nudged him onto his back, straddling him again. She lifted her tee shirt up over her head and tossed it onto her jeans on the floor, then brought her hands up behind her and unfastened her lacy peach bra, peeling it slowly down her arms. With a flick of her wrist, she tossed the slip of fabric to the wayside as well.

He brought his hands around to rest against her lower back, bringing her close as he captured her lips with his. Rolling her onto the bed, he knelt beside her, tugging her peach lacy panties—the last barrier keeping her from offering herself completely to him—down her legs.

Moments later, he lay beside her once again and traced her forehead, cheekbone, and chin with his forefinger before bringing it to rest on her lips.

"You tell me if you want me to stop, okay?" he asked, placing a quick peck on the taut peak of her breast.

"I won't need you to stop. Trust me," she whispered with a soft moan as she reached around and cupped his butt, pressing into him. She could feel his desire growing, and she moved with him, wanting more.

Every bit of bliss she had forgotten how to feel was rekindled with his coaxing caresses. The heat of passion, the rise of ecstasy sang through her veins, danced along the silk of her flesh, and ebbed and flowed as his kisses explored and claimed the length of her body.

She was the hills and valleys, and he was like the clouds, soft and tickling, fierce and commanding, bringing her waves of pleasure, like the rolling tide along the beach is moved by the winds of time. She was the Earth Goddess, her blood the water, her coos of pleasure like wisps of air, the soft contours of her body the earth, and her fiery passion like molten lava, flowing from her most inner core. And, he was the God of the Hunt, luring her, capturing her, devouring her as he took her, growling fiercely with the union of their release.

Together, they lay spent, their breaths measured and in time, entwined in one another's arms and legs, imprinting the moment of their union for all of eternity.

~ ~ ~

Dawn was breaking as Josh and Brooke awoke, entwined in the tousled covers of his bed. The past two hours had been filled with lovemaking and sleep, until at last the two lovers greeted the day with the first soliloquy of songbirds.

Brooke stretched and curled into Josh's warmth as he whispered against her tousled head with a kiss, "Good morning."

Nuzzling his naked chest, she replied in kind. After a few moments, she said, "I was thinking about something we discussed last night."

"Yeah?" He drew her closer as she continued.

"I think, after comparing the dates of everything we went through . . . you know, in our past. . . do you realize it all happened the same weekend? If I'm figuring things out correctly," she offered slowly.

"Really?" was his only reply.

"Everything happens for a reason, I believe anyway." Her voice was a hesitating whisper.

"Hm. Maybe?" He nuzzled his nose against her hair, tightening his hold around her body as she cuddled closer to him not wanting to admit Sunday had arrived.

~ ~ ~

Loud shouting and laughter sounded out in the front yard, waking Josh first. As he did a quick take of his bedroom and down at the woman sleeping in his arms, the whole night came back to him.

He was leaving Earth and Sky. He was going home. "Wake up, Brooke, we gotta get moving." He nudged her gently, sliding his arm—now feeling like dead weight and creeping with pins and needles—out from under her head.

"Brooke, wake up." He kissed her forehead and she stirred again and groaned. "Time to get up." He stretched for his phone and checked the time. "It's seven-thirty."

"Crap!" Brooke shot up and glanced around her. "It's so late!"

"We're fine. Let's get moving so we can grab breakfast. I gotta pack up the last of my things and get ready to leave." He hugged her close one last time, then released her quick. "I don't want you to go, but I need a shower. Meet you in the dining hall in a half hour?"

"Yeah." She stretched, still not completely awake. "Gotcha. Half hour." She dragged herself up, pulled her clothes from last night back on, and plodded slowly to the door. Hand on the knob, she turned and whispered, "Thank you."

He smiled back, totally taken in with the sleepy picture she made, wishing he could tug her into his bed and spend the next 24 hours—correction, the rest of his life—with her. "No. Thank you."

Chapter 26

The minutes flew by way too fast, with the morning suddenly over and Josh rolling out of her life on the same bus he'd rode in on three short weeks ago.

Her cabinmates, thankfully, hadn't realized she'd spent the night with Josh as they were all in the dining hall when she crept in through the squeaky front door of their cabin. She showered, dressed, and was pouring coffee at the coffee station talking with Lance about photography when Josh strolled in looking even more gorgeous than the first day she'd met him. Feeling her knees buckle a bit, she excused herself from her conversation with Lance and slowly stepped toward the man who had captivated her heart and soul.

"Good morning." Her voice was overly loud and overly bright, and his response was a wink and a chuckle.

"Good morning to you, too. I trust you slept well." He stretched and flexed his arm, groaning a bit.

"I slept wonderfully." She grinned. "What's up with your arm?"

"Not sure. Feels like someone dropped a boulder on it." He winked again and reached out, hugging her tight. "You brought me coffee?" He peered in her mug.

"Nope." She chuckled and led the way to the coffee station, where Alyssa and Kyle had been watching their exchange.

"Well good morning, you two." Alyssa spoke first. "Did you get any sleep at all?"

Brooke felt her cheeks warm, and cast a furtive glance at Josh. "Of course. We stayed up pretty late by the fire though."

Busy pouring his coffee, Josh nodded in agreement.

"You all set to take off?" Kyle asked Josh, as he reached for a mug.

"Yep. I want to thank you all for this amazing experience. You probably saved my life." He looked from Kyle, to Alyssa, and lastly to Brooke, his tone somber and sincere.

"Yeah, well. We do what we can. You did the rest. You have to want to heal first and foremost. You got this." Kyle reached over and gave a quick, firm man-hug with a double back-pat.

"Well, I'll leave you two manly men alone with your bear hugs. I've got to set up the presentation. Alyssa, can you help me?" Brooke didn't want to lose a minute with Josh, as they were ticking by so quickly. However, this was her responsibility, and the sooner it was set up the sooner she could rejoin Josh and share their last breakfast together.

"Sure. What do you need?" Alyssa stepped up without hesitation as Kyle and Josh continued their conversation.

Within moments the screen was latched into place and the computer and projector were set. Brooke stood at the front of the dining hall and gave a whistle to catch everyone's attention. When all eyes were on her, she spoke. "Well, it's hard to believe these three weeks have come to an end. You all have taught me so much. I'm going to miss every one of you. But I know you've got this. I know you're going to get back to life and be the best you can be. The world is waiting for you, all of you. And you're each going to make it a better world than it was before.

"This presentation is our little going away gift. And you'll each have a copy of it in your 'goody bag' we've put together. They're on the back table, labelled by name, so make sure you grab yours before heading to the bus. Don't worry about your luggage. As long as you left it all on your porches it will be on the bus when you head out.

"So, I guess without further ado, grab your breakfast and in a few minutes the show will begin." She stepped to the back of the room as everyone clapped and hooted and hollered. Within moments, plates had been filled, coffees refilled, and campers and staff were seated back at their tables.

As the slideshow began, the hall settled down and soon all eyes were fixed on the screen. All the music featured throughout the three weeks was woven into the presentation, including Enya from the yoga classes and Van Morrison from the art classes.

At one point everyone started singing along as they watched slide after slide of their life transformation journey. As Brooke rubbed her eyes dry with the back of her hand, Josh brought his arm around her shoulders and gave her a firm, lingering squeeze. She tilted her head and rested it on his shoulder, closing her eyes, wishing she could capture this moment with her camera. But she couldn't, so she would have to hold it close in her heart.

As the last photo spun into view, the crowd grew quiet. It was a group photo of everyone standing around the fire where they had released their intentions the day before. Brooke had stood on a ladder she'd set up for the occasion and had caught a shot from on high. The ring of campers dressed alike in white yoga pants and tunics circled the fire as the flames leapt upward. Their bodies were silhouetted by shadow and light, creating an ethereal effect as the smoke rose high, wafting around them like one huge halo over the entire group.

A collective coo of "ooh's and ahh's" filled the room. Josh nudged her and whispered, "I'm impressed."

Her cheeks warmed with his praise as the final "Hail and Farewell from Earth and Sky" slide filled the screen. A round of applause clattered throughout the room and the presentation was over.

The lights flickered on and Kyle gave a 'fifteen minutes before departure time' head's up warning to everyone. He urged the campers to take a final trip to the restroom, collect their goody bags, and get their last goodbyes in. Some wandered off to the lake, others sat on the veranda outside the dining hall. Josh took Brooke's hand and led her to the rec room where she'd taught him how to drum.

"Why are we going here?" She laughed as he tugged her along.

"There's one more thing I want to do," he explained as he led the way.

"I don't think we have time to drum." She followed along at a hurried pace keeping up with him.

Once they reached the rec room, he wrapped his arms around her before she could say another word.

"I wanted to kiss you so badly after our drumming session. Remember?" He squinted into her eyes, searching.

She nodded, lost for words, as she studied his lips.

"Can I have the kiss I didn't steal, now?" He bent his head and nearly collided with her face as she tiptoed up and wrapped her arms around his neck, claiming his mouth before he could act first.

She kissed him like she was never going to kiss him again, because she probably wasn't. She kissed him as if she was branding the memory on her soul forever, because she never wanted to forget him. Ever. She kissed him as if he were the only man for her. Because he was. And he was about to ride out of her life forever.

When at last their lips parted, he spoke again. "I'll call you. I'll text you. We can visit. I'll come up. I'll get a limo to bring you down."

A wistful smile was all she could offer as a response. Her throat felt as though it had been stuffed with beach sand, leaving her unable to speak. She hugged him instead, resting her forehead on his chest, breathing in his scent. Imprinting.

The bus horn blew, signaling it was time to board. He chucked a finger under her chin and guided her to look up into his baby blues. "I'm not going away forever. I promise."

"Okay."

"I'll keep in touch."

She nodded again, forcing a bright smile. "Sure."

The horn beeped again, and the couple left the rec room, heading toward the bus. She watched him catch up with the other campers, the last to board. And as he did, he turned, sought her out, and waved. Oddly, from the time he'd left her side until the time he turned to her from the bus steps he had put his Ray-Bans in place. When she finally waved back, he disappeared up the steps and was gone.

Chapter 27

"Now what?" Brooke asked her reflection in the bathroom mirror later in the day, after checking her phone for the thirteenth time. Raising two fingertips to her lips, she brushed them lightly remembering his kiss. His touch. The ecstasy.

"He's gone. Forget him. He's not coming back." Her reflection was a bit snippy, but probably correct. Why would he come back? Why would he call or text? She was a tree-hugging hippy. And he was probably a multimillionaire. And face it, Earth and Sky had done their thing, and she'd done *her* thing. He had a company to save and a client base who needed to get laid. He was probably going to get laid, too. A lot.

Her phone buzzed and she reached for it so quickly it fell off the bathroom sink onto the tiled floor. It was Alyssa, asking if she was coming to dinner.

She texted her reply, staring in the mirror one more time, as she searched every shadow. "Rosalie?" she whispered, hoping and not hoping at the same time the dead woman would appear.

Nothing. Brooke sighed and shut the light, and headed to the dining hall.

The Sunday night after a group left was always a bit low energy. It was like walking away from a major train wreck, with the survivors dazed and wondering what had just happened. Tonight was no different for her team mates. However, for Brooke, her world had been derailed and turned upside down, and she was still stuck on the train.

Two tables had been pushed together and three boxes of pizza were laid out on a third. Paper plates, paper napkins, cans of soda and bottles of beer were set out on the third table also. This was the ritual giving everyone permission to let loose and laugh, cry, or vent. You name it. Normally Brooke joined in. This time around she sat out, content with nursing her IPA and nibbling on a slice of the best chicken wing pizza this side of the Thruway, delivered from Vinny's, the number one pizza shop in town. She spied Dan and Alyssa sitting together, slipping one another covert glances, joking quietly. At one point they shared a slice, and it blew Brooke away knowing Josh had been correct. And she'd never seen it. Alyssa and Dan. Go figure.

Kyle came up beside her and offered her another beer, which she took after draining the one in her hands of its last swig. "How are you holding up?" he asked with a knowing look and sympathetic hug.

"Good." She bobbed her head once and bit her lower lip, holding up her new beer. "Cheers."

"Cheers." Kyle clinked his beer against hers and took a gulp. Wiping his mouth with the back of his hand, he continued. "So. Any more visits from Rosalie?"

"Nope."

"How'd you and Josh leave off?" He waited for her reply, not taking his eyes from her face.

She squirmed and blinked a couple times, shaking her head side to side. "I dunno. He said he'll text. I dunno. What's the difference?"

"It seemed like you two had something going."

"No. He tried—" Her voice trailed off lost in the memories she was beginning to bury deep in her heart.

Kyle snapped to attention. "Did he hurt you?"

"No. Seriously. What can happen in three weeks?" She gulped, and blinked away the moisture collecting in her eyes.

"Ah. I see."

"I'm not holding my breath." She shrugged and lifted her beer for another sip. "Can we change the subject?"

Kyle nodded. "The presentation was fabulous. You've got an amazing eye for catching the perfect shot."

"Thanks. This wasn't as bad as I thought it was going to be."

"Yeah. I hear ya. Once we get the client reviews back, we'll know if this is going to be a regular thing."

"Oh goddess, I hope not." Brooke laughed and chugged her IPA, with Kyle following suit.

Her phone buzzed and she froze, her eyes locked on Kyle.

Amused, he chided her. "Don't you need to check your phone?"

"Uh." With a quick glance down she saw it was not a news notification or weather update. *It was Josh.*

Kyle lifted his beer in a salute and sauntered off.

*Hey. About to hit the city. Been thinking about you. Slept most of the ride. Probably gonna crash as soon as I get home. Thank you for last night-this morning. *heart emojis**

"How do I even reply?" She scoffed aloud to no one.

"To what?" Mandy leaned over as Brooke closed the thread and read the preview of Josh's text, and whistled. "Whoa lady! Baby blues is texting you? Hot damn!"

"You look like you've seen a ghost, Brooke," Dan said, laughing. "Pun intended."

"What did he say?" Alyssa asked, eyes pointed.

Shaking her head, Brooke shrugged helplessly. "Just telling me they made it back to Manhattan."

"And he can't stop thinking about her and adores her and wants to whisk her off her feet!" Mandy spoke again, giggling.

"He did not!" Brooke snapped. "She's making stuff up."

"Okay, maybe a little. Damn, girl. I'd take a dentist appointment reminder from him and turn it into a porn flick. He was freaking hot."

Brooke stared at her phone, not sure what to text back. *'Okay. Have a good sleep'*? Or *'Come back. I need you?'*

Instead, she tapped out something in-between.

Okay. Thanks for texting. Sleep well. *heart emoji*

Just before she hit send, she deleted the heart.

~ ~ ~

Monday morning provided another text waiting for her.

Big day back to work. It feels so weird wearing a suit. Not sure I like it anymore. What have you done to me? *heart emoji*

After thumbing out a few different flirty replies regarding him without a suit or anything on, she deleted each one and finally hit "send" with something a little less desperate-sounding.

Good luck at work. I'm sure you look great. Have a good day.

She curled up tight, hugging her pillow and wishing it was him. Wishing they could have had one more night of passion. After a moments' thought, she texted one more message, regretting it immediately.

Thinking of you. *heart emoji*

She fought the urge to text him throughout the rest of the day. Besides the fact she didn't want to look clingy or desperate, she had nothing productive to say. No new group of campers were scheduled to come in. And nothing new had happened since yesterday. She decided she led a truly boring life. And until Josh had popped up, she had never realized how boring it was. By lunchtime she could not contain herself any longer, and so she texted again.

Thanks to you I realize I lead a very boring life. What have you done to me?

He immediately replied with a smiley face emoji. Nothing else.

She didn't hear from him again until late that night, after 11 p.m. All his text said was:

You up?

Since she'd been sleeping, she didn't see it until the sun streaming in her window woke her up, just after seven o'clock. She wondered if he was okay. Or had Rosalie come to him? She searched her mind for any remnants of dreams, but none surfaced. She replied:

I am now.

No smiley face. No heart. No immediate text back. She hoped he was okay.

When she still hadn't heard from him by 6 p.m., she texted again.

Are you okay?

He replied five hours later. Once again, she was already asleep.

fuckin awesome out with my bud derrk cebelatin. lots to tell *kissy face kissy face* emojis.

When Wednesday morning came and she saw the garbled text, she considered calling him, but didn't. He'd obviously been drunk. But on a week night? Instead, she texted a thumbs-up emoji and left her phone in her bedroom while she went down to the lake. Her heart was sagging and she felt even more disconnected from him than she had since he left. Hopefully he would reply soon and explain himself.

She dragged a kayak away from the row lining the shore, grabbed a paddle resting on a nearby tree, and shoved off into the lake. She rowed out to the area where Rosalie had saved her, and she stopped paddling, allowing her kayak to drift with the mild current.

"Rosalie? I need you. Are you here?" She spoke quietly. Nothing sounded but the water lapping against the side of the fiberglass boat.

"Why? Why did you bring him to me?" she wailed, and her voice echoed against the trees lining the shore.

Silence.

"I hope you're happy!" she shouted angrily, hoping to coax a response.

After a while, Brooke paddled toward the shore, dragged the kayak back to its spot, rested the paddle on the tree, and headed wearily back to camp.

~ ~ ~

Josh's head ached, but it was nothing compared to the pain he felt in his heart. He'd gotten in shortly before midnight, after letting loose with Derek at their favorite pub, celebrating once again.

The Monday board meeting had gone great. They drilled him and questioned him on the spot. They rode him hard, and he'd had no coaching from Derek. And he aced it. In fact, he did so well they were keeping him as CEO, with a three-month probationary period. They would cease all requests for candidates and withdraw the petition for early retirement. Great news, right? Why did he feel so hollow? He wanted to share it with Brooke, but when he texted at 11 p.m., she didn't reply at all. He didn't blame her. Maybe she was sleeping and would reply more during the day.

He was correct, she'd been sleeping. But by the time she did reply he was in full swing, one meeting after another non-stop. Then he and Derek went out to celebrate and before he knew it . . . he was home. It was almost midnight and he'd just seen a text she sent around dinner time asking if he was okay. So drunk Josh proceeded to tell her how fine he was.

He cringed now, re-reading his typo-filled text, and wasn't at all surprised with her lack of an enthusiastic response. Any excitement in sharing his experience before the board on Monday, and his meeting-filled Tuesday had fizzled as he opened her text on Wednesday and saw only a thumbs-up emoji. Nothing else.

So much happened Thursday that he could not wait to share with Brooke, but her silence was paralyzing. By day's end he planned to provide a recap, to give her a head's up, but he couldn't find the words. Last minute dinner plans kept him out until after midnight and he knew she'd be sleeping. So why bother texting? He did anyway.

You up? Lots to tell.

Friday morning arrived and he still hadn't heard from her, so he spent fifteen minutes scanning through good morning gif's finding nothing that fit her. Her lack of interest in him starting his life over bothered him more than he realized it would. He wasn't the type of person to have doubts in himself, or worry about what others thought. But it was different with Brooke. It did matter. A lot.

After work he'd gone straight home, declining an invitation to the pub with a bunch of co-workers. As he sat at the island in his kitchen nursing a beer and eating a slice of pizza he'd grabbed from the corner pizzeria by his apartment, he thought about texting her again and apologizing for the drunk text. He also contemplated calling her to tell her the good news. Instead, he read through all her other texts, looking for something, anything to give him hope. There was nothing except a few polite responses and a few emojis. Maybe she wouldn't be interested in the good news after all.

It was 9 p.m., and he tried to visualize what she would be doing at this moment. Had she gotten on with life, back into the routine of Earth and Sky? If so, she'd be drumming right now. Or dancing. He closed his eyes and remembered her twisting gently around the campfire, arms lifted, hair flowing around her as she turned and undulated as if the flames had taken over her body and were directing her in their own eternal dance just for him.

Wow. When did he become a fucking poet? And so pathetic. He snapped a cap off another beer and chugged it until it was empty, then tossed his uneaten pizza in the trash can under the sink. He forced himself not to think about her body. Her curves, the soft cooing sounds she made when he pleasured her.

Pathetic.

It was then it dawned on him. He hadn't thought of Rosalie all week. He studied the wedding ring on his left ring finger, and slipped it off with a guttural sob. "I'll always love you, Rosalie," he whispered as he kissed the golden band. Slowly, he made his way into their—his—bedroom and put the ring inside Rosalie's jewelry box he'd left on her dresser.

Chapter 28

The Saturday Morning In-house Meeting brought some interesting news. The pilot adult program had been a huge success.

This information came from Dee and Doug themselves who unexpectedly popped in for a visit. The team had been gathered in the dining hall with the fireplace warding off another chilly, rainy morning when Doug and Dee's rented SUV rolled into camp and parked parallel to the porch. At first, the butterflies in Brooke's belly began to beat wildly, with the hopes it could be Josh. Within a few moments, reality stilled their wings as Dee and Doug emerged as the SUV doors swung open. Dee shrieked and tried to shield her head with her overly large Coach handbag as she dodged the raindrops and ran up the porch steps.

With most companies, surprise visits from the upper management would put everyone on guard and make them nervous. But at Earth and Sky, it was like homecoming.

"Oohhhhh!!! Look! We made it, Doug! They're still in their meeting!" Dee called to Doug who was climbing the stairs right behind her.

"Hey, everyone! Surprise!" Dee shrieked and waved her hands as she tossed her purse on the nearest table. "A fire! Excellent! It's freezing up here. We left 90-degree weather to come see ya'll!" She rushed up to the staff who had slowly started standing to greet their bosses, and began hugging each and every one.

"Hey, Dee! Hey, Doug! Have you eaten?" Kyle

welcomed them, pointing to the table offering bagels, fruit, yogurt, granola, and other easy to grab breakfast fixings.

"Great. I'm starved!" Doug followed Dee, offering bear hugs to all.

When things quieted down, Dee and Doug joined the group with their coffee and danish in hand. "Sorry to interrupt, Kyle. Please continue. We don't want to be a distraction."

"Well, actually. We were just talking about how I hadn't heard from you regarding our next session. We figured we'd gotten a bad review and were waiting to be canned." Kyle laughed at his joke, while the rest of the group twittered nervously because it wasn't far from the truth.

"Oh, wow. No need to worry. We wanted to share the good news—no, great news—in person! Five out of the six clients you worked with this time around gave you all five-star reviews. You guys knocked it out of the park. We wanted to tell you in person how awesome ya'll are." Doug spoke up, with Dee nodding in agreement beside him as she listened.

"And this is why we'd told Kyle not to give ya'll a head's up before this last retreat. Ya'll know you're our best team and our potential clients insisted you not change a thing in your program. And they-slash-we were right in not telling you. Congratulations," Dee added as she extracted a packet of envelopes from her black and white oversized handbag.

"We've been busy beavers these last few days, coordinating everything so we could present you with your bonuses and another super surprise we think you all will enjoy." Doug took the envelopes from his wife. "Thank you, darlin'," he added with a wink.

One at a time, he called out each staffer's name, thanked them, made reference to the client they'd worked with and something the client shared about their time at Earth and Sky. After acknowledging the mentors and Kyle, they turned to Alyssa and Brooke. "And finally, our sweet lil Deathwalker.

C'mere, darlin'. You too, Alyssa, we couldn't make any of this next part happen without you." Doug chuckled quietly as he held his arms outstretched, coaxing the two women to join him and Dee at the head of the table.

Brooke groaned inwardly, but outwardly she appeared composed and professional, thankful they had called up Alyssa to stand with her. Her face warmed under the attention, and she rocked from one foot to the other, anxiously wishing she could crawl under a table. Dee and Doug were generous and empathetic bosses. They were also a shrewd and cunning couple when it came to business. They rewarded their staff frequently, but with each reward came a higher level of expectation.

"Whatever you're doin', ladies, don't stop. The clients love it." Doug gave them each a bear hug, with Dee following his actions, sandwiching Alyssa and Brooke between the two of them.

"These ladies right here are the reason for our visit. Don't get me wrong, each and every one of you shines your own bright light. But Alyssa here did something with her client even the best and most expensive therapists have not been able to achieve in three years. Made someone want to live again. And we understand our Lil Deathwalker had a hand in it as well. Hm?" He turned his head to Brooke and raised his bushy eyebrows quizzically. When all she responded with was a shrug, he waggled a finger and handed her an envelope. Similarly, he handed Alyssa an envelope, and hugged them one last time before motioning them back to their seats.

"Now. By Tuesday we were getting calls from most clients who had reached out to us on behalf of the campers you worked with. And they had nothing except positive things to say about the progress those campers had made in three weeks. The conversations became so in depth I arranged a conference call with them, so we could all share our experiences and formulate a plan to move forward."

Kyle crooked his head, his brow knitted in confusion. "Move forward how?"

Brooke felt her stomach lurch as she listened to Doug present his business plan.

"Consultants! They want individualized services. They want classes on site. They want ongoing therapy, life coaching, everything ya'll do they want you to bring it to them front and center." He glanced around at their surprised faces. "Isn't this great?"

"No more Earth and Sky retreats?" Brooke's voice squeaked with the thought of leaving the Adirondacks.

"Oh, no, Brooke. We'll still keep them. But we'd expand our services and on occasion ya'll would take turns flying out to the corporations requesting additional services. They're prepared to begin with a two-year contract, paid by vouchers quarterly."

"And this was discussed with . . .?" Kyle asked quietly, clearly not as enthusiastic with this proposal as Dee and Doug were.

"The five clients who paid for the campers here for the last three weeks. The majority were board presidents, along with some CEO's and other board members. Of the two families who had sent loved ones here, only one family was present. They are not requesting consulting services in a contract form. Rather, they've asked for planned retreat dates—one every six months for their whole staff and family." Doug was beginning to look perplexed with the lack of enthusiasm meeting his proposal.

"I'm not getting the reaction I thought I would." He sat down, with Dee beside him, addressing the otherwise quiet group of employees before him.

"I like it up here," Brooke offered quietly. "I don't want to leave. Ever."

Kyle and Alyssa exchanged a glance, which Brooke intercepted, and it riled her because she didn't like the feeling of pity it carried.

"Brooke, darlin'. It's not healthy living here year-round. You need a break, too, sometimes," Dee spoke softly and Alyssa nodded.

"You all need a break. Which is why we didn't set up another set of campers 'til next month. We decided to give you all a percentage of the profit made from this last session. Check your envelopes. Consider it a thank-you bonus," Doug explained, leaning his elbows on the table and clasping his hands together before continuing.

"The rest of your bonus is in the form of a field trip. We're going down to New York City to meet the clients so they can get to know you better and hear what you all can offer-compliments of Quirkyflirt. Since it smells like work and feels like work, and actually will be work, your expenses will be paid, and you'll be on the clock when you're meeting with everyone."

He slapped a hand down on the table after receiving no response at all. "We thought you guys would enjoy the chance to get out of the sticks and hit the city." He scratched his head in confusion, looking at his wife, prodding her to say something.

"We've found this magnificent Historic Inn and spa in the heart of Greenwich Village. It's got a salt spa, wine tasting around the clock, all organically grown food, temples for meditation and worship . . . Everything you could want," she said, her voice sagging with confusion at the apparent lack of enthusiasm expressed.

"Sounds like fun. And exciting. And a chance of a lifetime, thanks Doug! I think it's taking everyone a few minutes to process. Right, gang?" Kyle fought to find enthusiasm as he spoke the words his bosses were expecting to hear.

"The hotel arrangements and itinerary can be found with your bonus checks in your envelopes," Dee added.

"When do we leave?" Mandy spoke, excitement stirring in her words.

"Tomorrow. Crazy, right?" Doug looked at Dee and back to the crowd. "If ya'll don't have any questions, we're going to head over to our cabin to rest up. We've been traveling since Wednesday when we flew into JFK to meet with the Quirkyflirt board and CEO. Great company there. Nothing but good things to say about ya'll."

"Oh, by the way. The presentation, Doug," Dee said, tugging on Doug's arm.

"Oh, yeah. Your So Long Sunday presentation, Brooke. Bring it when we head downstate. We'll be showing it at our little shindig. Thanks, darlin'." He leaned over and pecked Dee on her forehead. "Now. I need a rest. If ya'll need us we'll be in our cabin. Thinkin' we'll head into town for dinner tonight. What ya'll say?"

Everyone murmured their approval, still appearing a bit shell shocked with the news.

"Great. Can't be too late a night. We fly outta Albany at seven a.m. sharp and into LaGuardia by ten-thirty. Quirkyflirt's arranged to have their limo service pick us up and take us to our lodging. Thinking we can make dinner at what, six? Sound good?"

Kyle spoke for everyone, confirming 6 would be fine. "Do you need me to make reservations?"

"Yeah. Some place good. How's about the Mexican place? I hear they make the best burritos this side of South of the Border. And I'm dying for a margarita."

With his comment, Brooke snapped to attention and scanned the room, half-expecting Rosalie to materialize. She waited for the telltale goosebumps to cover her body. If Rosalie were there, she remained hidden.

"Mexican it is." Kyle saluted Doug, and the couple waved farewell to everyone and headed to the door. Once their SUV turned out of the camp base and headed toward Dee and Doug's cabin, Kyle slunk down onto the bench and stared everyone in the eye and spoke. "I swear I had no clue. I'm sorry, guys. Really."

"Looks like Baby Blues pulled some strings for you, hmm, Brooke?" Mandy grinned and winked at Brooke, who responded by closing her eyes and shaking her head furiously.

"I don't want to go, Kyle. Please." Brooke's voice was a whisper as she pleaded softly.

"We don't really have a choice, Brooke. I'm sorry." He lifted his shoulders helplessly.

"Don't you want to see your CEO?" Mandy poked at her again and Brooke really wasn't sure how to handle her chiding.

"As a matter of fact, no. I don't think he has anything to do with this or I believe he would have given me a heads up. Or at least some indication he wanted to . . . see me." Brooke hesitated and recalled the Thursday morning text she'd ignored, which now left knots in her gut. She thought he wanted to brag about his job and his life and how everything was coming up roses, so she ignored it. She needed to get on with her life, a life that was never going to include Josh Quinn, so why drag this out?

She looked at Mandy and continued. "Which he hasn't. So, it's done. Final word." Brooke stood up and walked away from the crowd, running out into the cool, cleansing rain.

Chapter 29

"Did you look at the itinerary, Kyle?" Alyssa asked once they had settled into the brown leather high back seats on the E&S bus taking them to Albany Airport the next morning.

Brooke sat behind the two, eyes closed, hoping to get a nap in before they arrived at the airport. It was only 4:30 in the morning, and her co-workers had all sacked out sporadically throughout the bus.

"Uh-huh." Kyle's voice sounded unenthusiastic at best. Brooke didn't bother suppressing a grin since it was so dark no would see it anyway.

"We're doing a tour of Quirkyflirt Headquarters tomorrow, and having lunch with their board and CEO. Did you see?" Alyssa whispered. With the bus so silent Brooke couldn't help but hear her.

"Yeah. I saw." Kyle yawned.

"Did Brooke say anything to you?"

"No."

"Do you think I should say something to her?"

"No."

The butterflies had awoken with Alyssa's news. Brooke struggled to calm her mind, wishing she had not deliberately avoided looking at the itinerary. All she could think about was having to face Josh again. *Ugh.* After she blew him off by not texting.

"I think we should tell her. She needs to be forewarned."

"No."

"Why not?" Alyssa asked, enunciating her consonants in agitation.

"Because she can hear you just fine," Brooke whispered back as she leaned over the seat between them.

"Oh, geez, Brooke! You startled me. I thought you were sleeping. Did you see the itinerary?"

"No. I really didn't have a chance to even open the envelope. I brought it with me to review at the hotel." She continued whispering, even though she was sure everyone on the bus who was awake could hear them.

"We're getting a tour of Quirkyflirt tomorrow morning. And it looks like they're hosting a full-day event, starting with breakfast, followed by a tour, and lunch. The whole afternoon is open, then there's some fancy dinner. Are you sure you didn't know about any of this?" Alyssa peered over the back of her seat to address Brooke, who sat clenching her hands tightly in her lap.

"No," she whispered. "I had no idea."

"Well. I'm glad I gave you a heads up." Alyssa turned around and inclined her head against the back of the seat. "I'm going to try to snooze for a bit before we get to the airport."

Brooke woke her cell phone with a flick of her wrist and searched the skimpy thread of texts she and Josh shared this past week. He hadn't replied to her thumbs-up until Thursday mid-morning. Then all he'd texted was that he had lots to tell, making her wonder if he was all right, or if he'd been fired, or retired early. Or quit. Or none of the above, since according to Dee and Doug, Quirkyflirt was overly impressed by Earth and Sky.

Rubbing her thumb over her iPhone's home button, Brooke contemplated texting Josh. She flip-flopped with the idea until finally, right before they arrived at the airport's passenger unloading area, she texted. It was Sunday morning, nearly 5:30. He couldn't possibly be awake.

You up?

She deliberately worded it this way, to mimic his similar texts earlier in the week. She put her phone to sleep and slipped it into her purse, ready to go through the motions all passengers at airports do before boarding. After handing over her baggage, she slung her camera and computer bag over her shoulder and headed to their gate. Dan and Alyssa walked beside her as she brought up the rear. Shoes off, computer out, through the metal detector, and next thing she knew they were boarding their flight and in the air. By the time she had a chance to check her phone there was no cell service.

It was only after landing at LaGuardia and were waiting to disembark Brooke was finally able to retrieve her texts. There were six. All from Josh.

I am now.
Are you ok?
;)
Seriously. Are you okay?
Did you need something?
Please let me know you're okay.

His last text was timestamped thirteen minutes ago. Brooke stared at the messages, and her heart sang. While he was definitely being cheeky in the first three, his concern was evident in his last three, she analyzed. Grinning at her phone, she prepared to reply, when the flight attendant announced passengers could begin to disembark. Her witty comeback would have to wait.

~ ~ ~

Josh could not stop checking his phone. He sat outside on his terrace, basking in the morning sun as it shimmered and reflected off the Hudson River. He'd drank four cups of coffee and read the *Sunday Times* front to back twice—including the Funnies and the Long Island section. Walking around in his boxer briefs and tee shirt, he delayed his shower so he wouldn't miss her text. Nothing came through.

He felt like a teenager waiting for his prom date to finish getting ready. By now Quirkyflirt's limo would have picked Brooke and the Earth and Sky crew up from LaGuardia. It was nearly noon.

Pleasantly surprised was an understatement of how he felt when he woke up and found Brooke's text, mirroring his from a few days ago. So, he decided to play along and responded with the same messages she had sent him earlier in the week. What did it get him? Crickets. Her lack of a reply made him nervous, wondering if something had happened to her on the way to the airport.

Was she angry? Was she excited about seeing him? It was amazing how fate had taken charge of their lives. After her noncommittal and unenthusiastic responses to his initial attempt to remain in contact, Josh thought he was never going to see her again. Wednesday he'd met with Dee and Doug, his board, and the clients who'd hired Earth & Sky to work with his fellow campers. Thursday, Derek informed him the board had held another special meeting and voted to contract with E&S based on his review and the evaluation he had passed with flying colors on Wednesday.

He thought about calling her, but opted instead to text her the great news. Which she never answered. Then he remembered his drunk text. Groaning, he was pretty sure she was done with him. What was her reaction when she was told they'd be seeing one another again? He hoped she was as happy as he was, so they'd have a second chance at trying to make *something* work. Even if she didn't want to see him again, who wouldn't jump on an all-expenses paid trip to New York City, compliments of Quirkyflirt?

It was going to be interesting to see how they got along on his turf. She'd made it clear she wasn't a city girl. How could you not love Manhattan? He wanted to whisk her off her feet and paint the town. He wondered if she'd ever seen the Statue of Liberty or the Freedom Tower or Empire State Building? He made a mental note to check Madison Square Garden's line up to see who was playing this week. Maybe he could take them all to a concert at MSG.

In reality, all he wanted to do was make love with her again. Just one more time.

He checked his cell phone. Nothing.

What if their plane had crashed? No. A plane crash was not an option. He refused to even go there. Fate could not be so cruel. More realistically, it would have made the news by now. He wondered if maybe she'd chosen not to come? Maybe this was why she was not responding. Finally, he couldn't take not knowing anymore.

Where are you?

And the moment he hit send, a text came through.

I'm okay. Are you okay?

His heart surged with the synchronicity of the moment. They had texted one another at the same time. If that wasn't a sign, what was?

~ ~ ~

Brooke stared at the text alert popping up on her phone a milli-second after she'd sent hers.

Where am I? What does he mean? Specifically, the address? Or general location? Or did he think she was supposed to show up somewhere else?

Heading to lunch. You?

Feeling giddy, Brooke glanced up at her co-workers sprawled out in the 20-seater, white leather interior Hummer limousine chauffeuring them to the hotel compliments of Quirkyflirt. It was ironic, and probably not coincidental, Quirkyflirt used Hummers for their company vehicles. Was this the kind of sense of humor Josh had? She giggled and shook her head and said aloud, "I can't believe they gave us a Hummer."

Dan passed a guarded look at her as the meaning of her words registered. "Where's your mind at?" he snickered. One by one her co-workers joined in until finally Brooke was laughing as well.

"I wonder how many hummers they have?" Rob asked, a cheeky look to his eyes. Again, more laughter.

"And do all their employees have to have Hummers in order to work there, or at least like them?" This question came from a very pink-faced Mandy, who had a hard time asking it between her peals of laughter as she gasped for air.

"Probably just the men," Cara added with a snort.

"Wow, guys, are you all overtired or what? I'm more excited about getting to my hotel room than I am about this vehicle," Alyssa said, staring openly at Dan. "Hummer or no hummer."

Dan shot her a very quick and subtle wink which did not go unnoticed by the other passengers.

Brooke's phone buzzed, distracting her from the game Alyssa and Dan were playing.

I mean where are you, location wise.

Still caught up in the raunchy mood of her co-workers, Brooke replied:

*I'm enjoying your Hummer. *Kissy face**

Immediately her phone buzzed.

*Do you want me to come join you? I wouldn't mind enjoying my Hummer with you. *Kissy face**

Oh, my goddess. What did I do? Brooke thought, her face flaming hot. He wanted to join her. With his own Hummer.

I meant I'm in the limo your company provided us. Sorry for the confusion.

He replied in nanoseconds.

I knew exactly what you meant.

Great. Now she felt ridiculous. Her cheeks were still burning as she chastised herself for trying to flirt. Never flirt with a professional flirter. Especially the CEO of a business called Quirkyflirt.

While she contemplated her way out of the mess she'd created, he texted again.

Would you like me to see you for lunch? I can meet you wherever. Hummer-free.

Her thumbs flew over her screen.

Are you allowed? Besides, it's Sunday. You shouldn't be working.

Josh again replied without hesitation. *Am I allowed? *smiley face emoji* I own the company. And I wouldn't be working, I'd be seeing you.*

And then, before she could reply, another text came through.

I miss you.

"Oh dear," Brooke said aloud to no one in particular. Of course, Mandy jumped on it.

"Lemme guess. Baby blues is texting you again."

If Brooke's cheeks weren't hot enough, now they were about to burst into flames. "He wants to join us for lunch."

"Awesome, Brooke! Ask him for a place in Greenwich Village and we'll meet him there. I liked him. He was cool." Dan called out as he casually placed his arm along the back of the seat behind Alyssa.

Everyone says yes.

Josh replied: *I'm not asking everyone. I'm asking about you. Do you want me to join you?*

Brooke was having a hard time admitting she wanted him to come with them, so she ignored his question.

We don't know where to go. Dan asked if you could recommend a place in the Village.

A few minutes later the driver called back over the intercom. "Mr. Quinn requested I take you to the Loring

Place. It's near the hotel you'll be staying at, in Washington Square. It's American cuisine. Does this accommodate everyone's food preferences?"

Brooke received one final text as the driver was speaking.

Robert has directions to take you to a place near your hotel. Enjoy your lunch. See you tomorrow.

Chapter 30

There was a buzz of excitement flowing through the Earth and Sky team the following morning, as they walked into the Quirkyflirt lobby and waited patiently at the main desk for the receptionist to finish a phone call.

"Why, hello! You have *got* to be the Earth and Sky gurus! Am I correct?" A tall woman with broad shoulders dressed in a periwinkle blazer and skirt stood up with open arms and exclaimed, "Welcome to Quirkyflirt! My name is Skye, and I use they/them pronouns. Now if you all could sign our guestbook; I'll give you your name tags. Put the name you like to go by and the pronouns you prefer, okay? I designed them myself, I hope you like them!" Skye slid a sleek pale purple and teal guest book toward Dee and Doug, who stood first in line at the desk.

"Well, hello to you, Skye. It's a pleasure to meet you. What great hospitality." Doug spoke as he scribbled his name on the first line. Taking a blank name tag he wrote, 'Doug,' and following Skye's directions, 'he/him/his' below it. "Like this?" he asked Skye, who beamed at him in affirmation. After handing the pen to his wife, he selected two purple and teal lanyards for his and Dee's nametags. He offered one to Dee after she handed the pen to Kyle. One by one the team followed suit until they were all adorned with their lanyards.

"Great! Now. Follow me to the board room and I'll get you set up with coffee. Is anyone hungry? We've got a great assortment of goodies fresh from The Doughnuttery down the road. They are WORLD FAMOUS for their doughnuts! We also have the BEST bagels you can get in Manhattan, from Jerry's Bagels on 13th Street. You have to try one, even if you already had breakfast."

The team had congregated at their hotels' restaurant at 7:30 that morning, filling up with pancakes, eggs, waffles, and coffee. Lots of coffee. It was a little after nine o'clock now, and Brooke was so anxious about seeing Josh again she felt as though she would throw up with the thought of trying to eat anything else. She offered an exaggerated grimace at Mandy, whispering, "I feel like I'm going to puke I ate so much at breakfast."

Echoing those same sentiments with a giggle, Mandy added, "I definitely want to try a New York bagel. I want to hear what everyone raves about. A bagel is a bagel, no?"

Skye peered over at Mandy and in a stage-whisper answered, "No. To even suggest such a thing is sacrilege."

The group chuckled collectively as Mandy's face turned pink. "Sorry. Didn't mean to offend anyone."

Brooke was relieved Mandy didn't whisper a different sort of gaffe, about Josh, as she had been teasing her all morning. Knowing now how voices traveled in this building, she hoped Mandy would be more careful with her thoughts.

"This way, guys." Skye led them to the elevator, which brought them to the twelfth-floor lobby. Opposite the elevator, Skye opened a teal door adorned with geometric shapes and took note of their names and their faces as each team member filed past.

"There are printed place cards for everyone, so please find your seats. First, help yourselves to some coffee and tea and some noshes. Have fun! I'll see you all again later for the tour!" Skye closed the door, leaving the Earth and Sky team looking around the room paneled by floor to ceiling glass windows on three sides. A garden terrace, accessible by doors on every wall, boasted lush plants, comfortable-looking couches, tables and chairs, and a magnificent panoramic view of Manhattan.

As Brooke took in her surroundings, her confidence began to shrink. There was no way, absolutely no way, she and Josh could ever find enough common ground to mean something to one another. What could he ever see in her with a lifestyle like . . . this?

She searched the room and found other men and women dressed in suits milling about with ceramic teal and purple coffee mugs in hand. No one was sitting yet. Instead, they mingled around making chitchat and enjoying the view and fare.

Quietly, she found her place card situated next to a Quirkyflirt notepad and pen, and slipped her purse on the seat. Also placed by the notepad were three business cards belonging to Jadyn M. Tremont, Derek P. Hendricks, and Joshua A. Quinn.

Looking around the room, she decided she did not want to make small talk with anyone, so she walked over to the coffee station and poured herself a mug of steaming hot coffee. Dan and Alyssa were talking with Kyle, while Rob, Paulie, Mandy, and Cara were milling over the doughnuts and bagels while filling their plates. Dee and Doug had started a conversation with four other men and women by the coffee station. Feeling totally out of sorts, Brooke found her seat, took her iPhone out of her purse, and headed to the terrace, via the closest double French doors.

She breathed deep the cool morning air, surprised with how different it smelled. Air wasn't just air around here, even from the terrace topping a 12-story building. It smelled of bacon and fresh baked bread, with a slight hint of sea water, and car exhaust. And, with a wrinkle of her nose, she picked out . . . trash. How she could so carefully decipher those unique scents was beyond her understanding.

She sipped her coffee, standing by the ledge, wondering how anyone could live and work in such chaos. Could she relocate here to be with someone if she loved them? Forget

Josh. Generally speaking. She thought hard about what it would take to move to the city. Finally, she shook her head dismissing the notion. All the money in the world could not make her a city girl. Even growing up in California, she'd lived close to the mountains, skiing in the winter, hiking in the summer. The coast was not too far either, and there she enjoyed many a late-night beach party, ending with bonfires burning until the early morn.

No. She was not a city girl. And would never be.

She checked her cell phone again, hoping for something from Josh. The phone remained silent. She hadn't heard from him since his last text about the restaurant the day before.

"Brooke," Dan called from the door. "We're going to be starting in a few minutes."

Tipping her mug and emptying the remnants of her brew, Brooke took one last deep cleansing breathe, well as cleansing as Manhattan air could be, and steadied her nerves. All she had to do was listen. And smile politely. And get through this day one moment at a time.

As she came in through the doors, she saw Dan was correct about starting time. She was the last person to be seated as a tall man with a close-cropped cut, dark brown eyes, and form-fitting gray suit stood at the head of the board room and asked for everyone's attention.

She slipped into her seat and waited. She'd missed his introduction, and every word coming out of his mouth was a blur. He seemed like a fast talker, someone she would not give a second thought to if she'd seen him in a bar or at a social gathering. The energy surrounding him was brackish, where Josh's was golden, even when he was at his most depressed and lost state.

As this man spoke, Brooke likened him to a snake oil salesman, and her stomach knotted tight. She *did not* like him.

"So, welcome to Quirkyflirt. I'd like to hand it over now to our Director of Communications, Jadyn Tremont." He sat in one of the last two empty leather swivel seats at the head of the table. Brooke noted, according to his place card, this was the so-called best friend and board president who had threatened Josh with early retirement if he didn't experience a major transformation at Earth and Sky. She wrinkled her nose and glanced at the sole empty seat. Josh Quinn's place card glared at Brooke and her heart dropped as she wondered if Josh was not going to make an appearance after all. Derek scribbled something on the pad located next to his place card, and pushed it in front of Jadyn. She read the note, nodded, and began.

"Hiiii, everyone." Jadyn gave a little dip and wave of her hand. She was beautiful, with glowing cinnamon-colored skin, and long, thick honey brown dreads cascading down her back and over her shoulders. She wore a golden short-sleeved tunic, leaving her bronze skin bare and displaying gold bangle bracelets covering two-thirds of her left forearm. They jingled when she spoke, gesturing with her hands. "Let's start by taking a moment to go around the table and tell a bit about who we are and what we do," she said in a singsong, lilting voice.

She prodded the room with a nod, glancing around as she waited for everyone to confirm they were all on board. "Yes? No? Everyone comfortable with sharing? Hope so! I'll start. I'm Jadyn Tremont. And as Derek said, I'm Quirkyflirt's Director of Communications. I use the pronouns she/her/hers and I've been with Quirkyflirt for, oh, I don't know, I think it's been what, ten years, Derek? Aside from Josh, and Derek here, and of course Marybelle, the Director of Finance, I'm considered senior staff since I've been here so long. I love it here, wouldn't want to be anywhere else." She offered a wide, sincere smile and turned to Derek, lifting her shoulders slightly. Turning back to the crowd seated around the table, she paused and thought for a quick minute.

"Does anyone want to get coffee or tea before we get started? Did you all get to try those delicious doughnuts? Don't they melt in your mouth? Right?" She nodded again, encouraging people to speak up in agreement. "Well." She glanced back at Derek, who grimaced.

"Well, I guess if no one wants a refill we'll go ahead and get started. How about we begin over here," she pointed to her left, "and tell our stories, including our—" Jadyn stopped speaking as the door to her right opened slowly and quietly.

Framed in the doorway, looking as handsome and powerful as ever, stood Josh. Brooke froze, and forgot to breathe as she watched him scan the room with a frown, his eyes flitting from face to face until he settled on her. And she breathed, and for a moment all was well in Manhattan.

"Hello, everyone! What a great turnout. Thanks for joining us today." He took his seat next to Derek, the lines of his deep-gray suit jacket emphasizing his broad shoulders and well-defined arms. "Please continue, Jadyn."

Another warm, sincere smile flashed across Jadyn's face as she directed everyone to share their information. "Let's start with you, ah . . . Joe!" She read the place card of the man sitting to her left, and after Joe shared his brief bio, one by one people provided their names, the companies they were affiliated with, how long they'd held their current positions, what their title was, and any other information they felt inclined to share, from their preferred pronouns, to their favorite color, or the name of their cat.

If Skye had been the one to lay the place cards, they had done so with the specific intent to mix everyone up as much as possible, leaving Brooke flanked by two strangers—BB, the sandy-haired young man serving as assistant director to Jadyn, and Rose, board president of the philanthropic group who had funded Renee's stay at Earth and Sky.

Feeling totally out of place, Brooke wanted only to be nestled between two of her co-workers, preferably Dan and Alyssa, whom she noted sat together, as did Dee and Doug.

As everyone introduced themselves, Brooke matched their face with their place card, since it was hard to see their name tags from a distance. She jotted down names and organizations, and tried hard to remember which details belonged with which face and name. It was difficult to retain anything with her brain continually shouting, "Josh is here." She couldn't stop stealing a glance at him, at least once a minute. But his attention remained on each individual as they spoke, making them the sole focus for the moment.

In addition to the Earth and Sky team, there were a smattering of employees from Quirkyflirt, along with four CEO's and four board presidents from each of the companies or organizations who had hired Earth and Sky to work with the other clients who had joined Josh. Everyone except Ned, the cult survivor, and any representatives for him were present. When BB, the Assistant Director of Communications with Quirkyflirt sitting next to Brooke finished speaking, it was her turn.

Not exactly someone well-polished at engaging with audiences, Brooke paused for a minute to collect her wits. "My name is Brooke," she began softly, stopping abruptly when a young woman near the front spoke up and interrupted her.

"Can you speak louder? I can't hear you."

With a lick of her lips and a deep breath, Brooke began again. "My name is Brooke, Brooke Meadows. And I've been with Earth and Sky for three years. And, um, I'm the resident photographer." She smiled faintly, dipped her head and turned to the person to her left.

Phew. She peered over at Josh and noticed he had not directed his attention to the person now speaking. His eyes were focused steadily and unwaveringly on her. And only when she caught his gaze and held it, did he nod and wink before turning his attention to the person who had the floor and was sharing their story. Brooke continued taking notes until finally, it was Josh's turn to speak.

"Hello again, everyone. As most of you know, I'm Josh Quinn, founder and Chief Executive Officer of Quirkyflirt. And it is so good to have each of you here today." He trailed his sights around the table, pausing momentarily on Brooke before completing the cycle. "Quirkyflirt began thirteen years ago, after I completed my Masters in computer engineering. I'd been a bit of a geek through high school and college, not very lucky with the ladies"—someone whispered 'ha' and he grinned and shook his head—"It's true, yes. The founder of the most popular, most successful dating app *in the world*"—he paused again as the Quirkyflirt staff members cheered and clapped—"was a nerd who never even went to his high school prom. So, by the time I got to college I was tired of spending every Friday night with a bunch of other online computer geeks who had no social life. So, I made an app. It was free at first. But it caught on fast. Yes, Quirkyflirt was the original swipcleft-er." More laughter sounded from the room.

"I met my wife, Rosalie, through Quirkyflirt. And with her 100 percent support we saw it grow. And grow. And grow to what it is today. Quirkyflirt brings romance and happy endings into peoples' lives. Sometimes both if they're lucky." He paused again, chuckling as people slowly caught the innuendo and chittered.

"We've won awards. We've been invited to weddings of clients who ended up getting married. We've received baby pictures from the resulting connections and relationships. Seriously. Quirkyflirt sells more than just sex. We give people the chance to fall in love, a love they can make last a lifetime if they want." He settled on Brooke, and she felt her face grow warm. When she could not hold the gaze any longer, she dropped her eyes and doodled on her pad.

"When we wrap up here, we will be taking a tour of our facility. We employ 300 people here, and nearly 1,500 throughout our five other worldwide locations. Our staff loves us. Once someone signs on here, they rarely leave. Right, Jadyn?" He turned to his communications director for confirmation, which she gave enthusiastically.

"It's a great place to work. Love the holiday bonuses!" She laughed and everyone joined in.

"Great. I'll hand the floor over now to Derek Hendricks, Quirkyflirt's board president. Derek?" Josh sat back down and waited for Derek to share his story.

"Yes. I was one of the online nerds playing Warcraft with Josh 'til all hours of the morning. When he came to me with this idea of a dating app, I believe"—he paused and pointed at Josh—"I believe you said something like, 'I think I figured out a way to get us girlfriends.' Right? It wasn't something crass a horny college guy would say. No. He was looking for the real thing. Which is what he wanted Quirkyflirt to be—a way for even the most hopeless people to find the real deal. It wasn't called Quirkyflirt at first. I think you called it, what? The Love App?" He chuckled and others in the room joined in as Josh covered his eyes with one hand and shook his head, laughing as well.

"With Josh, it was always about finding true love. With me, well, let's say I wasn't ready to settle down at yet. But he found Rosalie, and together they took off with this idea, changing it to Quirkyflirt and sinking every penny they made into its marketing and development. His dream came true, right pal? They got married, had babies. Quirkyflirt wasn't a hook-up app. It was a 'make a wish' app. It's a 'find your soulmate' app. It's not just for getting people laid. It's for getting people loved."

He paused for a second, and bit his lower lip before continuing. "And Josh did it. He found love. True love. With Rosalie, and his two daughters."

The room was so quiet you could hear the ticking of the battery-operated wall clock hanging over the door. "But then, three years ago, the unthinkable happened." He leaned over and put a hand on Josh's shoulder. "And Josh lost his whole family. Rosalie, Sophia, and Rhianna. And I lost my best mate. My cohort in crime. My warcraft warrior. For three years we here at Quirkyflirt watched him struggle to comprehend what had happened. Why Fate would take away the woman of his dreams, and his daughters."

Derek straightened up and shrugged. "No one but the man upstairs knows why. Therapists didn't. Psychologists didn't. Psychotherapists couldn't help him figure it out either. He was running out of time. Quirkyflirt was starting to falter. We needed our captain back." His voice cracked and he turned his attention to Josh. "You okay, bro?"

Josh nodded, his face set in stone. Brooke wanted to run up to him and hold him, whisper in his ear he was going to be okay. But it wasn't her place.

"When I heard from another board member about this amazing company called Earth and Sky, I reached out to Dee and Doug. I told them about Josh's dire state, and they said he was a perfect candidate for a pilot program they were putting together. And, well, the rest is history. I don't know how you guys did it, but I got my Warcraft buddy back, although we haven't played Warcraft for years. Most importantly, Quirkyflirt got their leader back. Josh wasn't the only one who was lost, and all I can say is, thank you. Thank you, Earth and Sky, for saving my mate's life."

He leaned over as Josh stood up, and the two hugged while everyone applauded.

Derek was smooth, Brooke thought, clapping lightly. She didn't trust him a bit. Not one bit.

Brooke didn't see Josh again until after the tour, as she and the rest of the Earth and Sky team waited out front for their Hummer to return.

"Hey," she heard him call out and her heart soared like one of the pigeons resting in the letter 'Q' above her head. She spun around to greet him, her heart hitching as he strolled over to Dee and Doug. "How'd it go today?"

"This is an amazing operation you've got here. Did you say five other locations around the world. And someone said you have more than 8,000 employees? I thought my eight in the USA was a lot to handle. How do you manage?" Doug crossed his arms and stroked his chin as he addressed Josh with unabated admiration.

"Delegate, delegate, delegate," he answered with authority and experience. "If you'll excuse me?"

He made his way over to Alyssa and Dan next, and Brooke watched on, a potted plant providing partial camouflage as Josh gave Alyssa a politically correct hug and shook Dan's hand. "Are you guys having fun yet?"

Alyssa nodded. "I had no idea who you were when I met you. I mean, I understood you were CEO of Quirkyflirt, but I had no idea Quirkyflirt was this huge. Not really business savvy, I guess."

He shot a quick check at Dan, then back to Alyssa. "Something tells me you guys won't be needing Quirkyflirt, eh?"

Alyssa's cheeks turned a rosy hue as she offered Dan a sidelong glance, and shrugged.

"If you'll excuse me? Nice seeing you." With a final scan of the crowd, he found Brooke by one of the stucco planters lining the walkway. They locked eyes as he sauntered toward her. "There you are. I found you," he said, his tenor matching the warmth in his eyes.

"Here I am," she replied in a breathless whisper as she searched his faced, not sure what else to say. "I had no idea."

"I'm glad you didn't. You might not have given me the help I needed. I'm surrounded by 'yes' people. I needed you and everyone up there to kick my butt. And you did. Thanks." He leaned over and gathered her up in a strong, 'I'm never letting you go again' embrace. He tilted his head ever so slightly and she felt and heard him take a deep breath.

"You smell so good. Exactly as I remembered," he murmured, finally releasing his hold. "Can I take you to this dinner I have to attend?"

"I can't. We have to work on a presentation we happen to be doing for your entire board tomorrow. Remember? Thanks a lot." She rolled her eyes in mock agitation.

"Drinks, after? You can't work all night, can you?"

"Well, we'll work 'til we're done, I guess." She felt the others watching them and a quick glance over Josh's shoulder confirmed it.

Leaning in, she informed him with a smirk, "We have an audience."

Sporting a broad grin, Josh turned around and waved at the Earth and Sky staff. He caught Brooke's eyes, mischief gleaming in his own.

"You're crazy." She scoffed and waved him away.

"Yeah, I think I am. Over you. So. Drinks? Tonight? I'll come to your hotel. Just tell me when."

Brooked watched the Hummer sidle up to the curb before her. "I have to go."

"Wait." He reached for her hand. "Not so fast. Drinks? Ten p.m.?"

She bit her lip and watched her friends now climbing into their limo, then down at their clasped hands. "Fine. Do you know where we are?"

"Yep. Washington Square in the Village. I'll text when I get there. Keep your phone on and nearby."

"Yessir, Mr. CEO. Thanks. See you later." She hesitated, unable to tear her eyes from his lips.

He leaned over and kissed her cheek softly. "Thank you."

The ride to the hotel was unbearable, filled with catcalls and whistles as Brooke tried to dispel any suggestions she and Josh were an item.

"He's very appreciative and wants to show it. Seriously, guys, knock it off." She fumbled for her phone nestled in her pocket and began swiping through Instagram.

Chapter 31

It was exactly ten o'clock on the dot when the promised text from Josh buzzed her phone alive.

I'm here.

She replied, *We're in the hotel bar.*

He responded: *I'll be right there.*

Brooke grabbed the mirror out of her makeup bag and touched up her lipstick with a quick outline and smack of her lips. She cast a furtive glance at the outfit she'd chosen—a tie-dye, short-sleeved, whimsical sundress with green, purple, and blue splatters, wondering what Josh would think and if it was too relaxed.

Everyone else had remained in the clothes they'd worn all day, a business kind of theme. She contemplated running up to her room and changing as she noted the V-neckline dipped a little lower than she remembered, and revealed a little more cleavage than she now felt comfortable showing. But, hey. She was in New York and about to see the person who'd helped her move beyond her inability to trust another man. Who, she noticed with a skittish kind of belly flop, she hadn't really spoken with since having sex more than a week ago. What if he was only looking at her as a practice fling? What if she was investing or read more into this than he was actually offering?

What if he wanted to make love again tonight? The memory of his words echoed, taunting her. *I make money offa people getting laid.*

She forced this line of thinking out of her head with a mental shove, and called out to her team who'd decided to come out for drinks and appetizers after finishing up the presentation. "Hey, guys. Listen up," Brooke called. "Josh is on his way. Please, please behave."

Mandy cleared her throat and smirked.

"Behave? You're no fun," a deep and familiar voice rumbled low in her ear from behind, warming her and sending goosebumps through her body at the same time. She whirled around in her seat as he brought his hands up to her shoulders and gave a squeeze.

Their eyes locked momentarily, before his gaze dropped lower to rest where her neckline dipped, revealing her soft curves. The way his eyes narrowed in appreciation melted Brooke into a puddle of colors. Forget drinks, she thought, wanting nothing more than to leave and take him with her. Back to her hotel room, preferably.

"You're fast. I figured you still had to park your car." She patted the leather seat beside her, unable to do anything except drink in his presence.

"I was already in the lobby when I texted you." His eyes were bright and fixed exclusively on her. He slipped off the gray suit jacket she'd seen him in at the meeting. His tie was off, she noted as he folded the jacket and placed it over an empty chair at the table next to theirs.

"Hey, everyone," he called out with a wave.

"We can't talk to you. We were told to behave," Mandy said as she stuck her tongue out at Brooke.

"So, I heard." Josh offered a slow wink at Brooke, the dimples in his cheeks etched deep in a smile meant only for her.

"Thanks, Mandy. I owe you one." She murmured to her co-worker, her eyes still glued on Josh. "Did you eat? You look like you came straight from work."

"Yeah, we had that dinner tonight. Made for a long day. Had to wrap up a few things so I just stayed late and went straight to the restaurant." He grabbed a menu and viewed the entrees as their server came over and delivered their most recent order of drinks.

"Hey, there. I'm Gigi and I've been keeping this motley crew in check for most of the night. Can I get you anything to drink? Or eat?" Gigi asked Josh, her pen poised.

"Glenmorangie smooth, please." He eyed the offerings before asking, "The kitchen's still open?"

"Yep, 'til midnight," she called out over her shoulder as she walked away.

The table resumed their buzz and became a blur as Brooke watched Josh peruse the laminated, leather-bound menu.

After a moment he lifted his eyes and asked, "Yes?"

"I can't believe we're sitting here. I have to be honest. I don't know what to do." Brooke leaned in and spoke softly.

"Do about what?" He asked, his eyes teasing.

"You know. Us." She waved a forefinger between them.

"Just let it happen. See where it goes. Who knows?" He reached out for the glass of whisky Gigi brought back from the bar. As he did so, he handed her his charge card and motioned to the table with a barely visible wave of his hand, before adding quietly, "I got this." She nodded discretely and tucked his card in her pocket.

"See?" Brooke struggled to find the words she needed to convey her emotions. Her head was spinning for two reasons. First, the easy way he offered to pay for the whole table's bill, not even knowing what they'd ordered. Secondly, most importantly . . . *Josh was not wearing his wedding band.*

"What?"

She flipped a hand toward Gigi, rubbing her thumb and two fingers together.

"Brooke. Relax. Remember. Life is for living." He raised his whiskey and eyed her nearly empty wineglass. "What are you drinking?"

"Just merlot." She couldn't say anything about the ring. She didn't even know where she would begin, so she picked up her glass as he replied.

"Drink up. We have a lot of catching up to do." He held up his glass and saluted her.

"Yeah. A whole week's worth," she said, draining her glass.

~ ~ ~

Gigi, the ever-attentive waitress who kept Brooke, Josh, and the rest of the E&S team plied with alcohol and appetizers, came up to the four diehards still sitting around their table at 3 a.m. The North Square restaurant was otherwise empty of any patrons, both those staying at the hotel as well as locals. The rest of the team had gone to bed leaving Dan, Alyssa, Brooke, and Josh to close the place down. The last hour had been spent listening to Dan talk about the Pacific Crest Trail adventure he was planning, and how it would be more fun if he had people to share it with. "Hint, hint," he said, casting a glance around the table.

"I've always wanted to try this kind of trip. We used to hike. Nothing as extensive, though," Josh began slowly, reviewing the information and photos Dan hadn't stopped sharing on his iPhone the entire time.

"Is this something you think you'd like to do, Brooke?" Josh asked, as Gigi interrupted the conversation and informed the quad the bar was closing.

"Sorry, gang. You look like you're having such a good time, I hate to tell you we're closing out the register now." She handed the receipt to Josh for his review.

"Understandable," he offered as he took the bill, reviewed it, and handed it back. "This looks fine." He waved her off as he drained the last of the amber liquid flowing into his glass for the past five hours.

Brooke eyed him and asked hesitantly, "Are you okay to drive?"

"Are you asking me to stay?" His narrowed eyes held a wicked gleam, tinged with a healthy dose of humor. And hope.

Alyssa sputtered her beer as she started laughing. "No beating around the bush there, Josh."

With a quick wink at Alyssa, he returned his full attention to Brooke, who sat speechless and unsure how to answer.

"Well. No. I mean. Yeah, no. I don't want you driving, assuming you drove? Unless you have a limo driver chauffeuring you around?" She squinted at him, her face growing warm as he laughed at her suggestion.

In mock dismay, he asked, "Seriously? You think I would use a chauffeur? C'mon."

"Things were just getting fun!" Dan pointed to his half-full IPA. "It's still cold!"

Gigi came back and handed Josh the receipt and his card, waiting for him to sign. After calculating the tip, he handed it back and asked her if it was possible to buy one last round to go. "We'll be taking it up to my room."

"Sure," she said, as her face lit up after looking at the tip. "Yes, sir, Mr. Quinn. I'll have room service bring it up."

"Actually, I have to get a room yet," he said as he looked pointedly at Brooke. When she remained silent, he added, "Let me go check in now." He addressed the other three and asked, "What do you say? One more for the road?"

Brooke, Alyssa, and Dan exchanged looks, then Dan reached out and fist-bumped Josh. "You're the man!"

"You realize it's after three? Some of us have to work," Alyssa said as she checked her smart phone, "in five hours."

"The presentation won't start 'til I'm there. And we'll all ride over together." Josh chuckled as he pushed away from the table. "Don't worry. I've got connections."

After he was out of earshot, Alyssa whispered, "This is not the man we met a month ago."

"Nope. Definitely not." Brooke chewed her lower lip as she watched Josh saunter away, her belly full of the butterflies she'd thought had been left back at camp.

~ ~ ~

Dan and Alyssa stood up as if on cue, both calling it a night as Dan reached out to shake Josh's hand. "This was great, man. Next time I buy."

"Deal. Thanks. I needed this," Josh said as Alyssa led Dan to the door. After it had clicked closed behind the departing couple, he asked Brooke, "You want me to walk you to your room?"

The hungry look in his eye told her the only place he wanted to take her was to bed. Brooke curled deeper into the corner of the linen cream-colored love seat, situated at the far end of the room, by the table Josh and Dan had sat at exchanging hiking stories earlier.

"Or do you want to stay here with me tonight?"

Sitting up straight, Brooke answered quickly, "You should probably walk me to my room. I—I . . ." her voice trailed off. The fact of the matter was simple. She *did* want to be with him tonight, just not here. She looked around his suite, which was very similar to hers, although reversed in layout, with two king-sized beds instead of her one queen, and a sitting room off to the side. The decor was identical, a paisley print of rusty autumn hues. But there were no personal items, nothing saying someone was staying here. It felt cold and detached.

"We don't have to do anything. I just want to talk. I don't want tonight to end." He searched her face, his expression earnest and genuine.

"Hm. I remember what happened the last time you didn't

want the night to end." She drew her knees up and hugged them close.

"Yeah. You took advantage of me." He tossed back without blinking.

"Oh. Oh, my." She shot him a cheeky grin, bit her lower lip, and looked away as he laughed outright.

"Honestly, Brooke. I can't stop thinking about you."

She hugged her knees harder as he took a seat on the edge of the bed facing her. "You don't say, huh?" Her voice grew husky.

He patted the bed and crooked his finger toward her. "C'mere."

"Are you going to try something funny?" She dipped her head and studied him through her lashes as she accepted his invitation and joined him on the bed.

"Only if you want me to," he said as he closed his eyes and leaned in, brushing her mouth in a brief, questioning caress. He paused, unmoving, waiting for her consensual response.

Her answer came without hesitation as she gave a long peck and pulled away. "I don't want the night to end, either."

There it was. The two looked at one another, neither one knowing what to do next.

Inhaling a deep breath, he spoke. "Just for clarification. No mixed messages. I don't want to just talk for the next four hours. Or sleep." He lifted a hand and tucked a strand of hair behind her ear. His thumb lingered on her tender skin, caressing her cheek as he searched her eyes with an intensity hot enough to ignite an Earth and Sky bonfire.

"I think I need to talk a bit before we 'don't sleep'?" She turned into his palm, planting slow, sensuous kisses along his heart line, down his life line. She trailed the tip of her tongue along his thumb and kissed the end of it, her eyes never leaving his.

He cupped her face and claimed her lips thoroughly, whispering her name. His hands smoothed down over her shoulders, and down her arms. He cradled her hand in his, bringing it to rest against his lips. "What do you want to talk about?" he murmured, giving the same attention to her palm she had paid to his. While he held her eyes and waited for her response, he placed slow, light kisses as he flecked his tongue over her skin.

His lips trailed along her fingertips, as she caught her breath and struggled to speak. "You make it hard to remember," she chuckled and exhaled, wondering if the a/c had automatically shut off.

"Hey. We're even. You make it hard. Period."

She loved the way his eyes gleamed when he was naughty and she threw him a questioning glance, lowering her hand tentatively, searching for proof. "Oh, goddess. You were serious."

He nodded. "See what you do to me?"

Wide-eyed, she grinned. "Yeah, but from a kiss?"

"I told you I've been thinking about you all week." He nuzzled his nose against her neck, the day's stubble lightly shading his face sending shivers through her core.

"When you said you were thinking of me, I didn't realize you meant 'thinking' thinking. So much for appealing to the scholarly aspects of this relationship." She felt herself beginning to babble, recognizing her defense mode. Chatter away or crack jokes, best way to kill the mood.

"I can be scholarly. Just not at three a.m." He straightened up, resting his hands against his thighs. "So, what's up?"

He'd read her mood change; she could tell by the quick way he'd cooled off.

Needing more space, she left his side and moseyed around the room, looking in the empty drawers, picking up the remote, laying it back down, checking the room thermometer and clicking it down a notch.

"I'm not sure how to put it into words."

"Look. We don't have to do anything. I thought—" He lifted his hands in confusion. "I'm sorry."

"No, don't be sorry. I do want this. I just . . ." She closed her eyes, took a steadying breath, then focused her gaze on his reflection in the mirror hanging over the dresser. "We barely texted all week."

"We were both guilty of not communicating. But that's fine. I'll take you back to your room." He stood up, adjusted his pants by tugging at the waist as he walked toward the door.

"Stop, Josh! You're not listening," she called out as he brushed by her.

"Brooke. You're not telling me what you want or what's wrong. I don't know what to think. We're together again. In a hotel room. And I don't know what you're thinking or what you want. It's not me not listening. It's you not saying what you want." He came to her side, keeping his hands to himself. "I thought you were feeling it too."

"I guess I'm tired. And overwhelmed." She rubbed her forehead and closed her eyes, unable to look at him.

"I went too fast. I'm sorry." He opened his arms, offering a hug and she went to him.

"It's just . . ." She mumbled into his chest, heady with his scent. Bringing her arms around him she held on for dear life. "Your ring."

"My ring? My wedding ring." He spoke into the crown of her head. "I took it off. First time in three years." He rubbed his lips against her hair.

"Does this mean . . . you're dating again?" Her voice squeaked and she felt like she was going to throw up. Still, she held her ground.

"Ahhhh. No, Brooke. I see. No. I'm not dating again." He held her at arms-length, a look of sympathetic amusement painting his features. "You're seriously worried about me dating again?"

Unable to bear his scrutiny, she avoided his gaze, feeling so foolish and so immature, and so unworldly.

"You're this mega-rich, mega-corporate CEO dude who can have any woman in the world now. And I'm little old Brooke who can no way compete with all of this." She twirled around the room. "What the hell am I doing here?"

She watched as his CEO brain clicked into gear, analyzing the issue, then figuring out a solution. Isn't this what CEO's did? She got her answer as he walked to the table.

"Let's work through this, so we can get past it and move on, okay?" He motioned for her to take a chair, as he sat down at the other side of the table. She joined him.

"We both did a lot of healing this past month, no?" He folded his hands in front of him as she nodded. "You as well as me? I mean, what we did last week, we did together, no? And making love with me was as . . . monumental an event for you as it was for me, no?"

"Mm-hm."

"So, I can assume the same thing you're assuming, I take it, about me?"

"What do you mean?" Her face scrunched up with her question.

"Are you going to start dating? You probably have the guys lined up at your door." He leaned back, his expression serious and questioning.

"Don't be ridiculous."

"Exactly." The two sat unmoving for a few moments as his conclusion sank in.

The butterflies in her belly were gone. They had now all fluttered up her esophagus to her lungs and were batting wildly around her heart.

When she failed to answer, he did. "It's late. Why don't

we get some sleep?" He motioned to the beds. "You can stay here. Or you can go back to your room. Either is fine."

"Sooooo. We're done?" Her confusion had to be evident. It was late, she was tired. She wasn't understanding. "What are you saying?"

"You're so adorable and I'm so tired. And I don't want to do anything you're going to regret in the morning. I'll wait for as long as you need me to," he reached across the table and found her hand, entwining his fingers around hers. "And don't worry. I won't date."

She inspected his room. It was so impersonal. "I think I want to go back to my room."

His shoulders sank slightly, as he wearily consented. "Sure. I'll walk you." He grabbed his suit jacket, pocketed his extra room key, and followed her toward the door.

~ ~ ~

Josh held Brooke's hand, their fingers woven tightly, as they worked through the maze of hallways, as the elevator rose upward to the next floor, then down and around a bend until finally, they stood in front of her room. He watched her raise her key fob, slipping it into the slot above the door handle, and releasing it when the light flashed green.

"You want to come in?" she asked, after stepping over the threshold, while he remained in the hall.

"It's late." He glanced past her, noticing she'd left the light on. The ironing board was out, clothes had been piled on a chair, the television had been left on. "Are you sharing a room with the girls?"

"No. C'mon in. I leave the TV on so people think there's someone in here. Something I got used to doing back home." He followed her in as she tossed her purse and key on the dresser. "Sorry for the mess. It makes it feel homier."

He followed her in and allowed the door to swing closed behind with a solid thud. This could go two ways, he thought, watching her slip her shoes off. He followed her actions, and toed his way out of his gray leather Magnanni dress shoes, nudging them up against the wall.

She glanced at his shoes, then up at his face, and moved to the refrigerator tucked behind an armoire door. "You want something to drink?"

"You got any water?" He followed her, stopping when he reached her side as she handed him a bottle of Evian. He unscrewed the cap, downed a long gulp, then held it out to her. "Want some?"

"I can grab my own, thanks. After all. Dee and Doug are paying for this." She pointed to a sheet listing the prices of the refreshments and basket of goodies offered with each room. "Ten bucks a pop is crazy. Hey, it's not my penny."

He waited until she had grabbed a bottle and taken a drink, watching as her eyes slipped around the room, settling on the bed. Not moving, he waited until she was seated, legs curled up as she leaned against the pillows propped against the head board. Finally, she patted the mattress and crooked her finger, looking like a deer in the headlights. He went over to her, sitting beside her. A glance at the clock radio by the bed said 4:07.

"It's late. Or early, depending on how you want to look at it." He moved his chin in the direction of the digital clock.

"The night still hasn't ended. So, we're good. Right?" She took another drink of water, and set the bottle down.

"Scoot over," he said, prodding her with an elbow.

After they were sitting side by side, his arm curled around her as she rested her head on his chest, she spoke. "I felt like a prostitute in your room. I'm sorry."

"A prostitute."

"Yeah. Weird. I know. There it is."

"And how do you feel now?"

"Like I want to make love with you." She lifted her face up, licking her lips with her invitation.

Chapter 32

"You realize it's after four." He nose-kissed her, his eyes sultry with sleep and desire.

"I know," she offered meekly, sounding apologetic as she rubbed his nose back.

He made a throaty sound, sinking his hands into her arms as he gently guided her onto the bed, claiming her with a lingering, searching kiss.

Toes curled, pulse quickened, her heart pummeled as he lifted his head and studied her through veiled eyes. "Is this what you want?" His words came softly, his baby blues delving deep into her soul. "And this?" He drew the tip of his tongue along the hollow of her throat, nibbling his way to her ear. "And this." His words sounded thick as he traced his hand along her thigh, up across her hip and over her belly, resting in the valley between her breasts. He circled one of the tiny nubs hardening beneath her shirt with his touch.

All she could muster was a breathless, "Yes." She wrapped her arms around his neck, her body warming, unchecked with her desire as every cell came alive, waiting for the nourishment of his touch.

"I love this dress on you," he said, raining kisses along her flesh where her neckline dipped and promised. He lit a fire in her belly as he playfully tugged the material back with his teeth, exposing more of her skin. His other hand came up, teasing and coaxing her body to life as he groaned again and claimed her lips in a commanding kiss.

Instinctively, she brought her knee up, crossing her leg over his as her body molded against his length. He traced a finger along the curve of her hip, uttering a throaty moan as his hands rested on the soft mound of her bottom. She felt the thin cotton fabric of her dress wisp across her body as he lifted it up around her waist, her legs suddenly chilled in the cool hotel room air. He found the waistband of her panties, tugging them down her thighs, searching for and finding the warm, moist heat of her treasure. She exhaled a moan of pleasure as he slipped inside of her, literally holding her in the palm of his hand.

His lips roved over her shoulders, pushing the straps of her dress aside, losing himself in the rising mounds of her breasts, causing her to cry out as he raked his teeth lightly over the tautened peaks.

Cradling his head in her palms, whispering his name, she guided him to her lips, claiming him deeply and urgently, wanting him inside her. His hand moved between her thighs, within her, coaxing her pleasure to crest like wave after wave crashing on the shore. She cried out his name as he brought her to a realm where time stands still, and the world and universe become one.

As she floated back to reality, she only knew she wanted him more than any man she had ever known. She kissed him hungrily, demanding, as she nudged him onto his back. While she unbuttoned his shirt, she ravished his mouth, raining kisses along his neck, and his chest as she tugged the fabric away. She knelt beside him, pausing for a moment, before lovingly placing a lingering kiss on his chest.

"I want you," she whispered, as her hand deliberately and slowly moved lower. She fumbled for a moment with his belt and zipper. Finally, when his pants were undone and she slipped her hand down to feel his hardness.

With a long exhale, she breathed his name against his lips, slowly trailing her hand up and down the length of him, over the strained fabric of his boxer briefs. He groaned, and called her name out, his hands smoothing over her arms, around her waist, pulling her to him.

"I've missed you so much," he said softly, covering her forehead, her cheeks, her lips with feather soft kisses.

"I've missed you too," she echoed, sliding down along his length, tugging his pants and boxers down, off his legs. His hand remained on her lower back, her bottom and as she scooted back to him, he mirrored her actions with her panties. She lifted her dress up and over her head, straddled him, and leaned forward to claim his mouth.

Like a magnet and steel, they found one another without hesitation. And as she slipped lower onto him, his hands came to her hips, guiding her slowly.

She never wanted this moment to end, she thought, throwing her head back as she reveled in the feel of him against her, inside her. And as they danced this timeless dance, he moved with her, within her, rolling her over onto her back. Together, they both became lost in the giving and taking, the commanding and surrendering, the satisfying and being satisfied two lovers experience when their souls collide.

~ ~ ~

"Brooke! Wake up! It's seven-thirty." Josh nudged the woman beside him. He peeled out of bed and headed to the bathroom. Moments later, she rapped on the bathroom door. "Is that going to be your customary wake-up phrase?" she grumbled over the flow of water.

"Good morning, to you, too. It does seem to be the norm with us," he called from the shower as the water cascaded down his body. "Care to join me?" He peeked out around the shower curtain, watching as she put toothpaste on her toothbrush in front of the sink.

"Are you sure we have time?" she asked with a grin, after rinsing and spitting and rinsing again. "You can use this complimentary toothbrush if you want. I brought my own." She lifted a tan toothbrush wrapped in plastic, resting in a basket that offered other complimentary toiletries.

"It's a fantastic idea. And yeah, thanks. I'll need it." He held the curtain back and invited her in with a sweep of his arm. "Welcome, milady."

"Mmmm. Such hospitality," she murmured as he gathered her into his arms, embracing her fully beneath the stream of hot water.

Moments later, they dressed in unison, with Josh yanking on his clothes from the day before. As Brooke zipped up a pair of dress slacks, tucking her blouse into the waistband, she pointed out in an amused voice they never did get to catch up over how their week had been. "I know you get to keep your job. And you seem really happy," Brooke offered slowly, waiting for him to agree.

"Yeah, I guess." He dismissed her comment with a wave of his hand. "Even more importantly, for the first time in three years, I have hope. I can feel again. I have dreams and desires. And it's all because of you."

"Whoa. No. Not me. Earth and Sky." Brooke raised her hands. "Please don't give me all the credit. We have an awesome team and we did it together. If Dee and Doug heard you give me all the credit . . . Please don't."

"It *is* because of you. And the message you delivered from Rosalie. Derek couldn't believe it when I told him. I can't wait to see his face when he hears it from you." Josh gave a quick whiff of his socks, wrinkled his nose, then shrugged as he slipped them back on his feet, followed by his shoes.

"What do you mean you told Derek? The guy who was sitting next to you at the meeting?" Brooke slipped on her flats, and froze in place, her voice oozing dismay. "Why? Why would you tell him?"

"I had to. I told the whole board. They needed proof I was healed and good to go."

"Oh, my goddess. Is this what we're all about? Proving you're healed? On to the next?" Brooke grabbed her purse off the bed and attempted to leave.

Josh reached into the closet for his jacket and quickly slipped into it as he followed after her.

"Brooke. Wait. It's not what you think." He came behind her and clutched her shoulder as she reached for the door handle.

"You know how I feel. You yourself asked me to make sure Earth and Sky didn't use our Rosalie story as a marketing ploy."

"We aren't using it as a marketing ploy."

Brooke's cell phone buzzed with a text from Alyssa. "They want us to meet them for breakfast downstairs." Her voice was a monotone as she stared at him.

"Don't worry. It's going to be okay. Derek won't say anything. And I'll make sure I tell him not to before the presentation begins. Okay?" Josh dipped his head and caught her gaze before brushing her lips in a quick peck.

"My portion of the presentation is about being the camp photographer. Nothing else."

"I know. I know. We're good. Your secret's safe with me. Trust me." He wrapped an arm around her waist and guided her to the elevator.

~ ~ ~

The presentation was far more than Brooke or any of her co-workers, even Dee and Doug, had imagined. To begin with, it did not take place in the board room. Instead, it was held in the conference center adjacent to the board room on the top floor. Despite its capacity to seat 100 in stadium-seating fashion, every seat was filled.

The program began with Josh, handsome as ever in one of the navy-blue Armani suits he kept in the closet in his office, welcoming everyone to the program. He explained this was the kick-off event for the new conference center, which had been completed a few months prior. And while this had been in the making for some time, they had a special surprise to share. "In addition to thanking our Mayor of New York City and representatives from all the local Chambers of Commerce, I'd also like to welcome our last-minute guests, President and Vice President of the New York State Psychological Association, and the New York State Association of Naturopathic Physicians. Thank you all for joining us today."

With a quick inhale and glance around the auditorium, he introduced the topic of the event, the completion of the auditorium conference center available not only for Quirkyflirt business, but for any events local businesses reserved it for, as part of the Hand-in-Hand networking program Quirkyflirt and other area businesses had created in partnership with the Chambers of Commerce. After numerous speakers approached the microphone congratulating Josh on the success of Quirkyflirt, for sharing the wealth he brought with the hundreds of jobs he provided to the area, and the dedication to this networking program they would put forth, Josh called up the Mayor to offer a few words.

When the first portion of the program was completed, Josh took the microphone once more. "Okay. We've got more reasons to celebrate, so don't go anywhere. In addition to the Hand-in-Hand program we've started, Quirkyflirt has another announcement to make regarding the strides we take to be the best employer in this great city."

He scanned the audience, spotting the Earth and Sky team before continuing. "I've spent the last month working with an amazing crew hiding away in the Adirondack Mountains in Upstate New York. And now, as a result of seeing their success firsthand, the board and I have agreed this would put our benefits package we offer to our staff above and beyond anything anyone else offers."

He raised his hands, gesturing to the Earth and Sky team, and continued. "Earth and Sky, ladies and gentlemen."

The audience responded slowly at first, and as Josh motioned for the Earth and Sky team to stand, the applause increased.

"I believe in the amazing program Earth and Sky provides because I experienced it," Josh continued, motioning for everyone to sit and be quiet. "This is another gem Upstate New York has hidden away and it's time we as a state recognize this treasure. So, without further delay, I'd like to introduce Quirkyflirt's board president, Derek Hendricks, to tell you more about our initiative."

Cameras flashed, and it was then Brooke realized the media hadn't left yet. Her stomach rolled, thinking of having to get up in front of all these people. She leaned over the seatback in front of her and hissed in Kyle's ear, "Are you really prepared for this?"

He raised his hands in a futile gesture and she sat back with a thud, crossing her arms in front of her with a scowl.

As angry as Brooke was at Josh for trying to exploit her, she felt a bubble of pride burst in her mid-section as she watched him commandeer the crowd. He was powerful, and thinking back to the broken man who she met a month ago, she was astounded by the change. If this was Josh in recovery, she couldn't begin to imagine what he was like before Rosalie and his daughters had died. There had to be some demi-god energy flowing in him somewhere.

With Josh's invitation, Derek took the stage and presented Dee and Doug on behalf of Earth and Sky with a plaque from the Quirkyflirt Board of Directors. The plaque, as Derek read, recognized them for their outstanding achievements in non-traditional healing practices and their contributions to the overall good of mankind. Derek made another grand, heart-wrenching speech, and Brooke wanted to cringe with every word. Why was she the only one who could see through his BS? Even her own team thought he was Mr. Wonderful, with Mandy making sure to be as close to his side as possible once she found out he was available and not gay.

Each of the CEO's and/or representatives from the agencies that had sent clients to Earth and Sky were also on hand, to provide testimony and praise to Earth and Sky. Next, the mayor addressed the crowd again, followed by the director of the chamber of commerce. A few distinguished researchers, physicians, and therapists talked about the powers of conventional and non-conventional healing, and how optimum health is achieved when both fields work together.

Once this was wrapped up, the next surprise portion of the program unfolded. Somehow, Quirkyflirt had managed to bring back Louisa, Renee, Craig, and Lance, along with an array of the young children Earth and Sky had helped over the years.

The tributes they offered left not a dry eye in the auditorium, as one after another presented plaques, framed photographs, flowers, plants, and all sorts of other items of gratitude to Dee and Doug and their staff.

Finally, her team was called up to the stage to begin the presentation they'd worked on all afternoon and evening. Despite her desire to run from the auditorium and hide in the bathroom, Brooke joined her peers and relocated to a row of seats behind the podium. One by one they spoke, talking about their personal experience, schooling and degrees, how they were led to Earth and Sky, and what they liked best about the company and the work they do. The recently created PowerPoint they'd worked on the night before, provided examples of past art projects, some of the ceremonies performed, the buildings and grounds, and the team at their best: working with children.

When it was Brooke's turn to speak, her most recent slide show made from the adult campers flashed behind her. "Being the camp photographer has to be the most fun job at Earth and Sky. I get to know each and every camper personally, sharing their joys and sorrows, highs and lows, successes and, well, their bad days. We laugh and we cry together. We yell and scream. We dance and drum. And in the end, I get to put all of our memories into a slide show, like this. I'm so grateful to Dee and Doug, and my team at Earth and Sky, for bringing me into this family."

The crowd applauded her, and the cameras flashed as Josh came on stage to join her. Putting his arm around her shoulders, he peered into her eyes, beaming with pride. It felt so right to have his arm around her, for them to be standing together on stage. She didn't move until he thanked her, her cue to step back with the rest of the team.

"Thank you, Brooke, Mandy, Cara, Alyssa, Dan, Rob, Paul, Kyle, and Dee and Doug for a great presentation and for all you do at Earth and Sky," Josh said, encouraging everyone to give another round of applause.

When they finally quieted down, he grabbed the microphone, lifted it off the podium, and clearing his throat, addressed the crowd. Every now and then, he'd walk from one end of the stage to the other, making sure he connected with every part of the auditorium.

"So, you all are probably wondering why we're still here. Am I right?" He nodded. "Yes? Ha-ha. Okay, well, we've got some amazing news. And we're hoping with our announcement and actions, we'll continue to lead the way with innovative ways of showing appreciation to our staff. Quirkyflirt has decided to branch out a bit and try something new. Hey, we can't let the moss grow under our wheels here. No, sir." He paused while the audience chuckled. "We're teaming up with Earth and Sky to make all six of our locations the best places to work around the world. Currently, we've been acknowledged by Forbes as the number one employer in the U.S. We provide the best medical insurance and life insurance benefits, the best vacation and personal and sick time packages, day care, family leave, education supplements, and now, *now*, we will be providing employee wellness and alternative healing services where members of the Earth and Sky team will be working with us to bring all sorts of retreat programs to our employees. And like our health benefits, all this will be at no cost to our team. What better way to show you care about your staff's well-being than with work incentives and company-funded self-care services? We'll continue to be the number one company to work for in the United States and around the world! Thanks to Earth and Sky Retreats!"

The audience stood at this point, hooting and whistling and stomping and clapping, giving Josh and Earth and Sky and Quirkyflirt a standing ovation lasting for a good minute. Josh gave a salute and left the podium, taking the empty seat at the end of the row of chairs along the back of the stage where the Earth and Sky team now sat. "Isn't this amazing?" he asked, leaning into Brooke as he whispered in her ear. His smile dazzled her, and it was difficult to not share in his enthusiasm.

Derek took the stage once more and opened up the audience for questions and answers. "There are ushers walking around with paper and pens. If you have a question, please write it down and give it to the ushers, and they'll bring them here to be answered by a member of the Earth and Sky team. We have a few already," he said, waving the postcards in his hand high for everyone to see. "I'll ask the question, which the members of Earth and Sky team can come on up and answer. Ready?"

The questions varied, touching on every subject. "Are all the services the same at each Earth and Sky?" "Where are the different locations?" "This one is for Dee, where is your favorite Earth and Sky?" "Will you ever add more locations?" "Do you need an activities director?" "How do you apply?" "Does the photographer need an assistant?" The list of questions went on and on until Derek finally ended it by saying, "Okay. We'll take one more question. Let's see . . ." He shuffled through the cards before deciding.

"Ahhhh. Here's a good one! Ready? It's two parts. 'What's a Deathwalker? And can you tell us about the scariest encounter you ever had with a dead person?' Wow. So deep. Let's see . . . Who wants to take this one, hm?" He spanned the Earth and Sky team with a bright, welcoming, inquisitive smile, honing in at last on Brooke.

She sat there immobile, unable to think or breathe, hands clenched in her lap. She heard Josh whisper an expletive under his breath, although he did nothing to stop this. *Not a blessed thing.* When it was clear she was not moving, Doug stood up and went to the podium. As he started speaking, Josh leaned over and spoke softly in her ear, "I had no idea. I'm so sorry."

Unable to move or say a word, Brooke swallowed thickly and tried to focus on Doug's answer.

"Wow. I'm not sure where this question came from. Hm. Well. Deathwalker's actually a nickname for one of our sweethearts who works at the Adirondack location, and it's not as scary as it sounds. Not sure how it got out. It's really not one of the services we officially offer." He looked pointedly at Josh, who sat as still as Brooke.

Brooke noted the muscle in Josh's jaw pulsing as he clenched his teeth. "How could you betray me?" she hissed, through a false smile.

"I told him not to bring this up. Someone else must have asked the question. Maybe a previous client's family member? He wouldn't blatantly go against my wishes." Josh sounded furious and his cheeks were a rosy hue. She'd never seen him this angry before. Then again, she hardly knew him. And the Deathwalker question, this whole horse and pony show, proved how little she knew of him.

"So, really," Doug continued, "I've given you the gist of it. I'd say just about everyone I know has at one time or another thought they'd gotten a comforting message or sign from a loved one who passed. And this is kind of what deathwalking is, being able to receive messages from beyond the grave."

Someone yelled out, "Like a medium?"

Doug hesitated, turning back to his team. Covering the microphone, he asked in a pleading whisper, "Does someone—*anyone*—want to help me out here?"

He was doing his best not to reveal her identity, and because of his loyalty, she couldn't let her beloved boss flounder alone on stage. With every step she took toward Doug, her legs felt like Jell-O. She thought for sure she was going to collapse into a wobbly, wiggly puddle right there in front of everyone.

"I can help you out, Doug. Thank you."

Doug leaned over and hugged her tight, whispering, "I'm sorry, darlin'."

Standing under the blaring stage lights, Brooke bit her lip and forced herself not to cry. Being front and center, with flood lights on her, brought her back to the days she had accused her rapist, with the media following her around constantly trying to get a picture or trip her up. She remembered how it felt to not be believed. To be called a liar. To be laughed at. And now, she was going to be on the front page, national media once more. Would family and former friends back home call her out and accuse her of lying again?

"Thank you, Doug. I appreciate your effort. Hello again, everyone." Brooke's voice was soft and sweet as honey as she spoke into the microphone. "I'm not sure who asked about my personal nickname, or even why. As Doug said, it's not an official service we provide. At least, I've never seen it on any of our pamphlets or brochures. So, Derek, I'm not really sure where you came up with your question." Her icy glare was evident for all to see as she hunted down and singled out the board president who had gone to sit beside Josh. Josh, she noted, looked like he wanted to kill the someone. Contained rage was the phrase ringing in Brooke's head as she turned back to the audience. "I'm the camp photographer before anything else."

"What's it like talking to dead people?" someone shouted.

Brooke was silent, unable to find her voice. She lifted a hand to shade her eyes from the glare of the stage lights as she peered into the dark depths of the audience.

"Are you a medium?" someone else called out.

She shook her head and as the seconds ticked by, she struggled to think of something coherent to say. "No, I'm not a medium." She searched for simple words to describe what she did, so it didn't sound fantastic or exaggerated.

"I'm also a certified spiritual mentor and life coach, and counselor, with my LMSW," she said, pausing as she wiped her forehead with the back of her hand. The damn lights were so bright, so hot, and almost as annoying as Derek.

The audience waited, as camera flashes popped like fireworks.

Out of the corner of her eye, Brooke watched Josh whisper something in Derek's ear.

Josh betrayed her. To prove he had healed and was moving on. He said so himself.

"I don't call myself a medium. I don't call myself anything, actually. The name Deathwalker started as an endearment. I never realized it became a job description or title until now." She glared at Derek again as he offered a slight wave of his hand.

"Yes, I talk to people who have passed on. Or better, they come to me when they need me to relay messages to their loved ones. It doesn't happen at will. It's all totally random. They usually talk to me when I'm asleep. The dreams start way before the person even arrives at camp. There's not much else to it. Thank you."

Brooke put the microphone back into its stand on the podium, as other questions were shouted out behind her. All eyes were on her as she passed by the Earth and Sky team, as she grabbed her purse off her chair, and continued backstage. Josh tried to grab her hand but she sidestepped his effort. She did manage though, to give Derek one hard, spot-on, swift kick to his shin as she passed him by, beelining for the exit.

As she reached the corridor, she heard Josh call out.

"Where are you going?" His voice echoed behind her as she walked swiftly toward the elevator.

"Away from you." She didn't slow down for him.

"Brooke, hold up. I can explain. Or actually, I can't explain. I don't know what happened. I told him not to bring it up. Derek said he had no—"

"Screw Derek! Go back to your Warcraft buddy. He may need you to kiss his booboo." She jabbed at the elevator's down-arrow button.

"Brooke. Listen."

"No!" She whirled around to confront him. "You betrayed me. I trusted you and just like Richard—no, worse—you betrayed my trust and left me to fend for myself in front of all those people. In front of the cameras, in front of everyone!" Her voice cracked as she fought back her tears and turned away, struggling to catch her breath.

"It wasn't me!"

"You promised it wouldn't come up. You said so this morning!"

"Yes, and I spoke with Derek this morning and specifically told him the Deathwalker topic was off-limits. He betrayed me, Brooke. He *will* answer for it." Josh spread his hands in frustration. "I did not betray you. Trust me on this."

Fumbling through her purse for a tissue, she muttered, "You told me to trust you once already. And I did. My bad." Part of her heart tugged with his words, and for a nanosecond she reconsidered that he might actually be telling the truth. Maybe she *was* being unfair and owed Josh the benefit of the doubt.

The elevator pinged and the doors opened, and Josh followed Brooke into the nearly packed elevator. She blew her nose loudly and people recoiled from her. Josh moved closer, serving as a shield between Brooke and the curious, though slightly repulsed, onlookers. He hit the 11th floor button and the doors opened. Tugging at her hand, he directed, "Come with me."

Rather than make a scene, she followed. When no one was looking, she jerked her hand free and asked, "Where are we going?"

"To my office suite. There's a bathroom there where you can clean up in private and go back to the event."

"I'm not going back."

"Fine. I'll let Doug know where you are, and when they're ready to leave they can come get you." Josh led her down a hall, past a café, a lobby area, and his receptionist.

"Hold all calls," he barked as he pushed open his door so hard it slammed against the wall.

"I want to go home," she vented as he held her in tow behind him, her wrist clasped in his vise-like grasp. "I'm so done with New York. Everything is about money and impressing people. You can have your stupid Quirkyflirt and big city. It's all so fake. I don't know how you can even live here!"

"It's my home," he said quietly.

She paused for a brief moment, realizing without a doubt she'd viciously stabbed some really vulnerable part of him. She exploded, "Well, you're fake too! Can you leave me alone? Go away."

"There's the restroom." He pointed to the left as he walked past the small corridor and into his office.

She went in and locked the door behind her and crumbled into a heap on the floor and cried.

Chapter 33

The ride back to the hotel took forever, thanks to the endless traffic creeping along overcrowded streets, pedestrians and cyclists weaving in out and of the vehicles, and fender benders crumpled up at every other corner. Brooke stared out the window of the Subaru Imprezza ignoring all attempts at idle chitchat by Tony, her Lyft driver, as she contemplated where she was going to run and hide next. It was time to leave Earth and Sky.

Initially, she had planned to wait for her team until the presentation and lunch were over, but Josh refused to leave her alone. Although he stopped trying to reason with her, he'd sat at his desk working as if nothing had happened at all. He even had the audacity to order lunch for her, which she refused to eat.

"At least talk to me. You're acting irrationally," he said, finally breaking the silence as he watched her from his desk.

Glancing up from the Solitaire game she was playing on her phone, she acquiesced. "You want to talk? Okay. You have the worst taste in friends, let me tell you." She rolled her eyes, her tone sharp.

"Brooke. He's my best friend. I went through a major transformation because of you. I had to tell him, there's no one else." His words were taut and weary. "It just came out. I was telling him I'd met the most amazing woman in my life and next thing I know, I'm spilling everything. About the fire. Kayaking and the lake. You showing me how to drum. Everything. Even my bow drill. I told you, I couldn't get you or the last three weeks out of my head." Pushing away from his desk, he stormed out of the office.

As the door slammed, her phone buzzed, notifying her that her Lyft ride had arrived. As she hurried down to the first-floor lobby, she swore she would do everything in her power to never see Josh again.

~ ~ ~

"Are you sure you don't want to come with us? Skye is taking us all over Manhattan." Alyssa, Cara, and Mandy had poured into Brooke's room the next morning and were now sprawled across her bed trying to convince her to change her mind.

Brooke remained buried under the white linens and thick downy comforter, burrowing her head beneath the fluffy down pillow. "Guys! Just go. I really don't feel like it, please!"

"It was pretty shitty what he did to you, Brooke. I'm sorry he turned out to be such an asshole," Cara offered. Mandy piped up, adding, "And his president's an asshole, too. To think I was going to date him."

"Really guys. I'm going to hang, work out in the gym here, maybe go in the pool. And relax. I need to nurse my pride, and try to get rid of some of the negative energy."

"We're supposed to be shopping for dresses for the gala tonight. You won't have anything to wear," Mandy said. "We're going to Macy's!"

"I'm not going to the gala." Brooke swung out from under the covers and went to the bathroom. "Now go. Have fun." Without waiting for their answers, she slammed the door behind her.

Doug texted her a half hour later.

If you want to take a sick day today and skip the sightseeing, fine. But you WILL be at the gala tonight. I suggest you do some local Village shopping and find something pretty to wear. I left the company charge card at the front desk.

With a loud groan, Brooke considered leaving her resignation at the front desk and taking the card to buy a train ticket back to camp.

Instead, she replied childishly with an angry face emoji and powered down her phone.

~ ~ ~

Middle East Emporium was the most perfect little shop Brooke could have ever hoped to stumble upon during her outing. Just as its name implied, it was filled with all sorts of unique goods imported from the Middle East. Bronze statues of gods and goddesses, all sorts of exotic incense blends and censors, drums and singing bowls, woven rugs, ponchos, dresses, blouses, yoga pants, boxes, and baubles galore filled every inch of the shop, leaving barely any wall space visible. After enjoying a thorough study of every last item on display, she ended up in the clothing section, perusing through the wide array of dresses. There were elegant gowns of lime green chiffon and lavender lace, and skimpy slips of cotton passing as sun dresses, alongside floor-length, embroidered summer evening wear gowns.

Her first choice was a long black linen dress with spaghetti straps and embroidery around the neckline and down the line of buttons running from the V-neck bodice to the floor. Simple and elegant. She thought about her nickname and hung it back on the rack. No need to perpetuate a stereotype.

She chose a similar dress in a deep bluish/lavender hue, which really accentuated her green eyes she realized as she stared at her reflection in the dressing room. The price was modest for New York City shopping, so along with the dress, she purchased a pair of laced up goddess gladiator sandals and a black lace shawl. Too bad if she wasn't dressy enough.

This perfectly fit her personality, and she was not going to conform for anyone.

After grabbing a slice of real New York pizza, Brooke made it back to the hotel, had a swim, enjoyed the hot tub, took a shower and was dressed and ready to go when Doug rapped on her door.

"I'm ready," she called out, grabbing her purse and shawl. The self-care had worked and she felt really good. And maybe even a little excited about going out tonight.

Earlier, after her co-workers had returned from sightseeing, Doug came to her room to check on her. He'd told her she shouldn't let anyone rain on her parade. And he was right. She was going to have a good time this evening, despite Josh.

"Josh!" she exclaimed as she opened the door. "What are you doing here?"

"Can I come in?" He peered in her room and sidestepped around her.

She watched him enter, and as he closed the door, she retorted with a sarcastic, "Sure. Make yourself at home."

"I wanted to make sure you were coming tonight. Even if I had to drive you myself." He stood by the bed and checked her out head to toe. "You look beautiful."

"What do you want?" She tried to ignore how gorgeous he looked in his black suit with pale lavender dress shirt.

"I want to apologize. Again. And I'll keep apologizing until you forgive me." He ran a hand through his close-cropped hair.

"Why? What do you care?"

"Hasn't anything I've said to you, all the time we spent together, what we've shared—doesn't any of this mean anything to you?" He squared off to her, looking tired and worn.

"Oh, really? You're going to throw it all on me? I'm not

the one who betrayed a confidence. If this is what the start of our relationship looks like, what's going to happen down the road?"

"I said I'm sorry. I can't regret trusting Derek any more than I do already. If I could, I'd take it back. I can't. All I can do is prove to you I will never betray your trust again." He came to her side, lightly placing his hands on her upper arms. "You have to believe me." He bent his head to kiss her as she stepped away.

"Nope. Don't even go there." She walked to the door, stating, "You said your piece, now leave. I'll see you at the gala."

"I'm taking you."

"No, you're not. I'm going with my team."

"Your team left when I met them in the lobby. I told Doug you'd be going with me."

"They wouldn't!" Brooke cried as she searched for her cell phone buried in her purse and texted Alyssa.

Where are you?

That answer came almost immediately.

On our way to the gala. Josh said you two were going together. Are you okay?

I guess I have to be. I don't have a choice.

With her face scrunched up in displeasure, she spat at Josh, "Let's get this over with."

"We match," Josh said, his voice filled with hope and satisfaction as he held open the door. "I like when we match."

"Yeah, well. Don't flatter yourself, you know it was pure coincidence." She gave a sideways glance, taking him in as he walked next to her. She had to admit, they did look good together.

A few minutes later, after buckling up in Josh's black Bentley, Brooke flipped the passenger visor down and checked her makeup, attempting to be unaffected by the car she was sitting in, or the demi-god she was sitting beside.

Once they merged into traffic, Josh spoke.

"I missed you today. I took the day off to go sightseeing so I could be with you. And you weren't there."

"Awwww. It must be tough when you can't always get your way, hm?" She stared out the window, then back to the mirror to inspect her face.

He ignored her and went on. "I about got my ass handed to me the whole time, by everyone on your team, beginning with Dee and Doug. Do you have them all bewitched or something? You're loved beyond comprehension, in case there was any question."

"Good." She retorted with a smug look. "I earned their love, by being honest and not betraying them."

"God-mmph." He tapped the steering wheel impatiently. "Are you ever going to let it go?"

"Nope." She snapped the visor closed.

"No second chances?" He made a right into traffic and wheels screeched and horns honked. "Damnit," he snapped, swerving to avoid hitting a car he didn't notice changing into his lane a second before he merged into traffic.

"Mmmmm. Let me think. No." She studied the bumper of the car he'd barely avoided sideswiping, realizing she was ruffling cool Josh's normally unruffled feathers. She couldn't help but giggle.

"Well, we'll see," he countered, staring straight ahead, focused on traffic.

After a few minutes of silence, he pointed out, "Back in the hotel you said we were in a relationship."

She lifted her chin and focused her sights out the window, ignoring him.

Within a half hour, they arrived down at the western tip of Pier 61, where the gala was underway at The Sunset Terrace. The Bentley idled patiently, keys left in the ignition for the valet, as Brooke unfolded herself from the luxurious embrace of what was probably the most expensive car she'd ever ride in for the rest of her life. Josh walked around to her door, as Brooke took in her view of the well-lit reception hall nestled cozily along the Hudson River. The smell of the sea, the soft clang of a bell in the distance, the hum of distant chatter and laughter offered Brooke a chance to collect herself with a deep and steadying breath. When he reached her side, Josh held out his arm, which she refused with an ever-so-slight shake of her head.

They walked together, side by side, through the glass doors held open for them by a uniformed doorman, and headed into the lobby. Josh paused momentarily, waiting for direction to the area their affair was located. Following the maître d' who had joined them, Josh guided Brooke by gently placing his hand behind her elbow.

This was the picture they presented as they entered the ballroom, with Derek the first to greet them. "Hi! Glad to see you could make it, um, Brooke, right?" His dazzling smile would have charmed the skin off a fellow snake.

In a monotone, she asked politely, "How's your shin?" then turned to Josh. "Thanks for the ride. I'm going to find my team," she said, leaving without waiting for a reply as she set off in search of her co-workers.

As Brooke walked away, Derek's laughter carried over the din as he exclaimed, "Dude, you got your work cut out with her." She wanted to go back and kick him in his other shin, but she summoned as much restraint as she could and concentrated on scanning the crowded room for a familiar face.

She waded through the throng of guests, many decked out in fancy evening gowns, suits and ties, and even some tuxedoes. The stagnant cloud of perfume and cologne choked her. The close contact with human bodies overwhelmed her. Done with the city, she just wanted to go home to her woods and creatures and silence.

Her co-workers were all gathered at one table laughing

and chatting among one another, with two empty seats to spare. Their effort to keep Josh in her life could not be more blatant, and it annoyed the crap out of her. She sat in one seat and put her purse and shawl in the other. "Thanks for waiting for me, guys," she blew out in a sarcastic huff.

A few of them exchanged sheepish looks, saying nothing. Dee, who she was sitting next to her, patted her back. "Sorry, sugar."

"Can I talk with you for a minute, Brooke?" Doug pushed away from the table and motioned Brooke to follow him. They walked to the bar, where he proceeded to order an IPA and a merlot. He handed the wine glass to her and she nodded her appreciation.

"Let's go outside and have a little chat," he suggested, leading the way.

"Yeah?" Brooke was not happy, and didn't feel like faking it, even for her boss.

After propelling her to a spot on the deck overlooking the river, city lights sparkling on the mirror-like surface, he spoke. "This is a great business deal for Earth and Sky. A really great deal. And I can't back out of it. What I can do is thank you for opening my eyes to who we're dealing with. These city-folk play by different rules. We don't have to follow those rules. We have our own rules. Here at Earth and Sky, we're family—*chosen family*. My team comes first. Especially you, young lady. What they did was wrong. But I don't think Josh intentionally tried to hurt you. In fact, I think he's quite taken by you. Not sure what kind of magic spell you cast on him, but it worked." He winked at her and continued when she remained unyielding and silent.

"Now, thanks to you, I see what we're up against with the other feller, Derek," Doug paused, carefully choosing his words. "He's as slippery as a mudpuppy after an Arizona Monsoon."

"I kicked him in the shin. I couldn't help it." She didn't

bother hiding her enjoyment.

"Yeah," he chuckled. "The whole auditorium saw you. Great aim," he added, offering another amused chortle.

Brooke shrugged. "I'm not sorry."

"Didn't expect you would be," he said with a wink. "Now, just because we're moving forward with our deal, it doesn't have to impact you at all. You don't ever, ever, have to work with Quirkyflirt or any of the players again. You hear? There is no obligation for you to ever engage with Josh. Ever. After tonight, I mean."

"Why tonight?"

"We need to make nice for the media, and we leave first thing tomorrow, so tonight's it. Can you do this for me?" Although it came across as though he was asking for her permission, Brooke knew when her boss was issuing an order.

She took him in, and everything he'd said, and nodded slowly. "Yeah. I guess, considering you bought this really super cool dress." She twirled. "How do you like it?"

"You look delightful. Thank you for being such a great asset to our team, Brooke. Now go have fun." He took a swig of his beer and headed toward their table.

And while she didn't exactly have *fun,* she did have a difficult time not enjoying herself. She even danced with Joshua A. Quinn, Chief Executive Officer and Founder of Quirkyflirt.com, whose dance card was beyond full. Even as busy as he was with networking and schmoozing his board members and the rest of the partygoers, he managed to enjoy dinner by her side, joking and flirting and doing his best to get her to like him again. Yes, it was pretty obvious.

And by the end of the night, she managed to flirt back. *A little.*

It was nearly midnight when the band called out a 'last dance and last round at the bar' warning. Brooke rested her forehead against her folded fists, relieved the night was finally over. As the band plucked out the opening chords to the last slow dance of the night, she felt the warm breath of a whisper over her shoulder, just above her left ear. Josh gently rested a hand slightly below her neck, the warmth of his touch heating her exposed skin, and asked softly, "May I have this last dance?"

She glanced up with feigned adoration. "You mean me?" She batted her eyes and held her hand shyly in front of her mouth. "Oh, I'm so happy you chose lil ole me for your last dance."

"You're such a wise ass, you know?" He swooped her around as he guided her to her feet, holding her so close she thought he was going to lift her off the floor.

"Yeah, it's what you like best about me, isn't it?" She wrapped her arms around his neck, and leaned into him so she would not fall. Too much merlot, feeling incredibly sexy in her slinky little dress, and being desired by the richest, not to mention most handsome, man in the room did wonders for her confidence and made it way too easy to forget how angry she was with him.

As they swayed to the strains of "A Thousand Years," he locked eyes with her, leaving her powerless to look away. "This could be our song. About us, you know," he said.

"I don't think I'm going to make it past a hundred and fifty, sorry." She leaned away a bit, still unable to redirect her gaze.

He leaned in closer and whispered, "May I kiss you?"

"No, kind sir. You cannot." She licked her lips anyway.

"I believe you're giving me mixed messages," he accused as he dipped her.

"I believe you're trying to break my back. Warn me next time." Her hands dug so deeply into his shoulders for balance and support she surely would have drawn blood if he'd not been wearing a shirt and suit jacket.

He twirled her around and brought her in close again,

asking, "Now can I kiss you?"

"Maybe a little peck. Like a 'thank you for the dance' kiss. Nothing more." She lowered her eyes, gazing at his mouth, and when their lips failed to connect, she peered up through her lashes in confusion.

"You're beautiful." His energy was so intense she felt as though he was about to devour her. Her pulse quickened as his eyes trailed from her lips to the soft curve of her skin revealed by the dip in her neckline.

"Oh, look. The song is over." She tossed her head toward the band as the lead singer said goodnight and the house lights brightened the ballroom.

"But we've only just begun," he crooned, studying her with bedroom eyes.

"In your dreams." She reached up on tippy toe and kissed him lightly on the lips, summoning all her strength to not linger. "Thanks for the dance," she added. With every ounce of willpower she possessed, Brooke reclaimed her personal space, removing herself from his embrace. Without a glance back, she left him on the dance floor with his empty arms still outstretched following her hasty retreat.

Chapter 34

As Brooke and her team were boarding their 7:30 a.m. flight to Albany out of LaGuardia Airport, she received a text from Josh.

Can I call you quick?
No.
Okay. Can I text?
Apparently so.
Thank you for last night.
Last night? I was a bit abusive. I'm glad you enjoyed it.
I meant the kiss.
Good bye, Josh.

~ ~ ~

It felt good to be home, Brooke reflected as she slowly placed one booted foot in front of the other. With each step up the familiar, well-worn path to her rock, and with her trip to Manhattan three days behind her, Brooke understood how much of her home Earth and Sky had actually become.

Being in the city had been quite the change of scenery, she recalled as she breathed deep the sweet scent of pine and grass and wildflowers. And, had things played out differently, it could have been way more enjoyable. It was probably a good thing she and Josh didn't work out. Yeah, New York City was a helluva town, but definitely not a place where she could ever live.

Her cheeks grew warm at her recollection of the horrible things she'd said to Josh the other day in his office. In all honesty, she admitted grudgingly now to herself, she truly did not believe most of what she'd hurled at him in anger. She'd been rip roaring mad. And, yes, downright cruel. Maybe one day she would apologize to him, she thought. Realistically, it was probably eons into the future. If ever.

The last three days had been cleansing—*really cleansing*—for her heart and soul. She spent most of her waking hours fasting and meditating, doing yoga, journaling and writing poetry, or drumming. Really what she was hoping to do was purge. Purge all the pain, all the false sensations of love she thought she was beginning to feel; all the mundane, materialistic concepts she'd began measuring her life against this last week. The Bentley. Silk suits. Egyptian cotton sheets. Waiters. Doormen. People to pour her coffee and cut her freaking steak if she'd wanted. And the attention.

She hated attention.

Now, here it was Sunday morning, and at least she was beginning to feel like she had recaptured her routine. A week away from home. Two weeks since she'd hiked to her rock. It felt like a year. So much had happened. As she passed by the familiar patch of pale blue forget-me-nots, she thought of Josh, and how excited he'd been to be able to identify the plant. Sometimes the simple pleasures in life are the most rewarding. Too bad he'd never understand.

Josh. He'd been the last one to climb this trail with her, two short weeks ago. It didn't seem possible. She counted back the days and it still seemed wrong. Halting in her tracks, she played back each day. Yup, only two weeks, she confirmed before continuing on with her trek once more.

As she neared the top of the summit, still protected by the last bit of oak, maple, and birch limbs and leaves, she took pause, catching her breath in awe. A tumultuous thick blanket of clouds promising rain rose before her. Misty mountain tops were barely visible in the distance. Lush greenery rolled for miles like a velvet carpet. And the air. She breathed deep and felt dizzy with unfettered happiness.

Air. Oxygen. Clean air. What a treasure. What a precious, precious commodity she would never, could never take for granted again. A slight breeze had picked up, and it carried a hint of precipitation, caressing her skin like a feather-soft veil. It smelled like rain, she thought as she lifted her nose to the sky. She contemplated turning around, but never even stopped. This was the best form of grounding she knew, and right now she needed grounding more than ever. She'd brought a journal to read through some of what had transpired in this last whirlwind of a month, to sort through it all and figure out what she was truly feeling. She was feeling something akin to a broken heart and she wasn't sure of the cause. Was it triggered from the event because she'd been cornered and displayed like a freak at a circus? Or was it the fact she had started falling for Josh, a man who she would have gladly given her heart to, only to be exploited. Would she ever see him again? Did she even want to?

Unfortunately, the answer to both questions was probably 'yes.' More than likely she would cross paths with him in the future because of the business deal struck with Earth and Sky. And, if she was honest with herself, she wanted to see him again. She wanted to talk this out, maybe see if they would be able to work things through. But it was only a silly fantasy. Hopefully, she'd not see him anytime too soon. It would be too easy to fall in love with him and make a fool of herself. Her proof was what almost happened this past month. He was too smooth. Too polished. Too handsome. Too sexy.

As she continued to climb those last few steps, she reflected on Josh's path. He had needed her here to complete his journey of healing. It was their destiny. First, she came into his life to relay his wife's message freeing him of any guilt, and to share with him her permission to move on. She was here to teach him life is for living. She was also a safe testing ground to ease into the dating scene because she was some backwoods photographer playing camp. He no doubt knew she could never have had the power or ability to hurt him. He was too suave. The flirty stuff came naturally for him. She didn't believe for one moment his story about being a geeky computer nerd with no love life during his youth. No Ugly Duckling tale of woe for him. No freaking way.

Her heart sped up a bit thinking about him. How he moved her, made her feel things she'd never felt before. How he kissed, oh, how perfectly he kissed her. Their lips were made for one another.

No. No, they weren't, she argued.

Why are you tormenting yourself? Stop!

Did she blow it? Did she throw away a love of a lifetime?

No. She was his rebound love, in a sense. A delayed rebound love affair. Which would be way worse than an immediate rebound, because neither of them saw it coming.

Stop thinking. You're ruining your hike. You're up here to freaking heal!

Brooke focused on the air she was breathing, and the clearing a few yards ahead showing her the summit was within reach. It had started to rain a bit harder. She could hear it splattering on the leaves. No worries. It was still summer and even at this altitude, the rain was usually not too cold this time of year. She'd be fine.

Unless it was windy. But she didn't see any signs of a strong wind.

Yes, she'd be fine.

Up ahead was her beloved rock. She couldn't nap on it and soak up rays with such a thick, overcast covering of rain-soaked clouds. She could sit there and tap into its beautiful, solid, trustworthy energy. And let the rain wash away her tears.

She paused at the clearing and sighed, after spotting trash someone had left on the gray slab she'd come to think as her very own personal property. As she walked closer, she saw it was actually a piece of paper with a small stone resting on it, which kept the note from blowing away.

Well. She knew she hadn't left it, so whatever it was, it was none of her business. So, Brooke climbed up and sat off to the side a bit, taking extra care to not disturb the rock and note. However, she kept looking at it, wanting to move it so she could have more of the surface for herself. If she moved it, she'd want to read it.

Oh, hell.

Brooke picked up the rock and lifted the note, unfolding it. Maybe it was intended for someone down at camp, and if she left it here the rain would surely wash it away. It was her obligation to read it.

Since you didn't want me to call, or text, I figured the only way you wanted to communicate was in person. So here I am.

She stared at the note, amused at first believing someone had had a lover's spat. As she studied the scrawl, it dawned on her. It was for her. Slowly she lifted her head and pivoted in place. And there he was, half-hidden by a thicket of bushes.

Josh.

She jumped off the rock and ran to him, nearly knocking him down as she flung her body onto and around him so hard, so thoroughly, all he could do was laugh.

She clung to him, bewildered as to how he was here, in her arms.

"I missed our ole fella," Josh said, untangling himself. Laying an arm around her waist, he walked over to the rock with her at his side. He placed his hands on it, palms down, just as she'd taught him, his eyes void of Ray-Bans and glued to her face.

"You're crazy," she said, staring at him through watery eyes. *Don't cry.*

"Yes. Without a doubt I am absolutely crazy." He lifted a shoulder and tilted his head unapologetically.

"Are you here for a meeting? Doug and Dee left this morning." She waved a hand toward the path to camp.

"A sort-of meeting. With you. Let's sit. I have something to tell you." He reached out a hand and beckoned her to their rock, now dampened with the misty rain.

"Yeah?" She studied his face as he climbed up and took a seat, patting the wet, slick surface beside him.

She noticed it was beginning to drizzle a bit harder.

"Life is flying by. I'm getting old."

"How old are you?" She climbed up and settled down beside him, taking care not to slip off.

"Forty-two."

"Whoa. Ancient," she replied with a roll of her eyes.

"Yep." He nodded slowly. "Which is why I've decided to retire."

"Retire?" She clasped her hands mid-chest. "I'm so sorry! They pushed you out after all?"

"No. I went voluntarily." He grasped both her hands and held them close to his heart.

"Why?"

"Because I can't do it anymore. Your words hit home. It's a lot of fake, not much substance. I did what I set out to do. But, it's not me anymore. You helped me see it's not who I am, who I've become."

"Well. I'm glad I can be of help." Her heart hiccupped with a twinge of guilt, as the butterflies batted all unnecessary emotions away.

"I'm going to need a lot of help. I bought the old Meyers Mansion on the other hill." He pointed to the west.

"I didn't know there was a Meyers Mansion on the other hill. I definitely didn't know it was for sale." She followed his finger to the adjacent roll of land, laying her eyes on the thick growth of trees, and nothing more.

"Neither did they. I made them an unbeatably good offer for the whole 100 acres. It was a steal." His eyes, reflecting the gray clouds, were stormy with emotion.

"I see. And what are you going to do on the stolen lands?" She feigned consternation as she felt a raindrop trickle down her cheek. She wiped it away, never taking her gaze from his face.

"Drum." He contemplated for a good moment, before answering emphatically, "A lot."

"Well. This should be interesting. You better not keep us up with all the racket. What else?"

"I want to grow a garden and raise chickens. Do you know anything about gardens and chickens?"

She stretched her legs out in front of her and laughed. "Some."

"I'll hire you."

"Oh. I already have a job."

"You'll do it for free?" He cocked his head and waited.

"Not free," she said, pursing her lips thoughtfully as she tapped her slender pointer finger lightly against her mouth. "Maybe I'll barter."

"Sounds good to me. We can work out the details later." He held out his hand as if to shake on the deal.

When she took it, he leaned in close and kissed her.

Tilting her gaze slightly, she asked, "Did we just seal the deal?"

"Nope. I owed you one for Wednesday night. I never got to kiss you back. You just left." He wrapped his arms around her as she rested her cheek on his rain-soaked Earth and Sky sweatshirt now clinging to his broad chest.

"Gotta admit it was a nice effect." Her voice was muffled.

"Yes, you have a penchant for dramatic flair." He spoke against her crown, placing a light smooch on her head.

"If the occasion requires it." She snuggled closer.

"As far as sealing the deal, I'm hoping we can cross those T's and dot those I's later tonight." He whispered his wish into her hair, leaving another light kiss on the top of her head.

She answered by tightening her embrace.

The clouds grew darker as heavier drops started splattering around them and Josh leaned back from her, looking around. "It's raining harder."

She locked on his eyes and licked her lips.

"You have this certain tell when you want to be kissed," he said, his eyes darkened with desire.

Mesmerized, she leaned in slowly, as if she were magnetically being drawn closer. "So, what are you waiting for?"

"I want to tell you something."

"Then will you kiss me?" she whispered, suddenly unable to find her voice.

"Undoubtedly," he whispered back.

"Okay. Go for it." She could barely feel her breath as she spoke, or feel her body, or even think. Her lifeforce clung to his essence, his every word.

He drew in air and exhaled slowly. "My old life didn't fit anymore, only I didn't realize it until the event. And what happened to you opened my eyes. Up here, I'd seen what reality could be like—your reality—and I liked it. I liked it so much better than mine. What happened at the event proved it to me."

He paused, as the splattering threatened a downpour. When she didn't say anything, he continued. "I thought you were going to come down and I was going to win you over with this great city and everything I could give you. But then, I felt so foolish at the Quirkyflirt event. The bragging, the bullshit move Derek made, your words. All of it made me realize I don't belong there anymore. I belong up here. With you."

"Oh."

"You have nothing else to say?"

"No." She smiled and scooted closer, wrapping her arms around him again as she looked up at him. He came across so earnest, so vulnerable, his anticipation etched in tiny worry lines around his eyes.

"Well, what?"

"Now you can kiss me."

And he did.

They kissed as the clouds opened up in a full downpour, cleansing away all the pain and sorrow of the past, washing away the doubt, the differences, the confusion.

Sitting on their rock, completely unphased by the storm, wrapped in one another's arms, they held each other tightly, silently promising to never let go again.

When at last they drew back, she blinked away the threat of tears, as droplets cascaded down her face, and kissed him tenderly on his lips before whispering, "Life is for living."

"Yes, it is," he whispered back. "And I want to live every moment for the rest of my life with you."

"If we want to live, period, we should probably get out of this storm," she noted. "I don't want to die of pneumonia or get struck by lightning before we even get a chance to say I love you."

"Good point." He jumped down off the rock, held out his hand, and she took it.

They jogged to the canopy of the trail heading down to camp, where she stopped and tugged him to a halt. "Josh?"

She grew a bit shy as he searched her eyes, waiting for her to continue.

"I love you," she blurted out as her butterflies danced something akin to Swan Lake in her belly.

"I love you, too, Brooke with an 'e'." Gone were the worry lines, his expression filled with relief.

"I can't wait to raise chickens with you," she said as she walked down the path beside him.

"Well, let's just focus on teaching me how to drum."

"Deal."

"And the property has a lake, too," he offered slowly.

"Kayaking!" she exclaimed.

"No tandems," he offered in warning.

"Deal." She nodded. "How long do you get to stay? When do you have to go back to the city?" Her voice trembled and she wasn't sure if it was from the chill air and her damp clothes, or the thought of being without him again.

"I don't have to go back. Well, not right away. I was hoping maybe I could rent my old cabin until I get things sorted with the property. The old owners have a place in Florida, and they were getting ready to do their snowbird trip as it is. It should only be a couple weeks at most. I'm paying cash for the place and funding their move." He tightened his grasp but continued walking.

"Wow. You don't waste time, do you?"

"Not anymore. I have so much to make up for. I already spoke with Dee and Doug. They'll allow me to stay here based on your decision. Think you can put in a good word for me?" He tucked his arm around hers, their hands clasped closer to his side.

"Maybe? Hey, we could be neighbors." She shot a cheeky grin at him leaning into his side.

"Well, I was hoping for more than neighbors." When she didn't answer right away, he added, "Eventually maybe move in together? If you want."

"This is kinda fast. I just said 'I love you.' Now you want me to move in? I dunno, Mr. Quinn. Let's see where this goes," she said half-joking. All things considered, she still needed to take baby steps. This had to all sink in.

"You're right. I just don't want to be alone anymore." His voice cracked.

"Me either." She intertwined her fingers with his and squeezed hard.

They walked in silence until they reached the head of the trail leading into basecamp. "Hey. I have something I've been meaning to give you, but it never seemed like the right time. Here." Josh held out a small light brown box tied with a thin piece of hemp cord.

After tugging on the cord and lifting the lid, Brooke gave a soft squeal at the contents, an oval bloodstone pendant set in silver with a silver piece of fir dangling from the bottom. "I love it. It's just beautiful," she said in a hushed whisper as she lifted the chain and pendant from its resting place in the box shared by a real baby pine cone.

"Do you? It's called 'Love in the Forest.' I bought it on that trip into the village at the shop you like. Nurtured by Nature?" He took the necklace and came to stand behind her as she held up her hair, waiting patiently for him to clasp the chain around her neck. As he lifted the pendant, she noticed a cut-out in the silver backing, revealing a heart-shaped bloodstone image.

"Yes, I absolutely do love it. I've eyed that piece for a while now." She grinned broadly, lifting her chin. "How does it look?"

"Perfect." He leaned down and kissed her softly on her nose. "Just like you."

She leaned up on tiptoes, and kissed him sweetly as she grasped his hand. "Let's go tell everyone the good news."

With a gentle tug, he halted her in her steps. "Are you sure about this? We still have a lot ahead of us."

Nodding, she agreed, adding, "Yeah, we do, don't we? Like, I don't even know your middle name."

"You don't need to." He laughed and shook his head.

"Yeah, I do." She halted in her tracks. "Not budging 'til you tell me."

"In due time. There's got to be some mystery or else you'll grow tired of me."

"Good point. You're so smart." She hugged his arm as they continued walking toward the dining hall.

"No. I'm lucky. Unequivocally lucky." They stood at the bottom of the porch steps leading to the dining hall, where they could hear the clamor and clatter of the Earth and Sky team getting ready for dinner just beyond the wooden screen door. Josh looked at Brooke, then peered inside, hesitating.

"You okay?" she asked, recalling these were the first words she'd ever spoken to him. *My, how things had come full circle in just a few weeks.*

"Perfect," he said with a contented sigh. He leaned over once more and brushed a tender kiss across her lips. "Let's do this."

Together, they climbed the steps and burst through the wooden, squeaky screen door.

"Guys, meet our new neighbor!" Brooke called out, laughing, as everyone turned to face her and Josh standing united, hands clasped until the end of time. A momentary wall of silence greeted them as the sight registered in each one of her teammates.

"Whoa, dude!" Dan called out, the first to run over, followed by Alyssa, and the rest of the gang.

As everyone crowded around in a hubbub of excited chatter, Brooke caught Josh beaming at her, soaking up the unabashed acceptance embracing them both.

Brooke stared wide-eyed, struggling not to weep, as she thanked Goddess for her life, her gift, her chosen family, and most of all, for the healing love she found in Josh.

He held her close, squeezed her hard, and whispered, "I love you," against her head as the crowd urged them to come eat, since dinner was about to be served. Aloud, he stated, "I think I'm gonna like this hippy life. Thank you."

"Wait 'til you see Woodstock." She laughed outright and led him to their table, where it all began.

"I can't wait." He bent his head and placed a lingering, slow kiss on her lips. "Maybe we'll conceive a baby there."

Her face grew warm at the thought of what conceiving a baby entailed. "We can call her Moonunit."

"Deal." They shook hands and spoke in unison as they sat down to share the first meal of the rest of their lives together.

~ ~ ~

i got this thing about blues . . .

losin' myself in memories—
summer sea,
autumn sky eyes.
bury the blues in my garden;
up come forget me nots,
the last lobelia.

i got this thing about blues.

losin' myself
in the cool feel of Levi's
losin' Levi's
findin' skin against skin.

a smooth sweet jazzy beat
lickin' my veins
like your tongue on my honey
mmmmmm meltin' me . . .

i got this thing about blues.

always hopin'
for a blue moon

*that for once
really looks blue.*

*always searchin'
night skies.
midnight blue skies.
winter midnight sky eyes.
hauntin' blue eyes,
so blue. so blue. so blue.*

i got this thing about blues.

Also from **Soul Mate Publishing** and **Janina Grey**:

TEN BUCKS AND A WISH

All it took was one wish and ten bucks, and Deanna Drake was falling in love all over again with her high school sweetheart.

Returning to her Olde Westfield home ready to battle the proposed development of her family legacy, Deanna learns that the man she despises most is behind the takeover.

Cord stole her heart five years earlier and now plans to steal her rightful heritage and turn it into his next successful moneymaking venture.

Falling in love again wasn't even on her radar as she boarded the LIRR and headed east out of Manhattan.

Michael McCord knew he messed up bad when Deanna moved away to the city, never to return. Since then, he has been dealing with the realization that he lost the only love of his life forever.

But when Deanna's father dies and leaves Cord executor of the debt-ridden and failing Drake estate, the budding developer does what he does best—he takes something that is broken and molds and mends it back to life.

The only question now is what is he hoping to heal? The farm, Deanna's heart, or both? And where does he even begin?

He soon decides the best way to find out is to start with ten bucks and a wish.

Available now on Amazon: [**TEN BUCKS AND A WISH**](#)

Janina Grey:

Janina Grey has been writing since she could hold a crayon, and there has been no stopping her since. Journaling, short stories, poetry, newsletters, news, feature, columns, Op/Eds, and press releases have kept her busy her whole life. But it was the sweet romances she read in her downtime that stayed forever in her heart and gave her the inspiration to write her own.

Growing up on Long Island and living periodically in Tennessee as a youth has given her the opportunity to meet many different types of people and experience many different lifestyles. After moving from Long Island to settle in upstate New York with her family, she found the support needed to pursue her writing endeavors.

When Janina is not writing, she may be marching for women's rights, kayaking, camping, drumming, or dancing around the fire.

With her two children grown, she and her husband, David, share their 110-year-old Mohawk Valley farm house homestead with a few resident spirits and a very squawky murder of crows.

CPSIA information can be obtained
at www.ICGtesting.com
Printed in the USA
LVHW080405150821
695353LV00009B/380